PENGUIN BOOKS
Monday's Child

Cardiff Libraries
www.cardiff.gov.uk/libraries

Llyfrgelloedd Caerdy
www.caerdydd.gov.uk/llyfrgelloe

Monday's Child

LINDA FINLAY

MICHAEL JOSEPH
an imprint of
PENGUIN BOOKS

PENGUIN BOOKS

UK | USA | Canada | Ireland | Australia
India | New Zealand | South Africa

Penguin Books is part of the Penguin Random House group of companies whose
addresses can be found at global.penguinrandomhouse.com

First published 2016

001

Copyright © Linda Finlay, 2016

The moral right of the author has been asserted

Set in 12.5/14.75pt Garamond MT Std

Typeset in India by Thomson Digital Pvt Ltd, Noida, Delhi

Printed in Great Britain by Clays Ltd, St Ives plc

A CIP catalogue record for this book is available from the British Library

ISBN: 978–1–405–92875–5

www.greenpenguin.co.uk

For my lovely Monday's Child, Maxine Jane,
my daughter, my friend.

'Monday's Child is Fair of Face'

I

Torquay, Devon, 1900

Sarah stared at the substantial house with its reddish-grey stucco walls and elaborate quoins, then frowned. This couldn't be the place, surely? Moving closer, she squinted through the gaps in the iron gates and saw extensive gardens spreading down towards the sweep of the bay. A cool breeze, wafting up from the sea, sent tendrils of hair dancing from under her bonnet. Although the fresh air was welcome after her stuffy train journey from Plymouth, she didn't wish to arrive looking like some frowsy frump and hastily pushed the wayward locks back into place.

'What you staring at?'

The gruff voice took her by surprise. Peering down, she saw a freckle-faced urchin with hazel eyes scowling at her through the railings. He was dressed in an assortment of mismatched garments, and from his size, she guessed him to be about twelve, yet his candid gaze lent him the air of someone much older.

'I was looking for the Red Cliffs Ragged School,' she replied.

'Why you here? 'Cos if it's a home you want, you're too old. They don't take them as big as you and . . .'

'That's enough of your cheek, pipsqueak,' her godfather's voice called out from an open window. Sarah breathed a sigh of relief. It seemed she had come to the right place after all. 'Let Miss Sullivan in, please, Pip.'

'Righto, guv,' the urchin replied, pulling open the gate for Sarah to enter. 'Can't be too careful round here. You gets all sort of riff-raff hanging about,' he added, grinning cheekily up at her. She couldn't help smiling at his irrepressible nature, and it was only as she followed him up the driveway that she noticed his hunched back and limping gait.

From close up, she could see the once-grand building was in sore need of attention, but there was no time for speculation, for her godfather was waiting at the front door.

'Sarah, my dear, welcome to Red Cliffs,' he said, holding out his hand in greeting. Although his smile was warm, Sarah was taken aback at his appearance. His once-dark hair was now completely white and his bright blue eyes were faded, the skin around them etched with deep lines. 'Please ask Mrs Daws to bring a tray of tea through to my office, Pip,' he said, addressing the young boy.

'Thank you, Master Squeak,' Sarah added.

'That's a good 'un, miss,' he chortled, disappearing down the hallway.

'Did I say something funny?' she asked her godfather. He shook his head and ushered her into a large, airy room, but not before she'd seen his lips twitching.

'Take a seat, and let me look at you,' he invited, gesturing to an upright chair with its horsehair spilling from a tear in the cover. 'Why, it must be eight years or more since last we met,' he exclaimed, squeezing between the clutter of boxes and folders to reach the other side of the desk.

She stared at the plaque on the wall behind displaying the words *Love Never Faileth*.

'What a lovely sentiment,' Sarah said.

'The Red Cliffs' motto,' he said proudly. As he pointed towards it, she noticed his threadbare jacket with its fraying cuffs and suddenly felt overdressed in her best bonnet and sprigged cotton dress. Yet this morning it had seemed important she look her best to meet her father's dearest friend.

'My condolences on your sad loss, my dear. Your father was a fine man. We kept vowing to meet up, but time . . .' He shrugged.

'Thank you, Uncle Samuel. He had been ill for some time, and his death was not unexpected, yet it still came as a shock. Silly, isn't it?' She shook her head to blink away the tears that threatened whenever she thought of her father.

'Not at all. I was greatly upset myself when I heard the news. We'd known each other a long time, since medical college, in fact, when we were both young and had idealistic notions of curing the world of all its ailments.' He smiled gently, and she realized he was giving her time to compose herself. 'Then, of course, he married your lovely mother and had you. Proud as punch, I was, when they asked me to be your godfather. Only wish I could have visited more often, but you removed to Plymouth, and I was busy with the school. Still, that's water under the bridge of life, as they say.' Sarah nodded, for her father had always been busy working with his practice, as well.

'You've grown into a fine-looking woman, if I may be so bold,' Samuel said, his eyes twinkling in the way she recalled. 'Why, I remember when . . .' He stopped as a tiny, bird-like woman hurried into the room, carrying a laden tray.

'Thought the young lady might be hungry after her travels,' she chirped. 'Although you'll have to move some of these papers, Doctor. I don't know how you can find anything in this mess.'

'I know, Mrs Daws, but there's always something more important than tidying up to attend to,' he replied, duly sweeping papers to the centre of the desk. 'There.'

'Thank you, Doctor,' she said. 'Would you like me to pour?'

'If you would, please. That was most thoughtful of you,' he replied, eying the plates of sandwiches and cake, before turning to Sarah. 'Mrs Daws here bakes the finest sponge this side of the English Channel.'

'Oh get away with you, Doctor,' the woman chided, pouring tea into their cups and pushing the sugar bowl towards Sarah. 'If that's all, sir, I'd better get back to the kitchen before young Maisie puts the carrots in the swill bucket and boils the tops.'

'Oh dear, that bad, eh?' he grinned.

'You don't know the half of it, I'm telling you.' She shook her head, then smiled indulgently. 'Still, she means well, bless her.'

'The girls take turns helping Mrs Daws prepare the meals, although I use the word "help" advisedly,' he explained as the door closed behind the woman. 'Don't know how the place would function without her, and that's a fact. Salt of the earth, she is, bless her.' He proffered the plate of sandwiches but Sarah shook her head.

Despite her long journey, she had little appetite. Besides, she was anxious to know why he'd summoned her here.

'It's nice to see you again, Uncle, but . . .' she paused, not wishing to seem rude.

'You would like to know why I sent for you?'

She nodded. Although a suspicion of his motive was already forming in her mind, she had her own problems to attend to.

He took a sip of his tea then carefully placed the cup on its saucer. 'The truth is I need your help, my dear. I have been told by my own doctor that I must take things easy.' He patted his chest. 'The old ticker is slowing.'

'I'm sorry to hear that, Uncle.'

He shrugged. '*Anno Domini*, I'm afraid. However, my concern is not for myself but for the school and, more importantly, the children. I have spent the past twenty years or more building up this place. It is one of the finest schools for ragged children in the country, even if I do say so myself, and I'm not prepared to see it go to rack and ruin.'

'Forgive my asking, Uncle, but what is a ragged school exactly?'

'Sorry, my dear, I've been here so long I naturally assume everyone knows. A ragged school is somewhere orphans or children of poor families can come to receive a basic education as well as food. Of course, acquiring the necessary funds to run the school can be a problem, but that's another story. The children rely on me, as do the staff, and . . .' He broke into a fit of coughing.

As his face grew redder, Sarah jumped to her feet and poured water from the carafe on the desk. Holding the glass to her uncle's lips, she gently urged him to take a sip. Gradually the spasm passed, and he sank back in his chair with a wheezy sigh.

'Is there anything I can get you, Uncle?'

He shook his head. 'No, I'm fine now, thank you,' he rasped. 'Look, I'll come straight to the point. Sarah, I need the assistance of someone competent, and I'd very much like you to take over the administration here.'

'Me?' she gasped. 'But I don't know the first thing about . . .'

He held up his hand. 'Please hear me out. I know you are eminently capable, my dear. You have been running your father's home since your mother was taken, dealt with his patients and nursed him through his final illness.'

'That's as may be, but I don't know the first thing about teaching children.'

'You don't need to. We have a resident schoolmaster and travelling mistress who see to their lessons. Tell me, Sarah. With your father gone, do you have any ties in Plymouth?'

As he fixed his direct gaze upon her, she slowly shook her head. Until recently, she'd been betrothed, but Rodney, tired of the constant calls upon her time, had moved on to someone able to give him the undivided attention he demanded. Now she found herself as free as the proverbial lark, albeit she didn't feel much like singing.

'I realize I have sprung this upon you, but time is of the essence, and I won't be able to rest until I know everything's sorted. Before you make up your mind, why don't you let me show you around the place? You can meet some of the staff and pupils and see what miracles we endeavour to achieve,' he said, laughingly. But as her godfather struggled to his feet, Sarah saw just how much he had aged, how gaunt and frail he was.

'I would like to see what you do here, Uncle,' she replied. Having enough problems of her own to sort out after the recent death of her father, she had no intention of becoming involved, however she was curious to see the school she had heard so much about. 'Father always spoke highly of your work.'

She followed him along the hallway, noticing the polished parquet flooring that gleamed beneath threadbare rugs. Although the house was spotless, the decor was shabby with furnishings that sorely needed re-covering, and there seemed to be piles of boxes everywhere.

As he opened the door into a kitchen, warmth from the range welcomed them. A young girl was standing on a pail, washing dishes at the sink, but as soon as she saw Sarah, her eyes widened in fright, and she promptly wet herself. As the drips rained down on to the tin, she cowered in fright. Mrs Daws, who'd been making pastry at the scrubbed table, sighed.

'There, there, don't take on so. It's only a bit of water after all. Maisie's still settling in, Doctor,' she added, wiping her hands on her apron. 'Come on now, 'tis not the end of the world,' she soothed as the girl stared at the door, ready to take flight.

'Sorry to interrupt you, Mrs Daws. I'm just showing Sarah around but we'll come back later.'

Poor little mite, Sarah thought, darting a sympathetic glance in the girl's direction before following her godfather into the adjoining room. It was light and airy with

7

two long tables down the centre and bare wooden benches at each side.

'How many pupils do you look after here?' she asked.

'Usually about thirty or so,' he sighed. 'Of course, it varies because we never say no to a child in need.' Sarah nodded as she glanced around, taking in folded trestles resting against the walls.

'Those are for our drop-in visitors, for this serves both as dining room and soup kitchen,' he said by way of explanation.

'Goodness, I had no idea you catered for so many,' she exclaimed.

'All are welcome here, Sarah. One never knows when one might be in need of help oneself.' He frowned, as if he'd expected her to be more understanding.

'Of course, Uncle,' she said quickly. 'Father was always saying the same.'

He nodded, as if reassured. 'Now, back to the school itself. The children and staff all eat together so that we can instil at least basic table manners. It's an ongoing battle though. Some of them are literally starving when they arrive, and it can take time for them to realize each meal that's put before them won't be their last. Most are used to scavenging and have never even sat down to eat before.' He walked over to the wide sash windows that overlooked the back garden and pointed. Sarah caught a glimpse of the sea shimmering in the distance and the red cliffs that ran around the bay, then realized it was the vegetables neatly arranged in plots that he was gesturing towards.

'The children grow all the produce for the school and Sunday soup kitchen, with a little guidance from us, of course. It's important for them to feel they are earning their keep. You will find our regime includes plenty of fresh air and therapeutic outdoor activity.'

Sarah nodded as she stared out over the garden. Seemingly, the vast grounds she'd caught sight of earlier were used to cultivate produce.

'So this is really more than a school?' she asked.

'Indeed. We endeavour to make the children feel it's their home too. The squalor we find some of them in beggars belief, if you'll excuse the terrible pun. Our aim is to remove them from bad influences before they can commit any serious crime. We provide bed and board, together with elementary lessons and, for those that stay the course, some form of trade so they can try to make their way in this harsh world.'

'Where do they sleep? Sarah asked, staring at him in surprise.

'There are two dormitories upstairs, a bit basic but clean and certainly better than the wretched conditions they've been used to. Come on, I'll show you those and then the schoolroom and workshops. I started the Ragged School in an old ramshackle shed but it was soon filled to bursting. When my parents passed, I was fortunate to inherit this large house, and everything developed from there.'

'They must have been very proud of what you were doing,' Sarah commented.

His harsh laugh made him cough. 'Not really. They expected me to set up my own practice for gentlefolk in order to make a comfortable living, but I wanted to help the people who really needed it.'

'Like Father,' Sarah replied, thinking of all the patients who'd been unable to settle their bills. Often her family had lived hand to mouth, but her father claimed people mattered more than money. Rodney had voiced his disapproval of her father's largess, as he'd called it, saying he should insist his fee be paid up front. Although he'd never had the courage to voice his opinion directly to her father, he'd spent many an evening pontificating to her about them being taken advantage of.

Yet it had been those very patients who'd rallied around when her father was poorly, turning up on their doorstep each day with pots of broth or stew, while of Rodney there'd been no sign. He'd sent a short, impersonal note of condolence when her father died and that had been it. Biting down the bitter memories, she forced her attention back to the present and followed her uncle up the long flight of wooden stairs.

2

The two dormitories were lined with rickety beds and a motley selection of covers. Like the rest of the house, the room was spotless despite its shabby furnishings. As Sarah ran her fingers over the nearest coverlet, which at one time had clearly been a dress, Samuel pulled a face.

'We rely upon the generosity of the good ladies of the parish for much of the clothing and bedding. Now come and see our schoolroom,' he said, leading the way slowly back down the stairs. By the time he reached the ground floor he looked worn out and was struggling for breath.

'Why don't we sit a while?' Sarah suggested gently. He nodded and let her lead him back towards his study, where he slumped into his chair. With shaking hands, he fumbled in his inside pocket and drew out a little bottle of pills. Sarah pushed his glass of water within reach then tactfully walked over to the window, which overlooked the front garden. Was it really only an hour since she'd walked through those gates? It seemed like a different world here.

'I'm sorry, my dear,' her godfather wheezed a few moments later. As he struggled to his feet, Sarah hurried across the room and perched on the chair in front of him. Although she was pleased to see his colour had returned, it was evident the coughing fit had exhausted him.

'Why don't you tell me more about the school?' she encouraged. 'How many children do you have here at the moment?'

'Ah, got your interest at last, have I?' He gave a wry smile. 'Well, as I said earlier, it varies from month to month. Currently, I guess we have around eighteen who bed here, then there are other poor children who come in daily for lessons and luncheon. We have to insist those children spend at least the morning in the schoolroom before they can receive any food, for despite the Education Act we know jolly well if they weren't fed we wouldn't see some of them at all. It's down to their parents, of course, for they'd much prefer them to be out earning than learning.'

Sarah nodded, knowing how hard it was for some families to survive. 'Presumably those who live here are orphans, then?'

'In the main, although there are some who have fathers fonder of the bottle than of them, and then there are those born to prostitutes. As I said earlier, our job is to remove them from these bad influences and give them a chance.'

'It's admirable work you do here, Uncle,' Sarah declared. 'I thought I'd seen something of life but of course Father mainly dealt with the poorly, although some were needy too.'

'I knew you'd understand, my dear,' her uncle nodded. 'There is so much poverty in the world, and I've only scratched at the surface. I hope you now understand how important it is for the school to remain open and why I need your assistance. As I said earlier, you have the right attributes, if you would be willing to help, of course.' He sat back in his chair, steepled his fingers and fixed her with a searching look.

Although she was sympathetic to his plight, Sarah still had to sort out who was going to take over her father's surgery and whether her services would be required. Yet she couldn't help thinking her problems seemed insignificant by comparison with those of the children at Red Cliffs.

'I appreciate your confidence in my abilities, Uncle, but I'm still not sure what I could do. I might have assisted Father in the running of his surgery but that's very different to your work here.'

'Is it, my dear? It seems to me both concerns involve helping human beings who are in need. Of course, I don't blame you if you think all this paperwork would be too onerous, although I do remember your father saying your organizational skills were second to none.' Sarah smiled wryly, knowing her father had been as loath to waste time on futile form-filling as her uncle obviously was.

'It's not as if I have any family to call upon,' he continued.

'What about your nephew? Surely he'd be happy to come and help?' she asked, remembering the young lad she'd sometimes met at family gatherings before they removed to Plymouth.

He gave a harsh laugh. 'Christian? Now that's a misnomer if ever there was one. Sorry, that was uncharitable. Christian would indeed move here like a shot.'

'Well then,' Sarah smiled, pleased to have found a solution.

'Except Christian doesn't give a fig about the plight of the children. He likes the good life and would probably throw lavish parties or try to persuade me to sell to one of those developers who are keen to get their hands on this place. Your faith in Christian is misplaced, I'm afraid. I need someone by my side to help with the running of Red Cliffs. Someone I can trust, and I would trust you implicitly, Sarah.'

'I'm honoured, Uncle, but you forget I'm a female and, now Father's dead, am expected to take on a more domestic role than the responsible position you are suggesting.'

'Helping me run this place requires certain qualities, I agree. The person would need to be diligent, caring and conscientious, but who says that person need be a male? Your father, God rest his soul, did intimate in one of his letters that you concur with these lady suffragettes who believe women should have more rights and responsibilities.'

Sarah sighed inwardly, for it had long been a bone of contention that women didn't have the same opportunities as men, even in this new century. 'That's true,' she conceded.

'Well then, what better opportunity to put some of those principles into practice? And as for being expected to take on a more domestic role, well, you're not betrothed, are you?' Sarah shook her head, ignoring the pang in her chest as she thought of the evening Rodney asked for his ring back. Her uncle took out his pocket watch and frowned 'You did say in your letter you needed to return home this evening? Are you sure you won't change your mind?'

'I have things I must attend to back home,' she said quickly. Not for anything would she admit that, having paid for her train fare, she didn't have money for a room for the night, and she hadn't liked to presume her uncle would offer to accommodate her. Although, after what she'd seen today, her pride now seemed misplaced.

'Let me show you the classroom before you leave,' he insisted, getting to his feet and leading her outside through the front porch and down some steps. It was then that Sarah realized the property was set over three stories. 'We can only access that and the workshops from out here, which is mixed blessings sometimes,' he grinned then gave a sharp rap on the door. It was opened by a rather harried-looking young man.

'Good afternoon, Higgins. Forgive the intrusion but I've invited my god-daughter Miss Sarah Sullivan to see what we do here.'

'Miss Sullivan.' The man, who had a mop of sandy hair and nut-brown eyes, nodded politely, but Sarah could tell he was put out at having his lesson interrupted. As she followed her godfather into the room, she noticed another plaque bearing the school motto prominently displayed on the wall above the blackboard. There was a scraping of stools on the stone flags as the children jumped to their feet and stared curiously at her. She just had time to take in the rows of narrow benches that clearly served as desks, when the teacher clapped his hands and immediately the children turned to face him.

'Where are your manners, children? Say good afternoon to Dr Lawrence and Miss Sullivan.'

As they intoned their greeting, Sarah smiled, noting they were of varying ages, all with shorn hair and wearing an odd assortment of clothing. Then, as she stood studying the higgle-piggle of children in their ill-fitting garments, the ice that had encased her heart since Rodney left cracked, and something stirred deep inside her. She could see why her uncle was so driven, so passionate, and she too was filled with the overwhelming desire to make a difference to their lives too.

'Would you like them to recite the alphabet or their tables, perhaps?' Mr Higgins asked, breaking into her thoughts. She could tell from the glint in his eye, he was mocking, probably regarding her as some superficial goody two-shoes. Well, she'd show him, she vowed.

'Please don't let me disrupt your teachings. There will be time enough for me to see what the children know when I return.' It was only when she heard her uncle's intake of breath that she realized what she'd said.

Samuel watched as Sarah walked briskly down the driveway and turned left as she made her way back down the hill towards the station. She'd grown into a fine young woman, and he was confident she'd be the right person to take over the running of his beloved school when the time came. Of course, he hadn't put it quite like that as he hadn't wanted to scare her away. There'd be time enough to explain everything when she returned. As long as she came back. As if someone had walked over his grave, he shuddered. Supposing she changed her mind once she got home and thought things over? Even though he'd explained it was the administration he needed help with, it was still a huge undertaking, after all. While she had no responsibilities at the moment, there was no denying she was a very attractive woman and would likely marry and have a family of her own in the future.

She had been quick to suggest he call upon his nephew to help, but then she didn't know Christian had grown up to be a hard-hearted, greedy man who enjoyed the pleasures only money could buy. Samuel knew he would have no compunction about throwing them all out onto the streets, staff included, if he got his hands on the property.

Red Cliffs might be run down but it was in an area that had become desirable. With fashionable people descending in their droves to bathe in the sea or partake of the temperate air, there was now a demand for hotels and other comfortable accommodation. Developers, keen to cash in, were willing to pay good prices for substantial properties that overlooked the bay. A fact Christian knew only too well and wouldn't hesitate to capitalize on.

Feeling weary beyond words, he drew out his kerchief and wiped his brow. The responsibility for the welfare of these children hung heavy, and he could only hope and pray his god-daughter would keep her promise. In the meantime, he would see his lawyer and get him to draw up the necessary documents. He hadn't been joking when he'd told her time was of the essence. He hoped she'd forgive him for not being entirely truthful, but he couldn't afford to risk his property getting into the wrong hands. His beloved school must stay open; he would do anything in his power to ensure that happened.

Squeals of laughter and excited chatter filled the air as the children bounded out of the classroom like puppies, ready for their afternoon recreation. He smiled, revelling in the happy sounds, but as the noise grew ever louder he knew he needed to repair to more peaceful surroundings.

Reaching for his hat and coat, he slowly made his way down the driveway. As he turned right towards the quieter part of town, he noticed for the first time that the leaves on the trees were turning to russet and gold. Shivering as a cool autumnal breeze blew in from the sea, he realized the changing season had crept in without him even noticing. As ever, winter would follow close on its heels.

Returning to his home in St Marychurch, a small village bordering the fashionable resort of Torquay, Christian Lawrence poured a large brandy then threw himself onto the chesterfield. His meeting with the bank manager had not gone well, and he was in a foul mood. Confound that Collings; he'd only asked for a measly few thousand until his luck changed. It wasn't his fault the cards had gone against him these past few weeks. The man was an imbecile and a fool. Of course, there was still equity in his property to stand as collateral. He took a large slug of his drink, the liquor warming his insides while inflaming his temper at the same time. When his fortune changed and he was rich, Collings could go hang. He'd be sorry when Christian put his money where it was appreciated, he declared to the empty room as he slammed his glass down on the table.

He, Christian Lawrence, was cleverer than that half-wit, two-bit bank manager. Why, he had a thriving business running throughout the whole of the Torbay area, even if he hadn't been able to explain to that man exactly what it was. He couldn't exactly voice his opinion that the fancy toffs who descended on the area had more money than sense and that he was happy to help relieve them of it.

Money; he needed more of it and fast. Tomorrow he would call upon his 'agents' and find out how his enterprise was faring, put the pressure on if necessary. He picked up his glass then cursed when he saw it was empty. Struggling to his feet, he poured himself another generous measure.

He couldn't wait for the day when he didn't need to concern himself with finance. When he could re-engage the staff he'd had to let go and live life in the manner to which he was accustomed. One day, he'd claim his rightful inheritance and send those ragged urchins packing. After all, he was an orphan himself, wasn't he? His harsh laugh echoed around the empty room. Thank heavens he'd been on a shooting holiday when his parents contracted that virulent strain of influenza or he might have died too. The thought made him shudder, and he took another large slug of his drink. Apparently, he'd had an older sister who'd died before he'd been born. Just as well, really, or he'd have had to share even this modest inheritance. He stared around the small but elegantly furnished room and grimaced. This place was far too ordinary for his liking and in completely the wrong location for him. He needed to be living in Torquay itself where everything was happening.

Enough of these depressing thoughts, Christian, he chided himself. You are not yet thirty, and the night is young. Get out there and enjoy yourself, man. He'd call on the lovely Lil, he decided. He could do with some loving and she was the best at giving it. If she was busy there was always the playful Patsy. Grinning at the prospect, he finished his drink and made for the door. It was going to be his lucky night. He could feel it in his body.

3

Determined to keep her promise to her godfather, as soon as Sarah returned home, she set about closing up the house that had been both the family home and her father's practice. Although it was upsetting going through his things, whenever she felt any qualms that she was doing the right thing, the memory of those children's earnest little faces spurred her on. Now, a month later, having handed the house keys back to the agent, she was boarding the train for Torquay. Carefully stowing her bag in the rack above her seat, she checked the purse she'd stitched into her pocket was safe, then took a seat in the corner of the carriage. The other seats filled quickly, and she found herself squashed tightly into the corner. She spent the journey staring out of the window at the passing scenery as she pondered her future. Although tired after her exertions, she was bubbling with excitement and felt more alive than she had for ages.

As the train rocked and swayed its way through the Devon countryside, her head buzzed with plans. The plight of the children at Red Cliffs had awoken something deep inside her, and she was determined to help them. If she assisted her uncle with the administrative side of things, he would have more time to devote to the children. Then she remembered the supercilious expression on the schoolmaster's face and frowned. Obviously he'd thought her some do-gooder and, worse, that being a woman she wouldn't be up to the job. Well, she intended showing him exactly what she was capable of.

After changing trains at Newton Abbot where the kindly porter hefted her bag into the luggage rack, Sarah settled back in her seat. Although she was eager to take in the vastly differing landscape, tiredness finally overtook her and she felt her eyes growing heavy. She was rudely awoken by a loud hiss of steam and the jerking of the carriage as it shuddered to a halt. Disorientated, she opened her eyes to see the other travellers were gathering up their things ready to disembark. Realizing she'd reached her destination, she jumped to her feet and reached for her bag. Only it wasn't there. Frantically, she stared around the now-empty carriage, then checked under the seat in case it had fallen whilst she'd been asleep, but to no avail. A feeling of dismay flooded through her, for everything she possessed was in her bag.

'Hurry up please, miss, I've to shut the door now.'

She looked up to see the guard peering at her through the open door.

'My bag, it's not here,' she explained, pointing to the empty rack.

He shook his head. 'Had a lot of thefts recently, we have, although someone could have taken it by mistake,' he added, looking dubious. 'Best report it to lost property over there.' He pointed to a narrow door next to the ladies' waiting room. 'If someone hands it in that's where it'll be. Now I'm sorry but I must insist you get off.'

'Yes of course,' she muttered, stepping smartly onto the platform.

The clerk in the office sighed as she recounted her story. 'Giving me nothing but extra work, all these blinking thefts. What's your details?' he asked, opening a log book on the counter in front of him. Biting down a retort, Sarah told him her name and where she would be staying. 'Oh, Red Cliffs Ragged School,' the man scoffed. 'Probably be one of them beggars, then.'

'At least they have good manners,' she retorted, giving him a level look. How different the staff were here, she thought, remembering how helpful the porter had been at Newton Abbot. Marching briskly from the noisy, steam-filled station and out into the fresh air, she took a steadying breath.

Incensed by the man's high-handed attitude, it was a few moments before she heard someone calling her name. Looking up, she saw her godfather waiting in a pony and trap. Wearing an old-fashioned topper and long-tailed coat, he looked like a figure from another era.

'Looks like you've lost a shilling and found a farthing,' he quipped. Then, seeing she had nothing with her, his smile turned to a look of consternation. 'No luggage? You haven't changed your mind about joining us, have you?'

She shook her head. 'No, of course not. I fell asleep on the journey, and when I woke my bag was gone,' she explained, climbing up beside him.

'That's a terrible thing to have happened, my dear. You did report it?' he asked.

'Yes, but they don't hold out much hope of it being found,' she sighed, thinking it prudent to keep the comment about the school's pupils to herself. 'All I have is what I'm wearing and my purse,' she replied, patting her pocket. 'Can you imagine that?'

Her godfather gave a rueful smile. 'Regrettably, I can, Sarah. Nearly all the children who come to Red Cliffs don't even have that luxury. Most arrive in rags, hence the term Ragged School, and, well, I can't remember one ever wearing shoes,' he said, looking pointedly down at her leather boots. 'Don't worry, Mrs Daws will be able to help in the clothing department but I'm sorry you've had such a terrible introduction to Torquay, my dear.' He looked so forlorn, Sarah forced a smile.

'Luckily I'm wearing mother's cross, but father's bible was in my bag along with the only picture I had of them.' She swallowed down the lump that had risen in her throat.

'They'll always be in your heart, my dear,' he said, leaning over and patting her hand. She nodded, hardly daring to confess that her ritual of kissing them goodnight each evening had brought them closer.

He joined the line of traffic waiting to turn onto the main highway, and then the sweep of Tor Bay was spread out like a shimmering carpet before them. The bay was filled with boats going about their business while further out larger ships lay at anchor. As she smelt the tang of salt on the breeze, her spirits lifted.

'How are you, Uncle?'

'Can't grumble. Probably got as much vigour as this old mare here,' he laughed at the pony's slow gait. 'Now, let's breathe in this restorative ozone.' As Sarah inhaled deeply, her uncle smiled. 'That's better. The colour's already returning to your cheeks.'

'Goodness, I can't believe how busy it is,' she cried, staring at the well-attired people promenading along the sea front and the long queues for the paddle steamers, which were waiting to take others on a day's excursion. Samuel smiled at her expression.

'Torquay's known for its equable climate and attracts visitors nearly all year round. It has become a health and pleasure resort, a sort of retreat for the elderly and playground for the young. Why, only this month they introduced mixed bathing, provided the all-concealing costumes from neck to knee are worn, of course.' He frowned.

'Don't you approve, Uncle?' Sarah laughed but he appeared distracted and didn't answer. Suddenly he leaned forward, then pulled hard on the reins. As they jerked to a stop, she stared at him in surprise, but he was staring at a spot further along the beach.

'Take these,' he said, handing her the straps and jumping from the cart. Before she could ask what was wrong, he was darting between horses and carriages as he ventured across the highway. Then she saw him jump down onto the stones and crouch beside what appeared to be two piles of clothes fluttering in the stiffening breeze. He stayed liked that for what felt like ages. Worried he needed help, Sarah jumped down, tied the mare to a nearby lamp-post, then hurried to join him.

'Oh,' she gasped, her eyes widening in horror.

'Stay back, Sarah,' he ordered as she made to crouch beside him. She stopped, her hand flying to her mouth when she saw the blood-soaked pebbles upon which the body of a young woman was sprawled. As she stood there, her stomach churning, she heard a pitiful cry. Then, to her astonishment, the smaller pile of rags moved.

'Gracious,' she whispered.

'Here, take this,' her uncle urged. Automatically, Sarah reached out and took the trembling bundle from him. Gazing down, she saw terrified periwinkle eyes staring out of grimy skin.

'Take her to the cart, while I get someone to attend to the . . .' Her uncle's voice tailed off. 'Go,' he urged before calling to two policemen who were parading along the front.

Carefully cradling the little girl, Sarah cautiously made her way back across the road. As she placed her gently in the cart and climbed up after her, she saw those periwinkle eyes watching her warily. Pulling her onto her lap, Sarah couldn't help wrinkling her nose at the dreadful smell. Then the girl cowered into her rags as if she was trying to hide, and Sarah's heart went out to her.

'I'm Sarah,' she said. 'What's your name?' The girl stiffened, twirled her matted hair around one finger, but remained silent. 'You're safe now,' Sarah added just as the cart lurched and her uncle climbed in.

'What happened?' she asked.

He stared pointedly at the girl then shook his head. 'I expect you're hungry, little one,' he said breezily. The girl studied him before nodding. 'We'll take you home with us, and Mrs Daws will find you some bread and broth. Would you like that?' Again the girl nodded yet didn't say anything. As if his exertions had tired him, Samuel sat back in his seat and closed his eyes.

'Are you all right?' Sarah asked.

'Yes, I'm fine,' he assured her, but she could tell from the pallor of his skin, he was anything but. However, he picked up the reins and urged the pony on.

When they pulled up outside Red Cliffs, the urchin Pip appeared and pulled open the gates.

'Thank you, Pip,' Samuel said. 'You'll see to the pony?'

''Cors, guv, you know you can rely on me,' he grinned, looking curiously at the girl on Sarah's lap. 'Another waif, eh?'

'Indeed, Pip,' Samuel nodded, steering them around behind the house where steam was billowing from one of the brick outbuildings.

'The wash-house,' he explained. 'Luckily for us it's Monday, so Mrs Laver will be doing the laundry.'

Sarah glanced down at the little girl, wondering why her uncle should mention this seemingly inconsequential detail now. Then the back door of the house opened, and Mrs Daws stood frowning in the doorway.

'Another one, Doctor?' she sighed.

He nodded. 'Found her on the beach. A rum business and no mistake. Will you take her please, Mrs Daws?' But as the woman made to lift her down from the cart, the girl clung tighter to Sarah.

'Now, come along, little 'un, you can see Miss Sullivan when you're all clean,' she said firmly, prising the girl from Sarah and leading her into the wash-house.

'Why is she going in there?' Sarah asked, making to follow.

'She'll be fine with me, Miss Sullivan,' the woman told her. 'She needs a good scrubbing.'

Seeing her puzzled look, her uncle sighed. 'Goodness knows what she's harbouring. We have to make sure all the children are disinfected and deloused before they can come inside the house.' Seeing her shocked look, he smiled. 'Don't worry, Mrs Daws will ensure Mrs Laver is gentle with her. We built the bath-house next to the wash room for a reason, you know. Come along, let's go indoors,' he said, jumping down on to the path.

'What happened on the beach?' Sarah asked, not really wanting to hear yet needing to know.

'Looks like the woman, presumably her mother, died giving birth. I think the baby was stuck.' He sighed. 'Not particularly unusual, yet harrowing to think it might happen in broad daylight.'

'But there were all those people walking along the front. Surely someone must have seen something?'

'If they did they would have turned their heads away. Folk don't want to get involved in anything that's not nice, my dear. It's harsh but a fact of life, I'm afraid,' he added, seeing her horrified look. 'Come along.'

She followed him into the kitchen, ready to pursue the subject, but before she could say anything else he was overcome by a bout of coughing. Collapsing into the nearest chair, he fumbled in his jacket pocket, and as he brought out the little bottle of pills, Sarah hurriedly filled a glass from the jug on the table.

'Stupid chest,' he rasped, his eyes looking large in his gaunt face. Sarah was dismayed to see how much weight he'd lost in the short time since she'd last seen him. 'Well, don't stand staring,' he muttered. 'The kettle's boiling, and I'm dying for a cuppa.'

Sarah set about making the tea, glad of something to do. While she waited for it to brew, she stared around the room. The range was spotless, and a pot simmering gently on top wafted a savoury aroma her way. Despite the recent traumas, her stomach rumbled in hopeful anticipation, reminding her she hadn't eaten since snatching a hurried breakfast at first light. Assorted crockery, with its various patterns, was neatly stacked on the old dresser alongside pots that gleamed in the sunlight filtering in through the window. The large deal table was scrubbed, and even the flags on the floor looked freshly swept.

'Mrs Daws runs a good household,' Samuel wheezed, following her gaze. 'Been here nearly as long as I have, bless her, yet will she think of taking things easier?'

'Like you, Uncle?' she replied, pouring tea into cups. 'Do you take sugar?'

'At the price they charge, not likely,' he retorted, and she was pleased to hear the strength returning to his voice.

The door opened, and Mrs Daws bustled in carrying the little girl wrapped in a towel. Her matted hair had been shorn, and her face shone pink where it had been scrubbed. There was a defiant look in her eyes as they sought and found Sarah's.

'Right then, we'll put you in this,' the housekeeper said, pulling a dress from the pulley above the range and pointing to the number on the back. 'You'll be number eighteen.'

'She's to be known as a number?' Sarah gasped.

'Yes and no,' the housekeeper replied, helping the girl into the garment. 'She'll be called by her name when we find out what it is. However, all the children have numbered clothing and towels so they don't spread anything nasty. Right, that looks better,' she said to the girl. 'Now, come and stand on the mat by the door and let me check your scalp.'

As Mrs Daws ran a closed-tooth comb over the girl's head and inspected it closely, Samuel turned to Sarah.

'Don't look so horrified, it's not as bad as it sounds. We don't know where the girl's come from, and we need to observe scrupulous hygiene otherwise we might do more harm than good by spreading disease.'

'Good, all clean,' Mrs Daws pronounced. 'Now, come and sit at the table. I suppose you're hungry?' The girl nodded.

'Well, you've missed luncheon but you can sup some broth with the doctor and Miss Sullivan, how about that?' The girl nodded again. 'Where's your father, dearie? Does he live near here?' The girl looked glum and shook her head. 'Cat got your tongue, eh? Well, let's see if some food will help you find it. How about you, Miss Sullivan? Did you have a good train ride?' she asked as she bustled about setting the table and cutting wedges of bread.

'Call me Sarah, please, and do let me help,' she replied.

'Time enough when you've eaten. You look a bit peaky, if you don't mind me saying.'

'Sarah had her bag stolen on the journey, Mrs Daws,' Samuel explained.

'What a dreadful thing to have happened. Mrs Laver was just saying she heard there's a gang operating on the trains travelling to holiday resorts. Don't know what things are coming to, and that's a fact.' The housekeeper shook her head. 'Heard them new-fangled iron horses travel so fast they can fair shake the womb out of a woman.'

'I told Sarah you would find her some suitable clothing until she gets sorted,' Samuel said quickly.

'Of course, Doctor. That new verger called around with a large basket full of things just yesterday. We can sort through them. First, though, you both look filthy so get those hands washed while I dish up,' she said, ladling savoury liquid into their bowls. 'Now then, nipper, you need any help?' The girl looked affronted and snatched up the spoon in her left hand.

'Other hand,' she began but Samuel shook his head.

'Not now. She's had a harrowing experience.'

'Doesn't seem to have affected her appetite,' the house-keeper snorted as the girl lifted the dish to her mouth and gulped down the contents. 'I expect you'll want to check her over before she mingles with the others?'

'Indeed, Mrs Daws,' Samuel nodded.

'It's lucky for us we have Dr Lawrence to give them the once-over, Miss Sullivan. Couldn't afford the fees of the local GP, we couldn't.'

'I do hope this morning's experience hasn't put you off staying with us, Sarah?' her uncle asked, staring at her anxiously.

Sarah stared down at her dish, for in truth she'd been wondering if she was strong enough to cope. Then she felt the girl staring at her and, looking up, saw the silent pleading in those periwinkle eyes.

4

The room fell silent, and Sarah could feel three pairs of eyes staring intently as they waited for her answer.

'I promised I would stay to help, and that's what I intend to do,' Sarah replied firmly.

'Well, I'm very pleased to hear it,' Samuel said, relief replacing his worried look. 'I can't work out if there's more to do these days or if it's me taking longer to get things done, but there's no denying we need your help, is there, Mrs Daws?'

The housekeeper smiled warmly at Samuel. 'You do a marvellous job, Doctor. Why, those children are blessed with a roof over their heads and wholesome food in their stomachs thanks to you. But I agree, there's always more jobs to be done than hours to do them in. Suppose you'd like another slice of bread?' she added, turning to the child, whose eyes widened in disbelief.

There was a bang as the door flew open and a young girl of about thirteen, weighed down with a load of dirty bedding, staggered into the room. Her mop cap had slipped to the back of her head revealing a short crop of red curls which contrasted against the drab beige of her coarse cotton dress.

'The dormitories are spick and span, and this is the last of the washing for Mrs Laver. Shall I take it out to her?' she asked.

'Yes please, April, quick as you can, then you'd best tidy yourself up before I introduce you to Miss Sullivan here.' With a curious glance at Sarah, the girl nodded and hurried out to the wash room only to reappear almost immediately, smoothing down her dress with one hand whilst attempting to tuck her hair back under her cap with the other. It was then Sarah noticed the jagged scar running down one cheek.

'I was quick like you said, Mrs Daws,' she grinned.

'Good girl. This is April, Miss Sullivan. She finished her schooling here earlier this year and has stayed on as our scullery-come-maid-of-all. I don't know where I'd be without her, and that's a fact.' The maid beamed delightedly.

'Well, it's good to meet you, April, and what a delightful name you have.'

The girl grinned again. 'The doctor give it me 'cos it was the month he found me,' she said proudly. 'What job have you come for?'

'Manners, April,' Mrs Daws admonished.

'Miss Sullivan is going to help me with my paperwork,' Samuel explained.

'Hallelujah! 'Tis a nightmare trying to dust round all them letters and things,' April said, shaking her head.

'That's quite enough, young lady,' Mrs Daws said with a click of her tongue. Sarah turned away, trying to hide a grin at the girl's incorrigible nature. 'Now, I want you to take our new little friend here upstairs to show her where she'll be sleeping.'

April nodded. 'What's your name?' she asked softly, bending down to the girl's level. 'Cat got your tongue, eh? Well, never mind, until you find it I'll call you Monday seeing as how that's what day it is. You come along with April now, and I'll show you where everything is.' She held out her hand but the girl refused to take it and stood looking at Sarah.

Sarah knelt beside her and said gently, 'Would you like to stay here with us?' The girl nodded. 'Well, you go with April, and I promise I'll see you later.' The girl studied Sarah intently, then took April's hand and allowed herself to be led from the room.

'Has a way with the little ones, does April,' the housekeeper said. 'Course, she's not really more than a child herself, bless her. Now, let's get you some clean clothes sorted.'

'Please, there's no need, I can see you're busy,' Sarah said, as she began stacking their dirty dishes.

'April will see to those, and there's every need for you to change, my dear,' she replied, pointing to a dark stain on the front of Sarah's dress. 'Blood if I'm not mistaken.'

'Oh no,' Sarah exclaimed. 'And that's my only dress.'

'Nothing Mrs Laver can't fix, I'm sure. We'll go and see what the good ladies of St Nicholas' have given us. I dare say you'll be needing to look through your paperwork, Doctor.'

'Indeed I will. There's so much that needs attending to,' he said, rubbing his hand across his brow as he got to his feet. 'I'll leave you in Mrs Daws' capable hands, my dear. She'll see you have everything you need and show you where you'll be sleeping. I'll be in my study when you've got yourself sorted.'

'I'll bring you through a nice cup of tea when we've done, Doctor,' Mrs Daws called as she led Sarah through to the front room where the chairs were piled high with clothes, shoes and all manner of paraphernalia.

Ten minutes later, holding two dresses, an apron, a woollen shawl, two towels and a bag containing things for her toilet, she was following Mrs Daws up the stairs. Although she'd pointed out an apron was unnecessary for paperwork, the housekeeper had insisted she'd need one. As they approached the girls' dormitory, the housekeeper put a finger to her lips and beckoned. Peering through the door, they saw April cradling the girl in her lap and crooning to her softly. It was obvious the girl was sobbing her heart out, but as Sarah went to help, Mrs Daws shook her head.

'Let April look after her,' she whispered, walking further down the hallway and into the small room that was evidently hers. 'The poor little thing needs to let out her sorrow, and she might hold back if we interrupt.'

'I do hope I'm not inconveniencing you,' Sarah said, staring at the two narrow beds placed side by side, the small closet in the corner and the washstand with its flower-patterned jug and bowl.

'Don't worry about me, my dear. I fall asleep as soon as my head hits the pillow. Now, I asked Mrs Laver to bring up some warm water,' she said, pointing to the basin. 'You get washed and changed then bring that dress down for laundering. Just remember your towel number is twenty. It won't do to get it muddled with the children's. Which reminds me, school will be finishing soon, so I'd best get on.'

'I couldn't help noticing the scar on April's face,' Sarah said.

The woman's expression darkened. 'That were a rum do. The doctor heard pitiful squeals early one morning ten years back or more, went out to investigate and found her battered body by the gate. Someone had vented their spleen on the poor mite before dumping her and scarpering. Although the good doctor reported it, no one came forward, and, well, she's been here ever since. Happy little soul she is, but scared to leave here, which is understandable. Sleeps in the girls' dorm and takes care of the little ones, she does. Pip does the same for the boys. Of course, with his deformed body, nobody would employ him, so the doctor insisted he stay on and put him in charge of the gardens. Well, must get on. The doctor will be ready for his cup of tea. You get settled in and come down when you're ready.'

'Thank you for everything, Mrs Daws,' Sarah smiled, but the woman shook her head.

'No, thank you, Miss Sullivan. The doctor's not a well man. He needs to take things easy. You've come just at the right time.'

'I think what you are doing here is wonderful, and I'll do everything I can to help,' she assured her. The woman nodded then disappeared back down the stairs.

Sarah peered around the room, which was basic but adequate. Like the rest of the house, everything was shabby but spotless. Staring down at the things she was holding, she sighed. It wasn't wearing second-hand clothes that worried her or having to share with the housekeeper, much as she liked her privacy. It was the realization that the promise she'd made to help her uncle was going to have farther reaching effects than she'd envisaged. Come along now, Sarah, she chided, squaring her shoulders. Since when have you shied away from responsibility?

Catching sight of herself in the fly-spotted mirror above the washstand, her eyes widened in horror. The salt-laden air had caused her naturally curly hair to frizz under her bonnet, and it looked like an unruly bird's nest. Her cheeks were smudged with dirt as was her lace collar. Staring down at her dress, she saw it was rumpled and her black boots were caked with dried sand. The ravages of the morning had clearly left their mark. Goodness knows what her godfather must think of her.

Quickly, she rinsed her face and hands then changed out of her soiled dress and into the blue serge. It was still in good condition but very full on the hips, obviously having previously been worn by a lady of more rounded proportions. Sarah sighed. With her angular figure she was used to adapting patterns so that the garments she made fitted well, but her sewing things had been in her bag which had been stolen. Which reminded her, there was also the matter of her money bag she'd so prudently sewn into her pocket. She spotted a comb on the washstand, snatched it up and, using the tail end, began unpicking the stitches. Realizing that those coins were all she now possessed, she carefully tucked the pouch inside the placket of the blue dress's skirt.

Samuel grimaced at the piles of paperwork littering his desk then eased his aching limbs into the chair. To his mind, the events of the morning had once again proved there were more important factors to running the school than filling in official forms. That poor woman on the beach must have suffered terribly in her final hours, and who knew what that little girl had witnessed? Just how much she'd been affected remained to be seen, but clearly the shock had taken her tongue. He shook his head. And how had it affected Sarah? God knows he needed help but had he done the right thing in asking her to give up the life she knew to move in here? Yet what was the alternative? He couldn't, no, wouldn't let his life's work go to rack and ruin, or worse.

Seized by a fit of coughing, he reached for his bottle of pills. So much to do, so little time, he fretted, closing his eyes as exhaustion washed over him.

The cheerful cries of children woke him. Struggling to his feet, he made his way over to the window then smiled as he saw them spilling out onto the grass, happy to be free from the confines of the schoolroom. It never ceased to amaze him how soon they settled into the regime at Red Cliffs. Away from the harsh, cruel conditions most had been born into, they thrived on the food they received and were eager to learn. Higgins, a good master, forever pressed upon them the importance of grasping the opportunity they'd been given to forge new lives for themselves. Of course, for some the past never truly went away, and when darkness cloaked the dormitories, the terrors returned to haunt them.

'Here we are, Doctor,' the housekeeper said, coming into the room with a tray of tea things. 'I've put a cup out for Miss Sullivan too. I left her settling in upstairs and told her to join you when she's ready.'

'Thank you, Mrs Daws. Do you think I've done the right thing?' he asked sinking back into his chair.

'Getting her to help, you mean?' she replied, as ever picking up on his thoughts. 'Yes, I do, actually. From what you said, she's not had an easy time, what with losing her father after nursing him through his illness. A new start will be good for her and, from what I've seen, she seems a capable young woman. Besides, you need the help. You're looking more tired by the day, if you don't mind me saying. Now, it's been a day and a half, so get this tea down you.' Samuel grinned wryly as he accepted the cup she proffered.

An almighty crash made them both jump, sending the dark liquid spilling into the saucer.

'What the . . .' he began as something landed with a thud on the floor in front of them.

'Here's the problem,' Mrs Daws said, holding up a sock stuffed with sawdust and pieces of rubble. 'Those scallywags up to no good by the look of it. And just look at the mess on my clean floor.' They were both staring at the fragments of broken window when Higgins appeared, dragging two red-faced boys by their ears.

'Apologize at once, you scallys,' he ordered.

'We didn't mean to, sir,' the elder boy mumbled, squirming beneath the teacher's hold. 'Still, at least it's only the little one,' he ventured hopefully.

'Not good enough, Brown. What have you to say for your preposterous behaviour, Black?' he roared down at the other lad.

'Sorry, sir,' he muttered, staring at the broken window in dismay.

'You will both clean up the mess then spend the evening learning how to replace a window pane. The money for the materials will come from the wages you get delivering produce. It'll be an expensive business so you'll have to hope the good doctor will be gracious enough to accept payment by instalments. It will be the other side of Christmas before you see any money.'

The boys glanced at each other in horror. 'But it's only October,' Brown wailed.

'We're really sorry, sir,' Black declared to Samuel. 'It won't happen again, I swear.'

'Too right it won't,' Higgins muttered. 'And if I ever hear you swearing it'll be the tawse for you, hear me, boys?' They nodded and then stood there looking down at their feet.

'Well, no real harm done,' Samuel said.

'Except for disobedience and wilful damage,' Higgins stated, turning the full force of his glare on the culprits. 'Hungry, are you?' Two faces stared hopefully as they nodded. 'Well, what a shame 'cos it will take 'til supper time and beyond to clear up and repair. Perhaps a hungry belly will remind you to behave in future.'

'Surely it was an accident,' Sarah said, coming into the room and witnessing the scene.

'They have to learn that actions, accidental or not, have consequences.'

'They are only young boys and . . .' she began.

'Just what we need, a blinking do-gooder,' Higgins muttered, the glint Sarah remembered from before sparking in his eyes. 'I am the schoolmaster around here and know the importance of discipline. If you'll excuse us, Doctor, I'll see these reprobates clear the mess and make good the damage. They will of course be severely reprimanded,' he added, glaring at Sarah before marching the boys from the room.

39

'I'd best get back to the kitchen and see to the supper, Doctor,' Mrs Daws said, avoiding Sarah's eyes as she gathered up the tea things.

'It seems I made a mess of that . . .' Sarah began.

Her godfather regarded her silently for a few moments. 'Higgins is a very capable master, and the running of the schoolroom his domain. He has been with us six years or more, and we are lucky to have him. With his qualifications and experience he could easily go elsewhere and be paid a lot more too,' Samuel pointed out.

'Oh,' she murmured. 'I didn't realize.'

Seeing her crestfallen look, her godfather smiled. 'His ways might seem harsh but, believe it or not, he does have the interests of the children at heart. It will serve no purpose to Red Cliffs if you are at odds with each other, my dear.'

Although he spoke gently, Sarah could see he meant what he said.

'I understand, Uncle, and don't wish to fall out with him,' she replied.

Yet surely what those children really needed was love and tolerance?

5

Ignoring the jeers of the other children, Higgins frog-marched the two, now-subdued boys down to the workroom. He was fuming. How dare that woman have the audacity to tell him how he should treat his pupils? He'd been the master here for over six years and ran a good schoolroom. He was damned if he'd put up with some goody two-shoes telling him how to do his job, doctor's god-daughter or not. She'd probably never done a day's work in her life. Why, she'd even found time to change her dress in the short time she'd been here, for the one she'd been wearing when he saw her climbing out of the cart had surely been brightly patterned.

'Take a broom and pan up to the doctor's study right now and get that mess cleared up,' he barked at the boys. 'I'll follow when I've collected the necessary things.' He watched as they scuttled away then set about gathering together the materials needed to effect a repair to the broken window. It had been a long day, and he was hungry, but he knew the doctor would be working at his desk for a while longer, and the wind was already freshening. The man's cough had been worrying him for some time, and although he never complained, Harry could see it was getting him down.

By the time he got back to the doctor's study, the shards of glass had been brushed up, and the man was talking to the boys.

'So now you understand why you must be careful when you're having a kick around?'

'Yes, sir, and we're really sorry, sir,' they chorused.

'Well, here's Master Higgins. He's probably had enough of you already today so I suggest you apologize to him for making him work late.'

'We're really sorry, sir,' they chorused.

'We've checked there's no splinters of glass on the floor that could cut anybody's feet,' Brown added.

Higgins looked at the boys and shook his head. 'So I should hope. I'm sorry, Doctor, but I'm going to have to board up the window – unless we have the funds to purchase glass.'

'Boarding it will have to be, I'm afraid. We'll just have to hope the neighbours don't see and complain.' The doctor raised his bushy brows. 'Right, boys, I want you to help your master,' he instructed them. 'Use this as an opportunity to learn another skill. I'll leave you to it, Higgins,' he said, snatching up his hat and making for the door. 'Perhaps you would be good enough to let Mrs Daws know I am going for a walk and won't be in for supper. Good evening.'

'Yes, of course, Doctor. Good evening. Where are your manners, boys?'

'Good night, sir,' they chorused.

Back in her kitchen, Mrs Daws tutted at the dirty dishes still on the table. Calling to Maisie, she started collecting them then stood the girl up on her pail and told her to begin washing up. Maisie would take much longer than April but it couldn't be helped, for evidently she was still upstairs comforting the new girl.

With her thoughts in a whirl, she got out the remaining bread, sighed at how quickly it had diminished, then began slicing as thinly as she could to eke it out. To think when she'd woken that morning she'd thought things would become easier from today. Now, not only had they a new pupil to settle in, but the atmosphere between Miss Sullivan and the master was as icy as the coming frost. It was obvious they had different ideas, and she wasn't sure it boded well for the future of the school. No wonder the poor doctor looked more subdued than usual.

'What can I do to help?'

She started as Sarah appeared at her side. 'You fair made me jump, creeping in like that. Not helping the doctor with his paperwork then?'

Sarah shook her head. 'He said he had a headache and suggested I start tomorrow. Truth to tell, Mrs Daws, I think he's cross with me.'

'The doctor has a lot on his plate at the moment, and with him not being a well man, he can do without any upsets,' she replied, staring at Sarah pointedly.

'I haven't caused no upsets. I been a dry girl for ages now, haven't I, Mrs Daws?' a tiny voice piped up.

'Well, for all of two days you have, Maisie,' the housekeeper laughed and the tension was broken.

'Good girl,' Sarah said, trying not to smile at the froth of soap suds that covered more of her than the dishes. 'Look, why don't I wash those while you dry them.'

'That would be a help. The children will be in for their supper before we know it,' Mrs Daws agreed. 'Now you know why I suggested you'd need that apron. Maisie, whilst you're helping Miss Sullivan, why don't you tell her our morning routine? We find it helps them to settle in if they know what to expect,' she explained to Sarah, pointing to the wall where a timetable, printed in copperplate writing, was displayed.

'We gets up at 6 a.m., dress, make our bed, then empty our pots in the yard. Wash face and hands at pump. Then we do morning exercise and have breakfast at 7 a.m.,' Maisie recited proudly.

'Well done, Maisie, and can you remember what comes after breakfast?'

'We either help in the garden or kitchen before school starts at 8.30 a.m. Play at 10.30 then lessons again until lunch at 12.30.' She stopped as April came into the room holding the new girl's hand. Two periwinkle eyes regarded Sarah, and she smiled back.

'All right, dearies?' Mrs Daws asked.

April nodded then frowned at the clean dishes waiting to be taken through to the dining room. 'Shall we set the table, Mrs Daws?'

'Yes please, I'm all behind today. Any luck with the little 'un's name?' she asked, lowering her voice.

April sighed. 'We've looked everywhere but can't find that voice of yours, can we?' The girl shook her head then stared down at the floor. 'Never mind, perhaps it's in the dining room. You carry these spoons through, and we'll have a look.' Sarah watched as the little girl followed April through to the next room.

'Poor little mite,' she murmured.

'She'd have been a site worse off if the good doctor hadn't found her,' the housekeeper said briskly. 'Practical help is worth more than a peck of words, I find.'

'But we don't know anything about her?' Sarah frowned.

'The good doctor will make enquiries, and even if he doesn't find out anything, does it really matter? She's a little girl in need of care and attention, and that's what she'll get here.'

'You're right of course, Mrs Daws,' Sarah agreed, feeling chastened. Obviously love came before mere detail at Red Cliffs, and while she heartily endorsed their principle, it made Sarah realize how different life here was. 'Now, what can I do to help?' she asked, anxious to make herself useful.

'The farmer's wife dropped off some cheese she said was left over, bless her. If you'd like to get it from the pantry over there then grate it, the children can have it with their bread.'

To Sarah's surprise, the shelves in the pantry were quite bare considering the number of pupils and staff at the school, and when she returned with the cheese, she couldn't help commenting.

'I would have thought you'd have more stores in. Do you have regular deliveries?'

Mrs Daws shrugged. 'Depends what funds are available. We're very good at supplying our own vegetables and make our bread two or three times a week. Pip's been monitoring the Bramley tree and says the apples are almost ready for picking, so that'll be a treat.'

'That's good but surely the community help out?' Sarah persisted, thinking of the way her father's patients had rallied around with stews and casseroles when he'd been poorly.

'The church does, of course, and some of the more sympathetic traders, but we have also to remember the objective is to teach the children to be as independent as possible. In return for the cheese the master will take some of the children up to the farm to help out with the chores. Poor farmer Jim can't do much since his horse rolled over on him when he was ploughing. Anyhow, the children will like as not come back with a basket of eggs, which will have to be returned when more chores will be done. And so it goes on. It's a good way to teach the children that they don't get anything for nothing,' Mrs Daws pointed out.

'It's a sound ethos,' Sarah replied, vigorously rubbing the cheese down the grater.

'Can you use the finest blade on that?' Mrs Daws asked. 'Packs it out more. Then if you can make up the sandwiches, I'll see to the tea.' Turning to the hob, she confided, 'Trouble is there are those round here who think the school lowers the tone of the neighbourhood and would like it moved to the back of Torquay behind Torre station, if not closed down altogether.'

'Good heavens, why?'

'Ragged urchins are not a palatable sight to some, Miss Sullivan. Torre station's as far into the town as the railway's allowed to bring their freight, so I guess the powers that be think it would be more a more suitable place for the likes of us.'

'But Red Cliffs is by the sea. It's the perfect place for these poor children to take the air.'

'Ah, but this part of Torquay's becoming ever more fashionable, and these large houses have increased in value. They are being snapped up by people wanting holiday homes, and with the new sewerage having been connected, they are even having indoor bathrooms installed.'

'That would be nice for the children,' Sarah mused.

'But too costly for the doctor to afford, which means he can't keep up with those who are set on improving the area. If you take a look around, you'll see some of the large places are being turned into lucrative hotels, and this area is fast becoming the desirable part of town. This house might be sizeable but as the poor doctor spends all his money on the children rather than updating the building, its shabbiness has become a bone of contention.'

'Surely that's a rather shallow attitude?' Sarah asked, shocked by the venom in the woman's voice.

'It is, but then there are some very shallow people around. As ever, it is those that have the most who shout loudest so get heard.'

'But doesn't the doctor voice his opinion? Surely if he let it be known . . .' Her voice trailed off as she saw the schoolmaster glaring at her from the doorway.

'Mrs Daws, I just came in to tell you the doctor won't be in for supper. So, Miss Sullivan,' he snapped, his eyes narrowing as he turned to face Sarah. 'Not content with criticizing my discipline of the children, it appears you now see fit to question the way the doctor does things.'

'That's not what I meant . . .' Sarah began, but he was in full flood.

'Having only arrived here this morning, you cannot possibly know enough about the school to have a considered opinion on its running. The doctor is a busy man. He is also very principled and has neither the time nor inclination to explain his affairs to the busybodies around here. Nor should he be required to. Good evening.' He went out, slamming the door behind him so that the cups on the dresser rattled.

Sarah stared at his departing back in dismay. 'But I only said . . .'

'Seems you and he have got off on the wrong foot,' the housekeeper sighed. 'Oh well, we must press on. It's all right, young Maisie,' she crooned to the tiny girl who, on hearing raised voices, had cowered in the corner. 'Come on, supper's ready, so you can help me summon everyone indoors.' She smiled, and Maisie ran into the hall, picked up the striker and began beating the brass gong with all her might.

As Sarah walked through to the adjoining room, she found the pupils standing quietly behind their chairs. April was at the head of the girls' table, the new little girl by her side, whilst Pip was clearly in charge of the boys.

'Right, children, the doctor and Master Higgins are not joining us today so I shall say grace. Before I do, I would like to introduce Miss Sullivan who has come to help the doctor. I'd like you to welcome her and help her settle in.'

'Welcome, Miss Sullivan,' they chanted.

'Thank you, everyone,' Sarah said, smiling around at the children, who were eying the food hungrily, impatient to begin eating.

'Right, hands together and close your eyes,' Mrs Daws instructed. No sooner had she finished the short prayer of thanks than there was a scraping of chairs on the floor as the children sat down to eat. They had clearly been taught well, for their manners were good and they ate in silence. Together, Sarah and April looked after the new little girl and were gratified to see her eat something. It seemed no time at all before the sandwiches had been devoured and the children were sitting with their arms folded, ready to leave the table.

'Goodness, I am impressed,' Sarah said, as she watched them clearing away. Some stayed to help in the kitchen while others went outside to tend the garden.

'Well, as soon as they've finished their evening chores they have a free period before bed so they know what side their bread's buttered, if you'll excuse the pun. As the days are long and full, we all turn in about 7 p.m. I for one will be pleased to see my bed tonight.'

True to her word, no sooner had Mrs Daws' head touched the pillow than she was asleep. As gentle snores emanated around the room, Sarah lay back reflecting on the day. And what a traumatic day it had been, she thought. She'd had her bag stolen and now had to wear cast-off clothing, but that was nothing compared to what that poor little soul had witnessed on the beach. Whilst Sarah had kept her promise to return, in the few short hours she'd been here, she'd managed to fall out with the schoolmaster and upset her godfather. She sighed into the darkness. Hadn't her father taught her to keep her own counsel?

She stiffened suddenly, thinking she'd heard someone crying out. Propping herself up on her elbow, she listened intently, but the only sound was the creaking of the old house as it settled for the night. Then, as the housekeeper's snores reached a crescendo, she shrugged, lay back down and pulled the thin cover over her head. What wouldn't she give to be back in her own, quiet little room in Plymouth. Perhaps she could return, for what qualities did she really have to help with the running of the school or its children, come to that?

Then she heard something scrabbling at the doorknob and froze. Turning her head, she could just make out the outline of someone standing in the entrance. She shivered and was about to reach for the lamp when the bed creaked, and a small body crept in beside her. It was the new little girl, and by the way she was shaking, it was obvious she was scared. Pulling the trembling body close, Sarah knew she'd been given her answer.

6

When Sarah next opened her eyes, shadows of sunlight were dancing on the ceiling. She felt disorientated, and it was some moments before she remembered where she was. The space beside her was cold; there was no sign of the little girl who'd snuggled up to her the previous night. The other bed was empty, and it was clear Mrs Daws was already up and about her business.

Hearing the sound of footsteps on the garden path, she jumped out of bed and was just in time to see the tail end of a crocodile of children, towels under their arms, following Master Higgins towards the beach. Cursing herself for sleeping in, she quickly dressed in the blue serge dress, clipped back her wayward curls, then took her precious purse from under the pillow and carefully placed it in her pocket.

'Good morning, dear, did you sleep well?' Mrs Daws enquired as she entered the kitchen. The housekeeper was standing at the range stirring a huge pot of porridge, and the appetizing smell made Sarah's stomach rumble.

'I'm so sorry for sleeping in. You should have woken me,' Sarah apologized. 'What can I do to help?'

'You was slumbering like a baby. Not surprising really, when you consider the day you had yesterday, and obviously the new little 'un found her way into your bed. I got her up and dressed. She's gone with the others for their morning exercise.'

'Yes, I saw Higgins marching them down the path like soldiers, but do you think it's a good idea to take her back to the beach so soon after the tragedy?' she cried.

The housekeeper looked up from the pot and frowned. 'April's gone with her,' Mrs Daws said, as if that made everything all right.

'That's as may be but . . .'

'Look, Miss Sullivan, he's a good master and knows what he's doing,' she cut in.

'I'm not so sure,' Sarah muttered, remembering the terrified look in those periwinkle eyes. 'Won't it take her some time to recover from the ordeal of losing her mother?'

'Sometimes it's better for children to face things rather than let their fears fester,' the woman pointed out, giving the pot a vigorous stir.

'But she's so small and Higgins is extremely strict,' Sarah persisted, remembering the way he'd barked at the young boys the previous day.

The housekeeper sighed. 'Underneath that tough exterior beats a heart of goodness. Harry gives many more hours to the school than he's paid for. He might seem strict, but believe you me, he has the best interests of those children at heart. And they need the security discipline provides. They know where they stand then.'

'Hmm,' she murmured, doubtfully.

'Why not observe how things are done here before passing judgement, eh?' Although the woman smiled, once again Sarah felt as though she'd been reprimanded. Determined not to upset the housekeeper further, she smiled.

'You are right of course, Mrs Daws. Thank you for your words of wisdom.'

''Cors you could always join them next time they go,' the woman continued.

Sarah shuddered, for ever since a boy had held her head under the waves when she was a child, she'd been scared of the sea. However, having been found wanting once already, she wasn't about to admit her weakness.

'Shall I take these through to the dining room?' she asked quickly, pointing to the two large platters of bread on the table.

'Well, you're not officially here to do kitchen duties but we all tend to muck in, so thank you, that would be a help. Those children are always hungry after their exercise in the briny.'

Sarah was about to ask if it wasn't a bit late in the year for them to be swimming in the sea but bit her tongue. Mrs Daws was right. It would be prudent to monitor the daily regime here before commenting.

'Morning, ladies.' They looked up to see Samuel in the doorway. 'I've a meeting with the vicar, so can I leave it to you to supervise the girls at breakfast, Sarah?'

'Yes, of course,' she replied, happy to think he trusted her.

'And Higgins will see to the boys. I know it's your day for working your magic on replenishing our provisions, Mrs Daws.' He smiled then turned to leave.

'Now then, Doctor, I hope you're not thinking of going out without some hot breakfast inside you,' Mrs Daws clucked, placing a bowl of porridge on the scrubbed table and folding her arms. Sarah hid a smile as her godfather meekly sat down and began to eat.

'The kettle's coming to the boil so I'll make you some tea, Doctor, though them leaves have been mashed so many times gawd knows what colour it'll be.'

He shook his head. 'I've no time, I'm afraid. The vicar doesn't like to be kept waiting, and as I need to appeal to his better nature yet again, I'd best be on time. I'll have one when I return,' he added quickly when he saw the housekeeper open her mouth to protest. 'Perhaps you'll join me in the study then, Sarah, and we'll make a start on the dreaded paperwork.' He pulled a face as he got to his feet. 'Thank you, Mrs Daws, delicious as usual.'

'Surprised you've eaten enough to notice,' she sniffed, picking up the still half-full dish and scraping the porridge back into the pot.

There was a clattering out in the yard, and looking out of the window, Sarah saw the children jostling each other to peg their wet towels onto the snaking washing line to dry. Then the door burst open, and there was a deafening thud of footsteps as the stampede headed for the dining room.

'You go through, Miss Sullivan, and I'll bring in the porridge,' Mrs Daws said.

The children were already standing to attention behind their chairs, watched over by Pip and April. To Sarah's surprise, the little girl Monday was standing calmly beside her, looking none the worse for her trip to the beach. In fact, she actually had some colour in her pale cheeks. Maybe the master had known what he was doing, she mused.

There was a rousing cheer as Mrs Daws came in and placed a large pot before Sarah and another at the head of the boys' table. Then Higgins strode into the room, and silence descended like a bank of fog. He shot Sarah a wary look as he passed; she could sense the tension crackling between them. The children put their hands together while the master intoned the short grace in a soft yet meaningful voice that left Sarah wondering where he was from. It was certainly a different tone to the one she'd heard him using earlier, and she preferred it. There was little time for pondering, though, for no sooner had he finished than there was the sound of chairs scraping on the floor, and the girls stared expectantly in Sarah's direction. Following Higgins' lead, she hastily began ladling the porridge into their bowls while April passed around the plate of bread.

Sarah smiled as she watched the children tucking in as though they hadn't eaten for weeks. Then, satisfied everything was under control, she started on her own food. The porridge was good. She bent her head over her bowl and ate hungrily. Suddenly her spoon was snatched from her hand.

'What do you think you're doing?' she cried, staring up into the set face of Higgins. The room fell silent as, ignoring her protests, he leaned forward and fished something out of the bottom of her dish.

'Who is responsible for this abomination?' he demanded, staring around the table at each girl in turn. Nobody said a word. 'I shall ask just once more. If the culprit doesn't own up, every single one of you will go without luncheon and supper.' As horrified gasps ran around both tables, a red-faced girl of about nine raised her hand.

'It was an accident, sir,' she muttered.

'Oh, so this earwig just accidentally dropped into Miss Sullivan's bowl, did it, Edith Curdy?' Sarah stared from the girl to the milk-covered object the master was swinging between his fingers and shuddered.

The girl shook her head. 'It was only a joke, sir.'

'And it would have been funny if Miss Sullivan had choked, would it?' he persisted.

'No, sir,' she whispered.

'Apologize this minute, you miserable excuse for a human being, you,' he barked.

'Sorry, miss,' the girl muttered, staring down at the floor.

'Now, take this poor creature outside and bury it,' he ordered, thrusting the offending insect into the girl's hand. 'As punishment, you will wash and dry up all the breakfast things by yourself. There will be no play at all for you today. Instead you will spend your break times emptying the earth closets, which, I am reliably informed, are full to the brim. That will take you quite some time, during which you can reflect on your shameful behaviour.' Sarah opened her mouth to say that no harm had been done, but Higgins shot her a warning look and she kept quiet.

'Now clear,' he roared, banging his fist down on the table so that the spoons jangled against the bowls. Immediately, the children jumped to their feet and, dishes in hand, almost ran from the room.

'Sorry about that,' Higgins said, when they had the room to themselves. 'With these little horrors, you need eyes in your behind.'

'I can't deny I'm grateful you spotted the earwig but I'm sure there was no need to be so harsh . . .'

'There was every need, Miss Sullivan,' he cut in. 'It is our duty here at Red Cliffs to prepare these children for the outside world, and that means making them aware of what is acceptable behaviour and what is not.'

'Talking of acceptable behaviour,' Sarah replied, 'I was surprised you took the new little girl back to the beach so soon after her ordeal. It could have disturbed her.'

The master stared at her for a moment, that glint she'd come to recognize sparking in his eyes. 'Did she look in any way disturbed? I thought I saw her tucking into her breakfast quite heartily.'

'Well, yes,' Sarah replied, realizing this was true. 'But . . .'

'In my experience,' he began, stressing the word experience, 'it is better for them to confront their demons sooner rather than later. Good morning.'

As the door closed behind him, Sarah sighed. Were they destined always to disagree? She'd only meant to help, for sometimes women saw things from a different perspective. She was still musing when her attention was caught by movement outside, and she went over to the window. The children were now busy tending the vegetable plot, some digging, others emptying buckets of weeds into the compost heap. She noticed the miscreants from the previous day, Black and Brown, sweeping up the debris in the yard. Pip was keeping a watchful eye on the carrots and potatoes that were being harvested and scraped free of mud before they were laid out on the low wall to dry. They were all working diligently, which was more than she was, she realized.

As she passed by the table, she saw the seat where Maisie had been sitting was wet. Poor little thing, no doubt the upset had affected her, she thought, hurrying through to advise Mrs Daws.

The housekeeper was sat at the table writing a shopping list. When she saw Sarah her lips began twitching.

'Heard about your breakfast. Couldn't help earwigging,' she spluttered. 'Don't mind me,' she added, tears of mirth rolling down her face. 'It's their little pranks that keep me spirits up. You'd best keep your eyes open 'cos you never know what those little perishers are going to do next, and being new, you'll be their prime target. As will the silent nipper 'til she finds her voice. Still, April will keep an eye on her when she's not working.'

'Thank you, Mrs Daws, Higgins did warn me. By the way, I think Maisie had an accident during that upset at breakfast,' Sarah said.

The woman sighed. 'She was doing so well, too. Never mind, can't be helped. I'll see to it,' she said, getting to her feet and grabbing a cloth. 'The doctor's waiting for you in his study, by the way.'

Sarah hurried along the hallway, determined to show her godfather how amenable she really was. She owed it to her father to try and help his friend.

'Ah, Sarah dear.' Samuel looked up from the papers he was studying. 'Settling in all right?'

'Yes, thank you,' she replied, her eyes straying to the boarded-up window that threw shadows over the floor, darkening the room. 'Now, what can I help you with first?'

Samuel pushed the papers to one side. 'Before we make a start on this little lot, it would probably be helpful if I fill you in on how we do things here, the aims and aspirations for our pupils. Firstly, St Nicholas' contribute generously in all ways. You will have seen the church on the corner of the road, of course?' Sarah nodded, remembering thinking how incongruous the large building at the end of the road seemed, towering over its neighbouring houses in the road. 'Each Sunday after breakfast, the staff and pupils attend morning service before returning to help with the soup kitchen.'

'Ah, yes, you told me you have people who come here for their luncheon,' Sarah replied, remembering the trestle tables propped against the wall in the dining room.

'The waifs who live on the streets know they will get a hot meal, and of course there are those parents struggling to make ends meet who send their children along for free food. Anyway, it is our policy to help all those who come here. The good ladies of the church hold sales of work for Red Cliffs and will donate clothes and anything else they think suitable for us to distribute.'

'Like my dress,' Sarah said, looking down at the blue serge.

Her godfather smiled. 'That was fortuitous, was it not? The vicar introduced me to the new verger, Jack Wise, this morning. He seems an enthusiastic young man who has promised to help in any way he can. During the course of our conversation, I happened to mention that your bag had been stolen, and he told me about a gang operating in the area. It seems they prey on tourists who come here on vacation, for usually their luggage contains 'ripe pickings', such as jewellery and silver toiletry sets.'

Sarah gave a harsh laugh. 'Well, they certainly won't find anything like that in mine.'

'Jack knows someone in the local constabulary and will mention the theft to him.'

'You mean there is a chance I might get my bag back?' Sarah asked eagerly, her hand automatically going to the purse in her pocket. 'It's so demeaning to think these few coins are all I have.'

Her godfather frowned. 'We'll have to wait and see, but to be honest, I wouldn't hold out much hope. Whilst I agree the loss of your things was unfortunate, they are merely that, possessions, and as such can be replaced.' The last few words came out on a wheeze, and as if the speech had been too much for him, he slumped in his chair. A fit of rasping coughing seized him and he fumbled in his pocket for the bottle of pills. Sarah passed him his glass of water then sat there feeling guilty. She didn't remind him that almost everything she had to remember her parents by was in that bag.

7

As the coughing fit passed and Samuel's colour began to return to normal, Sarah shook her head.

'I'm sorry, Uncle,' she murmured. 'Perhaps I should leave?'

'No, it is me who should apologize. I've spent so many years concentrating on this place with little care for possessions, I sometimes forget my frugal ways aren't necessarily normal. Let me give you some money to replace your clothes. It was inconsiderate expecting you to be happy wearing other people's cast-offs,' he said, opening the top drawer of his desk and drawing out a cash tin. 'I do keep a modest amount here for emergencies.'

Sarah felt awful. 'Please, Uncle, that won't be necessary,' she said quickly. 'Use it to replace that glass.' She pointed to the boarded window.

'Well, if you're sure,' he said, frowning as he replaced the tin. 'I want you to stay here, Sarah,' he continued. 'Although your father was good enough to keep me informed of your progress, I would welcome the opportunity to get to know you better. Besides you have much to offer Red Cliffs.' He sat back in his chair and fixed her with his direct gaze.

'If you really think I can be of assistance,' she agreed. Even if she did return to Plymouth, she would have nowhere to live, for knowing a new doctor was taking over her father's practice, she'd handed over the keys. Besides, she was already becoming attached to the children and wanted to help. Staring down at the clutter on her godfather's desk, it was obvious he needed help. Besides, she liked a challenge; it wasn't in her nature to give up easily.

'Now, tell me, how is the little girl we found yesterday?' he asked, breaking into her thoughts.

'She seems happy following April around, although I was surprised Master Higgins took her to the beach this morning. I mean, it's so soon after . . .' Remembering Mrs Daws' advice, she stuttered to a halt. 'But I'm sure he knows best.'

'He does, believe you me. If he thought for one moment it wasn't the right thing for her he would have left her with Mrs Daws. Higgins swears bathing in salty water, along with deep breathing of the healthy ozone, is the key to attaining a strong constitution. I too believe hydrotherapy is nature's best cure, although my exercise is more likely to consist of an amble around the block these days. A healthy body makes for a healthy mind.'

'I agree outdoor exercise and swimming in the sea can be beneficial but surely the children go to the indoor baths in the winter?' she asked, remembering the bath saloons she'd seen on her way here.

Samuel gave a harsh laugh. 'I rather think the good folk of Torquay would have something to say about that. The pupils at Red Cliffs are tolerated rather than welcomed around here. They are deemed to lower the tone of the neighbourhood.'

'But that's preposterous,' she cried, then remembered Mrs Daws had said something similar the previous day.

Samuel shrugged philosophically. 'Yet that's the way things are. We have to ensure the children bathe in the most sheltered cove as it is. Now, back to the young girl. The vicar had already heard about the dreadful business on the beach and believes the deceased woman was a Romany, cast out by her folk when she eloped with a Gorgio, but we'll know more when the police have finished their enquiries.' Sarah nodded, thinking that would explain the girl's distinctive colouring.

'Do they know anything about the child's father?'

'Not yet,' he sighed. 'Although the police are trying to trace him.'

'What will happen if she continues refusing to speak?' Sarah asked. 'Mrs Daws said the other children might be cruel to her.'

Samuel narrowed his eyes. 'They might taunt her or play pranks but I don't think they'd actually be cruel. However, we'll keep a weather eye out, and if there's no improvement or she seems to be suffering in any way, we'll send her to the Deaconess. She has a home nearby which she opens for children with afflictions. A lovely woman who, with her loyal assistant, has achieved some remarkable results. Of course, she doesn't have the same cash constraints as we do here and, as numbers are fewer, is able to offer them a more comfortable environment. In fact, that might be the perfect solution for the little girl anyway.'

At this, Sarah felt a sharp pang in her chest, for she'd already become very fond of Monday, as April had christened her.

'Oh I hope we can keep her. Another move would unsettle her further, surely?' she cried.

'We'll see if the police can shine any light on the whereabouts of the little girl's father before speaking to the Deaconess. It could well be that when he finds out about the "accident" he'll turn up to claim her.' Seeing Sarah's expression, he sighed. 'Sarah, it is easy to get emotionally attached, especially under circumstances like this, but we must always do what is in the child's best interest,' Samuel said gently, giving her a knowing look.

'Very well,' she replied, understanding what he said was true. 'Does the Deaconess only take children with infirmities?' she asked, interested despite herself.

'Yes, she knows how difficult they can be to place, and her objective is the same as ours: to teach the children how to find their position in society. When I first took in Pip she offered to place him but the scallywag refused to go, saying he liked it here. Of course, that was some years ago now.'

'I noticed his limp and humped back. What is wrong with him, exactly?'

'Too long living in the dirt and damp of the sewers,' Samuel sighed. 'When we found him, we thought he'd contracted typhus, for he was covered in lice and had such a fever. We feared he would have to go into hospital, but Mrs Daws and I nursed him between us, and, well, his fighting spirit pulled him through, although his deformities remain. Still, as you saw for yourself, anyone more incorrigible you've yet to meet. He's bright and proved a good pupil but there was little chance of him being accepted in the workplace, so we kept him on to help with the children. They adore him even if he does keep them in line.'

'You obviously love children, Uncle,' Sarah said, seeing the soft look in his eyes when he spoke of them. 'Did you never want to marry and have a family of your own?' A look of sadness crossed his face, and he was silent for so long, Sarah wished she hadn't asked.

'These children here are my family,' he eventually replied. 'Which is why I need to ensure the school keeps running. Now, much as I hate it, we really must get down to this paperwork.'

Higgins was fuming as he made his way down to the schoolroom. In all the years he'd been at Red Cliffs he'd never had his judgement questioned. He knew he was a good master and had the best interests of all the children at heart. How dare that frizzy-haired, high-handed woman question his methods? He had been only too aware the new child might react badly when he took her back to the beach and had instructed April to keep an eye on her. He also knew how cruel children could be if they thought anyone was receiving different treatment, especially if it was perceived as preferential, and judged it better to treat them all the same.

Although the little girl had been hesitant at first, it was obvious she was used to the sea. With April's encouragement, she had soon been swimming along with the others and, on her return, had eaten a hearty breakfast. And had that wretched woman been grateful when he'd spotted Edith dropping that earwig in her porridge? Not a bit of it. Rather, she'd thought the punishment too harsh. Well, Samuel's god-daughter or not, she had a lot to learn and could jolly well look out for herself now, he thought, snatching up the bell and ringing it vigorously.

As soon as the children filed into the classroom his attention was focused totally on their lessons. If they were to have any chance of making it in the world, teaching them reading, writing, arithmetic and how to be careful with money was vital. He left it to the travelling teacher, Miss Letticia Green, to deal with the girls' moral guidance whilst he did what he could to teach the boys about respect. Of course, as she was wont to tell him, Miss Green was used to working in more salubrious surroundings and only agreed to come here out of the goodness of her heart.

He did a head count, surprised to find today was one of the largest classes he'd taught in a long time. Although he was pleased that children who didn't live at Red Cliffs were also seizing the chance to learn, it was challenging teaching a group of such diverse ages and abilities, especially with the limited facilities at his disposal. He grimaced at the second-hand books and slates he had to make do with. What a difference money would make.

'Good morning, class,' he greeted them, as if for the first time that day, for it was important they differentiated between school time and the recreational swimming.

'Good morning, Master Higgins,' they intoned.

He saw the new little girl standing timidly in the doorway and gently drew her towards a desk at the front. 'Sit next to Maisie here, and if you need anything put your hand up.' Two periwinkle eyes regarded him solemnly. 'Class, take your seats, slates at the ready,' he ordered.

'Remember always to use your right hand,' he added, leaning over and transferring the chalk from the girl's left hand. She stared at him in surprise. He saw her lips quiver but needed to press on as he had at least thirty other pupils to teach this morning.

'Me helps you,' Maisie whispered to the little girl. Whilst he usually insisted on a 'no speaking in class' policy, he decided to let it go this once. He was just thinking how challenging it was going to be if the girl persisted in remaining silent, when inspiration struck.

'Right, can someone tell me why it's important we know how to write our letters?' he asked.

'So we can write our name and address when we get out of this place,' Brown quipped.

'Correct, Brown. Can I take it from your comment that you have secured some employment?' he asked, fixing the boy with a steely look. 'If so, you'd best tell Mrs Daws you will not be needing any more of her delicious food.' As the boy's eyes widened in horror, he pushed the point home. 'And if that's the case, it would only be fair to let someone else have your place here at Red Cliffs.'

'But I'm only eight, sir,' Brown gulped.

'I am aware of that fact, Brown. However, for a moment there I thought it was you who had forgotten. And, of course, the best way to remember is . . .' He left the rest of his sentence hanging in the air and picked up the tawse from his desk. As he cracked the strip of leather against his hand, the boy paled.

'Besides, Brown, you can't leave until you've paid for the damage to the doctor's window, so you'll have plenty of time to remember.' He turned back to face the others. 'Now, we need to learn our letters so we can write our names,' he said, his voice softer as he moved towards Maisie and the new girl. 'What does your name start with, Maisie?' he asked.

'*Mmm*,' she sounded.

'*M*, that's right. And who can write an *M* on the blackboard for me?'

'That's easy, sir,' Black called.

'Then perhaps you would care to show us, Black,' he said, tossing a chalk to the boy.

The boy swaggered to the front of the class and wrote a capital M on the board.

'Easy peasy,' he smirked.

'I agree, for a nine-year-old such as you, it should be. Now, whilst the children in the first two rows copy this letter onto their slates, you will use the *M* to complete the word *manners*.' The boy's face dropped. 'Hurry up, boy, we don't have all day,' the master said, flicking the tawse.

Seeing the little girl shrinking down in her seat, he went over and crouched down beside her.

'Do you know what letter your name starts with?' he asked gently. Silently she surveyed him with those periwinkle eyes. Sighing inwardly, he tried another approach. 'In a minute I'm going to point to each letter of the alphabet in turn. If you recognize one, I'd like you to raise your hand.' Slowly the girl nodded and Higgins smiled. Progress at last. It was going to take patience but he was sure he'd get there.

'Me will as well, sir,' Maisie chirped up. He smiled again and returned to the front of the class.

'Right, Black, move away from the board, and we'll see how you got on with that easy peasy word. *M a n e r s,*' he sounded out. 'Spelt thus it reads "*mainers*". You need two *n*'s to make the "*a*" sound in the word. You should know that by now, boy. You will stay in at break and write out the correct word fifty times.'

'But, sir . . .' Black began, then fell silent as Higgins reached for the strap. 'Yes, sir,' he amended quickly as the master cracked the leather down on the desk beside him.

As he walked over to Maisie and her new companion, he heard a titter coming from the back of the room. Changing course, he strode over to where three girls had their heads bent together and picked up the slate that was causing so much hilarity. Inside the letter *O*, a grotesque face had been drawn, and it was evident from their guilty expressions that he was the object of their mirth.

'Thank you, girls,' he bellowed. 'When I require you to add drawing to your curriculum you will be the first to know. Miss Oram, I take it this is your masterpiece?'

'Sir,' the fair-haired girl answered. 'But it wasn't only me.'

'Evidently. All three of you will stay behind with Black and put your slates to their proper use by writing out fifty times, *I must obey.*'

'Does that mean I won't have to empty the earth closets?' Edith asked hopefully.

'Yes, it does,' he agreed. Then, as the girl gave a gleeful grin, he added. 'During this break. However, you will commence after luncheon, and as you two girls have helped cause the delay, you will assist.' As he treated them all to his sternest look, they gulped and stared down at their slates.

'Right, everybody out in the fresh air, apart from those who have their lines to do,' he ordered.

Having to mete out their punishment was bad enough but it also meant he was confined to the classroom during break. If only they had the proper materials, it would put a stop to these high jinks with the slates, for then they would have to pen their letters onto paper in ink, and in copperplate writing to boot. However, these materials cost money – money Red Cliffs simply didn't have.

8

'Come on, Lil,' Christian coaxed, nuzzling into the woman's neck, but she pushed him away. 'Don't kick a man when he's down. It wasn't my fault the cards were stacked against me. Now I could do with a little relief.'

'No pay, no play, you know the rules,' Lil muttered, a roll-up dangling from her painted lips.

'But I paid you last night, and we didn't do anything.'

''Twern't my fault all that ale you downed gave you the droops. Now, I needs to find meself a feller who does have money to spend. Come on, scarper before Madam Iniquity hears you saying you're broke and boots you out herself.'

Christian scowled at the woman, who in the cold light of morning looked rougher than any of the maids he'd seen touting for business around the docks.

'Pah, and to think I thought this was a high-class establishment,' he spat. 'I'll be rich one day, just you wait and see. And I'll be choosy who I spend my money on,' he called over his shoulder, then yelped as his scuffed brogues hit him hard in the back.

Be like that, he thought, snatching them up and hurrying away in his stockinged feet. He could get money any time he wanted. All he needed to do was pay a few visits to his men, scattered throughout the town, and find out how his little enterprise was faring. Word on the street told him business was booming, so he was expecting his 'agents' to hand over a sizeable sum. Then there were those new establishments needing protection. It hadn't taken long to send out the frighteners. He gave a loud laugh, for he fully intended to be rich sooner rather than later, then he'd buy up all the flesh dens in the town. That Lil would be sorry for throwing him out then. Reaching the park, he sat on a bench and bent to put on his shoes.

'Morning, Lawrence, still on your uppers, I see.' He looked up to see his bank manager doffing his bowler hat mockingly at him. 'Can't stop, just on my way to work. Don't call us, as they say,' the man sneered as, cane tapping on the path, he walked briskly towards the town. Christian gestured after him then stared down at his crumpled appearance. The black tail coat, once the height of fashion, was not only creased and splattered with mud but definitely outmoded, and as for his shoes, the less said about them the better, he thought, glaring after the dapper Collings. There was no way he could call on his agents looking like this, but he hadn't time to return home and change. Fumbling in his pocket, he grimaced at the pitiful handful of coins that remained from his night at the club. He'd been so sure he was going to win this time, too. Well, at least he had enough for a wash and spruce-up at the bath saloon. Once he'd smartened himself up, he'd collect his monies then pay a long-overdue visit to his tailor, after which he'd enjoy a long, leisurely luncheon and find someone who would provide the comfort his body was calling out for.

Feeling better at the thought, he made his way through the park and headed towards the baths. It was still early but already people were going about their business. Not wanting to be seen in this dishevelled state, he quickened his step. It was all that Lil's fault. If she'd been more accommodating they could have shared a bath in front of the fire and . . . what on earth was that? He wrinkled his nose as a crocodile of urchins approached, towels tucked under their arms. With their tatty rags and shaven heads, it had to be those tykes from the Ragged School his uncle ran. What a wicked waste of that splendid house with its panoramic view of the bay. Why, if he owned it, no, when he owned it, he would ensure it was put to better use. He supposed he should show willing and call on the old boy, but not today. He had more pressing things to do, he thought, quickly averting his head.

Saturday was Samuel's favourite day of the week, and with Sarah settling in and getting to grips with the paperwork, he could enjoy his evening with a free conscience. He was grateful for her help, for his mind was so overloaded with problems he'd become increasingly forgetful. Why, he'd clean forgotten he'd emptied his cash box so that Mrs Daws could purchase much-needed supplies. Thank heavens Sarah had declined his offer to help with the purchase of a new dress. And thank heavens for the good ladies of the church who provided Red Cliffs with donations of used clothing.

Letting himself out into the cool of the evening, he was surprised how misty it was. Obviously a sea fret blowing in, he thought, sniffing the air. He couldn't smell anything, though. Oh well, the wind must be coming from the other direction, he decided, as he felt his way down the path with his cane.

'Good evening, Doctor,' a voice called. Samuel closed the gates, then frowned at the hazy figure crossing the road. 'It's me, Jack Wise. We met the other day at the vicarage.'

'Ah yes, the new verger. Sorry, I didn't see you in this murky weather. How are you settling into your new position?'

There was a pause as the man gave him a funny look, before remembering his manners. 'Very well, thank you. Everyone has been most welcoming. How is the little girl settling in?'

'She seems fine, although she's still not speaking.' He shrugged. 'Shock can do that sometimes.'

'A terrible business. I was on my way to tell you that the police have found out about her family. The father's a stoker on the boats and away at sea at the moment. They had digs in a house along from the draper's, but apparently their landlady realized she could get more money by renting it out to holiday folk. No sooner had the man returned to sea than she gave the deceased notice to quit.'

'Despite her condition?' Samuel asked, incredulous that anyone should treat an expectant woman with a young child in such a manner.

The verger nodded sadly. 'Money is the root, as they say.'

'Tell me about it.' Samuel gave a heart-felt sigh. 'Well, the little girl is welcome to remain with us until the father returns.'

'It is good work you do at Red Cliffs, Doctor. The vicar was saying so earlier. However, the police have also located the deceased's parents and told them the sad news. They are presently camped out behind the old sheds at Torre, and the grandmother says she will pay a visit when she can get into town.'

'I will let Mrs Daws and my god-daughter, Sarah, know in case I'm not about. You will meet them both tomorrow when we attend church. The vicar usually joins us for a bite to eat after morning service, and you would be most welcome as well.'

'Thank you, Doctor, that is most kind of you. I shall look forward to seeing you all tomorrow then. I'll bid you good evening, sir, but mind how you go.'

The doctor chuckled. 'It will take more than a bit of sea fret to worry me, young Jack.' As he tapped his way along the road, he was too busy with his thoughts to notice the frown on the verger's face.

It had been an eventful week; truth to tell, the plight of the little silent girl had been playing on Samuel's mind. However, it seemed there was a grandmother who might take care of her, so that was a relief, as was the way Sarah had settled in to Red Cliffs. He'd been worried at first that she wouldn't stay, but as the week had worn on, she'd begun attacking the paperwork with a determined efficiency that amazed him. She'd been shocked at how behind he'd got, even reprimanding him about his tardiness when she'd discovered some important forms that should have been completed and returned some weeks earlier. Remembering the formidable look on her face, he chuckled. She was as refreshing as a summer breeze.

Then, remembering he had yet to explain the extent to which he required her help, he sobered. He really should have told her the truth from the outset, but he hadn't dared risk scaring her away. He'd tell her first thing on Monday, he decided. Decision made, he quickened his step and continued on his way to meet his dearest friend.

*

Sunday dawned and everyone was up early to help prepare the midday meal before they left for church. Sarah couldn't believe how industrious the children were as they chopped the vegetables for the soup that would be offered to anyone in need of a hot meal. Then, after their breakfast, they cleared away and helped set up the trestles in the dining room. Sarah was carefully setting out a pile of spoons and dishes when Pip appeared at her side.

'Yer can't put the best silver out, miss, it'll get nicked,' he said, taking the cutlery and hiding it in a drawer in the dresser. 'We hands out one spoon to each person when they gets their soup, then collect it back when they've finished. Otherwise they'll pocket 'em and flog 'em.'

'Oh, I see,' Sarah said. 'Thank you for telling me. I have so much to learn.'

'Yer telling me. Reckons you must be rich where you come from.'

Thinking of the few coins she had in her purse, Sarah shook her head. 'Believe you me, I'm not.'

'Well, yer speaks posh an' I likes it,' he grinned.

'Come along, Pip, I need more potatoes for the pot, and I haven't got all day,' Mrs Daws called.

'Gawd, I gets no peace in this place. 'Tis slave labour good and proper,' Pip protested as he limped back to the kitchen. Sarah smiled. Cheeky he might be, but he was clearly fond of the housekeeper and couldn't do enough to help her. Following after him, she began slicing the loaves she'd helped to make the day before. It had been an enjoyable morning, for she'd quite forgotten how soothing kneading dough could be.

'Steady on, they be right old doorsteps you're cutting, and that bread's got to feed the five thousand,' Mrs Daws pointed out. 'Well, it seems like it sometimes,' she grinned to soften her words.

Finally, the chores were done and the children sent to make themselves presentable. The previous night had been bath night, the time they received their set of laundered clothes for the week. Mrs Laver, a diligent woman, saw it as part of her duties to help with the bathing, before placing any stained clothing to soak in the remaining hot water from the copper, ready for the wash on Monday. Sarah had been surprised to see her using the urine collected from the chamber pots for this, until the woman had explained it was 'nature's clean-all', as she'd put it.

It was only when they returned and were lining up to be inspected by the master that Sarah realized she had yet to make herself presentable. Running upstairs, she rinsed her face and hands, then changed into the blue serge she'd put aside to air, ready for today. When Mrs Laver had handed her back her own dress, freshly laundered and pressed, she'd been embarrassed at how shabby it looked in comparison and had worn it for work instead. Taking out her purse, she thought about leaving it under her pillow then realized she had no idea who came into the room when she wasn't there. Deciding it would be foolhardy to put temptation in a child's way, she carefully placed it in the pocket of her dress.

By the time she made her way downstairs again, the children were filing, crocodile-fashion, down the path behind their master, and she was pleased to see Maisie and Monday, as she now thought of the little girl, holding hands at the back.

'Another sea fret, Mrs Daws,' she heard the doctor say as he closed the door behind them. Sarah looked at the clear blue sky and was about to comment but the housekeeper shook her head. 'Good job it's only a few yards to the church then, Doctor,' she said. How strange, Sarah thought, but soon forgot about it as the group walked along the road to the church.

The verger, a pleasant-looking man, smiled as he handed her a hymnal. She nodded then followed the others to the pews that were obviously allocated to the school. To her surprise, the children sang heartily, if not exactly in tune. The sun streamed in through the beautiful stained-glass windows, casting a wonderful rainbow glow on the flowers arranged on the altar. For the first time in a long while, Sarah felt a sense of peace steal over her, and she realized she was gradually coming to terms with the death of her father.

'If only you knew what a terrible state his paperwork is in, Father,' she whispered to him quietly.

After the service, the vicar was waiting to greet his parishioners as they left the building.

'Miss Sullivan, welcome to St Nicholas',' he beamed. 'Most appropriate, is it not, he being the patron saint of children? I understand you have come to assist our dear doctor in the running of his school. That is most commendable, my dear.'

'Well, I'm only helping him with the paperwork . . .' she began, but he'd already turned away and was speaking to the person behind. The verger, who was standing nearby, gave her another warm smile, and she found herself grinning back.

Hurrying to catch up with the children who were wending their way down the steep path, she passed a small group of women huddled together. They were soberly dressed, and by the way their glances kept darting in Sarah's direction, it was clear she was their topic of conversation.

'Good morning, ladies,' she called brightly. To say their smiles were forced was an understatement.

'Don't worry about them,' Higgins whispered, appearing at her side. 'All they need is a cauldron and Mrs Daws wouldn't have to worry about providing luncheon.'

So the master has a sense of humour, Sarah thought, grinning, but he was already shepherding the children along the narrow road.

Back at the school a crowd of unkempt urchins were waiting impatiently at the gates.

'Shall I let them in, Master Higgins?' Pip asked.

'Best let our tribe in first, I think. Right, you little lot,' he said, turning to the pupils in his charge. 'You know what to do.' To Sarah's surprise, the schoolchildren nodded and, hurrying through the gates, made their way around to the back of the building. 'Right, Pip, now you can let the others in,' Higgins instructed. Pip swung the gates wide open and was almost knocked off his feet as the crowd surged forward.

'Hey, easy does it,' Pip called, but the hungry children were so intent on getting to the food they took no notice. 'Blinkin' riff-raff,' he muttered, pulling the metal gates closed behind them.

9

By the time Sarah managed to make her way through the crowd of hungry waifs, the schoolchildren had already donned an assortment of aprons over their clean clothes and were handing out hunks of bread. Even Maisie and Monday were helping as they stood one on either side of Mrs Daws, passing her the bowls so she could ladle soup from the enormous pot. Then Pip appeared and, true to his word, handed each child a spoon before directing them to their place at the trestle tables.

'Wait, you little heathens,' Master Higgins' voice boomed over the noise of chairs scraping against the floor. 'This is Sunday, and even if you only do it today, you will thank the Lord for your food before you eat it.'

''Urry up then, guv, 'cos me stomach thinks me throat's been cut,' a voice muttered.

Higgins looked over at Sarah and raised his eyebrows. 'Lord preserve us,' he muttered, and the children fell on their food, eating as if their life depended upon it.

'I think they thought that was the grace, Master Higgins,' Mrs Daws said, trying not to smile.

'Heathens. I've a good mind to make them stand up and give thanks properly.'

'You'll have more chance of stopping one of them steam train thingys,' the housekeeper replied, staring at the children, who were shovelling food into their mouths as fast as they could.

'Discipline, that's what they need,' the master grunted.

'But they're starving,' Sarah protested. 'Discipline's not everything. Surely you must make allowances for . . .' she began, but he was striding over to a young lad who was stuffing his pockets with bread.

'Now, see here . . .' Higgins began, putting out a hand to stop him. But the boy was too quick and, dodging between the master's legs, made a dash for the door, bumping into Sarah as he passed.

'Oh,' Sarah cried, putting out her hand to steady herself.

'Stop him, miss,' Pip called, trying to hurry after him.

'He took yer purse, miss,' Black cried. As the master gave chase, Sarah felt her pocket. Sure enough, it was empty.

'But how did he know it was in there?' she gasped.

'Easy peasey, miss. Your frock was lopsided where the purse weighed it down. Me old man taught me to look for that when we was doing the markets.'

'The markets?' she murmured.

'Yeah, it was good pickings, 'til he got picked up himself,' he shrugged.

'Picked up?'

'Taken to the nick and banged up. 'Twasn't the first time, see, nor the second, come to that. Anyhow, he's inside. 'Course, it didn't help he had a knife at the time.'

'What about your mother?' Sarah asked, suppressing a shudder.

'Did a runner with the coal man. Said he might be dirty but at least he had a regular pay packet.'

'You mean she left you behind?'

He nodded. 'Yeah, said I wasn't part of the deal. Didn't bother me none 'cos she had a vile old temper, 'specially after a night on the sauce.'

'Sauce?' Sarah asked.

'The gin. Blimey, miss, don't you know nothing? I could have managed by meself, but it was winter and I had nowhere to shelter. The doctor found me picking scraps out of his swill bucket and here I am,' he grinned.

'Got clean away, the toerag,' Higgins gasped, hurrying back into the room. 'Reckon he shot out of the back gate 'cos the front's still shut. What was it you were saying about discipline not being necessary, Miss Sullivan?'

'Leave the girl alone, Master Higgins, she's had a nasty shock,' Mrs Daws said, coming over and patting Sarah's shoulder. 'You go and have a sit-down in the kitchen while we see to this little lot, dearie.'

'No, I'm fine, really,' Sarah insisted. 'But what a way to behave when you gave him food.'

'It's the way of things, especially with the likes of him,' Higgins muttered, turning back to the waifs, who were watching wide-eyed. 'Right, the show's over, so eat up before it gets cleared away.' There was a clinking of spoons against bowls as the children hastily finished their meal.

'I'll see if I can find out anything about that little tyke,' Higgins muttered, going over to one of the tables.

'Don't reckon they'll tell him nuffink,' Pip said. 'He don't speak their language.'

'Sit down,' Higgins barked as one little girl got up to leave. 'Nobody leaves before their spoon and bowl has been handed in.'

'See what I mean? I'd best go and help. Come on, Black, see if you can touch them kids up for some info, like who he was, where he's hangin' out.'

'Righto,' Black nodded, puffing out his chest importantly.

As Pip and April duly went around collecting everything up, Higgins clapped his hands loudly.

'Right, everyone, time to go, and don't forget to thank the good doctor for your meal on your way out,' he added as the doctor came into the room, accompanied by the vicar and verger. There was a scrabble for the door, cries of 'ta' and 'thanks', and then the room descended into silence.

'Right, pupils of Red Cliffs, that was a job well done. After you've washed the dishes and cleared away, you may be seated for your own meals.' As the children went about their tasks, the master came over, shaking his head. 'That rabble makes this lot look like saints, doesn't it?'

'At least it proves we must be doing some good here at Red Cliffs. Well done, Higgins. I don't know how we'd manage without you,' the doctor said warmly.

'Just takes a bit of discipline,' he replied, darting a look at Sarah as she came over.

'I wish we could do more than just give them a meal and send them packing,' she said. 'Some of them were absolutely filthy.' Higgins gave a harsh laugh.

'If you think you'll get that little lot in the wash tub, you can think again,' Mrs Daws laughed, as she came over to join them. 'Believe you me, they've just had one meal more than they usually get on a Sunday. Anyway, Sarah, have you told the doctor about your purse?'

'I heard, my dear. What a terrible thing to have happened,' he said, turning to his god-daughter. 'You weren't hurt, I take it?'

'No, only a bit shaken. It does mean I'm left with nothing but the clothes I was given when I arrived.'

'Just like the rest of us then, miss,' Pip said philosophically as he passed by with his hands full of the precious spoons. 'Better hide the family silver in case you have a notion to sell it,' he quipped, then dodged as Higgins went to cuff his ear.

'You're not my teacher now,' he called over his shoulder.

'Praise be,' the master muttered, raising his brows.

The doctor turned to the men by his side. 'Forgive me, I'm forgetting my manners. Gentlemen, allow me to introduce you to my god-daughter, Sarah. She has taken pity and come to help a poor, forgetful old man. Sarah, my dear, this is our esteemed vicar and his new verger, Jack Wise.'

'We saw you in church earlier, of course,' the vicar replied. 'I hope you will be happy here in Torquay, although I understand you have had rather a rude introduction to the area.'

'You must let us know if St Nicholas' can be of assistance in any way,' Jack said.

'Thank you,' Sarah replied.

'Jack, this is Harry Higgins, who you will have gathered is our esteemed schoolmaster. And last but definitely not least, Mrs Daws, our indomitable housekeeper without whom this place would not function.'

'It is a pleasure to meet you all,' Jack said. 'I've heard so much about your delicious stews, Mrs Daws, and cannot wait to sample one.'

'And so you shall, young Jack. I'll go and dish up.' She gave the verger a warm smile, and Sarah could see he'd made an ally.

The next morning, Sarah entered her godfather's study eager to attack another pile of paperwork.

'Good morning, my dear, did you sleep well?'

'Yes, thank you. I must admit, I find it quite comforting when Monday climbs into bed beside me.'

'Ah, yes, the little girl. In all the kerfuffle yesterday, I quite forgot to mention that the police have established where her family are.'

'Oh,' Sarah said, her heart plummeting. 'I mean, that's good, isn't it?'

'Yes, it is,' Samuel agreed, giving her a knowing look. 'However, the father is away at sea, and her grandmother is a Romany camping somewhere behind Torre station. Apparently the woman intends calling when she can get into the town.'

'How caring of her to rush over to see her grandchild,' Sarah couldn't help remarking. Before her godfather could reply, there was a knock at the door.

'The good ladies of the church wonder if you could spare them a moment, Doctor?' Mrs Daws said. 'I told them you were busy but they said it was important. Apparently something's been on their mind since yesterday.'

The doctor sighed. 'Sounds like trouble,' he groaned. 'All right, Mrs Daws, send them in, but please refrain from offering refreshment, or they'll be here all morning and we'll never get this lot sorted,' he said, gesturing to the pile of forms on the desk before him.

A few moments later, the door opened again, and the three ladies Sarah had seen huddled together outside the church stepped into the room.

'You know how we like our tea, Mrs Daws,' the one with the pointed nose sniffed.

'Oh, I know all right, but I'm afraid we're fresh out of lemons,' the housekeeper replied, smiling sweetly, as she closed the door behind her.

'Well, ladies, allow me to introduce my god-daughter, Sarah. She has kindly consented to help me with all this,' he said, pointing to the pile of paperwork. 'Sarah, this is Miss Snooper, Miss Prior and Miss Meddle, sorry, I mean Middle, of course.'

Sarah bit her tongue to stop herself from laughing out loud at their names. How appropriate, she thought, studying their features. Miss Snooper was the lady with the large hooked nose, Miss Prior had beady eyes that regarded Sarah as if she was some form of low life, whilst Miss Middle was so large she didn't have any waist at all. She gave a polite smile which was met with a look of disdain.

'Now, you know I'm not one to pry, Doctor.' That would be Miss Prior, Sarah thought, forcing her lips not to twitch. 'However, you must agree that we ladies of the church carry out our good works with the best of intentions. We give generously of our time and . . .'

'Indeed you do, ladies,' Samuel agreed, cutting her dialogue short. 'So how can I be of service?'

'As you well know, Doctor, we spend much of our time collecting clothes and other materials the ladies of our parish donate.' She paused and Sarah could see her uncle was struggling not to show his impatience.

'Mrs Daws showed me all the things you have generously given to Red Cliffs,' Sarah said quickly.

'I see, so you admit you have had access to our munificent donations,' Miss Snooper proclaimed grandly as if she was a magistrate addressing the court. The women exchanged complicit looks.

'Some of our donations come from distinguished people, such as myself,' Miss Middle said.

'And very grateful we are for your generosity,' the doctor said. 'Now, if there's nothing else . . .'

'Oh, but there is, Dr Lawrence,' Miss Snooper sniffed.

'I thought there might be,' he muttered.

'At first we weren't sure if we should mention it, but as stalwarts of St Nicholas', we feel it is our duty to warn you that this woman is taking advantage of your kind-hearted nature,' Miss Prior said, narrowing her beady eyes at Sarah.

'What? How?' Sarah gasped.

'By stealing my dress,' Miss Middle cried.

'But I've never stolen anything in my life,' Sarah spluttered.

Ignoring her protest, Miss Middle continued. 'That dress you are wearing is of the highest quality. Why, my dressmaker couldn't believe she was permitted to work with material so fine.'

'Miss Middle, I must stop you there,' Samuel said, getting awkwardly to his feet. 'My god-daughter is no more a thief than I.'

'But that is my dress she is wearing. I recognized it yesterday.'

'I believe you said you donated it to the church,' Samuel protested.

'I did. It is my duty to help the less fortunate . . .' Miss Middle's voice trailed off as Samuel held up his hand.

'Enough. For your information, Sarah had her bag stolen from the train on her journey here. Heedless of her own plight, she helped me attend a dying woman on the beach and in the process got her dress covered in blood. Mrs Daws suggested Sarah choose something from the jumble in our front room,' he said, looking at Miss Middle as he emphasized the word jumble.

'My dress is not jumble,' she muttered, her hand flying to her throat.

'And my god-daughter is not a thief,' he said, his face becoming redder by the moment.

'Well, we only meant to help,' Miss Snooper sniffed.

'As if having her bag taken wasn't bad enough, she also had her purse stolen when she was assisting with our Sunday luncheon for the waifs.'

'Well, what do you expect if you will invite all and sundry into your home?' Miss Prior said, shaking her head.

'I'd expect a little sympathy and understanding from ladies who profess to have the well-being of the community at heart. Now, we have important things to attend to, so I'll bid you good morning,' he said, opening the door and ushering them out.

'Goodness, how embarrassing,' Sarah murmured. 'No wonder you got rid of them so quickly. I'll go and change at once.' Samuel shook his head, and she noticed his lips were quivering.

'I had to get rid of them before I disgraced myself by pointing out that Miss Middle is quite twice your size and has no middle whatsoever. There is no way that dress could have been hers, Sarah.'

'I fear it might have been, Uncle, for I borrowed a needle and thread from Mrs Daws and altered it to fit.' To her amazement, her uncle burst out laughing.

'That's quite the funniest thing I've ever heard,' he roared, tears streaming down his face, but then his laughter turned to coughing, and he slumped back in his chair.

'Oh, Uncle, I wish you'd let me get a doctor to look at you,' Sarah cried, pouring water as he struggled for his pills.

'I see one every day in the mirror, my dear,' he wheezed. 'And it does me no good whatsoever.' He shivered and Sarah looked over at the boarded window then down at the fireplace, where an arrangement of dried flowers graced the hearth.

'I think we should get Mrs Daws to light a fire in here,' she suggested.

Samuel shook his head. 'No money for such luxury,' he gasped.

'Well, I'm going to get Mrs Daws to make us a hot drink.'

'All this fussing,' he whispered. 'You'll make someone a good wife one day, my dear.' Sarah opened her mouth to say her experience with Rodney had put her off that idea but his eyes had fluttered closed.

10

As Sarah opened the door to the kitchen, the warmth from the range welcomed her once more. Mrs Daws, who was kneading dough on the scrubbed table, took one look at her worried expression, and asked, 'What's up, Miss Sullivan?'

'I'm worried about the doctor. It's so cold in his room, yet when I suggested lighting a fire he said there was no money for such luxury. There's a right old draught coming through that boarded-up window as well. It doesn't seem right he should suffer when he does so much for everyone else.'

'Don't you fret, dear. Master Higgins has spoken to someone about that, and it is to be fixed this week.'

'But the doctor looks so frail, and as for that awful cough, I'm sure he's really ill.'

Mrs Daws eyed her sharply. 'Has he said he is?'

'No, he just muttered something about *anno domini* and having to take it easier when I first came to see him.'

'Well, there you are, then,' the housekeeper replied, punching the dough hard. 'Now, did you come in for anything particular?'

'I was going to get a cup of tea for the doctor but he had a nasty coughing fit and has fallen asleep.'

'Better leave him be, then. Rest is best, as they say, and goodness knows he never seems to sleep at night. April's always saying she hasn't had to make his bed 'cos it hasn't been slept in. Now, if you've nothing better to do, you can give me a hand with this lot. Those Sunday luncheons might be a good idea for them poor children but they play havoc with my supplies,' she said, thwacking another lump of dough on the table in front of Sarah.

The rhythmic kneading soothed Sarah's mood, but she had the feeling she was being watched. Frowning, she stared around the room and spotted a large ginger cat eying her from the chair beside the range.

'Oh, I didn't know you had a pet here at Red Cliffs,' she cried. The housekeeper laughed.

'Old Marmalade's a regular visitor. Only creeps in here when it's quiet, though. He'll scarper as soon as the children appear. Still, it's a bit of company for me, and we always find you a scrap or two, don't we, old chap?' she crooned affectionately. As if he understood, the cat opened his mouth wide then began purring. They continued their kneading in contented silence for a few moments.

'Are you settling in, dear?' Mrs Daws asked, turning to face her.

'I think so, although those ladies from the church were rather hostile when they saw me wearing this,' she sighed, pointing to her dress. 'Miss Middle said it was hers and this material was of the highest quality.'

'And what do you think?' the housekeeper asked. Sarah was quiet for a moment, wondering if she should voice her opinion. She decided against it. 'If you ask me, dearie, that serge came from the market, and whilst there's nothing wrong with that, it is hardly of superior weight. If you want my advice, you'll pay lip service to Hubble, Bubble and Trouble and no more.' The housekeeper grinned conspiratorially.

'That makes me feel so much better, Mrs Daws,' she said, smiling at the housekeeper's choice of names. 'Miss Middle accused me of stealing it, you know.'

'Well, a dog knows its own tricks. Anyhow, I don't reckon that colour does much for you. It's too harsh. I was sorting through one of the piles of donated clothes and came across a lovely dress in moss green which will suit you a treat. Mrs Laver is washing it as we speak. Of course, you'll probably have to take your needle to it but you made a beautiful job of altering that one to fit,' she said, pointing a floury hand towards the skirt of Sarah's dress. 'Better than that travelling schoolmistress, Miss Green, would have done, any road.'

'I remember the doctor mentioning that a lady teacher called a couple of times a week to teach the girls needlework and other skills they will need when they leave school.'

The housekeeper narrowed her eyes. 'Not sure how learning to sew fancy stitches on a sampler will help with that, I'm sure, and being a spinster who still lives at home, the extent of her knowledge of the skills required for running a home is purely theoretical. They learn far more helping out in the kitchen and growing vegetables in the garden.'

'Perhaps I could show them how to alter some of those clothes. If they wore things that actually fitted, they would look so much better and it would increase their self-esteem,' Sarah said, her spirits rising at the thought of being able to do something practical to help the young girls.

'Self-esteem, eh? Well, there's a thought,' the housekeeper replied. 'Now, let's leave the dough to prove. We've just time to have a cuppa before those children take their break and fill the yard with noise. Talking of children, I see young Monday, as you call her, is still creeping into your bed of a night.'

'I don't mind. It offers a bit of comfort,' Sarah smiled.

'Yes, but for whom? It won't do you any good if you get too attached, especially if they find she's got a family.'

'I know,' Sarah sighed. 'Apparently her father's at sea but she has Romany grandparents camping near Torre. Her grandmother is going to call when she can get into the town.'

'Kind of her to put herself out, I'm sure,' Mrs Daws sniffed. 'However, if she's family and wants to take the little girl home with her there's nothing we can do to stop her. Now, wipe your hands and get this down you,' she said, pushing a cup of tea in front of Sarah.

When Sarah took a hot drink through to the doctor, she found his study empty. Settling herself at the desk, she'd just opened a large, dusty ledger when there was a knock at the door.

'No doctor?' Mrs Daws asked, peering into the room. 'Well, perhaps that's a blessing 'cos Bert's here to mend the window.'

'But surely the doctor would be pleased?' Sarah frowned.

'Yes, well, if it's one of them fetey compli thingys it will be better, won't it, Bert?' she grinned, tapping the side of her nose. The housekeeper pushed the door wider open so that a round, cheery-looking man could enter. He was dressed in overalls, carried a battered tool bag and had a large wrapped parcel under his arm.

'Mornin', miss,' he chirped. 'Sorry, can't doff me cap 'cos me 'ands is full and I don't want to drop this 'ere glass. That's better,' he puffed, resting the pane against the wall.

'I'll get you a cuppa, Bert,' Mrs Daws said.

'You're welcome to the doctor's, it's still warm,' Sarah offered, picking up the cup and saucer from the desk.

'Ta, just the ticket,' the man grinned before downing the drink in one. 'Now, let's get this done before the doctor comes back. Luckily 'arry boy had the measurement so I could bring the right size glass to fit.'

''Arry boy?' Sarah asked.

'The master, Miss Sullivan. You see, he remembered Bert here saying if there was ever anything he could do for the doctor, he only had to say.'

'Ters right. Don't know what I'd 'ave done when my Dol was so ill if he 'adn't come round and give her that medicine. He's a right good egg. Knew I was out of work and wouldn't be able to pay, but he insisted.'

'And Master Higgins did your shopping when you weren't able to leave her, didn't he, Bert?'

The man nodded. 'An' 'e wouldn't take no money either, so here I am to pay me dues so to speak.'

'Well, this won't knit the baby a bonnet, so I'll leave you to it,' Mrs Daws said. 'There'll be another cuppa in the kitchen when you've finished, Bert.'

'Ta, Mrs D,' he called over his shoulder, for he was already busy taking down the temporary boarding.

Marvelling at the way these people's pride wouldn't allow them to take anything for nothing, Sarah bent her head back over her paperwork. How different to Rodney. As the thought popped into her mind, she pushed it firmly out again and went back to studying the doctor's figures. The scribble was almost impossible to decipher, and his bookkeeping seemed to consist of bills and receipts tucked inside the ledger rather than being entered.

'There, all done.' Sarah looked up to see Bert grinning as he pointed to the new glass sparkling in the window. 'Mind you, that there frame's warped and needs replacing as well, but that should keep out them draughts 'arry boy was talkin' of. You the doctor's god-daughter then? Good job you come to 'elp 'cos he needs it from what I hear. Anyhow, I'll go and get that cuppa from Mrs D.' He picked up his tool box, gave a little wave and whistled his way out of the door.

Sarah was still smiling at the thought of the stern master having a soft centre, when the doctor returned.

'That mist is really bad today. I know we live by the sea but I can't remember it being this bad before,' he said, removing his hat and placing it carefully on the stand. Although it had clearly seen better days, Sarah noticed he treated it as if it was new. 'Oh,' he exclaimed. 'Higgins has replaced the window. He must have found some glass in the workroom.'

Thinking it pertinent not to mention Bert's visit, Sarah smiled. 'It's much lighter, and not so draughty either.' Then, not wishing to dwell on the subject, she pointed to the ledger. 'Do you have time to help me with some of these figures before luncheon?'

'If I must,' he grimaced. 'I've just been talking with the vicar about our earlier visitors, and it would appear it's given him inspiration for his sermon next Sunday.'

Sarah looked at the mischief sparkling in her uncle's eyes and smiled. He was incorrigible; she could see how he'd managed to make a success of the school.

'I'm pleased to see you looking better, Uncle.'

'Thank you, my dear. It's just that wretched cough. It takes me unawares sometimes. Now, if we really must look at these wretched numbers, let's get it over with.'

Harry Higgins did a mental head count of his pupils and was gratified to see numbers had stayed consistent. Although it was harder teaching a large class, he knew the powers that be would use any excuse they could to try and close the school, especially as some of the more influential people residing in the area thought it lowered the tone of the neighbourhood.

For once, all the children were absorbed in the task he'd set them. Even young Maisie and Monday were trying their best to draw a picture of their ideal holiday. They were unlikely to have the luxury of a vacation but he knew it was important to give them something to dream about. Having spent the morning doing their sums and learning exactly how little money would buy them in the shops, he felt they deserved ten minutes of something lighter.

He walked around the room, murmuring encouragement at the inevitable drawings of boats, sandcastles and hokey-pokeys. Then he saw what Monday had drawn and almost did a double take. It was clearly a picture of a vargo with a campfire to one side.

'That's a very good gypsy caravan,' he praised. 'Have you seen one of those before?' Two periwinkle eyes regarded him seriously.

'Me's done a fairy castle,' Maisie piped up. Trying not to show his frustration at the interruption, he smiled down at the young girl's slate.

'And very good it is too,' he said.

'That's sissy. I've done a real castle,' Brown scoffed.

'Well, that's good, we can put you in the dungeon when you're naughty,' he replied. As the class rocked with laughter, he picked up the bell. 'Luncheon time,' he said, then stood aside as they thundered out of the room.

'Goodness, it's like a stampede,' Sarah said, hovering uncertainly in the doorway.

'Miss Sullivan, do come in. How can I help you?' he asked, trying not to show his surprise.

'Goodness, some of these pictures are quite creative,' she laughed, looking at the slates as she made her way to where he was standing. 'Whose is that picture?' she asked, picking up the slate and studying it.

'It's Monday's,' he replied. 'And I think it's very good for a little one. Their brief was to draw somewhere they would like to go on holiday, although of course for most it would be a dream, and that's what she came up with. You look surprised. I suppose you didn't expect them to have any fun in the classroom.'

'Well, yes, I am astonished at that,' she replied, a gleam sparking in her brown eyes, which reminded him of chestnuts. 'But my surprise was because Monday's grandparents are Romany and camping nearby.'

'So you think this was drawn from memory?'

'It would make sense,' she sighed, her heart sinking.

'You don't approve?' She was quiet for a few moments, and he could see she was searching for the right words.

'It's not that. The grandmother is to visit when she can get into town. I mean, she's not exactly hurrying to see her grandchild, is she?'

'Maybe not, but we don't know the family history so better to reserve judgement, don't you think? Now, I'm guessing you had a reason for paying a visit to my humble classroom. You were expecting to hear the howls of anguished children being beaten, perhaps?'

'No, of course not,' she gasped, then realized he was teasing. 'I thought you should know Bert came and mended the study window this morning. The doctor was out at the time and, when he returned, concluded you must have found a suitably sized pane of glass in your workshop.'

'Ah, I see. We don't usually hide things from him but as his funds dwindle his pride swells, if you see what I mean.'

'I understand, and your secret's safe with me. Mrs Daws knows I've slipped out to tell you and says you'll find an extra dumpling in your stew,' she grinned.

'Well, that was worth all the subterfuge, then,' he laughed.

As she smiled back, something sparked between them and her eyes widened in surprise.

11

'Grandmother's here, dear,' the woman announced, flouncing into the room, gold bangles jangling. 'Well, where is she then?' she asked, peering around. 'I haven't come all this way to be kept waiting.'

Samuel frowned, certain the plummy accent was as false as her smile. Before he could respond, the usually amenable Mrs Daws took him by surprise.

'Well, I'm sorry, I'm sure. We'd have rolled out the red carpet and had your grand-daughter ready and waiting in her best frock had we known you were coming,' she replied, narrowing her eyes. 'I mean, it has been three weeks since the doctor rescued her, and we weren't to know today was to be THE day.'

'I came as soon as I could, so you can bring her in now,' the woman replied haughtily, waving her hand at the housekeeper so the jangling started up again.

'She's in the schoolroom with the others, Mrs . . .?' Samuel said, quirking a white brow.

'The name's Rosa,' she announced grandly. 'Madam Rosa. You may have heard of me?'

'Nope,' Mrs Daws shook her head and pursed her lips to make her point.

'Well, Madam Rosa, perhaps you'd like a cup of tea whilst you are waiting?' Samuel offered.

'Ta, I am parched as it happens. It's a long way down from Torre.'

Seeing Mrs Daws open her mouth to protest, Samuel quickly intervened. 'Yes, it is a fair walk, Rosa.'

The woman gave a laugh. 'Walk? Came down on the wagon, dear,' she said, sinking onto a chair without invitation. 'Well, go on, it'll have to be a quick cup, mind, 'cos Baz is waiting outside.'

'The little girl's grandfather?' he enquired. The woman nodded. 'Well, why don't you ask him to join us for some refreshment?'

The woman laughed louder this time. 'Best not. The horse'll be in your garden munching them carrots' tops before you can blink.'

'Mrs Daws, perhaps you would be kind enough to make Madam Rosa a cup of tea?'

'I'll do better than that. I'll bring us all in some then Madam Rosa can read our leaves. That is what you gypsies do, isn't it?' the housekeeper asked, her lips curling into a passable smile.

'Being a Romany, I do have that gift. You'll have to cross my palm with silver first, though.'

'You don't say,' Mrs Daws muttered as she hurried away.

'Nice house you have here,' Rosa said, taking a good look around the room. 'Although shabbier than I'd have expected, especially compared to the others in the road. Seems quite a posh neck of the woods.'

'Indeed,' Samuel acknowledged. 'Now then, Madam Rosa, about your little grand-daughter . . .'

'Hope she's been behaving herself. I know what these little ones can be like. I remember when Holly, that is . . . I mean was, her mother was little. She were a right handful and . . .' She stopped as Mrs Daws came back into the room bearing a tray of cups and the brown pot.

'Here we are, tea up. The kettle was on the hob so it didn't take a moment to make. Now shall I pour or would you like to be Mum, Rosa?' she asked.

'You're the housekeeper so you can while I continue talking to Mr Lawrence here,' the woman said, waving her hand in the air.

'It's Dr Lawrence, actually,' Mrs Daws corrected as she picked up the teapot.

'Ooh, I likes a doctor,' Rosa pouted. 'So educated and with your high fees, worth a bit I'll be . . .'

'Let me do that, Mrs Daws, whilst you go and ask Sarah to bring the little girl in. What is her name, by the way?' he asked, placing the pot carefully back on the tray and turning to the woman.

'Gawd love us, Doctor, how would I know?' the woman snorted.

'You mean, you don't know your . . .' the housekeeper began.

'Now, if you please, Mrs Daws,' Samuel interrupted. 'I believe Madam Rosa said she was in a hurry.'

'And that is why I took the liberty of popping into the schoolroom just now,' Mrs Daws said. 'They are waiting in the hallway, Doctor. I'll show them in.' She opened the door, and Sarah came into the room, holding the little girl's hand.

'Ah, Sarah, do come in and meet Madam Rosa. Sarah has done a fine job of looking after our little visitor here,' Samuel said, smiling down at the little girl. 'Sarah, this is Madam Rosa, the grandmother.'

'Well, come on then, let's get a gander at you,' the woman said, getting to her feet and prising the little girl away from Sarah. As the girl stiffened and hid behind Sarah's skirts, Madam Rosa sniffed.

'Gawd love us, is it too much to ask that you look at your grandmother?' she cried, throwing up her hands so that the bangles jingled once more.

As Sarah crouched down and whispered something to Monday, the little girl put her thumb in her mouth then turned and stared shyly up at the woman.

'Well, that'll have to stop for a start. Can't be doing with babies who suck their dirty digits.' Monday sucked harder on her thumb and the woman sighed. 'Well, you've certainly got the Romany eyes, and that hair looks dark, from what I can see. Criminal, cropping a little girl's head like that,' she tutted. Before Sarah could explain, she went on. 'And there's a bit of our Holly in that defiant chin. Tell us your name then, ducks.' The periwinkle eyes darkened but the girl remained silent.

Seeing the woman scowl, Samuel intervened. 'I'm afraid she's been silent since we rescued her. Probably from the shock. It's quite . . .'

'You mean she's dumb?' Rosa asked, stepping back as if it was contagious.

'As I said, it's quite common . . .' Samuel began.

'But she'll be of no use at the fairs if she can't speak,' the woman wailed. Then her manner changed, and she stood staring at the child thoughtfully. 'She could still be useful, mind,' she said, stoking her chin. 'How much to take her off your hands?'

'I assure you we don't require any money . . .' Samuel began.

The woman gave a harsh laugh. 'Not you, *me*, you daft ha'p'orth. How much will you pay me to take her away?'

'Well, really . . .' Mrs Daws spluttered but Samuel was already on his feet.

'I have seen and heard all I need. The girl will remain here until her father is located. Good day to you,' he said, ushering the woman out of the room and into the hallway.

'May the curse of the gypsies be upon you . . .' she began, but the rest of her words were lost as the front door was slammed behind her. As Samuel stood, regaining his breath, there was a movement behind him.

'Oh, April, I didn't see you there,' he said.

'I heard what that bitch said about Monday, and, well, I was just about to come in and biff her one when you threw her out. Good for you, Doctor.'

'Yes, well, you'd better come into my study with the others,' he said. His cheeks were red with anger but he managed to control his voice. 'I don't think we'll see any more of them. It looked like a whole group of vans were parked outside so I'm assuming they are moving on.'

'Well, thank the Lord,' Mrs Daws muttered, sinking into a chair as April went over and threw her arms around the little girl.

'We'll look after you,' she crooned.

'Well, little 'un, I guess you'll be staying here with us until we find your father,' Samuel said, patting the little girl's head. 'Is that all right with you?' She nodded her head vigorously. 'Well, that's settled then.'

Sarah smiled. 'I can't tell you how relieved I am you saw that woman out. Why . . .' Her voice trailed off as Samuel shook his head and nodded towards Monday.

'Did you know that woman, Monday?' he asked, squatting down until he was level with her. Monday opened her mouth. There was a collective holding of breath, and Mrs Daws and Sarah exchanged excited looks. But then the little girl shook her head. 'Well, you go along to the kitchen with April and Mrs Daws. I'm sure they'll find you something nice to drink,' Samuel said, smiling encouragingly at her.

'I'll come too,' Sarah said quickly, ruffling the little girl's hair.

'I'd like you to stay here, please. We have things to do,' Samuel said.

As April ushered Monday out of the room, Mrs Daws began collecting up the tea things. 'For a minute there I thought the little girl was going to speak, bless her.'

'So did I,' Sarah sighed, passing the housekeeper a cup.

'She will, in her own good time, I'm sure,' Samuel said. 'Sometimes when one shock has triggered something, another unlocks it.'

'I'm that pleased you booted that woman out, Doctor, she were a nasty bit of stuff. Madam Rosa indeed,' Mrs Daws tutted. 'Well, I'll leave you to it.'

'I'm so happy Monday is to stay here, Uncle,' Sarah cried as soon as the housekeeper had left.

Samuel studied his god-daughter for a moment. He'd grown even fonder of her in the short time she'd been here and didn't want to see her hurt. 'I know you are, my dear. However, I must remind you to exercise caution, for we don't know how long she will remain here. When her father returns he'll probably want to take her home with him, especially as the poor man has lost his wife.' Seeing the mix of emotions crossing her face, he said briskly, 'Now, I must go straight to the police station and tell them what has happened.'

'But it's raining, Uncle,' she frowned, staring at the drops splattering against the window.

'I was going to ask you to accompany me, for we'll be passing the train station and could make enquiries about your bag. Still, I'll understand if you don't want to get wet.'

'I was thinking of you, Uncle,' Sarah cried. 'That rain will do nothing for your chest.'

'Then I'll put on my muffler,' he replied, his eyes twinkling so that she knew he was humouring her.

As Samuel steered the trap out of the gates, they saw Pip, shovel in hand, heading purposefully towards the road. Seeing them approach, he raised his cap.

'Afternoon, guv, Miss Sullivan,' he greeted them cheerily. 'Them gypos have left their calling card all over the place,' he said, waving towards the brown piles still steaming despite the rain. 'Good manure for the vegetables, though,' he grinned.

'Indeed, Pip, good work,' Samuel acknowledged. 'We're paying a visit to the local constabulary via the railway station, so look to Master Higgins if anything crops up.'

'Righto, guv.'

Despite the rain, it was refreshing to be out in the air, and Samuel felt himself relax for the first time that afternoon. The cheek of that woman. It still astounded him how some people sought to make money from innocent children. Then he caught sight of Sarah's pensive expression.

'Not still worrying about young Monday?' he asked.

She shook her head. 'No, I was thinking how lovely it would have been if she'd spoken, then that frightful woman's visit would have served some purpose.'

'Well, if I'm not mistaken she turned a corner this afternoon. Now sit back and enjoy this nice wet trip along the sea front. It's not often we get the chance to skip school,' he quipped.

Sarah smiled then turned her head to look at the sea. It was flat and grey. The promenade was deserted and had a dismal feel. Even the leaves drooping on the palm trees looked sad and out of place. It was so different from when she'd arrived.

'Have you settled into Red Cliffs?' he asked, hearing her sigh.

'Yes, the days seem to fly by. There is always so much to do.'

'Not working you too hard, am I?' he asked. 'Do say if I am. Mrs Daws reckons I can be a slave driver, albeit unwittingly.'

Sarah laughed. 'No one works harder than you, Uncle. Oh, we're here already,' she observed as he pulled up outside the station. Jumping down, she made her way towards the musty-smelling lost property office where she was greeted by the same clerk as before.

'Still roughing it with those urchins, miss?' he asked, looking up from his notebook.

'I am still at Red Cliffs,' she replied, ignoring his comment about the children. 'I called in to see if my bag has been found?'

The man put his pencil behind his ear then made a show of looking through his book.

'No, 'fraid not. Did warn you it was unlikely, didn't I?' he said, almost triumphantly. 'They reckon there's this ring, see, and . . .'

'Thank you so much for your help,' she cut in, anxious not to keep her uncle waiting in the wet.

'I can see by your face you've had no luck,' Samuel said as she climbed back into the cart. 'Now, I owe you an apology, my dear, for whilst you were gone it dawned on me that I still haven't given you any money towards purchasing new things. And then there's the little matter of your wages. I have been most remiss, especially after you've worked so hard on my paperwork,' he sighed.

'Uncle, please, there's no need. I have a nice bed, food to eat, and as for clothes, Mrs Daws told me she'd found a lovely green dress in the donations which she reckons will be better than this,' she said, patting the blue serge of her skirt, which showed from beneath her shawl.

'Well, I can understand you not wanting to wear that one after Miss Middle's dreadful outburst,' Samuel said, turning the horse towards the town. Remembering the woman's accusation, Sarah grimaced.

'Mrs Daws reckoned the green was softer and would suit me better.'

'You women and your colours,' Samuel laughed and shook his head. 'You look quite lovely to me as it is, Sarah. Ah, here we are,' he said, pulling on the reins.

As they entered the police station, a young constable peered importantly over the desk.

'How c-can I help?' he asked, flushing bright red when he saw Sarah.

'Good afternoon, I'm Dr Lawrence, and this is Miss Sullivan,' Samuel greeted him.

'O, o, S-sullivan,' the man repeated.

'No, not O'Sullivan, Constable, just Sullivan. I'm not Irish,' Sarah quipped. The constable blushed even more.

'I'd like to see Sergeant Watts, if you would be so good as to tell him I'm here,' Samuel said.

'Of course, sir, er, Doctor,' the constable replied before hurriedly disappearing through a door to one side of the counter.

Lips twitching, Samuel turned to Sarah. 'I think you've made quite an impression,' he said. 'Ah, good afternoon, Watts,' he acknowledged as a rather portly gentleman appeared, shiny buttons straining over the jacket of his uniform. 'This is my god-daughter, Sarah Sullivan. She has come to assist me at Red Cliffs.'

'Good afternoon, both,' the sergeant greeted them, peering through his wire-rimmed glasses. Then he turned to Samuel. 'About time you had some help with all them children. Don't know how you manage, I'm sure. Come through to my office,' he said, lifting the counter to allow them through. 'Potts, man the desk,' he called to the red-faced constable. 'I know, Watts and Potts, dreadful, isn't it?' he shrugged when he saw Sarah smile. The constable reappeared, surreptitiously glancing in Sarah's direction as he took up his place once more.

'Now, what can I do you for?' Watts asked as soon as they were seated. Briefly Samuel filled him in on the events of the afternoon. 'Blinking gypos. You should see the mess they left after we moved them on,' the sergeant grumbled.

'You mean they didn't leave voluntarily?' Sarah asked.

'Would've been a lot easier for us if they had, but sadly they never do, miss,' he said. Sarah looked at Samuel, and he knew what she was thinking. That dreadful woman hadn't made a special journey to see her granddaughter, at all.

Oblivious to the disquiet his comments had raised, the sergeant began sorting through his files.

'Ah, here we are,' he said, pulling out a report. 'Deceased found on beach, cause of death to be confirmed. Young girl, presumed to be daughter, approximate age five to six years, taken to Red Cliffs. Terrible business,' he sighed. 'Well, if you're sure you can keep her that'll be a help, Doctor. We'll contact the father when his ship docks and break the sad news about his wife.'

'Thank you, Sergeant. I believe the verger, Jack Wise, told you that Sarah's bag went missing on her train journey from Newton?' Sergeant Watts nodded. 'We called at the lost property office on our way here but the clerk said it hasn't been handed in. I don't suppose you've been able to find out anything?' Samuel asked.

'Afraid not, Doctor. Although we will continue with our enquiries, of course. We know there is some kind of racket going on with passengers' luggage and all sorts going missing. It's not just in Torquay, either. It's happening on trains everywhere around the local network. Looks like the work of an organized gang. We'll nab them in the end, of course.'

'That's reassuring to know,' Samuel acknowledged.

The sergeant nodded then turned to Sarah. 'I also heard from Jack that you had your purse stolen by one of them ragamuffins. And under the doctor's roof too.

Don't know what things are coming to, I'm sure.' He took off his glasses, rubbed them vigorously with his kerchief then put them on again. 'All this must be enough to make you think of going back home, Miss Sullivan, or do you have another reason for being here? A love interest, one of them rich holidaymakers perhaps?' He said it in such a condescending manner, Sarah felt the hairs on the back of her neck bristle. 'At your age, a pretty young thing like yourself must be thinking of settling down?'

A picture of Rodney flashed in her mind, but instead of being accompanied by the usual feeling of hurt, anger surfaced instead.

'I have come to Red Cliffs at my uncle's request and will leave when he no longer requires my help, Sergeant Watts,' she said crisply. Then, seeing her uncle frown, she added quickly, 'However, it is good to know you are making enquiries about my loss, and for that I'm truly grateful.' The sergeant puffed out his chest at her praise, and Sarah was sure the buttons would pop off at any moment.

'I don't suppose there's much chance of recovering Sarah's purse either?' Samuel asked.

'About as much chance as me being able to turn that gauche constable into a top-ranking officer,' Watts sighed. 'I understand you're from Plymouth way, miss. Not been much of an introduction to Torquay, has it? And now you've got another stray to look after.'

Stray? Sarah stared at him in disgust. Wasn't that how people referred to roaming cats and dogs?

'We've named the little girl Monday, and as long as she remains in the care of Red Cliffs, I shall ensure she is well looked after,' Sarah added.

'Oh, you're working at the school as some kind of nanny, are you?' Watts asked.

'Sarah is helping with the children, certainly, but her main purpose is to assist me with the paperwork and, in doing so, find out exactly how the school is run,' Samuel explained. Watts raised his brows until they disappeared under his hat. 'You find that surprising, Watts?'

'Well, Doctor, I don't mean to point out the obvious, but she is a female, and they're reared to marry and look after our needs.' He laughed and leaned forward. 'Women can help with the youngsters, certainly, maybe even sort out simple paperwork, but they don't have the brains to run anything. No offence, miss,' he said, turning to Sarah.

'Well, that's where our opinions differ, Watts. Sarah is eminently capable of running Red Cliffs,' Samuel stated firmly. It was only when he heard Sarah's sharp intake of breath that he realized he still hadn't told her of his intentions.

'Pardon me, I'm sure,' the sergeant sniffed. 'It's just that it's normal for a woman of your age to settle down and rear her own children, Miss Sullivan.'

'But things are changing, Sergeant,' Sarah told him. 'The National Union of Women's Suffrage is really gaining strength now.'

'Suffrage, piffle,' he shrugged. 'What do women know about suffering?'

'The word means the right to vote, Sergeant. And when women attain our right to vote in Parliament, we shall be eligible to hold important posts in society, such as sitting on School Boards, for example.'

'Never, my dear,' Watts scoffed. 'I appreciate your ambition, but a woman could never understand the complex way Parliament works.'

'And you do, Sergeant?' Sarah asked, staring unflinchingly at him.

'I am a man, Miss Sullivan, and that is the difference between us. Now, if there is nothing else, Doctor, I have places to be, people to see,' he said, getting to his feet.

'Oh yes, the important man,' Sarah muttered.

'Thank you for your time, Sergeant Watts,' Samuel said quickly. Seeing Sarah was about to continue arguing her case, he gently took her by the arm and led her from the room.

When he saw Sarah, the constable smiled, a blush creeping up his cheeks until he resembled a ripe tomato. 'G-good d-day Miss S-sullivan. I h-hope t-to s-see you again s-soon,' he said.

The sergeant, who was observing from his doorway, roared with laughter. 'See, Miss Sullivan, that is what you women are good for, attracting the interests of the male species. Good day to you.' And with a raucous laugh, he took himself back into his office.

'Insufferable imbecile,' Sarah muttered, striding out of the station.

'Good for you, Sarah. You certainly told him. I had no idea Watts was such a bigot. Much as I value the work he does for our community, I must admit I find his views outmoded.'

'Men like that belong in the last century,' Sarah huffed.

'I knew you were keen for women to get on in the world but never realized you were so impassioned,' Samuel replied, admiration sparking in his eyes.

'Yes, well, he annoyed me with his bigoted opinion on what women were good for.'

'Never mind, it was obvious Potts took a shine to you,' he chuckled then sobered quickly when he saw her scowl. 'Sorry, Sarah, I shouldn't tease. You've no idea how pleased I was to hear you tell Watts your opinion on women holding important posts in society.' He sounded so sincere that as soon as they'd climbed into the cart, she turned to face him.

'You believe women are capable, then?'

'I most certainly do and think society would benefit hugely. When we return to the school, I would like to hear more about your views on women sitting on the School Boards, for there is something important I wish to discuss with you.'

'We haven't got the vote yet, Uncle.'

'Ah, but if these suffragettes are half as determined as you, then it won't be long before they do,' he replied, giving her a shrewd look.

Lost in their own thoughts, they were silent on the journey back to the school. The gas lights along the promenade had been lit and were flickering long, eerie shadows on the mizzle that cocooned them in a damp blanket. Every so often a wail from a ship moored out in the bay sounded through the gloom, adding to the mournful feel of the late afternoon. Remembering that Monday's father was a stoker, Sarah wondered where he was headed and how long it would be before he returned for his daughter. Even though she knew this would be best for the little girl, she couldn't help the overwhelming affection she felt for her and knew it would be hard to let Monday go.

By the time they reached Red Cliffs, Samuel was coughing and wheezing. Relieved to see Pip ready with the gate open, Sarah called to him.

'Pip, the doctor needs to get inside straight away. Will you see to the pony?'

''Cors I will,' he said, hurrying over and helping Samuel from the cart. 'Best get a hot drink down you, guv. You take him through the front door, miss, and I'll tell Mrs Daws.'

Leaning heavily on Sarah's arm, Samuel made it into his office and slumped in his chair. He fumbled for his bottle of pills but even that was too much for him, and after counting out the correct dose, Sarah gently held a tumbler of water to his lips.

'I knew we shouldn't have gone out in all that rain,' she chided. 'The damp air's gone straight to your chest.' Too weak to reply, he nodded.

'Pip told me you've taken a turn, Doctor, so I've brought you in one of my specials,' Mrs Daws said, bursting into the room with a steaming mug. 'Now, sip this and you'll feel better in no time,' she crooned. It was just as if she was speaking to one of the children, Sarah thought, staring at the housekeeper in surprise. 'You go and dry yourself by the range, young lady, or you'll be ailing next,' she added, seeing Sarah watching.

'I'm fine, Mrs Daws,' Sarah replied.

'Well, you can go on through, anyway. I've left April coping with Maisie and Monday. They're supposedly helping her spread the scrape the butcher sent up but they're as much help as a chocolate teapot.' She shook her head. 'The broth's done, it just needs serving then you can all sit down to supper. It's nearly time for the gong to be rung anyway.'

'But I really don't want anything to eat, Mrs Daws,' Sarah protested.

'Maybe you don't, but the others do. Harry's gone to see his mother so someone needs to supervise the children,' the woman said, all but pushing Sarah from the room.

'Now then, Doctor,' Sarah heard her say, 'I've told April to put a warming pan in your bed, and I'm going to make sure you go upstairs and get some rest. I wouldn't put it past you to start working on them blinking papers as soon as my back's turned.'

Sarah smiled and waited for her uncle to protest but to her astonishment, he mildly acquiesced. Fighting down her growing unease, she shook off her wet shawl then hurried along the hallway to the kitchen where Maisie and Monday were licking their fingers with glee.

'Where's April?' Sarah asked.

'Putting pan in bed,' Maisie answered, pointing to the ceiling.

'I see. Have you finished spreading the bread for supper?' As the girls looked at each other and giggled, worry about her uncle surfaced. 'For heaven's sake, rinse your hands then go and ring the gong,' she snapped.

'There's no need to be like that, miss, they're only little,' April scolded, coming into the room. 'And Monday's had quite enough for one day, what with that horrid woman,' she added, glaring at Sarah accusingly.

'I know, and I'm sorry,' Sarah sighed. 'They're such lovely little girls.'

'Wish someone would call me lovely,' April muttered.

'Why, April, you're the most loving person I've met,' Sarah cried, horrified to think she'd upset her as well.

"Tisn't the same as being lovely though, is it?' April whispered, her hand going to the scar on her face as she stared down at her drab dress.

'Oh, April, you *are* lovely,' Sarah cried, pulling the girl close. 'And one day you will wear a pretty dress.'

'Now you're being stupid, miss,' April muttered. 'The likes of me wear other people's cast-offs. Always have, always will.'

'Well, that's where you could be wrong because I've had an idea, and . . .' The rest of her sentence was drowned by sound of the gong being bashed crazily. As it resounded down the hall, a stampede of children appeared from all directions and swarmed into the dining room.

It was still quite early when Sarah collapsed wearily on her bed. The children, noticing the absence of their master and the housekeeper, had played up over supper, taxing her patience to the limit. Perhaps Higgins was right about discipline and his insistence that children needed to have boundaries set, she mused.

She'd knocked at the doctor's bedroom on her way but Mrs Daws had opened the door, told her he was sleeping and wasn't to be disturbed.

'I shall sit in the chair beside his bed and watch over him,' she'd assured Sarah. It was obvious she was very fond of the doctor, but then they'd worked together for many years, so that was understandable, Sarah thought.

Although she was bone weary, her brain was buzzing like a bee on a rose bush. What a day it had been. That Sergeant Watts, calling Monday a stray, had really upset her. She thought of the dear little girl and the trusting way she looked at her and felt a warm glow inside. Thank heavens her uncle hadn't let that ghastly woman take her away. Madam Rosa indeed. She was about as genuine as that Miss Snooper. And then, afterwards, when Monday had opened her mouth, they'd all thought she'd been going to speak. She sighed into the darkness. And poor April not thinking she was pretty. She was sure, if she could get the girls adapting the cast-offs to fit, they would feel better about themselves. Of course, she'd need to speak to the travelling schoolmistress, but surely the woman would understand the value of teaching them something practical rather than sewing stitches on a sampler.

As for the sergeant's prejudiced attitude. Just the thought of it made her bridle. Women were on this earth to tend to men's needs, were they? She'd never heard anything like it. Or had she? Something tugged at the back of her memory as she recalled Rodney telling her he expected to come first in Sarah's life. He'd been adamant he wouldn't play second fiddle to her father, despite the fact he'd been ailing fast. *As my betrothed, it is your duty to attend my needs before anything else,* had been his exact words. His attitude had been the same as the sergeant's, she realized. Why had she never seen it before? Not like Harry. The thought came unbidden, and she shook her head in the darkness.

Remembering how her uncle had stood her corner when Watts had been spouting his chauvinistic opinions, she smiled. Her father had always encouraged her to achieve, and now it seemed she had an ally in his oldest friend. How fond she'd become of the man and how greatly she admired the work he tirelessly undertook for the school. She hoped he'd feel better after a night's rest.

Just as she was dropping off, she remembered her uncle saying he had something important to discuss with her. Well, it would have to wait until the morning, she realized as sleep finally claimed her.

13

In her dreams, Sarah was being pulled this way and that.

'Sarah,' she heard someone whisper in her ear. Thinking it was Monday climbing in beside her, she smiled. How she liked the comfort of the warm little body snuggling up to her. She reached out to cuddle her close, except there was no one there.

'Sarah.' The voice came again, more urgently this time. Sarah frowned. Monday didn't speak. As the thought penetrated her sleep-fuddled brain, she opened one eye to find an agitated Mrs Daws, candle in hand, bending over her.

'You must come quickly, the doctor's asking for you.'

'But it's the middle of the night,' Sarah whispered, glancing towards the window where the moon was shining brightly through the ill-fitting curtains.

'Now, Sarah,' the housekeeper urged, heading out of the room. Throwing her shawl over her nightdress, Sarah hurried after her. As they sped along the hallway, she was surprised to see the woman was still wearing her day clothes.

'Here she is, Doctor,' Mrs Daws crooned, leaning over the bed. Turning to Sarah, she whispered. 'He's in a bad way.'

'Goodness, Uncle, you're boiling up,' Sarah murmured, reaching for the damp sponge on the rickety table beside his bed.

'No time for that,' he croaked. 'Listen closely. I want you to take over the running of Red Cliffs, Sarah.'

'You need to rest, Uncle,' she soothed. 'We can talk about this in the morning.'

He took a raspy breath and fumbled feebly for her hand. 'Promise me you'll keep the school open,' he insisted, his rheumy eyes boring into her.

'Of course I will, Uncle,' she promised, patting his hand reassuringly. He gave a weak smile, closed his eyes and gave a shuddering sigh. 'Uncle?' she whispered. 'Are you all right?'

'He's going, my dear,' Mrs Daws sobbed as she bent and kissed her employer gently on the forehead. 'But he'll soon be at peace, thanks to you.'

Sarah stared from the housekeeper back to her uncle, shaking her head in disbelief. 'No!' she cried, sinking into the chair beside him. 'Oh, please, dear heavens, no.' She watched, as if in a trance, as Mrs Daws went over and opened the little window.

'To let his soul fly free,' the housekeeper whispered. 'Oh, look, a full moon. They say the souls of saints are carried to heaven by them moonbeams. Knowing his time was near, I saved these to pay for his safe passage to the afterlife,' she added, pulling two shiny pennies from the pocket of her apron. Murmuring a prayer, she carefully placed one over each eye.

Sarah stood staring at him, the tears cascading down her cheeks as she tried to come to terms with his passing. She looked at Mrs Daws and, even in the flickering light of the candle, could see how distraught the woman was. Making a concerted effort to pull herself together, Sarah took the woman by the arm.

'Come along, Mrs Daws, I'll make you a hot drink,' she said, gently leading her from the room.

Down in the kitchen, Sarah sat the trembling woman beside the range then riddled the embers into a blaze. As she put the kettle on the hob and set out the tea things, Marmalade, as if sensing his mistress' distress, sprang onto the housekeeper's lap.

'He's gone, Marmy, the doctor's gone,' she sobbed, burying her head in the ginger fur.

As Sarah automatically poured the water into the big brown pot, her thoughts kept returning to the same question. Had that damp been the last straw for her ailing godfather? With a sob, she sank into the nearest chair and buried her face in her hands. Suddenly she was aware of a hand on her shoulder.

'Don't cry, Sarah. Thanks to you, he was able to pass peacefully,' the housekeeper whispered, as the ginger tom snaked between their legs.

'But it's my fault he's dead. If only I'd insisted that he stayed indoors yesterday afternoon.'

'Once the doctor decided to do something you could no more change his mind than stop the tide from turning,' Mrs Daws smiled wanly through her tears. 'It was his time. To be honest, I've been that surprised he hung on so long, but he wouldn't give in until he knew his beloved school was in safe hands.'

'I still can't believe he trusted me to take over the running of the school,' Sarah cried.

'He has . . . had a high regard for you, Miss Sullivan,' Mrs Daws said, reaching for the teapot. 'Tut, tut, while we've been wallowing, this tea's stewed worse than prunes.

I'll make us another brew then go and sit with the doctor. I don't like to think of him all by himself.'

The cold light of dawn was creeping over the horizon as Harry hurried towards the school. Always an early riser, he'd woken with the feeling he needed to get to Red Cliffs as soon as possible. Letting himself into the hall, he sensed the stillness and knew.

Sarah was hunched over the kitchen table, her blotchy face and red-rimmed eyes confirming his suspicion.

'The doctor's gone, then,' he murmured quietly so as not to startle her from her thoughts.

She nodded without looking up. 'Mrs Daws is sitting with him.'

'I'll make us a hot drink. It'll help revive you,' he said, going over and putting the kettle back on the hob.

'Why does everyone think a cup of tea will make things better?' she asked.

'Probably because it does. We'll need to be strong for when the children come down, you know,' he pointed out.

'I couldn't possibly face them yet,' she cried.

'Sarah, this has been a shock, even though it's been on the cards for some time.' In her misery, Sarah hardly noticed he'd used her Christian name. 'However, the children will still need looking after, feeding, reprimanding probably,' he said with forced cheerfulness. 'You have to be strong for them. Drink this,' he instructed, pushing a cup towards her. 'I'm going upstairs to see Mrs Daws. April will be down in a moment. She idolized the doctor, for all she teased him, and will need comforting. Can you do that?' As his hazel brown eyes stared directly into hers, she felt something stir within her.

'Of course I can,' she replied. 'And I'll make a start on the porridge for the children's breakfast right away.'

He nodded approvingly and strode from the room. Once out of Sarah's sight, he had to stop in the hallway and wipe the tears from his cheeks. Taking a deep breath, he made his way upstairs. He knew he must be strong, for Mrs Daws had adored the doctor and was going to need his help for the next few days. And there was still another shock to come.

'He's gone isn't he?' April whispered as she came into the kitchen. 'I know he has 'cos the house feels dead and still.'

'Oh, April, I'm so sorry,' Sarah said, going over and pulling the girl close.

'Blimey, two cuddles in as many days. Aren't I the lucky one?' she quipped, but her lips were quivering, and her eyes looked desolate. 'We're going to have to be strong for the little ones, you know.' Sarah nodded at the girl who, despite not being that grown up herself, was already thinking of others.

'Have a cup of tea,' Sarah offered, pouring the liquid from the pot, noticing as she did that Higgins had used fresh leaves. 'It's nice and strong and will make you . . .'

'Feel better, miss? Not yet, it won't. He were good to me, the doctor was. Treated me like a daughter, which is more than can be said for me own sodding father. Pardoning my language, miss,' she added quickly before taking a sip from her cup. 'Still, it warms yer insides, I suppose.' Then she frowned. 'You don't think we'll all be thrown out on the streets now he's gone, do you?'

'Over my dead body,' Sarah exclaimed. Then realizing what she'd said, she clapped her hands over her mouth.

'Guess that's one each then,' April muttered just as Pip came into the kitchen, his limp more pronounced than usual.

'Thought you should know the vicar's been and said his bits. He's coming back to see you later, miss, to talk about his service. The men have arrived to take the doctor away. They're loading his body onto their cart,' he said quietly.

'Already?' Sarah exclaimed.

Pip shrugged. 'Waiting won't change nuffin', will it?' Although he tried to be nonchalant, his words came out as a sob.

April rushed over and threw her arms around him. 'That's right, you let it out, Pip. He were a right good 'un, weren't he?'

Realizing the others would be appearing soon, Sarah left them consoling each other while she set about preparing the breakfast. She wondered who would tell the children the sad news, but when they came downstairs it was apparent by their glum faces they already knew.

Although they were subdued, the children's instincts prevailed, and they tucked into their porridge as usual. Sarah had insisted April and Pip should sit in the kitchen while she supervised in the dining room. Having been at Red Cliffs the longest, they'd been hit hardest by the doctor's death, so she thought it better to give them time alone to come to terms with the news. By the time Master Higgins appeared, the children had finished their meal.

'Right, children,' he said briskly. 'Although this is a sad day, the doctor wouldn't want us to waste it, so it's lessons as usual. Please leave the table in an orderly manner and clear the dishes. I will see you in the schoolroom in fifteen minutes.'

As the children groaned and got to their feet, Sarah turned to the master. 'Surely, you are not expecting them to work today?' she whispered in astonishment.

He gave her a level look. 'It will be better for them if they follow their normal routine as much as possible.'

'But they've only just heard about the doctor . . .' she began.

'And will adjust better if their minds are occupied,' he said firmly. 'Mrs Daws is having a rest in her room, so please see that she is looked after when she comes downstairs.'

'Of course,' she spluttered, indignant that he should feel the need to mention it.

'This is going to be a difficult day for us all, Miss Sullivan. The vicar is calling back at noon to speak to you, Mrs Daws and myself, so please have refreshment ready in the front room. Out of respect, we will not use the doctor's office today. I will get April and Pip to supervise luncheon and see you then.' With a brisk nod, he strode from the room, leaving Sarah gaping after him.

Knowing there was no way she could bring herself to go into the doctor's office so soon, Sarah prepared a vegetable broth. Whilst it simmered, she spent the rest of the morning baking bread. Although it took longer than usual for the kneading to soothe her frazzled nerves, in time she began to feel calmer. It was then that she remembered her promise to her godfather. Whilst there was no question she would do all in her power to see that his beloved Red Cliffs stayed open, she knew she was going to need the continued help of Mrs Daws and Master Higgins. They were stalwarts; Sarah knew she couldn't manage without them.

At a quarter to noon, April and Pip appeared to help supervise luncheon. Sarah decanted the broth into the serving dishes then set out the platters of bread. Whilst they were taking the things through to the dining room, Sarah laid the tea tray. She was just adding a plate of buttered bread when Mrs Daws appeared.

'Sorry, despite everything, I fell asleep,' the housekeeper said, looking sheepish.

'That's the best thing for you, Mrs Daws. Oh, there's the doorbell,' she exclaimed just as Maisie decided it was time to bang the gong.

'Nothing changes,' Mrs Daws grimaced, standing back as the children stampeded into the house. 'I'll let the vicar in if you bring the tray through.'

'Here, let me take that,' Master Higgins said, taking it from her. 'Are you all right?'

'Yes, I followed the normal routine and kept my mind occupied, just like teacher instructed,' she retorted. He grimaced but didn't reply.

'Good afternoon, Miss Sullivan,' the vicar greeted her as she entered the room. 'Please accept my condolences on your sad loss. The doctor was a very fine man indeed.'

'Thank you, vicar, won't you take a seat?' she invited. Mrs Daws poured their tea and Master Higgins passed around the cups. This was certainly the day of tea, Sarah thought as the room fell silent. She saw the vicar glance at Higgins then down at his feet. Seeking to break the awkward silence, Sarah picked up the plate of bread and butter and proffered it to their guest.

'You must be hungry, vicar. It is luncheon time, after all.'

'Thank you, but no,' he said quickly.

'Well, I expect you're in need of sustenance after teaching the children all morning,' she said, turning to Master Higgins. He shook his head.

'Mrs Daws?'

'I really couldn't,' the housekeeper replied. Sarah put the plate back down on the tray and silence descended once more.

'I suppose you're here to discuss the funeral service,' she said, thinking the vicar was being sensitive to their feelings.

He glanced at Harry and cleared his throat. 'Actually, I'm here to see what songs you would like sung at Samuel's memorial service,' he said, in a soft voice.

'Memorial service? I don't understand, surely we need to discuss arrangements for his funeral first?' she cried, turning to both men in surprise.

'There is to be no funeral, Miss Sullivan,' the vicar said.

'No funeral? I don't understand. If it's a question of finance for a coffin, I'm sure . . .' Her voice petered out as the master raised his hand.

'Miss Sullivan, there can be no funeral because there will be no body to bury,' he said quietly, staring uneasily at her.

'No body? I don't understand,' she gasped.

'The doctor left express wishes his body be donated to the hospital for medical science,' the vicar said.

'You can't mean it,' she cried, her hand flying to her mouth in horror. 'Why, they'll cut him up and . . .' Her voice trailed off. 'Oh no, tell me that's not true,' she implored, staring from the vicar to the master and back again.

'At the good doctor's request, the money received is to be put into the school's bank account. And,' the vicar paused, 'with there being no body to bury, the expense of a coffin and its burial has been spared.'

Whilst Sarah didn't agree with her godfather, she had to respect his selfless generosity.

'Goodness, trust the doctor to do things differently,' Mrs Daws said, admiration in her voice. 'He always was a selfless man.'

'Indeed he was, Mrs Daws,' the vicar agreed, clearly feeling better now the news was out in the open. 'I have brought my hymnal with me as the dear doctor expressly wished the children to choose those cheerful songs they like. That way, he reckoned they'd be sure to sing them so rousingly, he'd hear them from heaven.'

Higgins and Mrs Daws duly chuckled, and Sarah stared at them in dismay. Had they no concern that the person they professed to love and admire was to have his body dissected and used for goodness-knows-what? Stomach heaving like the sea in storm, she fled from the room.

14

Christian whistled as he swaggered down the street in his new clothes. He knew he looked good and couldn't help stopping to admire his reflection in a nearby shop window. Life was on the up and, on the strength of the news he'd received two days ago, he'd persuaded his tailor and shoemaker to let him wear their goods on approval. He'd had to promise he would settle their bills, with interest, as soon as he received his entitlement. They'd been hesitant at first but when he'd told them it was to meet an eminent member of the palace who could put prestigious business their way, they'd relented. It was amazing what the hint of a royal warrant could do, even if he had used the name of his local hostelry.

He took the route away from the railway station. It was slightly longer but he didn't want to be seen by any of his 'agents'. You never knew who was watching, and although those gypsies had taken his wares with them, he couldn't afford any connection being made. A stroke of pure genius, that, sweet-talking Madam Rosa into thinking she was the sexiest woman on two legs, then persuading her to hide his things in her van. Why, she was fifty if she was a day, he chuckled. Still, at a time of life when their own men treated them as if they were invisible, women liked to think they still had allure, and with a bit of flattery, he was adept at using this to his advantage.

Getting his men to pick a fight with the gypos so that the police moved them on was another stroke of genius, even if he did say so himself. He'd promised Rosa he'd catch up with her and, when he'd completed his business, he would.

Reaching the church without being spotted, he slunk inside. To his amazement the place was packed. When he was shown to a pew occupied by three pious-looking women, he had no choice but to squeeze alongside the enormous hippopotamus at the end. Whilst he liked a female with a rounded body, he couldn't abide one who had gone to seed. When she smiled benignly in his direction, displaying teeth the colour of ditch water, he turned quickly away.

Focusing his attention on the congregation, he wrinkled his nose at the ragamuffins in the front pews. What on earth were they doing, occupying prime position, when he, a relative no less, was consigned to the side? Well, those urchins from the school his uncle ran had better make the most of it, for as soon as the service was over, he'd claim his rights and send them on their way. He recognized that obnoxious schoolmaster Higgins and the housekeeper, Mrs Floors or something, but who was that wiry-haired woman in the green dress? Why was everyone wearing bright colours? Surely this was a funeral, he thought, staring down at his sober suit.

As the service began he let his mind wander. He had such plans for the future. All he needed to do was get through this bit and he'd be in clover. At last his fortunes were changing. He was jolted from his musing by a loud voice.

'And now some of the pupils of Red Cliffs would like to pay tribute to the wonderful man, Samuel Lawrence, who founded their school,' the vicar beamed from his pulpit.

'Right, children, remember this is your chance to show everyone how much the doctor meant to you,' Higgins whispered, ushering them towards the aisle.

'He were like a father to me, and I shall miss him every day,' April's voice sang out.

'I'd like to say thank you, guv, for saving me from the sewers when I had typhus then nursing me back to health,' Pip said, staring up at the ceiling as if he could see the doctor.

Typhus, that meant rats, didn't it? Christian gave another shudder. If he kept the place, he'd have to get it fumigated.

'The doctor gave me a second chance. Told me if I learnt me lessons and stayed out of trouble, I'd get on in life. Well, the lessons are easy but I'll try harder not to get into trouble,' Edith declared, smiling sweetly. Remembering the earwig incident, Sarah and Mrs Daws exchanged looks as they smiled through their tears. Then it was time for the terrible twins, as they were known, Brown and Black, to say their piece.

'He were a good 'un, an' no mistake,' Black said.

'Yeah, we kicked our sock-ball through his window and smashed the glass. He didn't holler like the master,' Brown grinned as a ripple of laughter went around the congregation.

'No, he told us about con-, conse-, oh, them things that happen when you've done somefink. Like, we might have hurt someone. Still, we copped it really, 'cos we're still paying for the glass out of our wages,' Black sighed, theatrically.

'It is the school's ethos to make the children aware that things cost money and that they have a responsibility to respect property,' Higgins explained. This time the congregation murmured approval.

'He told me I was a good girl 'cos I didn't pee my pants no more,' Maisie said, clearly anxious not to be left out. A titter rippled around the church.

'And finally, we have our Monday child,' Higgins announced. 'She has only been at Red Cliffs for a few weeks and has yet to find her voice. However, she would like to show you, in her own way, how the doctor made a difference to her life.' As he turned to the little girl and smiled reassuringly, Sarah held her breath. Monday stared at the sea of faces then grinned and rubbed her tummy.

'Thank you, Monday, for showing us how much you appreciate the good food you have received at Red Cliffs. You see, everyone, it's purely because of the doctor's hard work and generosity that these children have a roof over their heads, food in their stomachs, receive an education and are thus given a chance to make their way in the world.'

'Thank you, Master Higgins. A fine tribute to a fine man,' the vicar nodded. 'We will now end this service with the children singing their school anthem during which the collection plate will be circulated. As the proceeds are going to the school to ensure the doctor's good work continues, I am sure you will all dig deeply into your pockets and purses.'

The organist struck a chord, and the children began to sing their school song:

God bless our Red Cliffs School
where love and truth do rule
We are taught to earn our bread
By working hard to be well read
and learn our sums to pay our way

While the pupils sang their hearts out, Christian watched the collection plate, his eyes widening at the ever-growing pile of pound notes. Talk about easy money, he thought, reaching into his pocket and drawing out his wallet. As the salver was passed to him, he made a big show of brandishing his note as he carefully laid it down.

Smiling benignly, he passed it to the large lady next to him, who added a small coin before quickly handing it on. Christian turned to watch the ragamuffins, his hand going to his pocket, where he placed the little pile of notes he'd lifted. Talk about a bonus. It had been worth suffering the service after all.

God bless our Red Cliffs School,
where love and truth do rule.

As the children finished their song, the vicar smiled down at them.

'Thank you, pupils of Red Cliffs School, for giving a fine rendition of your school anthem. The doctor would be proud of you. Now we shall finish our service with a prayer.'

After the service, Christian managed to dodge the outstretched hand of the vicar as he followed the crocodile of children out of the church. He then kept a discreet distance as they made their way back to Red Cliffs. He wished they would hurry for he didn't want to keep the lawyer waiting. By the time he reached the house, he could hear Higgins taking a well-dressed man to task.

'But surely it would be improper to conduct such business directly after the doctor's service?'

'I have my instructions, sir,' the man replied.

The master turned to the housekeeper. 'Mrs Daws, will you please take the children indoors whilst we sort this out.'

'Of course, Master Higgins. Come along, everyone, it's nearly time for luncheon.' The children cheered and pushed through the gates,

'I was given to understand we were meeting at your office on Wednesday,' Christian heard the woman in the green dress and shawl say. He frowned. Surely he recognized that voice?

'That was indeed the case, Miss Sullivan,' the lawyer replied. 'However, I received instructions that the will is to be read here, today, directly after the service.'

'Who gave such instruction?' Sarah asked.

'I did,' Christian replied, moving closer, certain now that this woman was the girl he used to play with at family gatherings. 'Goodness, that's never little Sarah Sulks,' he said, feigning surprise.

'Christian? Goodness, I would never have recognized you if you hadn't used that horrible name,' Sarah replied.

'Mr Lawrence,' Higgins frowned. 'I might have known you'd be behind this.'

'Might I suggest we go inside,' the lawyer said, shifting his oxtail leather Gladstone bag from hand to hand.

'Forgive me, you are Mr . . . ?' Sarah looked at him enquiringly.

'Fothergill. And you must be Miss Sullivan,' he replied.

'And I am Mr Lawrence, nephew of the late Dr Lawrence,' Christian announced, anxious to take charge of the proceedings. 'Higgins, perhaps you would lead the way to my uncle's office.' The master narrowed his eyes but Sarah touched his arm.

'Please?' she asked softly. 'I don't want there to be any trouble today.'

Harry stared at her earnest expression and nodded. 'As you wish, Miss Sullivan,' he replied, leading the way up the drive, but not before she'd seen his lips tighten into a line.

'Would you like some tea, sir?' Mrs Daws asked as soon as they entered the hall.

Mr Fothergill smiled. 'That is very kind but I think I'd rather conduct our business first.'

'Well, I'll go and see to the children then.'

'You are, sorry, were, the doctor's housekeeper?' he enquired.

'I had that honour, sir. He was a fine man,' Mrs Daws replied, her eyes glistening with unshed tears.

'He certainly was, and I am sorry for your loss. Now, if you would step inside with us, you will find this concerns you too.'

The housekeeper raised her brow. 'Really? I can't think how,' she murmured. 'Oh, well, April and Pip are in the kitchen so it should be all right.'

'Do you think we might get on with things?' Christian snapped. 'Some of us are busy, you know.'

'Quite so, sir,' Fothergill replied, making his way past Higgins, who was holding open the door.

'Right, if you would all like to be seated,' Fothergill said, sidling his way around to the other side of the desk.

'I'm sure there's really no need for the staff to be here,' Christian protested, glaring at Higgins.

'There is every need, sir. If you would kindly take your seat, we can begin,' the lawyer replied, opening his case and drawing out a sheaf of papers. Then he donned a pair of silver-rimmed spectacles, cleared his throat and, without looking up, began reading.

'This is the last Will and Testament of me, Samuel Ernest Lawrence, written this day . . .'

'Oh, do cut to the chase,' Christian interrupted.

'Very well, Mr Lawrence, if everyone else is agreeable?' Fothergill asked, staring at each of them in turn.

'For heaven's sake, get on with it,' Christian growled. The solicitor raised his brows then continued reading.

'I leave all of my estate including the house and school known as Red Cliffs to my god-daughter, Miss Sarah Sullivan . . .'

'What!' Sarah exclaimed, staring at the man in astonishment.

'No! I object, your honour,' Christian shouted.

'This is not a court of law, Mr Lawrence,' Fothergill said mildly.

'But Lawrence was my uncle. Red Cliffs is mine. It is my birthright.'

'I believe Dr Lawrence wanted to ensure the continued running of his life's work and as such appointed . . .'

'Never! I will contest it,' Christian spluttered, jumping to his feet. 'I suppose you came here grovelling and ingratiating yourself . . .' he added, glaring down at Sarah.

'Mr Lawrence, I must protest,' Fothergill interrupted. 'The doctor went to a lot of trouble to ensure his wishes would be carried out. I can assure you that his will is indisputable. You are named as a beneficiary, so if you will please be seated I will resume.' Reluctantly, Christian did as the man asked, then Fothergill cleared his throat and continued.

'Now, in addition to the estate, property and contents being left to Miss Sullivan, there are four named bequests. Firstly, to Mrs Daws. As a token of my thanks for many years' loyal service, Mrs Daws has the right to dwell at Red Cliffs for the rest of her years.' There was a sharp intake of breath and Fothergill raised his brow over his spectacles at Christian. 'She will also receive the sum of £100 to spend as she wishes.'

'Oh my,' the housekeeper murmured. 'I wouldn't know what to do with such money, so it can go straight into the school's funds, sir, if you would be so kind.'

'As you wish. I'm sure the doctor would have appreciated such a generous gesture. Now, to Master Higgins, the sum of £100 and the right to reside at Red Cliffs should he so wish.'

The master smiled. 'I think my mother might have something to say about that. However, like Mrs Daws, I would like my money to go to the school. It would hardly seem right taking anything from a man who dedicated his life so selflessly to Red Cliffs.'

'Admirable, sir. I can see why Dr Lawrence esteemed his staff so much.'

'But what about me?' blurted Christian, unable to contain himself any longer.

Fothergill looked back down at his papers. 'To my nephew, Christian Lawrence, I bequeath my gold watch and the sum of £100.'

'One hundred pounds!' Christian exclaimed. 'Why, that's . . .'

'If I might continue, sir,' Fothergill said. 'This sum is to be held in trust to be released on the birth of his first son.'

'What! That's preposterous. Why, I'm not even married, nor do I intend putting my head in the noose.' He turned to Sarah. 'This house is my birthright. It was promised to me, and I can prove it,' he shouted. 'You will be hearing from my lawyer soon, Fothergill.'

'As you wish, sir, However, I can assure you . . .'

'And as for you, Sarah Sulks, what the hell do you know about running a school? Have you any had formal training?'

'Well, no, but . . .'

'So you're not even qualified. Well, wait until the authorities hear about this. Mark my words, Sarah Sulks, your days here are numbered.'

Sarah opened her mouth to protest, but Christian had flounced from the room, slamming the door behind him.

15

They sat in stunned silence for a few moments then Higgins spoke.

'Good riddance, I say. That man has no interest in this place whatsoever.'

Sarah stared woefully at the master. 'Christian is right, though. What do I know about running a school? When my godfather made me promise to continue with the running of Red Cliffs, I had no idea he meant to actually bequeath it to me,' she said quietly. 'Am I up to the task, I ask myself?'

'You have a good heart, Miss Sullivan, and that's as good a start as any,' the housekeeper said. 'The good doctor wouldn't have asked you to run his beloved Red Cliffs unless he was confident you could. As for that no-good nephew of his, why, he never visited the poor doctor, even after Master Higgins sent him a letter saying he was ill.'

'Thank you for your faith in me, Mrs Daws,' Sarah said, smiling gratefully at the woman. 'With your help, I shall endeavour to ensure the school continues to run as my godfather wished. You will help me, won't you?' she asked, looking askance at the housekeeper and schoolmaster.

'Of course, my dear. That goes without saying,' Mrs Daws replied.

'And I will persist in trying to instil a modicum of learning and discipline into those little heathen heads.'

Higgins agreed gruffly, but Sarah saw the twinkle in his eye. 'I will also pledge my support to assist in any way I can with the running of Red Cliffs.'

'Thank you, Master Higgins. It will be a blessing to be able to draw upon your experience, for I owe it to my god-father to do my best for Red Cliffs.' They were all silent for a few moments, as the gravity of the situation sank in. The hush was eventually broken by the sound of a gentle cough.

'There will be the formalities and paperwork to go through, Miss Sullivan. However, I think that would be better left for another day,' Mr Fothergill said softly.

'Thank you,' Sarah replied, relief flooding through her. She'd had quite enough to take in for one day. Then a thought struck her. 'You said there were four bequests, I believe?'

'Indeed,' the lawyer nodded. 'The fourth beneficiary is to receive personal effects, estimated to be worth no more than £100.'

'And who might that be?' she asked.

The lawyer began gathering up his papers. 'I am afraid I am not at liberty to disclose the name, only the amount. The doctor entrusted these items to my safe keeping for onward transmission when he knew his health was fail-ing,' he muttered. 'Now, if you have no other questions?'

'I'm sure I will have, Mr Fothergill, but to be honest, my mind's whirling from shock at the moment.'

'I understand, Miss Sullivan. Perhaps you would like to arrange a meeting when you are ready to discuss the details.' He handed her a gold-edged business card. 'The doctor was a good friend as well as a client, and I have every admiration for the way he selflessly turned his family house into both school and home for the ragged children. Anything I can help with, you only have to ask,' he said, picking up his bag.

'Thank you, Mr Fothergill,' she replied.

He nodded, made his way to the door, and then hesitated. Turning back to Sarah, he cleared his throat before saying, 'Miss Sullivan, I think you should be aware that Mr Lawrence is likely to make trouble. I've seen it before when someone doesn't get what they think they are entitled to. Should you require any help before our next meeting, please contact me. Good day to you all.'

'Goodness,' Sarah murmured, sinking back in her seat.

'Well, I think we all need a cup of tea after that,' Mrs Daws said.

'Ah, the panacea of the English,' Higgins commented.

'Don't you use them fancy words on me, Harry Higgins. Come along, let's go and see what those children have been up to in our absence.' The housekeeper got to her feet.

'I'll just take a moment to go through some things in here,' Sarah said, staring at the paperwork that had been hurriedly pushed into a pile for their impromptu meeting. 'I haven't been in here since my godfather,' she paused and took a deep breath, 'passed on,' she finished quietly.

'Right, Mrs Daws, I for one could do with a cup of tea, so you can make it while I see to the children. Meanwhile, Miss Sullivan here can get used to playing boss.' Although his words were brisk, Sarah could see the sympathy in his eyes.

As the door closed behind them, she stared around the room, remembering the day she'd first come here. Glancing at her godfather's chair, she could picture him sitting there, telling her he'd like her support with the administration.

'You knew all along it would be more than that, didn't you, Uncle?' she whispered. 'If only I'd known, I would have spent my time getting to grips with the actual running of this place rather than trying to sort out the bookwork.' There's so much I need to know, she thought, staring down at the sea of papers and stacks of boxes full of she knew not what. Shaking her head to clear it, she caught sight of her uncle's muffler and battered old hat on the stand and felt the tears welling.

Suddenly the door flew open, and April and Pip burst into the room, followed by a worried-looking Mrs Daws. They were clearly distraught as they stood there, staring wide-eyed at Sarah.

'I'm sorry, Miss Sullivan, I told them you weren't to be bothered, but . . .' the housekeeper began.

'Mrs Daws said we should stay in the kitchen 'til you came, but we couldn't wait no longer,' April cried.

''Cos we needs to know if what that horrid man said was true,' Pip said.

'What man?' Sarah asked. 'You mean the lawyer, Mr Fothergill?'

'The geezer with the posh bag? Nah, the fair-haired toff,' Pip scowled.

'He said Red Cliffs was his and we should start packing 'cos he's going to sell it,' April burst out.

'I knew he was a rum 'un, but to tell the children that,' Mrs Daws spluttered.

'An' he said with our 'flictions we'd end up back on the streets where we belonged,' Pip muttered.

Sarah frowned. Flictions? 'Oh, you mean afflictions. What a nasty thing to say. Afflictions means . . .' she began.

'Does it mean we're going to be thrown outta here?' Pip asked.

'No, Pip, it most certainly does not,' she said firmly, staring at their scared little faces. 'Mr Lawrence was in a bad mood because he thought he was going to inherit Red Cliffs, but the good doctor has left the school to me instead.'

'Really, miss?' April cried.

'But you's a woman, miss,' Pip said. 'A very nice one,' he added quickly. 'But everyone knows it's men who run things.'

'Now, listen to me, young man. I may well be a woman but the dear doctor has entrusted the running of Red Cliffs to me, and I intend to take up the challenge. However, I shall need your help.'

'You can count on me, miss,' April replied eagerly.

'Me an' all if it means we can stay. The little 'uns will need extra looking after, especially at night when they thinks the bogey man's come to get them.'

'Yes, they've been right upset since the doctor died,' April agreed.

'The children look up to you and need to believe what you tell them,' Sarah said, staring from April to Pip. 'Master Higgins is going to explain that things are to continue as they always have, but the doctor's passing has come as a shock, and they will need you to comfort and reassure them. Can you do that?'

"Cors we can,' Pip said, puffing out his chest.

'The doctor said he could rely on us and you can too,' April assured her.

'Thank you. We will work as a team and keep Red Cliffs running in the same way the doctor did. Now, there's the gong. By the crazy way it's being banged, I'm guessing Maisie's hungry,' she laughed to lighten the mood.

'Oh, blimey, I'm meant to be dishing up,' April said, flying from the room.

'You really think you can do this, miss?' Pip asked.

'Yes, I do,' Sarah assured him. 'And, Pip, no more about me being a woman, eh? The world is changing, and females are going to have more of a say in how things are run.'

'If you say so, miss,' he replied, then followed quickly after April. Sarah sighed then saw Mrs Daws was shaking her head.

'You don't think I'm up to it?' she whispered.

'I think you're more than up to it, Miss Sullivan. Only minutes ago, those children were petrified, and now look at them. If I could get my hands on that good-for-nothing Christian, I'd . . . well, let's just say I'd teach him a lesson he'd never forget.'

To all intents and purposes, things carried on as normal at Red Cliffs over the next few days. April helped Mrs Daws with the household and kitchen duties while Master Higgins continued the running of both the schoolroom and workshops. Pip went about his duties, deferring to the master as he had previously to the doctor. Meanwhile, Sarah started to attack the paperwork with renewed enthusiasm, and began to make some sort of order of it all. While everyone was very sad at the passing of the doctor, life had to carry on.

'Mrs Laver has laundered them few clothes of the doctor's and wonders if she could take them to the poorhouse. They're not up to much but might serve a turn for some old soul,' Mrs Daws said, placing a cup of tea on the desk beside Sarah.

'Of course, he would have approved of that, wouldn't he?' The housekeeper nodded but instead of leaving as she normally would, stood there looking anxious. 'Is something wrong, Mrs Daws?'

'I don't want to trouble you when you got all this to sort out, but it's that travelling schoolmistress.'

'Miss Green? What's the matter with her?' Sarah asked, putting down her pen and giving the housekeeper her full attention. 'Sit down and tell me what's worrying you.'

'Wouldn't say no,' the housekeeper said, sinking into a chair. 'Been on me feet since before dawn, not that I'm complaining, Miss Sullivan,' she added quickly.

'You really must say if you've too much to manage. I've been thinking it wouldn't do Edith any harm to be given some more responsibility. Might channel some of that excess energy,' Sarah said with a smile. The housekeeper just nodded. 'Come on then, tell me what's worrying you.'

'That Miss Green has always had a spiteful side, I've thought. Anyway, since the doctor passed, I've noticed she's become more heavy-handed with the girls, and I don't like it,' the housekeeper said. She sat there, wringing her apron in her hands, and Sarah could see it was serious.

'She is due here this afternoon, is she not?'

'Always manages to arrive in time for luncheon even though her hours don't officially start until afterwards.' The housekeeper sniffed.

'Really? Goodness, I don't remember seeing her in the dining room,' Sarah replied.

'No, well, you wouldn't. She demands that a plate of food be brought to her in the schoolroom when she arrives. Master Higgins says I shouldn't pander to her but she makes such a fuss if it's not there. Then she takes it out . . . well, let's just say she's not very nice to the girls.'

'I see,' Sarah said, her lips tightening. 'Leave it with me, Mrs Daws. I think it's high time I paid this Miss Green a visit.'

'Thank you, miss. I don't want to cause trouble but it's been playing on my mind,' the housekeeper said, getting up to go.

'You did the right thing coming to me, Mrs Daws. The children's welfare is paramount.'

'That's how I feel,' she agreed. 'Well, I'd best get on.'

Sarah continued working her way through the pile of papers until she heard the dinner gong, then made her way to the schoolroom.

'Miss Green?' she asked. A smartly dressed woman in her mid-twenties, with a cap adorning her dark brown hair, looked up from eating her luncheon and frowned.

'I didn't hear you knock,' she said, narrowing her eyes.

'That's because I didn't,' Sarah replied, taking an instant dislike to the woman's superior attitude.

'Well, it's only manners to,' Miss Green replied, turning back to her luncheon.

'When I feel the need to knock on the door of my own schoolroom, then I will,' Sarah replied. 'As for manners, I think you should be looking towards your own behaviour before questioning others.'

'How dare you . . .' the woman spluttered, spraying crumbs of bread in the air. 'I am the schoolmistress.'

'And I am Miss Sullivan, the new proprietor of Red Cliffs. It has been brought to my notice that your treatment of the girls is somewhat heavy-handed, Miss Green.'

The woman sneered. 'Want them wrapped in cotton wool like babies, do you?'

'No, but I expect you to treat them fairly,' she paused to let her words sink in. 'I have also been looking up your terms of employment, Miss Green, and nowhere can I find reference to your entitlement to a free meal.'

'Is everything all right in here, Miss Sullivan?'

Sarah looked up to see the schoolmaster standing in the doorway. 'Yes, thank you, Master Higgins. I was just acquainting myself with the schoolmistress here. Please will you inform Mrs Daws that Miss Green no longer requires food to be brought to the classroom for her. Her terms of employment don't mention a free meal, though if she finds herself in need of food, she can of course join the others in the dining room, and the cost will be deducted from her salary.'

'No!' the mistress protested.

'I insist. We never let anyone go hungry at Red Cliffs, Miss Green.' Hearing a muffled chortle from the doorway, she looked up to see Higgins staring at her admiringly.

'Now, Miss Green, I would be interested in hearing what you intend to teach our girls this afternoon,' she said, turning back to the schoolmistress.

'Nobody has ever questioned me before,' the woman hissed.

'As the new headmistress, I feel I should know exactly what goes on in my school,' Sarah replied. The slight emphasis she put on the word 'my' didn't go unnoticed by the mistress and her mouth tightened.

'This is my afternoon for instructing the girls in the sewing of their samplers,' she replied.

'May I see one?' Sarah asked. Reluctantly, the woman went over to the cupboard at the front of the room and drew out a slim parcel. With a heavy sigh, she placed it on the nearest table then slowly pulled back the cloth to reveal a dozen or so samplers. Sarah picked one up and studied it carefully. 'A fine example of cross-stitching, Miss Green.'

The woman smiled graciously. 'I do pride myself on my instruction of the perfect needlepoint, Miss Sullivan.'

'So there are examples of other stitches, then?' Sarah asked, flicking through the other samplers, which all proved to be identical.

'Alas, no. Only when they have mastered the cross-stitch to my satisfaction will I allow them to progress to something more difficult.'

'Surely the older ones should have learnt more than one stitch by now,' Sarah said.

'These unfortunate children are slow to learn, Miss Sullivan,' the mistress sighed.

'Really? You do surprise me,' Sarah replied. 'From what I've seen, they appear to be rather bright at picking up things.'

'Picking up their spoons, maybe, but as for learning?' She shrugged her shoulders theatrically. 'It takes all my time to discipline them.'

Sarah pointed to the plaque on the wall. '*Love Never Faileth*, Miss Green. Isn't that the maxim Red Cliffs abides by? Well, the bell will be ringing for lessons in a moment, so I'll leave you to it.'

'Once more unto the fray,' the mistress sighed. 'Do feel free to call into my classroom again, Miss Sullivan.'

'I will indeed be paying another visit to my classroom, Miss Green. Good day to you,' she said, sweeping from the room. 'Sanctimonious little prig,' she muttered.

'Really, Miss Sullivan, I'm surprised at you, although I couldn't agree more,' Master Higgins said, grinning as he passed by on his way to the workroom. Then he stopped and retraced his steps. 'A word to the wise, Miss Sullivan. Be careful not to get on the wrong side of Miss Green, for she has friends in high places.'

16

Back in her office, Sarah was unable to settle after her confrontation with the schoolmistress. The woman's superior attitude had riled her, but should she have handled the situation differently? Knowing she needed to eat or she wouldn't be able to function properly, Sarah nibbled half-heartedly at the bread and ham Mrs Daws had insisted she bring back with her. The housekeeper had been delighted that she would no longer have to kowtow to 'her ladyship', as she'd put it, and had taken April's hand and danced a jig around the kitchen.

Well, this won't help me sort out the paperwork, Sarah thought, pushing her plate to one side and returning to the form she'd been reading earlier. It was a typically confusing local authority document setting out guidelines for school funding; she knew it was important, but she was distracted and couldn't concentrate. When she'd re-read the paper for the third time and still hadn't really taken in a single word, she put it down and rubbed her eyes. The heated exchange of words with the schoolmistress was playing on her mind, and she knew she wouldn't settle until she'd smoothed things over. Maybe if she shared her idea of the girls using their sewing to adapt donated clothing to fit, she and Miss Green might find some common ground. Particularly if she pointed out that this would also help towards them gaining some of the practical domestic skills she had just learnt the school was required to teach in order to qualify for one of the available grants.

She would go to the schoolroom right now, she decided, picking up her plate and taking it through to the kitchen, where April was scrubbing the deal table.

'Thank you, that was delicious as always,' she told the girl.

April beamed. 'I made that bread, miss,' she said proudly.

'Well, you've certainly the makings of a fine baker, young lady.' She was about to ask how Monday was, then remembered her godfather saying all the children should be treated the same. Not wanting to be showing any favouritism, she changed her mind. 'I'm just off to see Miss Green if anyone wants me,' she said instead. April grimaced but didn't pass comment.

Outside, the air was cold with a fresh wind blowing in from the sea. Sarah stared at the lowering clouds, wondering if she should go back for her shawl. Deciding it was more important to get things sorted with the mistress, she made her way around the back of the building towards the schoolroom. Suddenly, a scream stopped her in her tracks. Frowning, she peered around. Another shriek was followed by heart-rending sobbing. It sounded as if it was coming from the coal house, Sarah thought. Rushing over to the windowless store, she tried the handle but it wouldn't turn. From inside, the sound of hysterical crying was growing ever louder.

'Who's in there?' Sarah called, banging on the door. All went quiet and then a pitiful voice wailed.

'Miss, oh please help me, miss.'

'Edith, is that you?' she asked, recognizing the girl's voice. 'Have you shut yourself in?'

'M-Miss l-locked me in for w-wanting to learn m-more s-stitches. S-she s-said I w-was an un-ungrateful p-pig. It's s-so c-cold and d-dark in h-here, I'm f-frightened.' The pitiful wailing started up again.

'Is there a problem, Miss Sullivan?' Harry Higgins called from the doorway of the workroom.

'Edith's locked in the coal house,' she called. Even from a distance, she could see the master's lips tighten.

'Wait there,' he ordered.

'It's all right, Edith, Master Higgins has gone to get the key. Do you know where it's kept?'

'Sh-she's g-got it,' the voice wailed. 'I'm s-so c-cold.'

The master appeared, brandishing a key. No sooner had he pulled the door open than the girl shot out of the dark and threw herself into Sarah's arms.

'It's s-so h-horrid in there,' she shuddered. Heedless of the black dust clinging to the girl's clothes, Sarah pulled the trembling child closer.

'There, there,' she soothed. 'Who would do such a thing?' she asked, turning to the schoolmaster.

'It was her, L-lettuce L-leaf,' Edith whispered. 'F-first I c-couldn't fred the n-needle then I asked to l-learn n-new stitches . . .' The rest of the sentence was lost in a burst of frenzied sobbing.

'Take Edith inside, Miss Sullivan, I'll see about this,' he said, removing the key from the lock and holding it up.

'Can you make Edith a hot drink, please, April?' Sarah asked as soon as they entered the kitchen. 'Now, Edith, let's get you warm,' she murmured, leading the shivering girl over to the chair beside the range. 'I presume the girls call Miss Green "Lettuce Leaf",' she whispered to April as she passed.

'Yes,' April giggled.

Sarah pursed her lips. She'd certainly have something to say to that woman when she next saw her.

'My, my, Edith Curdy, just look at the state of you,' Mrs Daws said, coming into the room and staring at the young girl. 'Whatever have you been up to, young lady?'

'That wicked woman locked her in the coal house,' April told her, pouring boiling water into the big brown pot.

The housekeeper pursed her lips. 'Worst thing that could happen to her an' all,' she muttered to Sarah. 'Well, you'd best save some of that hot water, April. This young lady needs a thorough sponging down, not to mention clean clothes. And as for the state of you, Miss Sullivan,' she clucked, gesturing towards Sarah's dress.

Sarah grimaced down at the black grime that was clinging to the material. 'Oh well, it'll be the blue serge for me later, then,' she joked, trying to lighten the atmosphere, even though she was seething inside.

'You go and change, Miss Sullivan. April and I will see to Edith. I'll pour you a nice cup of tea for when you return,' Mrs Daws added. 'Now, come on, young Edith, you drink this, and we'll see if we can find you a biscuit.' As the little girl's face lit up, Sarah thanked her lucky stars that the kind-hearted woman was here to help.

By the time Sarah returned to the kitchen, she could hear the sound of the children running around outside. The master was sitting at the table, talking to Mrs Daws. There was no sign of April or Edith.

'That child was so filthy, she needed a right good scrub down. April's taken her out to the wash-house. There's tea in the pot so sit yourself down and have a hot drink, Miss Sullivan.'

'Thank you, Mrs Daws, but I really must speak with Miss Green first.'

'I've already had a word with her,' Higgins said. 'Told her that in view of that unfortunate incident, it would be better if she went home early. She wasn't too pleased when I also told her she would only be paid for half the afternoon, but . . .' he shrugged.

'I hope you told her such cruel behaviour will not be tolerated,' Sarah replied. 'Why, I'd half a mind to dismiss her on the spot.'

'Which is why I thought it better that I speak with her. As I mentioned earlier, she does have influential contacts,' Higgins pointed out. Already disturbed by the afternoon's events, his mild manner enraged Sarah even further. Storming around to his side of the table, she glared down at him.

'I suppose I should have expected you to take her side, Master Higgins. With your attitude to discipline and that repulsive tawse you keep on your desk, you would condone her behaviour. Well, let me tell you this, locking a defenceless child in the coal shed is the most despicable thing I have ever heard.'

'I agree, which is why I sent Miss Green home. I told her it is time she realized that schools have moved on since the days of incarcerating children for minor misdemeanours. Now, if you think I'm harsh, Miss Sullivan, perhaps you would like to hear about the days when pupils were made to use finger stocks and back straighteners,' Higgins said, quirking his brow.

Sarah shuddered. 'That's as may be, but that poor girl was scared out of her wits.' She sank into a chair as the anger drained from her.

'That was unforgivable and certainly not the way to deal with a miscreant. However, you need to understand that punishment and correction are very much part of the role of a schoolteacher. Children will always try and push the boundaries, Miss Sullivan, and it is our duty to show them right from wrong. I may threaten the pupils with the tawse, but it is merely a deterrent. One look at me swishing the leather and they very quickly remember to behave.'

'He knows what he's talking about, Miss Sullivan,' the housekeeper said, pouring tea from the pot and sliding a cup across the table towards Sarah. 'Them little perishers can try the patience of a saint at times, bless them.'

Sarah smiled wanly, then remembered the housekeeper's earlier words. 'Why did you say that being locked in the coal shed was the worst thing that could happen to Edith, Mrs Daws?'

The housekeeper sighed. 'Her mother was one of them, how can I put it, colourful ladies of the night.' Sarah frowned.

'A prostitute,' the master supplied.

'Oh,' Sarah muttered. 'But what does that have to do with the coal shed?'

'She used to lock Edith in the cellar whilst she went about her business. The doctor, God rest his soul, heard frightened screaming and found her in there, filthy dirty and with rats running over her little feet. She were only three. Had nightmares for months, poor little love, and she still hasn't really got over it.'

'You mean the mother let the doctor bring her to Red Cliffs?' Sarah gasped.

'Let him? She practically threw the child at him. Even offered the doctor a free . . . well, let us just say he got away as quickly as he could.'

'That's terrible.' Sarah took a sip of her tea and was quiet for a moment. 'It sounds to me as though it's the parents who need disciplining.'

The master nodded. 'I agree. However, put under pressure, adults will up and disappear, leaving their offspring to fend for themselves. At least by showing the children here right from wrong, we are giving them a chance to lead a decent life when they move on.'

'And hopefully by giving them affection there's a good chance they will want to marry and have their own families,' Mrs Daws added. 'The doctor was emphatic they should learn how decent adults behave. He were such a good man.' They nodded and fell silent once more, each lost in their own thoughts.

Then the master stared out of the window and smiled. 'I think young Edith must be feeling better for she's running around outside with the others.'

'Shouldn't she be tucked up in bed after her ordeal?' Sarah asked.

The housekeeper laughed. 'I'd like to see you try and get that one tucked up before the night bell goes.'

'But it's cold outside and . . .'

'Children are tougher than you think, Miss Sullivan,' Higgins said quickly, cutting off her protest. 'Running around the grounds gives them a sense of freedom after they've been cooped up inside. There's not much work they can do in the garden at the moment, so we let them have more free time to play. They are getting exercise in the fresh air without realizing it.'

'Runs off some of them high spirits,' Mrs Daws laughed.

'Children live in the moment, Miss Sullivan. As long as they are fed and watered, they are generally happy. Don't worry, I'll keep an eye on Edith in the schoolroom over the next few days to make sure she has suffered no ill effects,' the master reassured her.

'And I'll get April to make sure she's all right at night,' Mrs Daws said. 'Which reminds me, Miss Sullivan. Now the good doctor's room has been cleared and cleaned, perhaps you would like to move in there. It would give you space.'

Sarah stared at the housekeeper in dismay. The thought of sleeping in her godfather's room filled her with disquiet.

'Oh, I couldn't possibly,' she protested. 'It's only right that you should, Mrs Daws.'

The woman shook her head. 'I've had the same room since I came to Red Cliffs and it serves me just fine.'

'How about you, Master Higgins?' she asked, turning to the schoolmaster.

'I think my old mother would have something to say about that. She moans she sees little of me as it is,' he said ruefully.

'Besides, you're the head of Red Cliffs now, Miss Sullivan, so I'll get April to move your things across after supper. Talking of which, I'd better get on,' Mrs Daws said, getting to her feet and making for the pantry.

Well, it seemed that was that, then, Sarah thought, staring out of the window at the children, who were happily letting off steam. Edith was in a clean dress and seemed to be having fun with the others, apparently having forgotten her earlier ordeal.

'I still don't think Miss Green should get away with treating Edith so harshly,' she said, turning to the master.

'She won't,' Higgins replied. 'As I said earlier, Miss Green has connections, but as Mrs Daws is always fond of saying, there is more than one way to skin a cat.' He smiled gently.

'I'll take your word for that then, Master Higgins.'

He nodded then stared directly at her. 'Couldn't you call me Harry when we're alone?' he suggested.

She smiled, remembering him making a similar suggestion before her godfather died. 'Very well, Harry, but only if you call me Sarah. When the children aren't present, though, or they might get the wrong idea.' She laughed, then could have bitten off her tongue. He was staring at her in a speculative way, a little grin tugging at the corner of his lips. Why on earth had she said such a ridiculous thing?

'Well, I managed to get that blinking coal dust off Edith's dress, but I've had to put it out for Mrs Laver to wash,' April announced, bouncing into the kitchen. 'Oops, not interrupted something, have I?' she asked giving a mischievous grin as she stared from Sarah to the master and back again.

'No, of course not,' Sarah replied quickly, thankful to see Mrs Daws reappearing with a loaf of bread.

'If you say so,' April said sceptically. 'Well, I've numbered that other one Edith's wearing. Right cock-a-hoop, she is, to think she's got an extra frock to her name.'

Harry quirked a brow at Sarah, and she smiled, getting his meaning. He was right. Children were more resilient than she gave them credit for.

'Well, this isn't getting those forms sorted,' she remarked, getting to her feet. 'I'll see you at supper. You don't need any help, do you, Mrs Daws?' she asked.

The housekeeper shook her head. 'No, the soup's almost done, and April here can see to the bread and scrape. You get on with that paperwork. Sooner it's done, the sooner that frown will disappear from your face. We don't want you getting wrinkles, now do we?' she chuckled.

Harry watched Sarah leave the room and sighed. He didn't think for one moment she understood what she'd taken on with Red Cliffs. She was competent enough to cope with what she was doing and had her heart in the right place, of that he had no doubt, but there was a naïvety about her that troubled him. She didn't seem to understand their financial predicament or realize the place took a lot more than fresh air to run it.

17

'Good morning, Sarah,' Harry said, poking his head around the office door. 'May I come in?'

'Goodness, is it time for school already?' she asked, looking up from the form she'd been reading and blinking at him.

'I thought I'd make an early start, though not as early as you by the look of it,' he said, frowning down at the papers strewn across her desk.

'What with the comings and goings of all the children, I seem better able to concentrate either first thing in the morning or after supper,' Sarah smiled, not wishing to admit that since moving into her uncle's room, sleep had eluded her. Even Monday hadn't sought the comfort of her bed these past few nights, and Sarah had missed the warm little body beside her, although of course, it was good the little girl was feeling more settled.

'Ah, a crepuscular creature, eh?' he grinned.

'A what?' she asked, staring quizzically at the schoolmaster.

'It means one who is more active during the hours of dusk and dawn,' he smiled.

'Well, you must forgive my ignorance,' she laughed.

'Not at all. How boring life would be if we weren't constantly learning. It's blowing a right old gale out there,' he added, rubbing his hands together in an effort to get them warm. 'That's one of the reasons I wanted to speak with you.'

'Sounds serious. Why don't you take a seat,' Sarah invited.

'Thanks,' he said, straddling his long legs over the leather chair in front of her. 'Come winter the children are unable to spend much time outdoors, so we devote the extra hours to craftwork. In previous years, the pupils have made things to sell at the Christmas Fayre that St Nicholas' hold, with some of the profits going to the church and the rest into school funds. Your godfather was keen the children should give to others less fortunate and . . .' He trailed off.

'You wondered if I'd be agreeable to you continuing?' she finished for him. He nodded and looked at her expectantly. 'Of course, I think it's a splendid idea. What do they make?' she asked, trying not to be distracted by the gleam sparking in his hazel eyes.

'The boys fashion simple things from wood, toy boats, whipping tops, stilts, diabolos and containers for spills, that kind of thing.'

'Splendid. And the girls?' she asked.

'They help serve the refreshments and wash up on the day,' he replied.

Sarah's eyes widened. 'But surely they make things to sell as well?'

'Actually, they don't. Mrs Daws hasn't the time to oversee craftwork as well as teach them the household skills they're required to learn,' he explained.

'But sewing is Miss Green's remit and . . .' Remembering the samplers, Sarah broke off.

'Precisely,' Harry replied, as ever quick to follow her train of thought. 'The doctor did mention it but she told him they weren't capable of making anything worth selling.'

'Surely it is the teacher's job to encourage competency?'

He nodded. 'I agree. However, the doctor was too busy to pursue it.'

'But I am not, Master Higgins,' Sarah replied. 'I was going to speak to Miss Green about the way she conducts her classes, anyway. Do you know why she locked Edith in the coal store?'

Harry opened his mouth to reply but before he could say anything, she went on. 'It was because she said she was bored with doing cross stitch and dared to ask if she could learn something new. You'd think any teacher worth their salt would encourage such enthusiasm. Miss Green completely overstepped the mark, and I will not tolerate such behaviour,' she burst out, throwing her pen down on the desk. To her consternation, she saw the master's lips twitch.

'You think that is funny, Master Higgins?' she asked.

'No, I don't. It's just refreshing to see someone as passionate about the pupils' education as I am. And it is Harry when we're alone, remember?' He stopped and sniffed the air appreciatively. 'Smells like the porridge is ready. Come along, you must be famished after your early start.' Sarah sighed and shook her head.

'I've a meeting with Mr Fothergill this afternoon and have a mountain of forms to go through before I see him.'

'Very well, I'll get April to supervise the girls if you promise to eat some breakfast yourself?' he asked, staring at her until she nodded.

Sarah tried to concentrate, but her grumbling stomach kept reminding her she was hungry. By the time she went through to the kitchen, breakfast had already been served.

'It's hard to think there's twenty or more children in there,' she said to the housekeeper, inclining her head towards the dining room, where they were all eagerly tucking into their porridge.

'Only time they're quiet, the little loves,' Mrs Daws clucked. 'You sit yourself down at the table and enjoy yours in peace. The master said you've been slaving away since dawn. And don't think I didn't hear you creeping downstairs afore it were light.'

Sarah grimaced as she watched the woman go over to the large pot. 'Thank you, Mrs Daws,' Sarah said moments later when the woman placed a steaming bowl in front of her.

'Master Higgins was telling me about the Christmas Fayre. Before I speak to Miss Green about it, I wondered if Edith had suffered any ill effects after her ordeal the other day.'

'I'd lock that woman in the coal store and throw away the key, if I had my way,' the housekeeper snorted. 'April said Edith's had a couple of night traumas since. Apparently little Monday crept into her bed and cuddled her 'til she stopped screaming. Bless her. And although Edith didn't cry out last night, when April went to get them all up this morning, there they were, snuggled up together like a couple of dormice.'

So that was why Monday hadn't crept into her bed, Sarah thought, tucking into her porridge.

'April said she's almost certain she heard Monday say *sshh*, although she couldn't swear to it 'cos Edith was making such a racket. Even so, if the little 'un is thinking of others, that's a sure sign she's turned a corner herself.'

'Let's hope so, Mrs Daws. It was a terrible thing for her to experience.' She was quiet for a few moments, remembering the day her godfather had found Monday on the beach. Then she shook herself. 'Now, about this Christmas Fayre. I was thinking the girls should make something to sell this year. Do you think aprons, purses and peg bags would go down well?'

The housekeeper gave her a level look. 'Happen they would, Miss Sullivan, but you'd have to use unmarked or even new material if you were going to sell them and we don't have any, nor the money to purchase some neither.'

Sarah smiled. 'Leave that to me. As you know, I really think the girls should be tackling something more constructive than samplers. I had a mind to get them adapting the donated clothes, but this might be a better way to get them started. If they feel they are making a contribution to the school funds like the boys do, it will help to boost their morale.'

'Well, it makes sense, but if you're hoping to get that Miss Green to help, I wouldn't hold your breath.'

'*Carpe Diem*, Mrs Daws,' the master said, appearing by their sides.

'What's fish got to do with anything, Master Higgins?' the housekeeper frowned. 'Honestly, how you can be thinking of your stomach straight after breakfast is beyond me.'

'It means "to seize the day" or make the most of the opportunity, Mrs Daws,' Harry explained, winking at Sarah.

'Well, why didn't you say so?' the housekeeper muttered.

Harry raised his brow then looked serious. 'May I suggest you get Mrs Daws to send Miss Green to your office when she arrives, Miss Sullivan? If you speak to her in the schoolroom she will be on her own ground and think she has the upper hand.'

'Oh, yes, I hadn't thought of that, Master Higgins,' Sarah replied, but he'd already turned away and was ushering the children from the dining room.

'Right, those not on kitchen duties, run three laps around the grounds then make your way straight to the schoolroom. Now get a move on and no stopping,' he shouted.

'Goodness,' muttered Sarah.

'Can't swim in this weather, Miss Sullivan, they'd get pneumonia. This way they'll only catch a cold,' he grinned before jogging after his pupils.

Suppressing a smile, Sarah turned to the housekeeper. 'Would you send Miss Green to my office when she arrives, Mrs Daws?' she asked.

'It will be my pleasure,' the housekeeper grinned. 'Now, come along, Maisie and Monday, those dishes won't get themselves clean.'

Sarah had only been back at her desk a short while when there was a knock at the door and Mrs Daws appeared.

'That new young verger wonders if you can spare him a moment, Miss Sullivan.'

Suppressing a sigh, Sarah nodded. 'Show him in, Mrs Daws.'

'Miss Sullivan, lovely to see you again. I do hope I'm not interrupting?' Jack Wise asked.

'You'd like a cup of tea, Mr Wise?' the housekeeper asked.

The verger looked at Sarah and then at the pile of papers in front of her. 'Thank you, but no,' he replied quickly. 'The vicar asked me to call in to see if you knew about the Christmas Fayre. What with us both being new, he thought . . .' His voice trailed off, and Sarah could see he was struggling to put his thoughts into words.

'That we might need apprising of the event?' Sarah asked. 'The master was talking about it only this morning, Mr Wise.'

'Could you, er, I mean, if you would like to, er . . . Mr Wise makes me feel ancient, so could you call me Jack? I mean, if you wouldn't mind,' he finished awkwardly.

'Yes, let's be forward and use first names, Jack,' she said, giving him a wicked grin. He looked so delighted, Sarah went on quickly. 'Master Higgins has already got the boys started on their woodworking projects, and I would like to get the girls making things to sell too. I just wondered . . .' She let her voice trail off.

'Yes?' he asked eagerly.

'Well, I know how the good ladies of the church admire you.'

He raised his brows in shock. 'They do?' he squeaked.

'Indeed they do, Jack, so I was wondering if you could use your charm on them for me?'

'My charm? How?' he asked, raising his brows until they met his hair.

'The Misses Snooper, Prior and Middle are most generous ladies, are they not?' Jack frowned, opened his mouth to say something then thought better of it. 'They were only saying recently that they wished they could do more for Red Cliffs,' she told him, crossing her fingers behind her back. 'To be honest, they could, and you'd be the perfect person to point out what it is they could do. You see, I am eager for the girls to make some items to sell. Obviously the school will provide the materials, well, I say obviously but really I mean hopefully,' Sarah paused. 'What I really mean is the school doesn't have funds to actually buy any cloth . . .' She shrugged helplessly. Just as she'd hoped, Jack smiled.

'I'm sure the good ladies could help there,' he assured her. 'What kind of cloth, exactly?'

'I was thinking cotton. You know the sort with checks? I think they will sell well, thus generating a fair amount for church and school funds. Regrettably, we cannot run to any decoration, like ribbon, buttons, braiding, but . . .' She shrugged and let her voice trail off again.

'Leave it with me. I'm sure I can persuade those ladies to help.'

'That would be such a relief, Jack,' Sarah gushed.

He flushed with pleasure, stared up at the plaque above her and read aloud, 'Love never faileth.' Then, realizing what he'd said, he flushed even redder and bounded towards the door. 'I'll go and see them straight away.'

Surprised at her audacity, Sarah shook her head, then returned to her paperwork. An image of Rodney flashed before her. Whatever would he have thought of her boldness, she wondered. Immediately, the picture of her smiling betrothed was replaced by an angry-looking Rodney. Yes, he would have been horrified, but then, he wasn't here, was he? Besides, she'd changed a lot since they'd last met.

She was trying to fathom out the jargon of an official form when she was interrupted by the door banging open. Looking up, she saw the schoolmistress glaring at her.

'Apparently you want to speak to me. It will have to be quick because I've a lot to do,' the woman declared self-righteously.

'Yes, Miss Green, that is correct. Come in and close the door behind you,' she replied, remembering the schoolmaster's advice. The woman swung the door shut, then flounced down on the chair in front of Sarah.

'I want to speak to you about something serious,' Sarah began, staring her in the eye.

Miss Green glared back, her chin lifting defiantly. 'If it's about that Curdy child, I'll have you know she is a rude, arrogant, high-and-mighty little . . .'

'Child, Edith is a young child, Miss Green. And whilst you are in the schoolroom she is under your care.'

'Now, look here!'

'No, Miss Green, you look here. The welfare and morale of the children is my responsibility and . . .'

'Well, isn't that lucky,' the schoolmistress sneered. 'Seeing as this is my afternoon for teaching them moral issues,' the woman said haughtily. 'Now, if there's nothing else . . .' She began, getting to her feet.

'There is, actually, Miss Green, and whether you wish to stand or sit, you will not leave my office until I have finished what I have to say.' The woman sniffed but sat down again. 'Firstly, I would like your assurance that nothing like that dreadful incident with Edith will occur ever again,' Sarah demanded.

'Children need discipline, Miss Sullivan. You ask old Higgins, he'll tell you,' the schoolmistress replied, chin in the air.

'Discipline, yes, cold-hearted cruelty, no. I have spoken with Master Higgins, and he assures me he uses deterrent rather than deeds.'

'He would, he's all talk,' Miss Green scoffed. 'There's other schools that would be happy to have me. I don't have to stay here and listen to this, you know.'

'Well, naturally Red Cliffs would be sorry to lose you, but if you feel it would be better to leave then . . .' Sarah paused.

Miss Green's eyes widened, and she sat bolt upright. 'Here, I never said I was leaving,' she cried.

'Well, then, do I have your assurance that you will never treat any child so cruelly again, Miss Green?'

The schoolmistress sighed. 'Very well,' she said, getting to her feet.

'Secondly, Miss Green, can you confirm that you are qualified to teach needlework at a level suitable for girls up to the age of thirteen?'

'Of course I am,' she snapped.

'Good. You will understand, then, that in order to make a garment of any note, one needs to be able to sew more than a single style of stitch.' Sarah paused and waited for the mistress to answer.

Miss Green narrowed her eyes. 'Well, of course, any fool knows that.'

'Then that is what is required of you, Miss Green. From today you will be teaching the girls how to over-sew and hem.' The teacher opened her mouth but Sarah put up her hand. 'I am sure you will want everyone who attends the church Christmas Fayre to see perfectly finished aprons on the Red Cliffs stall.'

'Aprons? Who said anything about aprons?' Miss Green asked.

'Oh, did I not say?' Sarah smiled sweetly. 'The girls will be selling aprons along with other simple items they have made during your lessons.'

Miss Green's eyes narrowed to slits. 'There's at least twelve of them little misses in my class. I won't have time to help them all,' she protested.

'We shall be teaching them together, Miss Green.' The woman pursed her lips into a tight line. 'Regrettably, I have an appointment in town or I would accompany you to the classroom right now and assist. However, rest assured I shall be at your next lesson, and will look forward to seeing what progress the girls have made. Now, I'm sure you are anxious to begin, so I'll bid you good afternoon.'

Sarah looked down at her papers but could sense the woman glaring at her. She refused to look up, though, and finally the door slammed behind the schoolmistress. What had she let herself in for? she wondered.

18

After her confrontation with the schoolmistress, Sarah welcomed the walk along the seafront. It was overcast, so there were no well-heeled holidaymakers out seeing the sights or taking the air. No doubt they were taking afternoon tea in one of the hotels, she thought, passing a grand building, its front bay windows overlooking the sweep of the harbour. How the other half lived, she mused, thinking of her work-filled days at Red Cliffs.

Despite the absence of holidaymakers, there was the usual perambulation of horses and carts going about their business. The incongruous sight of palm trees lining the promenade made her smile, and by the time she reached the town, her equilibrium was restored.

She was shown into Mr Fothergill's office at precisely two o'clock. It was on the top floor of an elegant Regency building built of pink brick, and the room smelled of beeswax and old papers. The smartly dressed man rose to his feet to greet her.

'Miss Sullivan, I'm sorry to have to ask you to come here, but there are so many documents to go through, it will be easier. I trust you have settled into Red Cliffs?'

'Yes, thank you, Mr Fothergill, I have, and I don't mind coming to see you at all. Truth to tell, I have been so busy since I arrived, it was lovely to get some fresh air on the walk here,' she replied, settling into the seat he indicated and placing a bag containing official forms on her lap.

While the man scuttled back to his chair, Sarah looked around. His desk, while no larger than her own, was of walnut and so highly polished Sarah could see her reflection in the gloss. It was also tidy, apart from the folders in front of him, and had an inkstand, pen tray and large blotter arranged in an exact row.

'Now, Miss Sullivan,' he said, pulling on his silver-rimmed spectacles and adopting a more official tone. 'You are obviously aware you are the sole beneficiary under the will of Dr Lawrence, apart from the four bequests mentioned when last we met?'

'Yes, although when my godfather mentioned about me taking on his school, I had no idea he intended leaving the actual property to me.'

'Quite,' he smiled briefly. 'In addition to the property known as Red Cliffs, its outbuildings, fixtures, fittings and contents, there are a number of matters relating to his estate I need to acquaint you with.' He sat back in his chair and stared at Sarah.

'That sounds serious,' she replied.

'You have been left a number of investments which will need to be transferred into your name.'

'Investments?'

'Your godfather was a shrewd man who looked after his money wisely. By taking advantage of the current high bank rate, he was able to use the interest towards the running of the school. If the property has any chance of continuing as it has, these investments need to be transferred, and to that end I have taken the liberty of arranging a meeting with the bank manager in,' he paused and took out his silver pocket watch, 'exactly thirty minutes.'

'You mean there's doubt about Red Cliffs continuing as it always has?' Sarah asked, frowning.

The solicitor cleared his throat. 'Expenditure is high, my dear, and despite your godfather's best endeavours, funds have been dwindling at an alarming rate.' Seeing Sarah's frown deepen, he went on quickly. 'There is, of course, the offer received from a developer keen to purchase Red Cliffs. It is quite a substantial sum and could, er, prove the answer to your financial, er, problems.'

'Problems I am sure we can overcome, for that was not my godfather's wish, was it, Mr Fothergill?' she asked, staring at him directly.

He shook his head. 'No, it wasn't, but as the new owner you should be aware that Red Cliffs, being a substantial property in one of the most desirable areas of Torquay, could realize a tidy amount.'

'Like I said, Mr Fothergill, that was not my godfather's wish.'

'No,' he agreed. 'In fact, Dr Lawrence thought you would be of the same opinion. We had some in-depth discussions about the ongoing management and running of the school. He wanted to make sure everything was in place, although unfortunately he passed away sooner than we expected.'

'He knew he was dying, then?' she asked in surprise.

The solicitor sighed. 'Yes, Miss Sullivan, he did. Now, to continue. The interest from the bank contributes a reasonable sum, although this will have to be monitored.

Then there are the sums received from the local authorities in respect of the number of children who have been placed in the school by order of the courts.'

'The courts?' she gasped.

'I'm afraid so. This is rather than them being incarcerated in a reformatory or the workhouse and covers their care, well-being and elementary education. Red Cliffs employs,' he consulted his papers again, 'a full-time housekeeper, part-time laundry woman, one full-time schoolmaster and the services of a travelling schoolmistress, part time. Now, of course, there will be yourself to add to the payroll.'

'Payroll?'

'Even the good can't live on fresh air, Miss Sullivan, although I have to inform you the wage will be minimal.' He paused and stared at her over his glasses. 'Now, about the children. For those who have voluntarily arrived at the school, or been taken off the streets by the good doctor, there are minor sums received from the Education Department to contribute towards their schooling. Red Cliffs will have been sent forms for this.'

'Ah,' said Sarah. 'You must mean the ones that were in the pile of my godfather's papers. I have brought some with me,' she said reaching for her bag.

Fothergill frowned. 'Perhaps we could look at those later? There is much I need to acquaint you with before we make our way over to the bank.'

'Of course,' Sarah replied. Although the man had spoken mildly, it was clear who was in charge of this meeting, and her admiration for the dapper little man increased. No wonder her godfather had engaged his services, she thought. There was a discreet cough, which brought her swiftly back to the present.

'While these minor sums contribute to the running of Red Cliffs, a significant element of income needs to come from other sources and to this end I am pleased to tell you that the benefactor, Char . . .' The rest of the name was lost in another cough.

'Benefactor? Who might that be?' she asked in surprise.

'I'm afraid I'm not at liberty to disclose any name at this time.'

'Why not? If someone is helping to finance Red Cliffs, surely I should know who they are? I mean, he must have been a friend of my godfather's?'

'A good friend, yes, but,' he glanced at his pocket watch once more, 'we really must move on.' Fothergill looked quickly down at his papers. 'In view of the training in crafts and skills the children receive in preparation for work in trade and domestic service, there are council grants available to provide boarding for some of them, as well as assisting in the remuneration of teachers.'

'It sounds as though there's money available to help with the continued running of the school, then,' Sarah replied, a feeling of relief spreading through her.

'Gaining access to these funds is not quite that simple, but then these things never are,' the solicitor remarked, looking serious. 'In order to obtain these grants it will be necessary to permit inspections by the local authority to ensure the skills are being taught.'

'Oh my goodness,' Sarah replied. Remembering her earlier discussion with Miss Green, Sarah could see it was vital the woman did as she'd been asked, although there was no problem with Master Higgins' teaching, from what she'd seen. 'Hopefully that shouldn't pose too much of a problem,' she added brightly, crossing her fingers.

'Now, I know the doctor would have been the first to admit paperwork was not his forte, for he preferred to spend his time looking after the children. However, he did successfully deal with the council in these matters, so must have maintained proper accounts.'

A vision of the scraps of paper she'd found inside the ledger swam before her, but she shrugged. 'Well, the books will need bringing up to date, when I have a minute, and there are still boxes of papers to go through,' she laughed, but the solicitor stared sternly back.

'Miss Sullivan, these accounts will be required for audit purposes.' Sarah gulped. 'Look,' he went on, his voice softer. 'I know latterly the dear doctor had trouble with his eyesight and was often unable to focus properly, so if I can be of help in any way, please let me know.'

'Thank you, Mr Fothergill,' Sarah cried, relief flooding through her. No wonder her godfather had thought it was misty when he went out; his sight was going.

'Now, it is time for our meeting with Mr Collings, so if you would like to follow me,' he instructed, rising to his feet and neatly placing papers in his Gladstone bag. 'Just one thing,' he said. 'Have you been contacted by the late doctor's nephew again?'

'Christian? No, thank heavens. Why?'

'You should be aware that he has instructed his solicitor to contest the will,' he advised, staring at her over his glasses.

'He did threaten to do that, but as we hadn't heard anything, I thought it was just bluster.'

'Although it probably won't come to anything, to make absolutely certain your uncle's will is watertight, I have taken advice from counsel. Although this is a formality, it does mean no sale of the property may take place until we receive verification.' He checked his watch again. 'Now we really must be leaving.'

As Sarah followed him down the stairs and over the road to the grand entrance of the bank, her mind was whirling from all the information Fothergill had imparted. She didn't see the man rushing out of the building until he shouted out.

'You'll be sorry for this, Collings. When I get my money, I shall be a man of considerable means and you and your bank will not see a penny of it. Out of my way,' he muttered, pushing Sarah aside. 'Oh, it's you.'

'Christian?' she replied.

'Don't you "Christian" me. You thought you could come here, sweet-talking my uncle out of my inheritance. Well I've got news for you . . .'

'Mr Lawrence, that is no way to speak to Miss Sullivan,' Fothergill interjected, taking Sarah by the arm and leading her through the line of customers who were watching the confrontation with avid interest.

'Ignore Mr Lawrence,' he advised, as Sarah took a look over her shoulder. 'I shouldn't be telling you this, but your godfather was a good friend of mine. I believe the reason Mr Lawrence is so upset is that the bank has had to call in their loan,' he whispered. Then turning, he greeted the bank manager, who was still standing outside his office door.

'Mr Collings, I think you are expecting us,' he announced. 'May I introduce Miss Sullivan.'

'Good afternoon. Please step inside,' said Mr Collings with a smile.

By the time Sarah left the bank, it was late afternoon, and her head was spinning, while her hand ached from signing a seemingly endless pile of official papers. Who'd have thought there'd be so much involved with the transferring of Red Cliffs into her name? As to the matter of the funding of the school, it all sounded horribly complex and not a little intimidating. And who was this benefactor, Charles, who had pledged his continued investment in Red Cliffs? Both Fothergill and Collings had been decidedly cagey about the man's identity. It seemed, for the time being, she'd have to respect his wish to remain anonymous.

Although a light mizzle was falling, Sarah welcomed the long walk back to Red Cliffs. The gentle onshore breeze helped to clear her head, and she stopped and leaned against the railings, staring out at the vast expanse of grey ocean. The bay was busy with shipping. Some vessels were taking on coal at the wharf, while naval and other freighters lay at anchor in deeper waters. The sight reminded her that Monday's father was out there somewhere, still unaware his wife and baby were dead while his daughter was in the care of Red Cliffs. She'd been so taken up with trying to sort out her godfather's papers, she'd not had much time to devote to the children recently.

Well, from tomorrow, she would make sure that changed, she thought, conveniently putting all thought of official forms and paperwork to the back of her mind.

'By yourself, Sarah Sulks?'

She jumped as a voice sounded behind her, and turned to see a man calling from the open window of a carriage.

'Christian? What are you doing here?' she asked.

'I've just been to see my new home,' he announced loftily.

'You're renting nearby then?' she asked politely.

He gave a harsh laugh. 'The likes of me don't rent houses, Sarah Sulks. We own them, and it won't be long until my solicitor confirms Red Cliffs is mine. I shall be moving in very soon, so you'd better start making plans to move out, goody two-shoes Sarah Sulks.' He raised his hat mockingly then called to the driver to move on. She watched as the carriage rolled away, a sinking feeling spreading through her stomach as she remembered how he'd always stopped at nothing to get his own way. It was only the lamplighter going about his work that brought her back to the present, and she began walking briskly back to Red Cliffs.

'How did you get on, dear?' Mrs Daws asked as Sarah made her way through to the kitchen.

The warmth from the range was welcoming after the damp outside, and throwing off her shawl, she went over and held out her chilled hands.

'I've never seen so many official papers in all my life, Mrs Daws,' she sighed.

The housekeeper clucked in sympathy then went back to spreading scrape onto the slices of bread. 'But you got everything sorted out? I mean, Red Cliffs can carry on as before?' she asked, giving Sarah an anxious look.

'Oh, yes,' Sarah assured her, not wanting to burden the woman with talk of funding and accounts. 'Although there was something curious Mr Fothergill said.'

'What was that?' asked Harry coming into the room.

'He said Red Cliffs had a benefactor, but couldn't or wouldn't reveal his name.' She turned back to warm her hands and didn't see the look the housekeeper and master exchanged.

'And is this benefactor to continue helping to fund the school?' Harry asked.

'Apparently so,' she replied.

'Thank the Lord,' Mrs Daws muttered. 'Ah, here's April,' she added quickly. 'Can you brew us a pot of tea, then take the plates of bread through to the dining room? I've made some dumplings to go on the stew, being as how there's precious little meat in it. The butcher wonders if he could have some money off his account, Miss Sullivan. He didn't like to ask but it's been mounting up. The doctor used to pay him something every month, you see.'

'Of course, Mrs Daws. I was able to draw a small amount out of the account today, but until everything's settled we are going to have to be careful.'

The housekeeper laughed. 'We're quite used to that, aren't we, Master Higgins?'

'We are,' he agreed. 'Might I suggest that you lock any money in the cash tin in the doctor's, sorry, I mean, your desk drawer, Miss Sullivan.'

'That's a good idea.'

'Have your meal first,' the housekeeper suggested.

'Your stew smells delicious, Mrs Daws,' Sarah said, sniffing the air appreciatively.

'It does but, regrettably, I can't stay,' Harry replied. 'Mother's been under the weather, so I promised to cook her something light for her evening meal. Pip is going to supervise the boys at supper and then help them with their woodwork projects. I'll come in early tomorrow so you can tell me more about your meeting with Fothergill, my little crepuscular friend,' he grinned at Sarah, then disappeared out of the door.

'He do come out with some funny things, that master,' Mrs Daws said, shaking her head. 'Right, April, if you've finished laying the tables, you can get Pip to sound the gong. I've got one of me heads, and I really don't think it would stand up to Maisie's vigorous bashing.'

Sarah glanced at the housekeeper and saw she looked pale and drawn. 'I'll dish the meal and supervise the girls, Mrs Daws. Why don't you take a tray up to your room and eat in peace?'

'That does sound tempting, I must admit,' the woman replied just as the gong sounded and there was the thundering of feet down the corridor.

19

By the time Sarah had dished up and said grace, she was ravenous. Despite her meeting with the solicitor and bank manager, and then that unfortunate confrontation with Christian, the sea air had sharpened her appetite. She was tucking into one of the housekeeper's feather-like dumplings when she realized a little group of girls at the far end of the table were huddled together.

'And when she said we had to look out for blood spurting from our belly buttons, I nearly died!' As the girl Sarah knew to be Ellen screeched and dug Edith in the ribs, the rest of the little group rocked with laughter.

'May I ask what is so funny?' Sarah asked mildly.

'It was old Lettuce Leaf. She decided it was time we learnt about sex,' Edith replied gleefully.

'I beg your pardon,' Sarah frowned.

'She said to save us from a life of whoring we should know how our body worked,' Ellen added.

Sarah gulped, then seeing the boys showing an avid interest in their conversation, knew she had to take control of the situation. Getting quickly to her feet, she rapped on the table with the wooden spoon as she'd seen the master do.

'Time to clear away. You boys will then go with Pip to the workroom while I speak with the girls from Miss Lettu . . . I mean, Miss Green's class in the front room,' she announced.

*

Upstairs in her room, Mrs Daws sank down on the bed and held her throbbing head in her hands. What a day it had been. And Sarah returning home and mentioning the doctor's dearest friend had been the last straw. Whilst it was reassuring to know the school would continue to be funded, and the good doctor's work could carry on as he'd wished, it had finally sunk in that she wouldn't be seeing Samuel ever again. Tears prickled at the back of her eyes and she shook her head. You're made of sterner stuff than this, Daisy Daws, she told herself.

Seeing Christian earlier had upset her equilibrium. In fact it had fair given her a turn. There she'd been, walking down to the compost heap with her peelings, when his face had suddenly appeared through the bushes, sneering at her like she was something old Marmalade would bring in. When she'd called out to him, he'd made a most ungentlemanly gesture and loped off.

Such a lovely boy he'd been too, until his parents had sent him away to that posh school. He'd been so upset when they'd told him, crying into her apron until she'd reassured him she'd still be here when he came home for the holidays. Why, she'd even promised to bake his favourite treacle sponge for him. She'd had a real soft spot for the doctor's nephew.

She sighed into the darkness, remembering how he'd ignored her when he had returned. That school had given him ideas above his station, and he wouldn't lower himself to communicate with a servant unless it was to snap his fingers. It had been his mother's nurturing he'd needed, not fancy ideas planted in his brain by some high-faluting schoolmaster.

Now, that Harry Higgins was such a lovely fellow and a good schoolmaster too. The way he looked after his widowed mother was a credit to him. Mind you, he'd recently begun using those funny long words. But only when Miss Sullivan was around. Perhaps he was trying to impress her. Now, there was a thought. She was a lovely girl, a bit naïve about the ways of the world, perhaps, but Harry would take care of that. A match between the two of them would be most acceptable.

If only the doctor had married and had a family of his own. He'd have made a wonderful father. She'd told him once, but he'd laughed and said the children of Red Cliffs were his family.

'Oh Samuel, I do miss you so,' she sobbed.

Christian needed some loving, and he was on his way to get it. He'd had one hell of a day and needed to forget his worries.

He'd watched through the carriage window as Sarah Sulks made her way along the promenade before crossing the road that would lead up the hill towards Red Cliffs. He couldn't believe the nice little girl he'd played with had turned into a conniving, thieving woman. How dare she try to con him out of his inheritance? Samuel Lawrence had been his uncle, and Red Cliffs was his birthright. He would move hell and high water to secure possession and couldn't wait to take ownership, he thought, banging his fist against the door. Immediately the carriage drew to a stop. For heaven's sake, he sighed. Was the driver an imbecile? He'd told him he wanted to be taken to the other side of the docks.

As it wasn't far, he decided to get out and walk. Striding angrily to his destination, he remembered his meeting with the bank manager and growled. How dare that Collings bloke have the audacity to tell him the bank had foreclosed on his house and he was required to move out immediately? Wasn't it enough the bailiffs had already taken most of his furniture? Of course he'd been cross, but there'd been no need for Collings to have him physically removed from the bank. And to have Sarah Sulks witness the scene was embarrassing beyond words. At least he'd had the satisfaction of being able to tell her that he would one day gain possession of Red Cliffs. Although his statement had been slightly premature, he intended to make it happen. He'd already contested the will. Now all he had to do was pay a visit to Rosa and collect what was his. Life is on the up, Christian Lawrence, he told himself as he made his way up the steps and gave his customary three long and two short raps.

'Blimey, look what the winds blown in,' the woman chirped as she opened the door.

'Lil, my darling. Your day has just got a whole lot better, for aren't I your favourite man of all time?'

'If you've got bucks to burn, then of course you are,' she chortled.

'I got bucks a plenty to spend on you, my darling Lil, so let me in and let the loving begin.'

Following her inside, he patted his pockets in triumph. He could think of no better way of spending the money he'd lifted from the collection plate.

'May I have a word with you in private please, April?' Sarah whispered to the girl.

'I ain't done nothing wrong, have I?' April asked, looking up from the tray she was carrying.

'No, of course not. But you are a sensible young lady and I need to ask you something. Can you come with me whilst the others clear away?'

As April followed her into the front room, Sarah closed the door firmly behind them.

'Take a seat,' she said, indicating one of the easy chairs, which had once been the height in luxury furnishing but now, with its moth-eaten covers, looked as awkward and uncomfortable as Sarah felt.

'I don't like leaving them by themselves with Mrs Daws not here to supervise,' April said.

'This won't take long, April. You heard the conversation at the table?'

April giggled. 'Old Lettuce really got them going, didn't she?'

'That's why I need to ascertain exactly what Miss Green has told them.'

'Oh, I wasn't there,' the maid said quickly. 'I was helping Mrs Daws with the vegetables. She makes a nice drop of stew, doesn't she? And she's promised to show me how to make those dumplings.'

Sarah smiled at the girl's enthusiasm. 'The thing is, April, I need to know who is responsible for seeing to the girls when they start their . . . I mean, now some of them are getting older.'

April frowned for a moment then chuckled. 'Oh, you mean their monthlys?' Sarah nodded, relieved she had understood. 'Why, Mrs Daws, of course.'

They were interrupted by a knock on the door and Edith and Ellen coming into the room.

'Do you want us in here, miss?' Edith asked.

'Yes, I wish to speak to all the girls who were in Miss Green's class this afternoon, please,' Sarah told her.

'Right, you lot, in you come,' Edith bellowed behind her and the other ten apprehensively filed in. As they stood staring at her quizzically, Sarah was reminded of the day her godfather had first shown her the schoolroom.

'Don't look so worried, girls. We are just going to have a little chat. I'm afraid there aren't enough chairs for you all, so perhaps you'd like to sit in a circle on the rug.' She waited until they'd settled themselves, then smiled at each of them in turn, praying the right words would come.

'We didn't mean to giggle at the table, miss,' Ellen ventured.

'I haven't brought you in here to tell you off, girls. When I heard you talking earlier, it made me realize I didn't know what you were being taught in your lessons with Miss Green.'

'Usually she gets us doing those boring stitches or tells us to beware of evil men who only want one thing, though she never tells us what that is no matter how many times we ask,' Ellen sighed. 'Do you know, miss?'

Sarah tried to swallow the lump that had risen in her throat. 'Why don't you tell me what this afternoon's lesson was about?' she suggested.

'Don't you know, miss?' Edith asked. 'Old Lett . . . I mean, Miss Green said you'd told her we need to know about our morals.'

Sarah frowned, trying to recall her earlier conversation with the schoolmistress. 'I think she got the wrong end of the stick. I was talking about morale, which is something different,' she told them. They stared blankly back at her.

'You mean the teacher got it wrong?'

'Don't be daft, Maggie, teachers never get things wrong do they, miss?' Ellen said.

'Well, sometimes there can be a misunderstanding,' Sarah said tactfully. 'Now, who is going to tell me what you learnt this afternoon?'

'She told us when we was ripe, blood would come out of our belly button,' Edith said.

'I don't want no blood,' Maisie whimpered, clutching at Monday's hand.

'There, there, don't fret, that don't happen to little girls like you,' April said quietly, going over and sitting down beside them.

'What else did Miss Green say, Edith?' Sarah asked.

'That's the weird bit. She started talking about rabbits and how they jump on each other's backs.'

'Then she said when that happens to us we have to cross our legs or we'd have a baby,' Ellen butted in. 'But why would a rabbit jump on our back? It don't make no sense.'

Sarah closed her eyes and took a deep breath. 'Look, girls, as I said, sometimes there can be a misunderstanding, and I think Miss Green has got things a bit crossed.'

'You mean her legs, so she don't have a baby?' Maggie asked.

'I just think Miss Green might have been a little confused about what we discussed. Anyway, I think that's quite enough about the subject for one night,' Sarah said.

'If Miss Green's got things wrong, does that mean you'll be teaching us now, miss?' Ellen asked.

189

'Although I'm not a teacher, I shall be spending more time with you. Since I came to Red Cliffs most of my time has been taken up with sorting out the paperwork.'

'Yuk,' Edith said, pulling a face.

'Yes, yuk indeed, Edith. However, if I hadn't paid attention in my lessons I wouldn't have been able to get things sorted out.'

'Was you clever in class, miss? 'Cos Miss Green says I'm as thick as two short planks. I guess I must be 'cos I don't even understand what she means,' Ellen sighed.

At this, Sarah had to bite her tongue. Whatever was that woman doing to these poor children? She'd speak to Master Higgins first thing in the morning. 'No, Ellen, I wasn't particularly clever but I wanted to be, so I made sure I concentrated during lessons.' Seeing their serious expressions, she decided it was time to move on to a lighter subject. 'Now, girls, I understand that St Nicholas' holds a Christmas Fayre every year to raise funds.' Immediately, the mood brightened, and they smiled.

'We helps with the freshiments,' a little voice piped up.

'Refreshments, June,' April corrected her. 'The boys make things to sell, and we serve the tea and cakes,' she told Sarah.

'So I understand. How would you like to make some things to sell?' Sarah asked them.

They stared at her in disbelief.

'Us? But we're girls,' Ellen cried.

'What on earth could we make?' Edith scoffed.

'Girls are just as capable at making things as boys, Ellen. I thought that perhaps you older girls could make aprons while the younger ones make purses or peg bags.'

'You think we could do that?' Ellen gasped.

'I do,' Sarah replied firmly. 'And I shall get Miss Green to show you how.' At this, the room fell silent. The girls looked at her in disbelief. 'Didn't she teach you any new stitches this afternoon?'

'Nah, she just talked about sex,' Edith replied, raising her brows.

'But I asked her to show you how to hem and overstitch.'

'More chance of them rabbits jumping on our backs, I'm thinking,' Edith muttered.

'Well, girls, from now on we shall use the time after supper each evening to work on our projects.'

'Miss goes home at four o'clock, sometimes earlier,' Edith pointed out.

'But I don't, Edith. As I was saying before, now that the paperwork is more or less sorted, I will have more time. Time I would like to spend getting to know you all, and what better way than by making things for the Christmas Fayre.'

'Gosh, miss, that would be real nice,' Edith said, looking around at the others. A murmur of approval ran through the room, and Sarah smiled.

'Now, if April agrees, I think we should all have a hot drink before we go to bed.'

As a rousing cheer ran around the room, April nodded. 'I'll make the drinks, but you lot are washing up the cups.' The girls rushed from the room, but April paused, looked at Sarah and shook her head. 'That Lettuce Leaf is rotten through and through, if you ask me. I don't know much about life, but sure as eggs is eggs, you don't get babies by rabbits climbing on your back, do you, miss?'

'You don't, April,' Sarah agreed.

'Everyone knows the stork brings them,' she chirped, bounding from the room.

Sarah stared after her. The maid had been joking, hadn't she?

20

Harry smiled as he handed his mother her bed-time drink.

'You spoil me, son,' she said, patting his hand. 'You should be out courting some pretty young girl, not waiting on me.'

'Nonsense, Mother. Now, drink your milk while it's hot and then it's up the wooden hill to bedlam.'

Mrs Higgins smiled. 'Your father always said that,' she said, staring into the fire.

Harry leaned forward and added a lump of coal, then poked the embers into a blaze. 'There, that's better. Dr Hawkins did say you needed to get more rest in order to regain your strength.'

'Piffle. I'm as strong as I ever was,' she protested.

'Well, I've put the stone pig under your bed covers,' he replied, knowing it was better not to argue with her. 'Now, you enjoy your drink while I clear away our supper things.'

'Leave them, Harry. It'll give me something to do whilst you're at work tomorrow morning. And don't argue,' she said, when he opened his mouth to protest. 'Sit down and tell me how things are at Red Cliffs. It's ages since we've had a proper catch-up. Are the children adapting to not having the good doctor around?'

'You know what kids are like. They were upset, naturally, but Mrs Daws has kept a weather eye out. She's even been baking them extra little treats, though how she does it on our budget, goodness only knows,' he said, sinking into the easy chair on the other side of the fire.

'She's a treasure and no mistake,' his mother agreed. 'And how about the new lady?'

'Miss Sullivan? She's settled in well. She had a meeting with the solicitor today, and it seems our benefactor has agreed to continue funding the school.'

'That's a blessing. So you think Red Cliffs will be safe?' she asked.

Harry frowned. 'I hope so. I'm not sure how much Miss Sullivan understands about the grants Red Cliffs has to apply for. She'd only just returned from the bank as I was leaving and seemed rather bemused. I told her I would go in early tomorrow and she could tell me everything then.'

Mrs Higgins quietly studied her son for a few moments. 'You like her, don't you, Harry?'

'Well, of course. She has the interests of the school at heart, and Samuel had a good regard for her.'

His mother smiled. 'As do you, Harry. It is high time you married and made me a grandmother, young man,' she said, finishing her drink and getting stiffly to her feet. As Harry went to help her she shook her head. 'No, don't get up. I shall need to be more active if I'm to be anywhere near fit enough to play with my grandchildren.'

'Really, Mother, you're incorrigible,' he exclaimed.

'Think on what I've said, Harry. You're a good man and would make someone a splendid husband. Of course, I might be a little biased,' she laughed and gave him a wink.

'Good night, Mother,' he said firmly, before settling back in his seat and sipping the rest of his drink. Really his mother did have some extraordinary ideas.

Yet, as he sat staring into the fire, where the coal was burning brightly, a picture of Sarah seemed to emerge from the flames.

Next morning, Harry left their little cottage on the outskirts of Cockington just as the sky was lightening to grey. Although it was November, the weather was mild, and he whistled as he made his way down the country lane towards Torquay.

'Morning, Master 'iggins. 'Ow's the new woman shaking down?'

Harry smiled as the head of the farmer appeared above the hedge. Nothing was kept quiet for long in these parts.

'Good morning, Jim. Miss Sullivan's settling in well, thank you. How's that leg of yours?'

The man grunted and pointed to his sticks. 'I be like a blessed cripple,' he grunted. 'No good to man or my beasts. I can just 'bout manage the milking, tho I haz to use one of 'em blinkin' maid's stools, mind.' He raised his bushy brows and shook his head. 'The wife does what she can, but she's that busy, what with making her cheese and seeing to the 'ens, the yard's in a right old state. Fair breaks my 'eart to see it.'

'Being Saturday, the pupils only have morning lessons, so why don't I bring them up to the farm after luncheon? They can tidy things up a bit, under your supervision, of course.'

'That's right kind of you, my boy, but I'm sure you've got better things to do,' the man protested, but Harry knew it was his pride speaking.

'You'd be doing me a favour, Jim. I've got a couple of lads still trying to atone for breaking a window and a few of the others could do with learning to do as they're told. Besides, the exercise in the fresh air will do them good,' Harry chuckled.

'Well, if you be sure, I can't deny it'd be an 'elp. I'll get the wife to put back some of 'er eggs 'er ye.'

'Mrs Daws would be very grateful. Talking of which, she wants to make vegetable soup for supper so I'd better go and check on the state of the garden. Then I have a meeting with Miss Sullivan, so I'll see you later, Jim.'

Harry continued down the lane, but for once it was thoughts of Sarah Sullivan that filled his mind rather than the morning's lessons. He was eager to hear how she'd got on with the solicitor yesterday, for something told him she was going to need his help.

All was quiet as he let himself in through the gates and made his way to the vegetable plot. The cabbages and parsnips looked healthy, pretty even, their leaves sparkling with the morning dew, he thought, carefully lifting some with his spade and placing them in a sturdy old trug. Steady on, Harry, he told himself. You'll be locked up, waxing lyrical over a few vegetables like that. He added carrots and onions from the store shed, then, whistling happily, made his way into the kitchen.

'Goodness me, someone's cheerful this morning,' Mrs Daws greeted him, straightening up from beside the range, where she'd been riddling the embers back into life.

'It's a fine day out there, Mrs Daws,' he said, placing the basket of produce on the kitchen table.

'Is it, indeed?' she asked, darting him a knowing look. 'I'll get Pip to bring in some potatoes to go with those, and we'll have the makings of a fine stew,' she added, nodding to the basket.

'I spoke to farmer Jim on the way here. He's out and about but hobbling on sticks. I said I'd take the boys up to the farm to help out this afternoon.'

'That's a good idea. Poor Bess is having a right old time of his moaning,' the housekeeper clucked. Harry was just about to tell her about the eggs when April came bustling in, a bundle of sheets under her arm.

'Maisie's wet the bed, so I'll put these out in the wash-house.'

'Oh no, and she's been dry for a while now,' Mrs Daws tutted.

'It wasn't really her fault, Mrs Daws, she was too scared to get out of bed and use the pot in case she was covered in blood.'

'Whatever gave her such a notion?' the housekeeper cried.

April opened her mouth to reply, then looked awkwardly over at Harry.

'Don't mind me, April, I'm off to see Miss Sullivan. No doubt she's already in her office.'

'Been up since before light. That woman works all hours on them papers,' the housekeeper sighed. 'She'll wear herself out at this rate.'

'I'll go and help,' he promised. 'See you at breakfast.'

Harry popped his head around the office door to find Sarah delving into one of the boxes that were lying alongside the desk.

'Finding more paperwork to play with, oh crepuscular one?' Harry laughed.

'You're a fine one to speak, Harry Higgins. Why, it's just past dawn and here you are, checking nothing untoward has happened to your beloved Red Cliffs,' she replied, grimacing down at the papers she had retrieved.

'A bit early to be hunting for treasure, isn't it?' he quipped.

Instead of laughing, she let out a long sigh. 'Both the solicitor and bank manager told me in no uncertain terms that I need to make sure the school's books are up to date. They have to be checked by the accountant before we can apply for any more funding.'

Picking up a handful of papers, he raised his brows. 'Cripes, you'll have a fine old job deciphering some of these. They're all foxed.'

'Foxed?' she asked.

'It means they're all yellowed and spotted with age.'

'Well, why didn't you just say that?' she snapped. Then, seeing his crestfallen look, she added in a softer voice, 'Sorry, it's just that all this seems horribly daunting.'

He stood there, taking in the dark smudges under her eyes and the tendril of hair escaping its braid, but thought it prudent not to mention the smut of dust on her nose.

'I hope you are not overdoing things, Sarah?' he asked.

'Well, we can't all have the sleep of the gods, Harry. How is your mother?' she asked, belatedly remembering she'd been poorly.

'Much better, thank you. She had a turn yesterday morning, but Dr Hawkins gave her some medicine, and she's right as rain again. Father and she were very close and she never really got over the shock of losing him,' he explained.

Sarah nodded. 'It took me ages to get used to the idea of not seeing my father again. Look, why don't we sit down? There's something I need to discuss with you.'

'Sounds serious,' he said, straddling the chair in front of the desk. 'Before I forget, though. Your godfather took the health and welfare of the pupils here very seriously. He made a point of examining them at least once a month but . . .' Not wishing to upset her, he let his sentence trail away.

Despite her fatigue, she was quick on the uptake. 'Now he's no longer here, we need to see about engaging the services of another doctor?'

He nodded. 'Dr Hawkins, who attends Mother, asked how the children were and mentioned he would be pleased to look after them, if it would be of any help. He was a great friend of Dr Lawrence and intimated he would be happy to accept a nominal fee.'

Sarah smiled. 'That's very kind of him. Everyone seems to have been a friend of my godfather.'

At this, his expression changed. 'Not everyone,' he replied. 'There are many around here who would like to see the school moved. They think the state of the building here lowers the tone of the neighbourhood. At the risk of sounding disrespectful, they do rather have a point,' he said, gesturing to the shabby decor.

'Perhaps we could draw on some of the funds in the bank or ask this benefactor for some, whoever he is,' she replied, looking at him pointedly, but he wasn't to be drawn. 'Apparently there has been an offer from a developer wanting to purchase Red Cliffs.'

'Yes, the doctor mentioned it. Over his dead body was his answer. Oh, I'm sorry,' he added, flushing at his insensitivity.

'It's all right, Harry,' she whispered. 'We couldn't sell, even if we wanted to. Christian has contested the will and everything's up in the air until it's sorted. I just can't help worrying about the pupils. I promised my godfather I'd keep Red Cliffs running, but . . .' Her voice trailed away on a sigh.

'Knowing the doctor, he will have ensured his will was drawn up correctly,' Harry replied, her crestfallen look tugging at his heartstrings so that he was seized with the urge to pull her into his arms.

'Of course,' she replied, making an effort to pull herself together. 'Mr Fothergill mentioned applying to the council for grants, but I was astounded at how much bureaucracy seems to be involved. The books have to be audited, Red Cliffs inspected . . .' Her voice trailed off. 'I had no idea it was all so complicated.'

Harry smiled gently. 'I wouldn't say it was complicated. Just that there are procedures to follow. The good doctor knew how important it was to keep on the right side of the powers that be. If I can help in any way, please feel free to ask,' he said, pulling out his pocket watch and frowning. 'Nearly time to supervise the feeding of the five thousand, as Mrs Daws puts it. Unless there's anything else you want to discuss with me?'

'Actually, Harry, there is.' She paused and seemed to cast around for the right words. 'Apparently, to save them from a life of whoring, the girls were given a supposed lesson on morals yesterday, and it left them very confused, to say the least. Miss Green not only misled them about the facts of life, she scared the wits out of the little ones.'

'Ah,' Harry nodded, the earlier statement from April suddenly making sense.

'Is that all you can say?' she cried. Then, after a concerted effort to control her emotions, she went on more quietly. 'I expressly told her to teach the girls stitches suitable for making aprons, and she completely ignored me. In the light of what Mr Fothergill told me about the conditions for funding to be granted, along with the incident in the coal store, I have decided the woman should be dismissed.'

'Oh, I don't think . . .' Harry began, but she held up her hand.

'My mind is made up on this. I will undertake to look after the girls until a suitable replacement is found.'

Harry looked at her determined face and felt his stomach sink. She really didn't have a clue about the way Red Cliffs operated, and it seemed he was going to have to enlighten her.

'You have formal training as a schoolmistress?' he asked.

'No, I do not. However, I do know how to prepare the girls for the outside world, and I am certainly more proficient in needlework skills. There is nothing Miss Green can do for Red Cliffs that I cannot.'

Harry swallowed hard. 'You were talking about school inspections earlier, Sarah.'

'What has that got to do with anything?'

'Everything. You see, the Mr Green who is employed by the local authority to carry out these inspections just happens to be the schoolmistress's father. So, you see, we cannot afford to fall out with Miss Green, let alone dispense with her services. The consequences for Red Cliffs would be catastrophic.'

'But that's blackmail, Harry,' Sarah spluttered.

'Not blackmail, just the way things are, I'm afraid,' he replied.

Sarah thought for a moment. 'Is that how she got her job here?' she asked, the light dawning.

Harry shrugged but said nothing. Better to leave her to draw her own conclusions, he thought, getting to his feet. 'Please do not do anything too hastily before you know how it all works around here.'

Although she nodded, the set of her face told a different story.

21

As Harry entered the kitchen, Mrs Daws looked up from stirring the porridge.

'Goodness, Master Higgins, you look like you've got the weight of the world on those shoulders.'

'Hmm,' Harry replied, still distracted from his conversation with Sarah. 'Truth to tell, I'm a bit worried about Miss Sullivan. She seems to have got it into her head that Miss Green's services should be dispensed with.'

'Have you told her about the connection between that girl's father and the local authority?'

'I explained about the school inspections and asked her not to do anything until she understands how everything works, but . . .' He shrugged.

'Well, perhaps when she's had a chance to think, she'll see you have to look at the wider picture, as the dear doctor always said. Mind you, that Miss Green has a lot to answer for. Young April was embarrassed to explain in front of you what the woman had told them. Apparently, she took it upon herself to illustrate how their body worked,' the housekeeper spluttered. 'She . . .' Her voice trailed off and two pink spots appeared on her cheeks.

'No need to explain, I understand what you mean,' he replied.

'You do?' she asked, looking surprised.

'I might be a bachelor, Mrs Daws, but I do have a grasp of the facts of life.'

'Really? Goodness,' the woman muttered.

'In fact, you could say I'm an authority on the birds and bees.' He grinned as the housekeeper's eyes widened in surprise.

'And the stork, Master Higgins?' April asked, coming through from the dining room.

'That's quite enough, young lady. If you've finished laying the table, you can take these plates of bread through.'

'Yes, Mrs Daws,' April grinned.

'I never know if that girl's winding me up or not.' The housekeeper sighed. 'You wouldn't believe the things that Miss Green told the girls. I'm thinking I'd best have a proper little chat with them whilst we're doing our house-keeping skills this afternoon. No good teaching them how to run a house if they don't know about . . . well, things,' she amended.

Harry chuckled. 'Good idea. They need to know who they can turn to if they have any questions.'

'Trouble is, this place is like a Chinese laundry, and if the boys get wind of what Miss Green's been saying, well, I'll leave you to draw your own conclusions, Master Higgins.'

'I'll have a little man-chat when we go up to the farm this afternoon.'

'You do that, but for heaven's sake, tell them the proper facts. I've heard enough about birds, bees and rabbits to last a lifetime. Not to mention that blinking stork.'

'It's a shame it's not lambing time,' he quipped, only half joking. Seeing animals being born often triggered questions at a level they understood. The housekeeper threw him one of her looks. 'Don't worry, Mrs Daws, I'll start by teaching them about showing respect for you wondrous women.' He chuckled again as he turned to go, then winced as her wet cloth hit him in the back of the neck. His protest was interrupted by a tapping on the door.

'Good morning, Walt,' he said, opening the door to find the poacher on the doorstep.

'Mornin', Master. Just happen to come by these,' he winked, holding up his knapsack, from which two fluffy tails poked. 'Thought Mrs Daws could make a nice stew or pie for you all.'

'I'm sure she'll be delighted. Go on in, the kettle's boiling,' he managed to say, turning away quickly before the man could see him laughing. He could just imagine the expression on the housekeeper's face. Normally she'd be only too grateful to receive rabbits, which would help her to eke out their precious provisions, but after their discussion just now, he couldn't help feeling Walt's timing wasn't quite right. Still, at least it had cheered him up, he thought, whistling as he made his way towards the schoolroom. He'd prepare the room for the morning's lesson then return for his breakfast. Hopefully, by then, Sarah would have had time to think things through and realize that getting rid of Miss Green was not an option.

His musings were brought to an abrupt halt when he came across the eldest boy in his class deep in conversation with the two youngest. As the boy wasn't known for his articulation skills, Harry's suspicion was aroused.

'Everything all right, boys?' he asked casually.

'Yeah,' Bunter muttered, nudging the others who quickly nodded.

'Hmm,' he replied, giving them a stern look. 'Well, you'd best get those hands washed ready for breakfast. The gong will be sounding in a few moments.' He watched them scamper to the pump, then sighed. That they'd been up to no good, he was certain; he could smell mischief at a thousand paces.

By the time he entered the dining room, the children were standing behind their chairs. He glanced at Sarah as he passed, but she was busy saying something to Monday and didn't notice him.

'Put your hands together for grace,' he instructed. No sooner had he finished than there was the usual scraping of chairs and buzz of anticipation as Pip and April served the porridge.

'What are you doing, Bunter?' he roared.

'Fort Byrd had somefink in 'is porwidge.'

'Well, concentrate on your own food. Brown, pass the plate of bread down this way, please.'

As the children tucked into their meals, Harry looked over at Sarah and saw she was berating April.

'I really don't think it matters which hand Monday holds her spoon in, April.'

'But we've been taught it's ignorant to use the wrong one,' the girl persisted.

Harry frowned and turned his attention back to his own breakfast. Surely Miss Sullivan knew that no child would ever be accepted by society if they didn't hold their cutlery properly, or their chalks, come to that. He sighed inwardly, and vowed to mention it after the meal when they were by themselves.

'Right, if everyone's finished, you may clear the tables. Apart from those on washing-up duty, you will run the customary three times around the grounds before making your way to your desks.'

Harry waited until the dining room had emptied then took his mug over to Sarah.

'I couldn't help hearing you taking April to task. She was right to correct Monday, you know. It's her duty to ensure the little ones eat properly.' He saw Sarah bristle.

'And properly means not letting a child use their dominant hand?' she replied.

'Etiquette dictates which hand should be used to hold cutlery correctly. We want the children to be accepted in society when they leave here. Most will seek employment in one of the big houses and it is our responsibility to ensure they are prepared.'

She stared at him for a long moment then sighed. 'Yes, I suppose you're right. It's certainly time society was more forward thinking, though. I mean, it's natural for a child to use their dominant hand and Monday can't help it being her left. It's not fair,' she declared.

Harry stared at her thoughtfully then finished his tea before replying. 'It's also not fair on April if she's told off for doing the very thing she's been asked to do.'

'I'll apologize, of course. I seem to be getting a lot of things wrong, don't I?' she sighed.

'And a lot of things right too,' he assured her quickly. He hesitated for a moment, not wishing to break the thin thread that had been spun between them, but he knew he would be failing in his duty as master if he didn't give the children all a fair chance. 'I notice Monday still isn't speaking.'

'No,' she sighed. 'I guess the shock of her ordeal must have gone deeper than we thought.'

'I have been watching her in class, and she seems quick on the uptake, which is why I think she would fare better if she were placed in the home of the Deaconess.'

'No,' Sarah snapped, then made an effort to control her feelings. 'She has settled well here and is great friends with Maisie. Couldn't we give it a little more time?' she pleaded.

'It's true, Maisie and she seem to be able to communicate without words,' he agreed, and her hopes lifted, only to be dashed again as he continued. 'However, Monday needs to be encouraged out of the shell she is hiding in, and it will take time and effort to do that. It is also important that dear Maisie learns to interact with the others. We are simply not being fair to either child.'

'I'll spend more time with Monday, then,' Sarah said quickly.

Harry smiled gently. 'You may have every intention of doing that, Sarah, but we both know the running of Red Cliffs makes considerable demands on your time. The Deaconess runs a much smaller establishment and would be able to devote more time to Monday.'

'Yes, I remember my godfather saying before he . . .' she blinked hard, ' . . . passed away.'

'Think about it, eh?' he urged gently. 'We want the best for all the children in our care, don't we?'

'Of course,' she murmured. She paused for a moment, then rose quickly to her feet. 'Well, this won't knit the baby a bonnet, as Mrs Daws always says. Or, in my case, get those flaming forms filled in ready for the accountant.'

'If you need any help, you only have to say.'

'I suppose you're an authority on everything here,' she replied.

'Not at all. However, I've been here for some time and have a general idea what makes things tick.'

'Well, you were right about April. It was unfair of me to take it out on her. I'll go and apologize immediately, sir,' she said, giving him a salute.

'Quite right too, Miss Sullivan,' he grinned. 'Can't have mutiny in the ranks.'

Feeling better for clearing the air with Sarah, Harry whistled his way down the path towards the schoolroom. However, his usual ability to sense trouble alerted him to a huddle of boys behind the compost heap.

'Leave me be,' he heard a young voice yelp.

''And it over, ven. You was warned.' Recognizing the voice of Bunter, he quickened his step and headed towards them.

'Leave him alone, you bully,' said another familiar young voice.

'Brown, Black, what's going on?' he shouted.

'It's Bully Bunter, sir. He's been threatening the little ones,' Black said.

Harry looked from the spoils in Bunter's hands to the two young boys who were now cowering behind the shed. 'What have you to say for yourself, Bunter, you serpulid little worm, you?' Harry said, gripping the boy by his ear.

'Oy! Vat 'urts,' Bunter yelled, his face growing red. 'I ain't dun nuffink. It woz vem,' he nodded towards Black and Brown. 'Vey jumped me.'

'So, you were just quietly walking down the garden, minding your own business when Brown and Black set upon you?' Harry asked, quietly.

The boy nodded. 'Yeah, vat's 'xactly 'ow it woz.'

'So why are Byrd and Dibble twitching like terrified mice behind the shed?'

'Search me,' he shrugged.

'I intend to,' Harry muttered, spying the bread sticking out of the boy's pockets.

'He made Sparrow Legs and Spittle save their bread for him. He spat in their food and said he'd do worse if they didn't, sir,' Brown piped up.

'Thank you, Brown. Whilst I agree Bunter's grammar leaves a lot to be desired, when I need an interpreter I will ask for one.' He turned and stared sternly at the oldest pupil in his class. 'Is this true, Bunter?'

''Cors not.' Harry stared pointedly at the bread in the boy's hand then pointed to his pocket.

'I was helpin' 'cos they couldn' eat it.'

'Lies slide from your tongue like butter off a hot spoon, Bunter. When we go to church tomorrow, I shall ask the vicar to keep you behind and train you up as one of his clerics. What do you think of that idea?'

'I ain't wearin' no poncy frock,' Bunter protested.

'You may not have any choice in the matter. I haven't got time to speak to you now. Go and see Mrs Daws, and tell her to set you to work in the scullery. I've a feeling she'll have a nice furry little job waiting. The rest of you, take yourselves into the classroom this minute.'

Back in her office, Sarah kicked out at one of the boxes. Blooming things, she muttered. If she didn't have all these blessed papers to sort, she could devote more time to Monday. If Harry Higgins thought he was going to send her to the Deaconess, he had another think coming. She spent the next hour moving the boxes to the far end of the room, out of her way. It wasn't a practical solution, but the physical exertion of pushing and pulling them out of her way made her feel better. There was a hesitant tap on the door. Sarah swore under her breath.

'Sergeant Watts is here to see you, Miss Sullivan,' Mrs Daws said, looking apprehensive.

Sarah forced a smile. 'Show him in, Mrs Daws.'

'He's brought a little girl with him and wants to know if Red Cliffs can take her in, temporary like. Poor little lass is filthy and looks fair starved. I'll clean her up then give her a bite to eat whilst you discuss things with the sergeant,' the housekeeper said.

Sarah looked at the good-hearted woman and felt ashamed of her earlier outburst. 'You're a treasure, Mrs Daws, the way you always put the needs of a child first, despite having so much to do.'

'Ah well, the chores can be done later whereas that poor little lass is scared out of her wits. Red Cliffs is all about priorities and seeing the wider picture, Miss Sullivan. At least, that's what the good doctor always said,' she added, giving Sarah one of her looks. 'I'll show the sergeant in, then,' she added.

As the woman bustled away, Sarah felt she'd been given some kind of message.

'Miss Sullivan,' Sergeant Watts said, taking off his hat as he entered the study. Then he looked around, frowning at all the boxes stacked under the window, their contents spilling over the floor, the forms scattered across her desk.

'Sergeant Watts, it's good to see you again.'

'Looks like you could do with getting yourself a house-wife,' he chuckled. Sarah smiled politely. 'I could always send Mrs Watts around to help you. She'd show you how to tidy up in next to no time. Proper good housekeeper, she is.'

'I'm sure she is,' Sarah replied, thinking the poor little woman probably wouldn't dare be otherwise. 'I understand you are here on business,' she said, anxious to get their meeting back onto its right footing.

He cleared his throat and remained standing. 'I am, Miss Sullivan.'

22

'I understand you have brought a little girl here?' Sarah asked.

The sergeant nodded gravely. 'Indeed I have. Saved from the wheels of a cart, she was,' he informed her, puffing out his chest so that the buttons on his jacket strained in the way Sarah remembered.

'Sounds like an unfortunate accident, Sergeant.'

'Oh no, miss. A man was chasing her with his belt and when the milk cart rounded the corner he pushed her right out in front. If it hadn't been for the driver being so quick-thinking, she'd have been squashed flat as the wife's smoothing iron either by the horse's shoes or the cart's wheels.'

'That's dreadful,' Sarah said, shuddering. 'And the man?'

'Vanished like the morning mist,' Sergeant Watts replied. 'Or probably scotch mist in his case, 'cos apparently he was as drunk as a skunk.' He sniffed. 'And at this time of day as well. Anyhow, I asked at the orphanage but they're full to bursting. Now, the good doctor never turned anyone away, so . . .'

'Of course she must stay here,' Sarah cried.

The sergeant looked relieved. 'Well, if you could give me the usual receipt, I'll be on my way.'

'Usual receipt? For what?' she asked, looking askance.

'Proof that you're keeping the girl,' he replied, shaking his head. 'The doctor always gave me a form, though how you can find anything in this mess, I don't know,' he added, grimacing at the array of forms, ledgers and papers on her desk.

Sarah groaned inwardly. Which form was she supposed to give him? As she stood there dithering, there was a sharp rap, and Harry popped his head around the door.

'Sorry, I didn't know you had a visitor, Miss Sullivan. Good morning, Sergeant Watts. The pupils haven't been getting into trouble, I hope?'

'No, Master Higgins. Your little lot could show some of them adults how to behave, and that's a fact. Why, only . . .'

'The sergeant has brought a little girl with him. She's in the kitchen having something to eat,' Sarah jumped in quickly, fearful the man might embark on yet another of his lengthy explanations. 'Apparently, he requires a receipt for her,' she finished, frowning down at the paperwork.

'Ah, yes, you need Form RT176,' Harry said, easing out a blue document from an open folder.

'Good job you know, Master Higgins. I was only saying earlier that Miss Sullivan should concentrate on house-wifely things rather than . . .'

'Here you are, I've signed in the usual place,' Harry said, scribbling something at the end of the form and handing it to the man. 'Is there anything else, Sergeant?'

The man shook his head. 'No, I'd better be off, lots to do, you know. I can see you'll have your work cut out teaching this one about paperwork, Master Higgins,' he said.

Harry took one look at Sarah's reddening cheeks and knew he had to act quickly. 'It took me ages to learn what each form was for, Sergeant Watts. However, Miss Sullivan is extremely quick on the uptake. At this rate, she'll soon be telling me what's what. Now, I must return to the school-room, so let me escort you to the front door,' he said, darting Sarah a look as he ushered the man from the room.

'I'll give Constable Potts your regards, shall I, miss?' the sergeant asked.

'Please do,' Sarah muttered. As soon as the man had gone, she sank into the chair and put her head in her hands. How would she ever learn which form was for what? As she sat ruminating, Harry returned, pretending to mop his brow.

'Watts is a good chap but hard going. Don't look so worried, Sarah. There might be a lot to get to grips with, but you'll soon learn.'

'But I didn't even know those forms had special numbers,' she sighed.

'They don't,' he replied, a mischievous gleam sparking in his eyes. 'It was the doctor's way of getting rid of him. He'd say, "Ah, yes, you need form bla, bla, bla, Sergeant", and would pull one out at random, scribble his name and hand it to the man.'

'You're joking?' Sarah gasped. 'Didn't the sergeant ever mention it to him?'

'Nope, so he can't even have looked at the forms, can he?'

'But that sounds highly irregular.'

'It probably is, but nobody ever questioned the doctor,' Harry laughed then looked around the room. 'I can see you've had a busy morning, but don't overdo it, will you?'

'No, I won't. I must check on the new girl. Mrs Daws said she looked starved and was taking her to the kitchen,' Sarah said, getting to her feet.

Harry chuckled. 'There's really no hurry, for that poor girl will have to be bathed, shorn and issued with clean clothing before she's allowed anywhere near Mrs Daws' pristine kitchen.'

'But she'll need my help,' Sarah protested, only to have Harry raise his brow.

'Mrs Daws is quite capable, and, besides, she has her own way of doing things. However, the girl will have to be examined before she can mix with the others, so I'll get Dr Hawkins to call in as soon as he can. It's about time the others were given the once-over again anyhow.'

'You make them sound like a herd of cattle,' Sarah said, pulling a face.

'Not much difference sometimes, which reminds me, I'm taking the boys up to the farm this afternoon to give old Jim a hand. Mrs Daws was worried about them hearing from the girls what Miss Green told them, so I've promised to give them a little pep talk on the way. Mrs Daws is going to explain about the moral thing properly to the girls when she has them for house skills later. Hopefully, that will clear up any misunderstandings. You might like to give her some moral support, if you'll forgive the pun,' he laughed.

Sarah smiled. 'I certainly will. I'd hate to think of them all going around believing they might be jumped upon by rabbits. Honestly, whatever was the woman thinking of?'

'I have no idea. Mrs Daws said she never wanted to see or hear about them again, but a couple arrived this morning, courtesy of our local poacher, Walt.'

'Oh no, poor Mrs Daws.'

'Don't worry. I've got one of the boys preparing them for the pot as penance for bullying a couple of the younger ones. He's making a right mess of it, so it's a good job it's bath night,' he chortled.

'That must mean it's Saturday. Don't they ever get fed up with doing the same things at the same time every week?' she asked curiously.

'Most have had such traumatic little lives, they find comfort in the routine, Sarah. What might seem monotonous to us gives them a sense of security. Talking of routine, I notice you haven't had a break since you've been here, so whilst those grimy little bodies are being scrubbed under the watchful eye of Mrs Daws and Mrs Laver, why don't we walk into town and have a fish supper? Unless I'm treading on the constable's size nines?'

'Goodness, no, heaven forbid,' Sarah spluttered.

'Can I take it that means you will walk out with me for a bite of supper?' Harry asked.

As he stood staring at her intently, despite their recent disagreements, Sarah felt the sparks fly between them once more. Not trusting herself to reply, she could only nod her acceptance. The warm smile he gave her as he left sent her heart spinning, like the Catherine wheels her father used to light for her on Guy Fawkes' night.

Come on, get a grip, Sarah Sullivan, she thought to herself, rising to her feet and hurrying down the corridor. The man's only asked you to share a fish supper with him. Only then did she remember she hadn't asked him what he had called into her office for.

*

April was busy preparing the luncheon when Sarah entered the warm kitchen. The enticing aroma of freshly baked bread and cooking vegetables made her realize it had been a long time since breakfast. Marmalade, curled up on the chair by the range, opened one sleepy eye and, having ascertained Sarah posed no threat, promptly closed it again.

'Mrs Daws is helping Mrs Laver with the new girl,' April said, looking up from the pan she was stirring. 'Luckily, she was here for her customary tea and blether before putting the soiled stuff to soak, 'cos that new one's a right firecracker and no mistake.'

'Poor thing's probably petrified after her earlier ordeal. Anyway, I'm glad we're alone, April, for I want to apologize. I realize now that you were only trying to help Monday with her cutlery and I shouldn't have snapped at you.'

The girl stared at Sarah thoughtfully for a moment. 'Happen I wish you was right, miss, about us using our domino hand.'

'Dominant, April, the word is dominant,' Sarah gently corrected. 'Why do you say that?'

'Well, I likes to use my left hand for writing and cooking. It comes natural, like,' she said, staring down at the spoon in her left hand. 'See, miss?'

Sarah nodded.

'That Miss Green said I was sinister. Always tied my left hand behind my back so I couldn't use it. I didn't want Monday to go through that, she's such a sweetie and too young to be called sinister.'

'Nobody should be called that, April. You are sweet and helpful and most certainly not sinister,' Sarah said, patting the girl's shoulder. 'Now, shall I cut the bread?'

'You're all right, you are, miss,' April smiled, then turned back to stirring her soup. They were working in companionable silence when a strangled sob came from the pantry. Sarah looked askance at April, who gave a funny laugh.

'That's poor Bunter. The master's sent him to prepare the rabbits, and he's making a right old song and dance about it. He's been in there for ages and hasn't even done one yet. I offered to help but Mrs Daws said it was his pennies and to leave him to get on with it.'

'I think you mean penance, April. It means he has to atone for bullying the younger ones.'

'I'll leave him to it, then. One thing I can't abide 'tis bullying,' she said, raising her voice. Immediately, the sniffling from the scullery got louder. The girl sounded just like the housekeeper, and Sarah had to bend her face over the loaf to hide her smile.

''Tis a shame Monday hasn't found that voice of hers yet,' April commented, turning and seeing the little girl run past the window.

'Is she still only friends with Maisie?' Sarah couldn't help asking, remembering her earlier conversation with the master about the Deaconess.

'Yeah. Maisie's the only one who can understand her. Though if Edith has a night trauma, the little poppet hops into her bed and comforts her. It's strange, really, 'cos they don't really mix during the day.'

A sudden screech and squawking, followed by the outside door bursting open, interrupted their conversation. The ginger cat opened its eyes, arched its back, then fled.

'You'll have to let me put some cream on those or they'll fester,' Mrs Daws said, leading the sobbing little girl firmly by the arm. Her hair had been shaved, and she was wrapped in a towel.

'But it hurts.'

'I know, but if you'll just let me rub this in, I promise it'll make your back feel better,' the housekeeper soothed, dropping to her knees on the mat. As she gently peeled away the cloth, the pervading smell of carbolic filled the room. Sarah and April stared at each other in horror. The girl's back was covered in livid purple wheals. They watched as Mrs Daws tenderly dabbed the skin with lotion, then eased a drab dress over the girl's bony shoulders, where it hung like a billowing tent over her skinny frame.

'Now can I have something to eat?' the little girl pleaded, then her eyes narrowed as she saw Sarah and April watching. 'This ain't a peep show, you know,' she hissed.

'Let me check your head, and then you can have some of April's nice, hot broth. How do you fancy that?' The girl nodded eagerly, then sighed as Mrs Daws began running the funny comb over her shaved head. 'Well, that's got them little varmints for now,' she pronounced, struggling to her feet.

The girl rubbed her scalp and shrugged. 'At least it don't itch now.'

'This is Miss Sullivan and April,' the housekeeper said, gesturing towards them. 'Now you know our names, are you going to share yours, dearie?'

Two clear grey eyes surveyed them all solemnly. 'Me name's Kitty,' she finally said.

'And do you have a second name?' Mrs Daws encouraged.

'Nah, only posh kids have them,' she replied.

'Well, Kitty's a pretty name,' Sarah said, giving the girl a bright smile.

'Pretty is as pretty does, me mam always said.'

Sarah opened her mouth to ask about her mother then closed it again when she saw Mrs Daws shake her head.

'Now, dear, you sit down at the table here and have your luncheon with me. We can have a nice little chat while April and Miss Sullivan supervise luncheon in the dining room. It can get a bit noisy in there, and I expect you'd like to have a bit of peace.'

'What I'd like is some grub,' Kitty replied.

Another sniffle came from the scullery. Before they could stop her, the girl ran over and disappeared inside.

'Blimey, you're makin' a bleedin' mess of that and no mistake. Give it me, boy, and I'll show you how it's done.'

'Well I never,' said Mrs Daws, staring through the open door. 'She's skinned that rabbit in half the time I ever could.'

23

Sarah was in a cheerful mood as she made her way back to the office after luncheon. The girls seemed more friendly towards her after their chat the previous evening, and she was beginning to feel she belonged at Red Cliffs. Then there was her fish and chip supper with Harry, which she was really looking forward to. It would be a good opportunity to get to know him better, and she couldn't deny a walk along the promenade appealed. She'd have to rake through her closet for something decent to wear, for the fashion-conscious visitors were sure to be out on a Saturday night. Then she laughed. Her wardrobe these days consisted of cast-offs, and whilst she was grateful to have them, they were hardly of the latest mode. It would still be nice to see more of Torquay itself, though, for she'd hardly left Red Cliffs since she'd arrived.

As soon as she opened the door, she noticed the letter propped up against the glass paperweight. Picking up the little brass opener with its incongruous pixie handle, she carefully slit open the envelope, noting the thickness of the paper. It was from Mr Fothergill, recapping the salient points of their recent meeting. She was about to put it aside to read later when the penultimate paragraph caught her eye.

As you have already been informed, Mr Christian Lawrence, nephew of the late Dr Samuel Lawrence, is contesting his uncle's will. You are now advised, he has lodged a complaint against Red Cliffs Ragged School stating that the dilapidated condition of the property lowers the tone of an otherwise respectable neighbourhood. Furthermore, Mr Lawrence claims the children, clothed in rags, their hair shorn like convicts, run wild in the streets and cavort in the sea when they should be attending class. As he has informed the local authority, they are obliged to carry out an inspection of the school known as Red Cliffs. They will pay a visit within the next twenty-eight days, and it is essential you lodge the school's accounts with Messrs Calculus and Arithmica forthwith in order that they may conduct an audit before said inspection takes place.

Please do not hesitate to contact me if I can be of any further assistance.

Yours sincerely,
A. Fothergill, Esq.

Well, of all the cheek, Sarah fumed. How dare Christian make such outrageous claims about the children of Red Cliffs? They weren't permitted out of the grounds without being accompanied by an adult, and a vigilant Pip ensured the gates were kept locked at all times. As for cavorting in the sea, didn't the authorities realize the benefit of taking exercise in the briny air? The pupils might not have uniforms in the conventional manner, and their hair had to be shorn for hygiene purposes, but they were always well behaved outside the school; Master Higgins made sure of that. She stared around the room, taking in the peeling wallpaper, the filling bursting from the chairs, the sundry boxes and files lined up against the walls, and sighed. Even if she could persuade the bank to release funds for redecoration, there wouldn't be time to make any real difference before the inspection.

Then her thoughts turned to despair. It seemed Christian would go to any lengths to get the school closed down and claim Red Cliffs as his own. Although she was prepared to fight tooth and nail to keep it open, could she succeed in the face of such formidable opposition? Hadn't Harry intimated the inspectors already had concerns? What would happen to him, Mrs Daws and the children if Red Cliffs were shut down?

Suddenly she was gripped by an overwhelming determination. Her uncle had entrusted the school into her care, and she would do everything in her power to keep it open.

'If Christian Lawrence thinks I'm giving up without a fight, he's got another think coming,' she muttered, screwing the letter into a ball and throwing it at the door just as it opened.

'Ouch,' Harry moaned as the missive hit him on the forehead.

'Sorry, Harry,' Sarah sighed. 'I didn't know you were about to enter.'

He stood there studying her for a moment. 'As you're looking incensed, I can only guess this contained unwelcome news?' he asked, quirking his brow as he handed her the scrunched-up letter.

'You'd better read it for yourself,' she sighed.

Carefully, he spread the letter out on the desk, then scanned the contents. 'Well, we've had inspections before so I am sure we can cope with another,' he commented, giving her a reassuring smile.

'But what about the state of the house? It does need a lot of attention,' Sarah said, giving a deeper sigh.

'The local authority understands the school's cash constraints. They also know that Red Cliffs can't fund uniforms, and we have never had any complaints about the children's behaviour outside the school. Well, apart from the odd comment in church when one of them got bored and decided to voice his own opinions on the vicar's rather long-winded sermon,' he grinned wryly.

'They want to see audited accounts, though. I've made some progress with the ledgers but my godfather's writing is not easy to decipher.'

'I'm more used to it than you, so why not let me help?' he suggested. 'Of course, it will mean we'll have to postpone our fish and chip supper,' he added quickly when she shot him a grateful look. 'We can treat ourselves by way of celebration when we've completed this onerous task.'

'Oh, Harry, you make it sound like the inspection will be a mere formality. If you're sure you don't mind helping me with the accounts, I'd be really grateful,' she replied, feeling happier.

He smiled then looked out of the window. 'The boys are lining up, ready for our visit to the farm, so I'd better go. Can't risk them laughing and joking; it might upset the neighbours.' He winked. 'I'll see you later.'

Sarah smiled as the door closed behind him, then opened the heavy ledger. If the local authority wanted audited accounts then they would have them, she thought, losing herself in the columns of figures. She was frowning over a faded invoice when she heard voices followed by the front door opening. Going to investigate, she found Maisie and Monday, rags in hand, standing on the front doorstep.

'Hello, girls, what are you up to?' she asked.

Maisie glanced at Monday then puffed out her little chest. 'Mrs Daws give us a very 'portant job to do, ain't she, Monday?' The little girl nodded and surveyed Sarah with her periwinkle eyes.

'Really? And what might that be?' Sarah asked, although the rags and polish gave her a good idea.

'We's to rub the doorknob and letterbox until they sparkle 'cos we's too little to learn about seeds in mummies' tummies,' she beamed. 'She said we was 'spons'ble girls and she nos we won't go no further than the step, didn't she, Monday?' Again the girl nodded.

'Well, that is an important job, girls, and it will make the front door look much smarter,' Sarah smiled. 'If anyone comes to call, I'll be in my office.'

Maisie shook her head. 'They gotta get past Pip first.'

'Of course they have. Silly me,' Sarah replied.

'Yeah, you gotta fink, miss,' Maisie replied, tapping the side of her head with her finger. She looked so serious, Sarah had to smother a giggle. The children at Red Cliffs were priceless, she thought, returning to her work with renewed determination. If Smarty Pants Christian Lawrence hoped to have them evicted, he was in for a fight.

She worked on until the room grew cold and long shadows crept into the corners. The empty fireplace stood testament to the state of the school's finances; Sarah could only imagine the warm glow of coals in the grate. Stretching her stiff back, she made her way along the hallway.

'Guess what, miss?' Edith asked as she entered the inviting warmth of the kitchen.

'You've promised to do all the washing-up by yourself?' Sarah teased.

'Don't be daft,' the girl snorted. 'We've been planting seeds in pots, and Mrs Daws has told us about how things grow.'

'Yes,' Maggie cut in. 'If you plant carrot seeds you's goin' to get carrots, ain't you?'

'Er, yes,' Sarah frowned, staring askance at Mrs Daws. The housekeeper merely grinned back.

'Well, that's how stupid old Lettuce Leaf is,' Maggie snorted.

'Stands to reason rabbits ain't goin' to make no little baby boys, are they?' Ellen said, staring seriously at Sarah.

'No, of course they're not,' she agreed.

'You lot are just plain stupid,' Kitty piped up, sneering at them. 'Everyone knows that a man gets out his tadger and puts it . . .'

'Right, April,' Mrs Daws cut in quickly. 'Perhaps you'd like to show Kitty where she'll be sleeping tonight. That's if you've decided to stay, missy?' she asked, giving the girl a level look.

'You say I won't be locked in?' Kitty asked.

'This isn't a prison, Kitty. You are welcome to stay or go, the choice is yours,' the housekeeper replied casually.

The girl thought for a moment. 'I'll stay,' she announced, as if she was doing them a favour.

'Well, off you go with April, then.'

'I was about to cut the bread,' April pointed out.

'I'll do that,' Sarah said, smiling at her.

As soon as they'd left the room, Mrs Daws shook her head. 'What that girl knows is fearful for someone of her tender years. She's had a right time of it from what I can make out, and as for those marks on her back, well, Dr Hawkins is calling by after supper to look at them and . . .'

'What's a tadger, Mrs Daws?' Edith interrupted.

'That's enough questions for one day. If we don't hurry and stir this into the mixture, we'll have no cake to offer the vicar tomorrow, will we?' Mrs Daws pointed out.

'We can tell him how babies get into their mummies' tummies, can't we?' Maggie asked.

'Erm, I don't think the vicar knows much about babies, Maggie,' Mrs Daws said quickly.

'You're telling me, he nearly dropped Billy in the bont,' she sniggered.

'Font, Maggie, the word is font,' the housekeeper corrected her.

'Well, whatever it was, he still nearly drowned the poor little blighter.'

Just then, a noise in the yard heralded the return of the boys. The door opened, and Harry appeared carrying a basket of eggs.

'Bess sent these, Mrs Daws. The boys are excited because Jim was so pleased with the way they tidied his barn and outbuildings, he promised they could help him plant his seeds when the weather warms up again.'

Mrs Daws snorted. 'The eggs are most welcome but don't you speak to me about seeds,' she muttered, Harry raised a brow at Sarah who was trying to smother a grin.

'Right, girls, supper's almost ready, so go and rinse your hands,' she ordered, picking up the eggs to take to the pantry.

As the girls clamoured towards the open door, Harry turned to Sarah.

'Did I say something to upset Mrs Daws?'

Sarah smiled. 'Not really. She's just spent the afternoon teaching the girls how babies get inside their mother. She was using seeds as an example,' she said, pointing to the rows of flowerpots on the windowsill. Did you know, if you plant carrot seeds you'll get carrots growing?' she spluttered. Harry frowned, clearly thinking Sarah had been overdoing things.

'Kitty, the new girl, tried to share her knowledge of a man's, erm, anatomy,' she stuttered, her cheeks going hot. 'I think it all got a bit much for Mrs Daws.'

'This Kitty sounds rather worldly wise,' he frowned.

'She is, Master Higgins,' Mrs Daws sighed, coming back into the room and giving the big pot a stir. 'This rabbit stew's about done, so if you've finished cutting the bread, you can sound the gong, Miss Sullivan. I can't be doing with Maisie's bashing and banging this evening.'

Sarah gently sounded the gong and then stood back as the stampede began. Kitty pelted down the corridor, pushing past in her haste.

'Hey, missie, that's no way to behave,' April called, following behind. 'Oh, I'll finish cutting the bread,' she added, staring at the half-empty plates on the scrubbed table.

Sarah frowned. 'But I know I cut enough slices,' she replied.

'Well, there's only enough to feed half of them,' April pointed out.

Harry stared thoughtfully at the children filing into the dining room then strode purposefully after them.

Supper finished, the children set to clearing away and tidying up before their bath. Sarah and Harry took their tea through to the office. Harry lit the lamps, and as their soft glow lit up the room, Sarah sank into her chair.

'Goodness, those children can certainly eat,' she said.

'Hmm. I was certain it was Bunter who'd taken those slices of bread, but I couldn't see any sign. Unless the little blighter had already eaten the evidence, of course,' he raised his brows.

'Well, it was only a few slices, I suppose,' Sarah replied with a shrug.

'That's not the point, I'm afraid, Sarah. We are here to teach the children right from wrong and cannot allow thieving in any shape or form.'

He looked so sternly at her, Sarah felt as if she'd been caught red-handed herself and quickly opened the ledger she'd been working on earlier.

'Right,' Harry said, taking out his pocket watch. 'Dr Hawkins is examining Kitty and all the others after their baths so we probably have a couple of hours.'

'I've entered the outstanding invoices I managed to decipher up until October when . . .' She paused as a rush of emotion threatened to overwhelm her. 'When my god-father passed away,' she finished. 'However, there are so many papers and forms that are either half completed or require signature. Poor Uncle; it wasn't his fault. He can't really have known he was dying,' she whispered.

'He knew, Sarah,' Harry said gently. 'He just wasn't expecting it to be so soon,' he said, briskly. She nodded, remembering then that Mr Fothergill had said the same.

They worked easily together, with Harry reading out the amounts and Sarah entering them in the ledger. Then, as Harry passed her the papers to file, she couldn't help noticing his long, artistic fingers. On one occasion, their hands touched, and she felt a delicious tingling sensation shoot up her arm. He must have felt something too because his hand lingered and his glance caught hers, before he quickly looked back down at the papers.

'Getting there,' was all he said, much to Sarah's disappointment. She watched as he concentrated on deciphering the scribble of figures, fascinated by the way his hair flopped over his eyes whenever he leaned forward. Finally, he leaned back in his seat and rubbed his forehead.

'Right, that's enough for tonight. If we make a concerted effort tomorrow after luncheon has been cleared away and the Sunday waifs dispatched back to town, we should have this little lot in a passable state for the accountants to do their stuff. Of course, those will have to wait,' he added, gesturing to the boxes under the window.

'I can start working my way through them on Monday,' Sarah said.

Harry shook his head. 'You won't have time for that, I'm afraid. You need to spend a period in the classroom, see what the children are learning and the methods we use here. The inspector is bound to ask questions, and you need to be prepared. It will also be beneficial for you to sit in on a couple of Miss Green's lessons.'

Sarah nodded. 'After she disobeyed my instruction, I fully intend to make sure she shows the girls how to make their aprons,' she said, thinking of all the other things she wanted to say to the woman. 'Do you know, she called April sinister because she uses her left hand? I mean . . .' Her voice trailed off as Harry shook his head impatiently.

'I think April meant sinistral, Sarah. It means relating to the left side of the body, while sinistrality refers to someone with a preference for using the left hand.'

'Oh,' Sarah muttered, wondering how he knew so much.

'Be careful, Sarah. Mr Lawrence is hell-bent on getting Red Cliffs closed down and will plumb the depths to do so. I hear he has recently made it his business to befriend Miss Green, and she has been seen walking out with him.'

The unlikely image of debonair Christian Lawrence with the skinny, crow-featured Miss Green on his arm made Sarah want to laugh. Then she saw Harry's bleak expression and realized he was telling the truth.

24

Christian glanced at the scrawny, shrew-like woman sitting opposite him and was glad he'd chosen an eating place away from his usual haunts. It would do his reputation as the suave, debonair man-about-town no good to be seen with someone as plain as her. Still, needs must, and the stakes were high, he reminded himself.

'So, tell me, Letticia,' he grinned, turning on his naughty-little-boy look. 'Forgive me; that was presumptuous of me. May I call you by your first name? It is so pretty.'

'Why, thank you,' she simpered. 'Of course you may and I shall call you Christian.' She fluttered her lashes at him, reminding Christian of the spider he'd squashed earlier. 'I've never been here before,' she said, looking around. 'Of course, Father was a little put out that you didn't call for me, but I assured him you would next time.'

Next time? Christian thought. Over his dead body! Then he remembered why he'd invited the woman here, and smiled as amenably as he could. Thankfully, he didn't need to answer because she was only halfway through her tale.

'I told him it was because you were a very busy man. What exactly is it you do for a living?' She leaned forward in her seat, scrutinizing him with eyes he couldn't quite determine the colour of.

'I'm a dealer,' he replied, taking a sip of his drink, then picking up the menu. 'Shall we order?'

She wasn't to be distracted, though. 'How fascinating, what do you deal in, exactly?'

'This and that. You know how it is,' he shrugged. 'I was thinking of having the haddock.'

'Who's a hungry boy, then?' she replied in that sing-song voice that was already getting on his nerves. He forced his lips into a smile then drained his glass. 'Oh, and a thirsty one too,' she giggled.

'Yes, well, as I said, I have had a busy day.'

'You didn't explain exactly what you do,' she persisted.

'I effect the transfer of items from one person to another, taking a healthy commission in the process.' When it goes right, he thought, remembering his 'agent' who'd nearly got caught the previous day.

'And does that make much money?'

'Enough. I also offer, er, protection too. That's lucrative.'

'Oh, goody. I love a man with plenty of readies,' she gushed. 'And you can protect me anytime,' she added, fluttering her spiders again.

'Are you ready to order, sir?' the waiter asked, appearing beside their table.

'Yes, the haddock and chips for me, please,' he said, grateful for the interruption. The waiter frowned, and Christian realized he should have let Letticia order first. 'What will you have, my dear?' he asked hurriedly, to cover his faux pas.

'Oh, Christian, you are forward,' she gushed. 'I'll have the same but with a double portion of mushy peas, please. Do you have any battered cod's roe?'

'Certainly, madam. Would you care to change your order?'

'Goodness me, no, I'm so famished I'll have that as well.'

What a pig, Christian thought, calculating how much (or, rather, how little) he had in his wallet. And he'd been hoping to have enough left to spend on Lil's favours later.

'Can I get you more drinks, sir?'

'Scotch, please, a large one,' Christian replied automatically.

'Well, if you're pushing the boat out, I'll have a large gin and pink,' Letticia grinned. 'I'm not really used to imbibing, so you might have to carry me home,' she giggled.

Christian's spirits lifted. Not used to drink, eh? Perhaps there was hope for later, and without paying for it. The park was really dark, and he knew the weak link in the chain they used to lock the gate.

'I've told you all about my job, Letticia, so why don't you tell me about yours. You're a travelling schoolmistress, I believe,' he asked, turning on the charm.

'Oh, Christian, I do believe you've been doing your homework,' she tittered. 'My little joke, get it?'

'Very droll,' he replied. 'You're obviously a clever lady. Now, which schools do you teach in?'

'Two local authority establishments in the town, and I also have to visit this place called Red Cliffs,' she pulled a face. 'It's horrid, full of evil, smelly little girls. Do you know, the other day one of them had the audacity to question my sewing instruction? Nobody doubts my methods, I can tell you, so I locked her in the coal store.'

'How terrible,' he exclaimed, thinking she must be a hard woman to do such a thing; even he wouldn't do that to a child.

However, Letticia thought he meant it had been terrible for her. 'It was. That new woman, Miss Sullivan, tried to take me to task, but I told her good and proper.'

'Quite right too,' he nodded, thinking that was a scene he'd like to have witnessed. 'I'm intrigued. If you hate working at Red Cliffs that much, why don't you leave? I mean, a clever young lady like you must be in great demand,' he gushed, and she flushed with pleasure.

'Your drinks,' the waiter said, placing their glasses before them. He watched in astonishment as Letticia downed hers in one, wiped her lips with the back of her hand, then placed her glass back on the tray.

'Another, please,' she told the waiter. If the man was surprised, he was too well trained to comment and, with a polite nod, went to replenish her glass. 'All this talking is giving me a right thirst,' she giggled at Christian, who was nursing his whisky thoughtfully.

'You were telling me why you don't leave Red Cliffs,' he prompted.

'So I was,' she replied. 'My father is employed by the local authority. He's very high up, you know. Well, anyway, he says that working for a charitable institution will look good on my character and might even improve my marriage prospects,' she giggled. 'As you're probably aware, I'm not the typical English rose you gentlemen seem to prefer.'

She paused, and Christian realized she was expecting him to demur. 'You have very interesting characteristics, Letticia,' he said.

'Goodness, do you think so?' she simpered. He nodded, and she leaned forward so that her top gaped, affording him a glimpse of her skinny bosom. Crikey, he'd seen more meat on a sparrow, he thought, remembering Lil's luscious, rounded curves. 'This is really nice, Christian. I'm having a lovely time and could sit here all night,' she sighed.

Heaven forbid, he thought, just as the waiter and waitress appeared.

'Your drink, miss, and your food,' the waiter said, stepping back so that the waitress could set down her loaded plate. Christian tried not to curse. What he'd envisaged would be a quick discussion about the failures of Red Cliffs looked like taking up the whole of his evening as well as rapidly depleting the contents of his wallet. At this rate, he'd end up without the wherewithal to enjoy some real comforts with Lil, which he was sorely in need of after the past half hour.

'This is what I call a decent portion,' Letticia was saying.

He eyed her piled plate with distaste and then looked quickly away as she began stuffing the food into her mouth.

'They are going to carry out an inspection at that so-called school,' she told him, spraying a mixture of batter and peas across the table and completely ruining the little appetite he'd had. He pushed his plate aside. 'You not going to eat that?' she asked. He shook his head, and she stabbed his fish with her fork and added it to her own. 'Be a shame to waste it,' she said, seeing his horrified look.

'Sure you wouldn't like the chips as well?' he asked sardonically.

'Oh, thanks,' she said, pulling his plate towards her. 'Good job you didn't have mushy peas as well 'cos anymore and I'd have wind something chronic.'

Charming, he thought, taking a sip of his drink and determining to get the conversation back on track. 'Is it usual for schools to have inspections?' he asked. She nodded but, to his irritation, continued stuffing large pieces of fish into her mouth. Feeling sick, he looked down at his glass and tried to ignore the revolting sounds coming from across the table. Then pushing both empty plates to one side, she gave an almighty belch.

'Oops, manners,' she laughed, taking a glug of her gin, which seemed to refresh her memory. 'You were asking about inspections,' she said. 'Well, Red Cliffs is a special case. I shouldn't be telling you this, but there has been a complaint, so of course my father will have to investigate.'

'Why will your father have to investigate?' he asked, looking at her intently.

'I already told you, he's the inspector,' she announced proudly.

'What will happen if the school is found wanting?' he asked.

'Then he could have them shut down. Still, knowing him, he'll probably give them a warning or something.'

'But if they were closed down you wouldn't have to work there any more, would you?' Christian pointed out. 'Surely that would be the answer to your prayers?' And mine, he thought, as a vision of the property developer handing him a wad of notes flashed before him.

She sighed. 'The trouble is, I would either have to find another job or marry.'

'Well, as I said earlier, you have attributes that make you very marriageable. Any man would be proud to propose . . .' he began.

'Goodness, Christian, I had no idea you felt that way about me. I mean, a proposal on our first date, well!'

'I didn't mean . . .' he stammered, taking a hurried gulp of his drink.

'I accept, you silly man. I was only trying to keep the school open because I thought I'd never get another position as convenient as that. Now, I don't need it. I shall tell father he must have Red Cliffs closed immediately. Then we can arrange our wedding,' she cooed.

'No,' he said, swallowing hard. 'That's not what I meant . . .'

'You're worried about those poor little children. Well, that's so sweet of you, I could kiss you right this minute,' she said, leaping to her feet and hurrying over to kiss his cheek.

The restaurant fell silent as the other diners looked on with interest. Christian rubbed his cheek in dismay. What the heck had gone wrong?

'Sit down. You're making a spectacle of yourself,' he hissed.

'Oh, I'm so happy, Christian. When we have our own family, you'll make a wonderful father,' Letticia gushed.

Unable to contain his dismay, he snapped his fingers at the waiter. 'Bring me the bill.'

Outside, a gentle drizzle was falling. Anxious to be rid of the woman, Christian seized upon the excuse.

'Driver,' he called, hailing a passing carriage. 'Take this, er, lady home,' he instructed as it pulled up alongside them.

'But darling Christian, you must come with me and speak to Father,' she pouted.

'These things need to be done properly, Letticia. It's too late an hour to respectably call upon him this evening,' he replied glibly. 'Besides, I have more business to attend to. Good weddings require money, after all. Now, hurry out of the wet,' he said, all but pushing her inside and hurriedly closing the door.

She lowered the window and leaned out. 'How long will it be before I see you again?' she asked.

'Be assured, I will attend to my business as quickly as I can. In the meantime, the sooner you can get Red Cliffs closed, the sooner we can set a date, can't we?'

'Oh, Christian, you really are keen. I will speak to Father first thing in the morning.'

'Until I can formally ask for your hand, you must keep our plans for the future secret. I don't want to start off on the wrong foot with my future in-laws, do I? Now, pull up the window, and I'll see you as soon as I can. Off you go, driver,' he called.

As the carriage moved away, he sank back against the wall. That was a close shave, Christian, he told himself. Silly cow! As if he'd entertain the notion of marriage to someone like her. He needed somebody warm, someone whose kisses filled him with passion. Not like that sloppy effort she'd inflicted on him. Still, at least it had given him the opportunity to lift her purse, he thought, pulling it from his pocket and testing its weight. Red Cliffs was within his grasp at last, he thought, whistling as he headed towards the nearest tavern to celebrate.

When Christian woke the next morning, his head was thumping, and his throat felt as rough as sandpaper. Despite his hangover, he was in high spirits, for Red Cliffs would soon be his. Checking he had enough of Miss Green's money left for a carriage, he hurriedly got himself ready. He would pay a visit to Madam Rosa, collect his valuables and get his agents to dispose of them. Then he would lie low while Miss Green dealt with her father's inspection. She was so keen to marry, he had no doubt she would ensure the school was closed down. Things couldn't have worked out better, he chuckled.

Buoyed up with his success, he decided to take another look at his inheritance. Giving the driver instructions to head for Red Cliffs and then on to the Yalberton area where he knew the gypsies had made their latest camp, he hopped into the carriage. Then he closed his eyes and settled down to sleep. It seemed only moments later when he was woken by the carriage juddering to a halt. Peering out of the window, he saw a crocodile of ragged urchins crossing the road in front of them. Sarah was laughing up at that Higgins fellow, and he couldn't help thinking she'd be quite a good-looking woman if it wasn't for that unruly hair of hers and those unfashionable clothes. A great improvement on that scrawny Miss Green, anyway, he thought with a shudder. Glancing behind, he saw the imposing property of Red Cliffs rising up from behind the iron railings. Not long now and it would be his, he smirked, rubbing his hands together with glee.

*

Unaware she was being observed, Sarah continued her conversation with Harry then fell silent as they entered the church. Determined to put all thought of the school's accounts and forthcoming inspection out of her mind, she opened her hymnal. A little hand crept into hers, and looking down, she saw Monday regarding her with those periwinkle eyes. Her heart swelled with love, and she gave the girl a warm smile. Then she looked at the other children from the school. Whilst they were clean from their bath night, their mismatched clothes set them apart from the rest of the congregation, who were dressed in their Sunday best.

'Ask and ye shall receive,' the vicar intoned, staring down from the pulpit.

I only ask that Red Cliffs is saved, Sarah thought.

'Whatever ye ask, ye shall be granted.'

'I want a wee wee,' Maisie's little voice piped up. As a titter ran through the congregation, Mrs Daws quickly led the little girl from the church. Aware that some people were tutting in disapproval, Sarah and Harry exchanged dismayed glances. Whatever would the vicar think of this interruption to his sermon?

They needn't have worried, for he was smiling. 'Trust a little child to show us the way. That little girl was not afraid to ask and nor should we be. Something to reflect on as we sing our final hymn, "All Things Bright and Beautiful".'

'Well, back to the fray,' Harry whispered as they led the children up the aisle. Sarah nodded. Truth to tell, however hard she tried to dispel it, the forthcoming visit to the accountants was playing on her mind, and she was anxious to get back and sort the rest of the papers. Unfortunately, as she hurried down the path, she was accosted by Hubble, Bubble and Trouble, as Mrs Daws had named them, and by the expressions on their faces she could tell they meant business.

25

'Good morning, Miss Sullivan,' Miss Snooper greeted her, sniffing as she looked Sarah up and down. 'The verger has told us of your requirement for new material so the girls can make items for the Christmas Fayre. I must say, we were most surprised to hear that, for they usually serve the refreshments.'

'And they still can, Miss Snooper,' she replied, making an effort to curb her impatience. 'It's customary for the boys to make things in order to raise funds, and I feel it is only fair the girls should be given the same opportunity.'

Miss Snooper sniffed. 'Really? Why? I mean, they are girls,' she said, emphasizing the word girls.

'And being girls, sewing skills will enhance both their employment and marriage prospects,' Sarah explained, forcing her lips to remain smiling.

'But do they really need new cloth?' Miss Prior asked, her beady eyes boring into Sarah.

Before she could reply, Miss Middle spoke. 'I see you are wearing yet another dress, Miss Sullivan,' she said, narrowing her eyes at Sarah's green skirts. 'Are our donations not good enough for you now, then?'

'Of course, Miss Middle, we are most grateful for your offerings. Actually, this dress is one which I have adapted to fit.'

'Oh, you sew, that explains it,' the woman muttered.

'It is a handy skill to have, Miss Middle, and as I said earlier, one that will benefit the girls throughout their lives. However, if we expect people to pay for the articles we make then the material really does need to be in pristine condition.'

As Miss Snooper sniffed and opened her mouth to say something else, Sarah noticed Jack Wise beckoning to her.

'Please excuse me, ladies. I believe the verger wishes to speak with me. But if you can assist with the materials, we will be most grateful. Good morning to you,' she said, smiling with relief as she hurried towards him.

'I do believe Miss Sullivan has set her hat at our dear verger,' Miss Snooper sniffed. Sarah couldn't resist turning and quoting the school motto.

'Love never faileth, Miss Snooper,' she called, stifling a giggle.

'I'm sorry for interrupting your conversation, Miss Sullivan,' Jack said, his eyes twinkling in a way that let her know he was anything but. 'I wanted you to know that, having given your request for new material my keenest attention, I have found the perfect solution.'

'Really, Mr Wise, er, Jack? That sounds marvellous, and so quickly too.' She smiled up at him and he beamed delightedly back.

'Let me introduce you to Mrs Knight and she will explain,' he said, ushering Sarah back to the porch where an elderly lady, sporting an elegantly trimmed bonnet, was waiting in a wicker Bath chair.

'This is Miss Sullivan from Red Cliffs, Mrs Knight. She is the person who has had the splendid idea that girls as well as boys should raise funds for the Christmas Fayre.'

'And quite right too,' the silver-haired woman, replied, giving Sarah such a warm smile, she knew she had an ally. 'Miss Sullivan, it is nice to make your acquaintance. I'm really interested in your project and might even be able to help. Do you have a few moments to talk?' Sarah looked down the path and saw the crocodile of children led by the master already making its way up the road towards the school.

'Yes, of course, Mrs Knight.' The woman beamed.

'Just give a wave when you're ready for me to push you home, Mrs Knight,' the verger said. Then, with another bright smile in Sarah's direction, he bounded over to where the vicar was now being interrogated by the three good ladies of the church.

'I do believe you have an admirer, my dear,' Mrs Knight chuckled. 'Now, I understand you are seeking new material for your girls to make aprons and other items for the Christmas Fayre.'

Sarah nodded. 'I feel it's important they should contribute to the fundraising, as well as serving refreshments. It would be good for their self-esteem and teach them a craft. Although there are some here who don't agree,' she added, looking over towards the three ladies.

'Don't worry about them, Miss Sullivan,' Mrs Knight said, following her glance. 'Everything's fine as long it is their idea. They consider themselves pillars of the community and hate to feel excluded.'

'Oh, I didn't realize,' Sarah muttered.

'Now, let's talk business. I quite agree the girls should raise funds too and would like to help. My husband, God bless him, was proprietor of a General Draper and Milliner's shop in the town until his death.' As Sarah went

246

to voice her sympathy, the woman held up her hand. 'It was a while ago now, and whilst I still miss him, life has to go on. Anyway, I managed to carry on running the business until last year when my rheumatics took a turn for the worse. I sold the shop to a Mr Day, would you believe,' she chuckled.

Sarah frowned. 'Oh, I see, Knight into Day,' she smiled, as the penny dropped.

'However, I still have a few bales of brightly coloured material along with boxes of trimmings languishing in my spare room at home. It would give me great pleasure to know they were being put to good use.'

'You mean you'd let the school buy them from you?' Sarah asked.

'Buy them? Good heavens, no, my dear. You are welcome to have them.'

'That's very kind of you, Mrs Knight, but we couldn't just take them. The ethos of Red Cliffs requires things to be earned.'

'Well, my dear, in that case you could say that Dr Lawrence more than earned the little I am offering. He was so kind when my George was ill, coming out at all hours even though he was busy with the school. Sadly, as he is now deceased himself, I can't pay that debt back. However, I can carry it forward, can't I?'

As the woman's clear grey eyes stared hopefully at her, Sarah found herself nodding. 'Thank you so much, Mrs Knight. Red Cliffs would be honoured to accept your kind gift.'

'Good, that's settled then. I understand from Jack that he lunches at Red Cliffs on a Sunday, so he can collect the things when he takes me home. He might have to make a few trips, but something tells me he would welcome the opportunity.' Mrs Knight laughed and gave Sarah the most outrageous wink. 'Now, I've kept you long enough,' she added, waving to Jack who immediately hurried over.

'I'll see you later, Miss Sullivan,' he beamed.

'Yes, you will, Jack. Thank you once again, Mrs Knight. I do hope you will visit the school to see how the girls are getting on with their sewing. Oh . . .' She stuttered to a halt as she remembered the woman was obviously an invalid.

'I'm not housebound, my dear, and I would love to visit. Now, come along, Jack. I'm ready for my luncheon.'

With another smile at Sarah, Jack began solicitously covering the woman with her blanket.

Pulling her shawl tighter against the brisk sea breeze, Sarah hurried back to Red Cliffs. How kind of Mrs Knight to let them have material, she thought, her brain buzzing with ideas for things the girls could make. She was impatient to share the news with them, but when she let herself into the house, the usual hectic round of dishing up of the Sunday lunches was already under way.

She watched the pupils serving meals to those children less fortunate than themselves and couldn't help marvelling once again at how insightful her godfather had been in setting up the school the way he had. The fragrant aroma of savoury stew made her stomach growl, and she was just about to comment when she saw the housekeeper scratching her head.

'Well, blow me, Miss Sullivan,' Mrs Daws said, pointing to the empty plate on the table. 'Knowing we were a bit short on bread, I specifically counted the number of slices I cut. April and Pip handed out the children's, but the slice I left here for you has disappeared.'

'Never mind, Mrs Daws, some of your delicious stew will suffice,' Sarah assured her, but the woman was not to be mollified.

'I'm happy to share what little we have, but will not tolerate stealing,' the housekeeper declared hotly.

'Perhaps there are more waifs here today than usual,' Sarah suggested.

'Pip did a head count for me. This is becoming a regular occurrence. Master Higgins thought it was Bunter but I'm not so sure,' the woman replied, sinking onto the chair next to Sarah. 'Between you and me, I've a feeling it's something to do with that Kitty. This began when she arrived, and April said she heard her slipping out of the dormitory during the night. Now, we have an open door policy, as you know, but it isn't natural or safe for a child to go wandering in the dark, and April said she was gone too long to have just slipped down to the privy.'

'She is getting enough to eat?' Sarah asked, remembering her godfather saying how starved some of the children were when they first arrived.

'I should say. I even did dumplings last night. No, I've a feeling something's not right. I can't put my finger on what it is, but I will,' she sighed.

'Did you find out about those marks on her back?' Sarah asked.

The housekeeper pursed her lips. 'Dr Hawkins reckoned she'd been lashed with a whip. Can you believe?'

'But that's terrible. Surely it wasn't her father?' Sarah gasped.

'No. When we had a little chat, she let on her father had died, and they'd had to move from the farm he tenanted somewhere near Dartmoor. Anyway, it seems her mother met a man who had no time for children and they both scarpered, leaving Kitty to fend for herself. Apparently a "gentleman" befriended her and set her to work thieving for him. On a good day, he'd feed her, but if her pickings weren't enough . . . well, you can imagine,' she sighed, getting to her feet.

'Poor girl, no wonder she's so worldly wise,' Sarah replied, thinking of the discussion the previous afternoon. 'We'll have to make her feel loved, give her cuddles, that sort of thing.'

'You've more chance of petting a wild dog,' Mrs Daws snorted. 'Now, I'd best take this pudding into the front room. Master Higgins was going to tell the vicar about the inspection over luncheon, so I thought it best they ate in there away from prying ears. I can't believe the things that Christian's accused Red Cliffs of. He was always such a nice little boy.'

'According to the master, he's walking out with Miss Green,' Sarah replied, not wishing to dwell on the past.

'Well, she'd better be careful, that's all I can say. Mind you, they're both conniving rats, so happen they deserve each other.'

As Sarah stared at the woman in surprise, the waifs began streaming out of the dining room.

'Fanks, missus,' one little lad chirped.

'Yeah, good grub,' another said.

'Well, that's the first sitting finished. Oh no, my poor head,' Mrs Daws groaned as Maisie began banging the gong with all her might. 'April will be supervising the girls, so can you dish your own stew?'

Sarah nodded. 'That's fine, Mrs Daws. I'm sorry I was late back, but the verger introduced me to Mrs Knight. She kindly offered us material and trimmings left from the sale of her shop.'

'Dorothy Knight, you were saying? Now there's a lovely woman,' Mrs Daws began, then broke off as Kitty came barging through the door. 'Hey, where've you been?'

'The privy,' she replied. Mrs Daws raised her brows, but Sarah noticed the little girl looked flushed and was breathing heavily.

'Well, enjoy your stew, Miss Sullivan, and I should have a rest while you're at it. I hear from Master Higgins that you've another evening of bookkeeping ahead.'

Sarah groaned. 'Don't remind me. It's good of him to help, though, especially as he can decipher the figures better than I can.'

By the time Sarah had finished her meal, the pupils were filing out of the dining room. Leaving them to clear away the dirty dishes, she went through to the office, ready to tackle the dreaded paperwork. Opening the door, she blinked in surprise, for spread out across her desk were bales of crisp gingham in the most beautiful reds, blues, greens and yellows. Perfect for aprons, Sarah thought, running her fingers over the material. There was also a carton of matching silks and buttons. A sudden thud in the corridor roused her from her musing. Jack staggered into the room, his head just discernible over a pile of boxes.

'Goodness, let me help you,' Sarah said, taking the top two from him.

'Thanks,' he puffed. 'I thought I'd manage these in one trip, as Mrs Knight always has a sleep after her luncheon, and I know you want to get started on the things for the Christmas Fayre.' He offloaded the rest of the boxes then gave her a dazzling smile. 'She has had a simply marvellous idea and wonders if she might take up your kind invitation to visit. Would tomorrow afternoon be convenient?'

'Well, yes, if she could make it about one o'clock, I'll see if I can get Pip to collect her,' Sarah said.

'No need,' he beamed. 'It's my afternoon for visiting the almshouses, so I can drop her off en route,' he explained.

'Perfect. I appreciate you dropping these materials in, Jack,' she began, but was interrupted by a knock on the door. 'Goodness, it's as busy as the railway station,' she exclaimed. 'Come in.'

'Sorry, I didn't know you were busy, Miss Sullivan,' Harry Higgins said. 'I can come back later.'

'No need, I'm just going,' Jack said, bounding towards the door. 'Until tomorrow afternoon then, Miss Sullivan, er, Sarah,' he added. With a final smile, he disappeared.

'He made it sound as if you have a date, Miss Sullivan,' Harry said, quirking a brow. Seeing his solemn expression, Sarah was tempted to tease him but thought better of it.

'Mrs Knight, who used to have a draper's shop, has given us these beautiful materials for the girls to make things for the Fayre,' she explained, gesturing to the bales on her desk. 'I invited her to visit the school, and Jack has kindly offered to bring her tomorrow afternoon, as she uses a Bath chair.'

'Oh, I see,' Harry replied, looking decidedly relieved. 'My mother used to sew, before Father died.' His face clouded for a moment. 'She'd love these bright colours.'

'Well, you can buy her one of the aprons we'll be making. It'll make an ideal Christmas present.'

'Don't talk of Christmas yet, please,' he groaned. 'Pip is doing a splendid job helping the boys with their woodworking projects but some of their results look rather odd to say the least.'

Sarah laughed. 'I have no idea how the girls' sewing will turn out. I know April will help but I've still got to get Miss Green to co-operate.'

'Please be tactful, Sarah. Whilst I don't agree with her methods, with this inspection looming we do need her on our side. And that brings me to Monday. As she's still not speaking, I called in to see the Deaconess earlier. She has a vacancy and will be happy to take the little girl as of this week.'

'So soon?' Sarah gasped, her heart sinking. 'Couldn't we give her a little more time?'

He gave her a sympathetic look, but shook his head. 'We have to think of Monday's welfare, Sarah, and we are not doing her any favours by delaying things, are we?'

26

Sarah hardly slept that night. The room was bitterly cold, with wind rattling the windowpanes and soughing down the chimney. She still felt uncomfortable being in her godfather's room, but Sarah knew Mrs Daws had been delighted to have her bedroom to herself again, so she hadn't mentioned her unease. While she should have been happy that, after a long evening working with Harry, the books were finally ready for the accountants to audit, she couldn't get Monday out of her mind. If only she could have spent more time with the little girl, perhaps it would have made a difference. She knew in her heart of hearts that Harry was right when he said they had to do what was in the child's best interest, but the thought of not seeing her dear little face each day cut through Sarah keener than the hooley raging outside.

She must have dozed off because the creak of the floorboard on the landing woke her. Knowing that Mrs Daws always made an early start, Sarah dressed quickly then stole down the stairs. The range in the kitchen was ablaze, its welcome warmth emanating around the room, whilst the kettle was on the hob to boil the first brew of the day. Marmalade, curled up on the chair, opened one eye, ascertained Sarah posed no threat, then promptly went back to sleep again.

'You're up even earlier than usual, Miss Sullivan,' the housekeeper said, hurrying through from the pantry and bringing with her a blast of cold air. Sarah could see the woman was looking disgruntled and wondered if she was put out at having her early morning peace invaded.

'Good morning, Mrs Daws. Is everything all right?'

'I don't know what this place is coming to, and that's a fact. This cheese is half the size it was when I put it away last night,' the woman grumbled.

'Perhaps it was mice,' Sarah suggested.

'Not unless they've learnt to use a blinkin' knife,' Mrs Daws snorted, pointing to the side of the cheese, which had been cut away neatly. 'Someone's been taking food when my back's turned, and I'm going to find out who it is,' she declared. Just then the kettle gave its welcome whistle.

'Shall I make some tea?' Sarah asked. 'It was so cold upstairs I'm surprised I didn't turn to ice overnight.'

The housekeeper let out a long sigh. 'Our coal stocks are dwindling fast. The good doctor always called November the month of mists, murk and managing. I just hope we have enough fuel to keep the range going until we get our delivery next month.'

Sarah looked up from pouring the hot water into the big brown pot. 'Shall I ask the coal merchant if he can call earlier?' she asked.

The housekeeper gave a snort. 'You can ask away, Miss Sullivan, but he won't deliver until he receives his money. Our benefactor pays for Red Cliffs to have the coal store filled in time for Christmas each year.'

'Oh, I see,' Sarah replied, thinking again how much she still had to learn about the running of Red Cliffs. 'Well, here's your tea. Now, what can I do to help? I've plenty of time before I have to leave for my appointment with the accountants. Which reminds me,' she said, staring down at the worn material of her dress, 'would it be all right to borrow something from the donation box, just for this morning,' she added quickly as the woman gave her a funny look. 'There's a navy blue coat that looks quite presentable, and as I shall be representing the school, I feel it is important to look as smart as I can.'

'This place is yours now, Miss Sullivan, so you hardly have to ask,' Mrs Daws replied. 'If you really want to lend a hand, you can help me knock up some bread, seeing as how we'll have to bake extra to make up for that cheese.'

The two women stood either side of the scrubbed table, mixing dough in companionable silence. The housekeeper was still looking pale, but Sarah couldn't determine if it was because of the theft of the cheese, the rapidly dwindling coal stocks or tiredness, for the woman did work exceedingly long hours. If only she didn't have to go into town, she could be of more help, Sarah thought.

Then she became aware of someone creeping into the room. Looking up, she saw it was Monday. Before Sarah could ask the little girl what she was doing, the child's eyes widened in amazement, and she made a beeline for the cat on the chair.

'Ginger, me pussy,' Monday cried. Sarah stared at the housekeeper in amazement, but as she opened her mouth to say something, the woman gave a slight shake of her head. 'Oh, Ginger, I knew you'd come and find me,' Monday murmured, picking the cat up from the chair and cuddling it tight. The look of pure happiness on her face brought tears to Sarah's eyes, and she saw the housekeeper hastily wiping her own with the corner of her apron.

'Well, I never,' Mrs Daws muttered. 'That cat has only ever let me pick him up before.'

'Ginger's mine, Sarah,' Monday cried. 'He lived with me before and must have come looking for me.'

'But he's . . .' Sarah began just as April came hurrying into the room.

'There you are, Monday, I've been looking for you everywhere,' she exclaimed.

'Ginger's come and found me,' the girl explained, giving April a beaming smile.

'And he's brought your voice too by the sound of it,' April chirped. 'Who'd have thought it was hiding in that old moggy all along.'

'He's thirsty and wants milk,' Monday announced, and to their astonishment, she placed the cat on the floor, picked up the jug and poured some of the white liquid into a saucer. 'Here you are, Ginger,' she crooned.

'Well, come along, it's time you were dressed ready for your own breakfast, young lady,' April insisted, bustling the little girl from the room. At the door, the maid stopped and winked. 'There'll be no stopping this one now, you wait and see,' she grinned.

As the door closed behind the maid, Mrs Daws shook her head. 'I do believe she's right, Miss Sullivan. It's times like these that make my job worthwhile. What's a bit of cheese compared to this? And as for you, Marmalade, if the little girl thinks you're her Ginger who am I to disillusion her? Since when have you drunk plain old milk, eh? You usually sulk if I don't give you the cream off the top.' The cat looked up from the empty saucer, licked its lips and gave a contented purr.

'Shouldn't we have kept Monday in here with us, Mrs Daws?' Sarah frowned.

'Good heavens, no. It's best she sticks to her routine. The familiarity will make her feel secure, although we'll monitor her progress, of course. Master Higgins will be delighted. He was bereft at the thought of her having to go to the Deaconess.'

'He was?' Sarah asked in surprise, her heart lifting. 'He seemed so matter-of-fact about it.'

'That's his way, Miss Sullivan. He always puts the interests of the children first, despite what he might be feeling in here,' the housekeeper said, patting her chest. 'Now, we'd best put this dough to prove or the children won't have any lunch.'

Sarah's meeting with the accountants went well, for she'd only had to hand over the ledgers and answer a few simple questions.

'We will ensure the accounts are audited before the local authority inspection, Miss Sullivan,' Mr Calculus advised her. 'Once again, please accept our condolences on the sad loss of your godfather. He was a fine man.'

'Thank you, Mr Calculus.'

Outside, Sarah dithered, wondering if she should pay a visit to Mr Fothergill. However, she didn't have an appointment, and he would probably be busy, she thought. As she turned towards the sea front, the biting wind stung her face, and she was glad for the warmth of the coat she'd borrowed. She was musing on the miracle of Monday finding her voice, when she caught sight of a little figure darting into Rock Walk. Surely that was Kitty, she frowned.

Weaving between carriages and traps, she hurried across the road and made her way through the sheltered walkway. Designed for those with a fashionably pale complexion to enjoy a pleasant promenade, the trees afforded a dense cover, and Sarah had to squint hard before she caught sight of the little girl dodging between the bushes. Stealing along on tiptoe so as not to alert her, Sarah gently parted the branches to find Kitty kneeling beside a skinny child of about five. He was covered in grime and, despite the cold weather, wore ill-fitting breeches and a torn top.

'I got you some bread and cheese, Luke,' Sarah heard the girl mutter.

'You bin so long, I starvin',' the boy answered, grabbing the food and stuffing it into his mouth. Then he caught sight of Sarah and froze. As he stared at her with bright grey eyes, Kitty spun around.

Her eyes widened in panic then she stood up and squared her shoulders. 'You bin following me?'

'No, I saw you from across the road and wondered why you weren't in class,' Sarah said gently.

'I 'ad to feed Luke, and that housekeeper's been watching the pantry like a hawk so I was later than usual. Oh,' she said, putting her hand to her mouth as she realized what she'd said. 'Suppose you won't want me back now, miss,' Kitty muttered, wrapping her hands around her bony shoulders as a sudden gust of wind whooshed up the walkway.

'Why don't we go back to Red Cliffs? You can tell me everything over a hot drink,' Sarah said.

'But I can't leave Luke, miss. 'E's got a bit of a fever and . . .'

'We'll all go,' Sarah said gently, holding her hand out to the little boy.

He stared uncertainly at Kitty, who nodded slowly. 'An 'ot drink would be nice, wouldn't it, Luke?' The little boy got to his feet and tentatively took hold of Sarah's outstretched hand. ''E's my bruvver, miss,' Kitty explained. 'I 'id him in the bushes 'cos it was warmest, but he's been coughing somefink chronic.'

'Let's hurry back to the warm kitchen. I'm sure Mrs Daws will know what to do,' Sarah reassured her. She could only guess at the little girl's anguish at having to leave her brother in the gardens. It seemed the mystery of the missing bread and cheese had been solved, anyway.

'Well, well, what have we here,' the housekeeper clucked as Sarah ushered Kitty and Luke into the kitchen.

'It would appear Kitty hid her little brother, Luke, in Rock Park,' Sarah explained. 'He seems to have a bit of a fever and must be hungry, for he's been surviving on the scraps Kitty took him.'

'And would that be my best bread and cheese, young lady?' asked the housekeeper, narrowing her eyes at Kitty.

'Sorry, Mrs Daws. I didn't know what else to do when the copper took me away from the guv. Will you tell on me?' she asked, turning to Sarah.

'No, I won't,' Sarah promised.

260

'April, love, can you come here a minute,' Mrs Daws called. 'It's a bath and warm bed for you, young man,' she told the young boy. He pulled a face and she laughed. 'When you're clean you can have a nice bowl of broth, how about that?'

The little boy's face lit up, and Kitty turned to the housekeeper. 'Can I have one too?' she asked.

The woman nodded. 'I dare say by the time this young man's clean and tidy it will be time for luncheon anyway. Ah, April there you are. It seems we have another new boy for Master Higgins to school. First, though, he needs the usual carbolic treatment. Can you take him out to Mrs Laver for me?'

''Cors I will. What you called, then?' April asked in her easy manner.

'Luke Matthew Bawden,' he replied.

'Well, Luke Matthew Bawden, just you follow me.'

As the door closed behind them, Sarah turned to Kitty. 'While Luke is being bathed, let's have that hot drink and you can tell us how all this came about.'

'I'd just made a brew when you arrived,' Mrs Daws said, pulling the big brown pot in front of her and pouring out three cups of weak tea. 'I'm afraid the leaves are past their best really, but . . .' she shrugged.

'Mam always said as long as it's hot and wet then you was in clover,' Kitty sighed, then took a large gulp of her tea.

Mrs Daws and Sarah exchanged glances.

'You must miss her,' the housekeeper said.

'Not much good if I do, is it?' The girl sighed again as if she had the weight of the world on her shoulders.

'So, if Luke Matthew Bawden is your brother then you must be Kitty Bawden,' Sarah said.

'Kitty Alice Bawden,' she replied.

'Now, that is posh,' Mrs Daws said.

Kitty looked shamefaced. 'Sorry missus, I didn' dare give you me full name in case you told that copper.'

'Why would that matter?' Sarah asked. 'I mean, the police are here to help.'

'You havin' a laugh? The guv made me steal from them people who got off the trains and 'e said if I told anyone I'd be banged up as an 'complice. 'Cors, I was never allowed to keep anyfink. But he fed me – sometimes.'

The housekeeper gave a horrified snort. 'Did he know about Luke?' she asked.

Kitty shook her head. 'He's a bit slow, like. Mam said she could have called him Simon like the rhyme. Vat's why I 'as to look out for 'im. Me middle name's after Alice in Wonderland. Now, she was right pretty.'

'Yes,' Sarah replied. 'Just like you.'

'Now you are 'avin a larf,' Kitty scoffed.

'No, I'm not actually. Looking after Luke must have been a huge responsibility,' Sarah said, sipping her tea thoughtfully.

'Yeah, well, I weren't much good at it 'cos we was almost always 'ungry.'

'Tell me about this guv. Was he the brains behind the thefts from the railways?'

Kitty hooted so much she almost spilled her tea. 'Oops, sorry, missus,' she said, glancing quickly at Mrs Daws. 'Na, he's a drunk, does what he's told by this posh toff. We dun the stealin', gave the stuff to the guv, who sold it or passed it on to the toff if it was something 'spensive, like.'

'And you never got caught?' Sarah asked.

'Nah, see, I worked with the flower seller on the station steps. When she had a customer choosing a posy, I'd nab his purse. Easy peasy,' she grinned.

'Goodness,' Mrs Daws said weakly. 'In all my years here I've never heard such a story. And this flower seller was in on the act?'

''Cors not, or she'd want a cut. Nah, I seed this toff lift a wallet once. Right posh he was. You'd never fink he'd need the dosh. Anyhow, it was all in the way he did it, see. He said somefink to this geezer, looking him straight in the eye while his fingers nab the purse.'

'Then you copied this, er, toff?' Sarah asked.

Kitty nodded.

'But how do you know which pocket to go for?' Mrs Daws asked.

'By looking for the bulge,' Sarah replied, remembering the day her purse had been stolen.

'Coo, 'ave you dun it too, miss? I wouldn't 'ave fort you was the type.' Kitty said, looking Sarah up and down with something close to admiration.

Just then, the door opened, and Master Higgins came in, rubbing his hands together against the cold.

'Ah, Kitty, I wondered where you'd got to,' he said. 'I suppose you think you know everything, do you?'

'Na, I don't. But I bet I know somefink you don't,' she replied.

'Oh, and pray what might that be?' he asked.

'Miss Sullivan is a fingersmith,' she hooted.

27

At this revelation, Harry and Mrs Daws chuckled at the unlikely image of the prim Miss Sullivan skulking around, picking people's pockets. Sarah was about to protest her innocence when Harry squatted down beside Kitty.

'You shouldn't judge everything by whatever has gone on in your past. That is all over, I hope. This is now your home, and as a pupil of Red Cliffs, it is important that you trust us. Along with Mrs Daws, Miss Sullivan is the most honest person I have met, understand me?' he asked.

Kitty studied him gravely for a moment, then nodded. 'I suppose you 'ave to be good to be in charge here.'

'I'm glad you understand that,' he said gently. Then the door opened once more, and April came in with Luke wrapped in a towel. Although he was shivering, his eyes were bright and looked even bigger now with his shorn head.

'A new pupil?' Harry asked, leaning over and feeling the little boy's forehead.

'Yes, Master Higgins. This is Kitty's brother, Luke Matthew Bawden, all carbolicked and deloused,' April chirped.

'The word is carbolated,' Harry corrected.

'That'll 'ave got rid of the itching and now yous can 'ave some grub,' Kitty told him.

'Right, young Kitty, you run along and get yourself cleaned up for luncheon, unless you want me to get

Mrs Laver to pop you in the washing copper?' Mrs Daws said, lifting the lid off the pan of broth so that the kitchen was filled with a tantalizing aroma. 'Well, go along then,' the woman urged.

'I goin', I goin',' the girl replied, disappearing outside.

'Don't leaf me,' Luke wailed.

'Kitty's only going out the yard, young Luke. She'll be back in a jiffy,' April said, pulling a woollen shirt over the yawning boy's head. 'Now we'll get you something to eat.'

'If he stays awake long enough,' Harry said as the boy yawned again. He pulled out the chair beside Sarah, and she was immediately aware of his nearness. Unaware of the emotions he was causing, he continued. 'I'll get Dr Hawkins to call in on his way back from surgery. That little boy looks like he's running a bit of a temperature. Where did he spring up from?' he asked, lowering his voice.

'I spotted Kitty making for the Rock Walk on my return from the accountants. Apparently she'd hidden her brother there and was taking food from here to feed him,' Sarah explained.

'Ye gods, so that's why the bread was disappearing. I have sorely maligned young Bunter,' Harry replied, shaking his head. 'So we have a full house now, then, as Monday will be staying. Do you know, that girl hasn't stopped chatting all morning?' He paused and smiled at Sarah. 'You must be pleased?'

'Oh, I am,' she cried. Then, remembering her god-father's warning, she quickly added, 'As I would be for any of them.'

He gave her a knowing look. 'How did you get on at the accountants?'

'I handed the books over to Mr Calculus, signed a few forms. He confirmed that everything appeared to be in order and that the accounts would be audited before the inspection.' She broke off as Monday came in followed by Kitty.

'I've been doing sums, Miss Sullivan, and drawing,' said Monday. 'This afternoon we're going to do stories. I love stories.'

'Coo blimey, girl, fort the cat 'ad got your tongue,' Kitty said, staring at the girl in surprise.

'No, silly, he's been hiding my voice,' she laughed. 'Oh Maisie,' she said, as the door opened again. 'I wondered where you'd gone.'

'Wee wees,' Maisie said. 'As I bin a good girl, can I bang the gong, Mrs Daws?'

'Go on, then,' the woman said, laughing. 'Right, you little lot, into the dining room.' She winced as the reverberating gong was followed by the usual stampede. 'Young Luke, are you going to sit here with me in the kitchen and have a bite to eat?' she asked, turning to the boy, but he had fallen asleep in April's arms.

'I think he should be put to bed in the room behind the kitchen, Mrs Daws. It will be warmer in there, and I want Dr Hawkins to check him over before he mixes with the others,' Harry said. 'Come along, Sarah, it looks as though you're supervising luncheon along with me. A word to the wise, though. It might be an idea to have Kitty sitting by you. It'll help her settle now that she doesn't have to worry about her brother.'

*

By the time the children had eaten and were exercising in the grounds, the verger and Mrs Knight had arrived.

'We'll go through to my office, shall we?' Sarah invited, but Mrs Knight, sporting another fashionably trimmed bonnet, was staring thoughtfully at the children.

'Do you mind if we stand here and watch for a few moments?'

'No, of course not,' Sarah said, trying not to show her surprise at the woman's interest. 'I can't thank you enough for the beautiful material and accessories. I couldn't believe it when Jack staggered through the door with it all.' The verger beamed but before he could say anything, Mrs Knight was speaking.

'It is my pleasure, and I've had an idea which might help you to prepare for the inspection. I hope you won't think me presumptuous, but I've invited the good ladies of the church to join us, Miss Sullivan.' She turned her candid gaze on Sarah, who forced her lips to remain smiling. Mrs Knight was watching the children with a gentle smile on her face. 'Those little darlings remind me of starlings, the way they flit about,' she observed.

'Anything less like a murmuration, I have yet to see,' Master Higgins laughed, coming up behind them. 'More like a stampede of crazy elephants, Mrs Knight.'

'Master Higgins, good afternoon to you,' the woman smiled. 'You might pretend to be stern but I can tell you are fond of them.'

'Well, I always was a glutton for punishment,' he quipped. 'Good afternoon, verger.'

'Good afternoon, Master Higgins,' Jack replied.

'Please excuse me, everyone, but I have to prepare the classroom so it's ready for the onslaught, so I'll bid you good afternoon.'

'Remember me to your dear mother,' Mrs Knight called after him.

'I feel we should go inside, Mrs Knight,' Sarah said, noting the rising wind and worried the woman would catch a chill.

'Very well, my dear. I have seen all I need. Would you mind, Jack?' she asked.

'My pleasure, Mrs Knight,' the verger responded cheerily and began pushing the chair towards the back door. 'It'll be easier this way.'

'Now, before the others join us, I would like to outline my idea, Miss Sullivan,' the woman said as Jack closed the office door behind them. 'I know how much importance the local authority places on uniform these days, and I have to say I agree with the principle. It places all the children on the same level.'

'But . . .' Sarah began.

'Just hear me out, if you would, Miss Sullivan. When I was looking out the gingham yesterday, I came across a quantity of heavy cotton material which could be used to make smocks for the girls and long shirts for the boys. Thus dressed, they would look uniform, would they not?'

'Why, yes, they would and it's a marvellous idea, Mrs Knight. However, that sounds like an awful lot of work, and we only have a matter of weeks before the inspection,' Sarah pointed out. 'Why, the cutting out and sewing alone would take many hours.'

'Hand-sewing, yes, but I have one of Mr Singer's wonderful machines at home and could run up the items in next to no time. It would be the trimmings and buttons that would take the time, and this is where the second part of my plan, the ladies, come in.'

As Sarah stared at the woman in surprise, there was a ringing of the front doorbell.

'The good ladies have arrived,' Jack announced, waving from his position at the window. 'Shall I let them in, Sar . . . I mean, Miss Sullivan,' he amended darting a quick look at the older woman.

'Do say you agree, Miss Sullivan,' Mrs Knight urged.

'Well, it's a very kind offer and I can see how it would give a better impression if the children were dressed in some kind of uniform, but are you sure?' she asked, thinking of the time constraints.

'Leave it to me,' she whispered, as Jack showed the ladies into the room.

'The Misses Snooper, Prior and Middle,' he announced grandly, bowing as he ushered them into the room. 'Do make yourselves comfortable,' he added, gesturing towards the chairs.

'Ladies, thank you so much for coming,' Mrs Knight greeted them effusively. 'As I am sure you know, somebody has called for Red Cliffs to be inspected again.' The ladies nodded in unison. 'Being smartly attired ladies yourselves, I hardly need tell you the importance appearance plays in creating a favourable impression.' The ladies nodded again, and Mrs Knight smiled. 'I'm sure you will agree the children would look better uniformly dressed.'

'Oh, indeed,' they chorused.

'Smart appearance, smart mind,' Miss Snooper added.

'Precisely, Miss Snooper, I knew a lady such as yourself would grasp the significance immediately,' Mrs Knight replied. 'So, ladies, we are all agreed that the pupils of Red Cliffs would receive a more positive reaction if they were similarly dressed?'

'Goodness me, yes, Mrs Knight,' Miss Prior replied, casting her beady eyes over Sarah's dress. Thanking her lucky stars that it was the beginning of the week and her clothing was clean, Sarah smiled. 'You only have to hear the comments in church on a Sunday to realize that local people would prefer the children to be smartly dressed. Not that we are ones to cast aspersions ourselves, of course,' she finished, smiling superciliously.

There was a muffled snort from the corner, and as the ladies turned towards him, the verger hid his face in his kerchief.

'I was just agreeing with Mrs Knight's splendid suggestion when we hit upon a snag,' Sarah said quickly.

'A snag which we cannot see how we can overcome.' Mrs Knight sighed deeply and stared down at her hands.

'Perhaps we might be of assistance,' Miss Snooper said. 'We good ladies of the church are renowned for our enterprise and pride ourselves on assisting wherever we can.'

'That is most kind of you, ladies,' Mrs Knight began. 'However, I think this might be beyond even your capabilities.'

'Well, if you don't tell us, we won't know, will we?' Miss Middle countered.

'That is true, Miss Middle. You see, I have this marvellous cotton material at home which would be suitable for smocks and shirts. Now, I am happy to run these up for the children, ready for the school inspection but, alas, would never be able to add all the trimmings and buttons on so many garments with such time constraints.'

As Mrs Knight shook her head and fell silent, Sarah inwardly applauded the woman's guile.

'I have it,' Miss Snooper cried. 'We, the good ladies of the church, can assist.'

'You can?' Mrs Knight gasped, clutching her hands to her chest.

'Goodness me, yes,' Miss Prior added. 'My sewing skills are second to none.'

'We can have them ready, just like that,' Miss Middle added, snapping her fingers.

'Are you sure, ladies? I mean, it would need a concerted effort over the next couple of weeks or so?' Sarah asked.

'We're sure,' they chorused.

'But where would you meet?'

'I could put my front room at our disposal, ladies,' Mrs Knight suggested. 'Then, as soon as I finish on the machine, the garment can be passed on to you for hand-finishing.'

'We can form a sewing bee,' Miss Snooper cried.

'Yes, we shall be busy, busy bees,' Miss Prior cried.

'Very busy, busy bees,' Mrs Middle added.

'There, Miss Sullivan, I told you we good ladies of the church would solve your problem,' Miss Snooper said, giving a sniff. 'We have the well-being of the community at heart and are always at the centre of its affairs, aren't we, verger?'

'Yes, ladies, I can safely say you are,' Jack agreed, his lips twitching.

'Well, now we've solved your little glitch, we'd better be leaving, Miss Sullivan. We are very busy ladies, you know,' Miss Snooper said. As one, the three ladies rose to their feet. 'Shall we say ten thirty tomorrow morning, Mrs Knight?'

'That would be splendid, Miss Snooper. I shall make a start as soon as Jack here has delivered me safely home.'

'Allow me, ladies,' Jack said, jumping up and opening the door.

As Sarah and Mrs Knight stared triumphantly at each other, the ladies could be heard outside, singing 'We are the busy bees' as they made their way down the driveway. No sooner had Jack re-entered the room than the three of them burst out laughing.

'That was a terrific performance, Mrs Knight,' Sarah cried.

The woman shrugged. 'You heard Miss Snooper. By her own admission, they are always at the centre of community affairs, and by now I should think it will be halfway around Torquay that they have solved our dilemma,' Mrs Knight smiled. 'Now, if I'm to make a start on cutting out, you'd better take me home, verger.'

'I'm so sorry if we've delayed you, Jack,' Sarah said.

'I wouldn't have missed the show for the world,' he admitted. 'Although if the vicar should ask, I was merely carrying out parish duties.' With a wink and smile, he wheeled Mrs Knight to the door.

'I can't thank you enough, Mrs Knight,' Sarah said.

'My dear, it has given me a sense of purpose as well as an opportunity to rekindle my love of amateur dramatics. Do please feel free to call around anytime to check on the progress of our sewing.'

With a final warm smile in Sarah's direction, Jack wheeled Mrs Knight out of the front door. As Sarah went back inside, she distinctly heard the sound of Mrs Knight, accompanied by the verger, singing 'We are the busy bees'.

Just wait until I tell Harry, she thought. Harry, goodness, she was meant to be sitting in on afternoon lessons. Quickly straightening her skirts, she hurried down to the schoolroom.

'Good afternoon, Miss Sullivan,' Harry greeted her.

'Good afternoon, Master Higgins. I'm sorry I'm late,' she apologized. It was only as a titter ran around the class that she realized what she'd said. Harry's lips twitched, and she realized he was wondering whether or not to pursue the subject. Darting him her sternest look, she was relieved to see him turn to the blackboard.

'Now, to continue with our sums, who can tell me the answer to this? If I had twelve iced buns and took one away how many would be left?'

'None, sir.'

'None, Black? How do you make that out?'

'If I saw twelve iced buns I'd have to eat them all so there'd be none left,' he chortled.

As the class dissolved into hysterics, the master opened his desk, took out his tawse and held it in the air.

'I ain't staying 'ere to be whipped,' Kitty cried, jumping to her feet.

'Sit down, Kitty,' the master ordered.

'Not blinkin' likely. I got enuf scars on me back already,' she sobbed. Before Sarah could stop her, she fled from the room.

28

As shocked silence descended on the schoolroom, Harry saw Sarah getting to her feet and motioned for her to remain seated. The look of disapproval she was giving him made him speak more sharply than he'd intended.

'Right, Black,' he snapped. 'This upset has been brought about by your mischievous bent so you will atone by continuing with the lesson.'

'Me, sir?' he squeaked, suddenly looking unsure of himself.

'Yes, Black, you. Come to the front of the class and take everyone through their tables, starting with two times two for the younger ones and continuing until you reach twelve times twelve.' As the boy blanched, Harry walked towards the door. 'Miss Sullivan, please take charge in my absence and report any mistakes Black makes when I return.' Without waiting for a response, he strode from the room.

Cursing himself for not remembering Kitty had been lashed by that callous brute, Harry peered around the grounds. He only ever used the tawse as a deterrent, but the poor child wasn't to know that. Suddenly, he caught sight of a movement and saw Kitty pelting hell for leather towards the end of the garden. By the time he reached her, she was leaning against the fence, watching seagulls wheeling and swooping across the bay.

'It would be lovely to be free like that, wouldn't it?' he asked softly.

'Not 'arf,' she sighed. 'I ain't comin' back to be whipped,' she added, her eyes narrowing. 'I had enough lashings from the guv.'

'That was unforgivable behaviour on his part. I just wanted you to know that I never actually use the tawse, Kitty.'

'Yeah, right,' she sneered. 'Why you got it, then?'

'To act as a deterrent to the pupils,' he explained.

'A whata?' she asked.

'It's meant as a warning,' he smiled.

'Well, why didn't you say that?' The way she stood staring at him reminded Harry of a cat sizing up an enemy. 'Why don't you just tell them off?'

'I do, but they don't always listen,' he sighed. 'Seeing the tawse makes them think twice about misbehaving in the first place. It acts as a reminder of what could happen if they do. I can't expect you to understand, but it's a big responsibility, ensuring they don't come to any harm whilst they're in my care.'

'I do understand, 'cos it were my duty to look after me bruvver and . . . Oh blimey, I'd forgotten about Luke. I can't leave without him,' she said, turning back towards the path.

'Luke has a fever, Kitty. He's sleeping at the moment, and Dr Hawkins is calling in to check on him after he's finished his surgery.'

'He will be all right?' she asked, anxiously.

'I'm sure he will. Better to get him looked over first, though,' he replied. 'Then, if he gets the all clear, you can leave before supper.'

'Before supper,' Kitty muttered, screwing up her face and staring back over the bay. She looked so forlorn, Harry's heart went out to the little girl. 'You couldn't leave after because it would be dark and unsafe for young Luke to be wandering around.'

'Nor safe for me, mister. You 'ave no idea what some men suggest. I mean, I might be poor but I got me morals. And I ain't no charity case, either.'

Harry swallowed hard. This was certainly one proud young lady; he'd have to take things gently if he was to persuade her to stay. 'Well, for a start you are deemed a minor by law which means the local authority have a duty to pay something towards your upkeep.'

'Ain't heard about that before,' she said, eying him suspiciously.

'Well, it happens to be true. Secondly, I'd be upset if you did decide to leave,' he murmured.

'Why? What's it to you?' she asked, glaring at him.

He gave a long sigh. 'Well, apart from the fact that I can see you are bright and would benefit from a good education, there's a pupil here who would gain from your help.'

'Me? 'Elp someone? 'Ow?' she asked, curiosity getting the better of her.

'This girl is desperate to be liked by the others so spends her time acting as though she's a hard nut. She thinks by playing pranks and being disruptive they will admire her, but in truth they generally tend to steer clear of her.'

'Not surprised. That's a daft way to go about things, ain't it?' she said.

Harry nodded. 'I agree, Kitty, but the thing is, she won't listen to a grown-up like me. She needs someone nearer her age to guide her. Someone with a more mature outlook who understands what makes people tick.' Seeing he had her attention, he shrugged his shoulders dramatically.

'Well, I nos 'bout people, that's for sure,' Kitty sighed.

'As I say, you would make the perfect friend for her. Still, as Mrs Daws has told you, we never keep people here against their will, so . . .' He let his words hang in the air and stared studiously out over the sea. As he listened to the waves being sucked into the crevices around the base of the red cliffs, he prayed Kitty would be sucked in by his plan. This little girl, with her shell-like exterior, needed the help and protection of the school more than she realized.

'Well, I bin finkin', like,' Kitty said after a few moments. 'Luke needs to see this doctor, and if 'e's poorly, it would be cruel not to let 'im 'ave' is supper, 'specially as 'e missed 'is lunch, so I could hang around and 'elp, as long as you promise not to use that whip.'

'Well, if you're really sure?' he asked, trying to appear nonchalant.

'What's 'er name?' Kitty asked.

'A teacher never divulges secrets, Kitty, but between you and me, she's the only girl in the class who has nobody sitting next to her.'

'Ah, got yer,' Kitty said, tapping the side of her nose with her finger. 'If you think she needs me then we'd better go back right now, hadn't we?'

As Kitty hurried back along the path, Harry let out a sigh of relief. If Kitty and Edith helped each other, he could get back to his task of ensuring the pupils were ready for the inspection.

By the time they re-entered the classroom, Black was struggling with his eight times table.

'So, Miss Sullivan, how does young Black here measure up as a teacher?' he asked.

'He tried very hard, Master Higgins,' she replied, diplomatically.

'But Miss had to keep putting him right,' Edith sniggered before turning in surprise as Kitty slipped into the seat alongside her.

'Right, then,' Harry said. 'If you have given the class their mathematical instruction for the afternoon, you may return to your seat, Black.' Immediately the boy scuttled back to his bench. 'It is important you can all write the letters of your name clearly when the inspector visits. I have penned the appropriate letters out for each of you to copy.' He went around the room handing each pupil their name card. 'You will spend the next thirty minutes copying the letters onto your slates.' He was about to give Monday hers when a thought struck him. Hunkering down beside the little girl, he smiled. 'Now you have found your voice, I wonder if you can tell us your real name?'

''Cors I can,' Monday nodded. 'It's Monday,' she cried.

'What a day,' Harry muttered as they made their way towards the kitchen for a much-needed hot drink.

'I can feel your frustration from here,' Sarah sighed, looking at the pupils, who, heedless of the cold wind blowing in from the sea, were running around enjoying the freedom of the garden.

'It was a stupid lapse on my part to bring out that tawse,' he admitted.

'To be honest, I was thinking more of the difficulty you face having to teach such a wide-ranging age group. It must take a lot of planning,' she said gently.

He stared at her in surprise. 'Fancy you realizing that. It is a challenge but . . .' He stopped as an agitated Kitty came hurtling towards them.

'I 'ate you, miss. You promised I could trust you,' she shrieked.

'And you can, Kitty,' Sarah assured her.

'Then why's that copper come back? I'm getting Luke, then I'm off. I ain't waitin' around to be banged up.'

As she began to run away, Harry's arm shot out and pulled her back. 'You are not going anywhere, young lady, until we get everything sorted out. Now, come along. We'll go and see exactly what the policeman wants. You never know, it could be good news,' he said.

'Like that's goin' to 'appen,' Kitty snorted but let him lead her into the kitchen.

'Good afternoon, Miss Sullivan, Master Higgins,' Sergeant Watts said, getting to his feet. From the look of the empty cup and half-eaten seed cake, he had been there some time.

'There you are, Kitty. Fancy running off like that,' Mrs Daws scolded. Kitty glared at the housekeeper.

'What can we do to help you, Sergeant?' Sarah asked.

'I'm here on official business,' he said, puffing out his chest importantly. 'Perhaps we should go through to your office, miss.'

Sarah stared from Kitty's scared expression to the policeman's pompous one and shook her head. 'It's much warmer in here, Sergeant. Anything you have to say can be heard by everyone.'

'Well, if you're sure,' he replied, looking doubtful.

'Shall we all make ourselves comfortable around the table?' Sarah suggested. 'Ah, April,' she added, as the girl came in and stared at them, open-mouthed. 'Would you please supervise the children and make sure we are not disturbed?'

'Yes, Miss Sullivan,' she replied.

'Right, Sergeant,' Sarah continued as soon as the door closed behind the girl. 'Perhaps you would like to explain why you are here.'

'Indeed, Miss Sullivan,' he replied, pulling out his notebook and flipping it open. 'We have apprehended a certain Mr Cedric Smith.'

'That's the guv,' Kitty cried. 'Is he banged up?'

'He is helping us with our enquiries, yes. He was caught taking a wallet from a gentleman as he alighted from the train at the station.'

'He never were no good at thievin'. That's why he got us to . . .' Kitty's voice trailed away, and she looked fearfully at the sergeant. 'Suppose you goin' to bang me up an' all?'

Sarah reached out and took hold of the little girl's hand. 'She is only a child, Sergeant.'

'Quite, miss, and we at the local constabulary pride ourselves on the fair and understanding way in which we conduct ourselves,' the man replied, staring sternly at her through his glasses. 'As I was saying, Miss Sullivan, we have apprehended one Cedric Smith and need more information from young, er, Kitty here.' He paused and stared solemnly at the girl. 'Now, young lady, I want you to tell me exactly what your business was with this Mr Smith.'

'He made me steal things,' Kitty muttered, looking down at her lap.

'What kind of things, where and when?' the sergeant asked, his pencil poised.

'Off the trains or at the station, mainly. There's good pickings from the swells coming here on holiday, and if I got him a decent amount of dosh, I'd get food and a straw bed behind the sidings.'

'So, this Mr Smith is the brains of the operation?' Sergeant Watts asked.

''Im? 'E ain't got no brains,' Kitty hooted. 'Just does what the toff tells him.'

'This toff, does he have a name?' the sergeant asked, pencil poised.

'Guv called 'im "that conniving bastard",' Kitty shrugged.

'Do you know what he looks like?' Harry asked gently.

'Yeah, I seed 'im once. Told you, didn't I, miss, how he 'ad the best sleight of 'and I ever seen. Suppose, with 'is smart cloves and topper, no one thought 'e were a fingersmith.'

'And this smartly dressed gentleman was Mr Smith's boss?'

Kitty nodded. 'And loads of uvvers. He 'ad all sorts workin' for 'im. Once 'e'd marked their card, that were it, they were in the net.'

'Marked their card?' Mrs Daws snorted. 'What kind of language is that?'

'It's street speak,' Kitty told the woman grandly. 'Means 'e had somefink on 'em 'e could shop to the cops if they didn't come up with the goods.'

'But how did you get involved with such a man?' Sarah asked.

Kitty sighed like an old woman. 'Caught me pinching off the barrow, did'n' 'e? Luke were starving,' she added, staring at the policeman defensively.

'Luke being your brother?' Sergeant Watts asked. 'And what would his surname be?'

'You ain't catchin' me like that. You said I was sharp, didn't you, Master Higgins?' the girl chirped gleefully.

'I certainly did, Kitty,' he agreed. 'Sergeant Watts, what exactly is it you want from Kitty?'

'I already have what I came for, sir,' the sergeant said, snapping his notebook shut. 'Kitty here has confirmed our suspicions that the thieving ring operating around the stations is being masterminded by a "toff", as she puts it. Wouldn't happen to remember the colour of his hair, I suppose?' he asked, turning to Kitty.

'Cors I do. Memory like an elephant, I 'as. Fair 'air and blue eyes 'e uses to charm the ladies,' she replied. 'Not me, though, 'cos I seed through 'im.'

'That's most helpful, Kitty,' Sergeant Watts replied, opening his little black book again and jotting down the details. Kitty beamed. 'Right, I'll be off. Is this young lady to stay here at Red Cliffs?'

'I is, 'cos I 'as to 'elp Master Higgins with someone, don't I?' she replied, staring at the master.

'You do indeed, Kitty,' he replied gravely.

'So does that mean you aren't pressing charges against Kitty?' Sarah asked.

'No, she has helped us with our enquiries and is free to go,' the sergeant replied, getting to his feet and snatching up his helmet. 'Hopefully, added to what we already know, this information will help to put the man at the top away for some time.'

'Will he and the guv be punished?' Kitty asked.

'Well, we will have to see what the magistrate decides, but yes, I think I can safely say they will be punished.'

'Good, well, give them both at least fifty real 'ard lashes each from me, 'cos they deserve it,' she said with feeling.

Trying to hide his smile, the sergeant turned to the housekeeper. 'Thank you for the tea, Mrs Daws. Good day to you, Miss Sullivan, Master Higgins.'

As the door closed behind him, Sarah turned to Kitty who was beaming like a beacon.

'Well done. You have done your duty, and as the sergeant says, you are free to stay with us now.'

'Yeah, but he ain't much good as a copper, though, is he?'

'Why do you say that?' Harry asked.

'Well, 'e never remembered I hadn't told him my surname, did he?' she hooted.

29

The next afternoon, it was with some trepidation that Sarah, armed with gingham and silks, made her way to the classroom. Hoping the schoolmistress would be amenable, she pushed open the door to find the girls sitting by themselves. A tiny fire was glowing in the grate but it wasn't sufficient to take the chill off the room.

'Where is Miss Green?' she asked.

'She hasn't turned up,' Edith called. Sarah just had time to register the girl was sitting alongside Kitty when there was a knock, and Master Higgins appeared in the doorway.

'It would appear Miss Green has been unavoidably detained,' he announced. 'Still, that could be convenient for you, Sarah,' he added, lowering his voice so the girls didn't hear. 'You can start them on their aprons and what-not, and it will be a *fait accompli* by the time she deigns to turn up.' He grinned conspiratorially, and Sarah felt her pulse quicken.

'It will certainly make life easier,' she agreed.

'Well, I'd better get back to the workroom and see if I can salvage those boats for the Christmas Fayre,' he chuckled. 'Actually, it's refreshing to have something creative to do rather than concentrating on the inspection. See you later,' he said, giving her a salute.

'Right, girls, as you've gathered, Miss Green has been detained, so let's make a start.'

'Hope it's at Her Majesty's pleasure,' Edith chortled, only to be dug in the ribs by Kitty's elbow.

'Shall we move these tables together so we can spread out the gingham?' Sarah suggested. At once, there was a lot of scraping and thumping as they were pushed together.

'What are we making?' Kitty asked.

'Aprons to sell at the Christmas Fayre,' Monday said proudly. 'Miss said she was going to show us how it's done.'

'Yeah, 'cos we're not just serving the freshiments this year,' June piped up.

'The word is refreshments, June, but well remembered,' she added as the little girl's face fell. 'Although serving the refreshments will still be an important part of our role, if you remember, we are also going to make items to sell at the Fayre. Now, I want you to watch carefully as I place this pattern on the material.'

'But it's only a plain bit of paper, miss,' Maggie pointed out.

'Ah, but it's cut out in the shape of the apron. This is so all the ones we make will be of uniform size. Now we pin this pattern to the gingham and cut carefully around it.'

'Can we choose what colour material we use?' Ellen asked.

'You can indeed. Then the ladies can choose which colour apron they want to buy. Now please keep quiet for a few minutes and watch.'

To her surprise, the room fell silent as a dozen pairs of eyes followed her every move. By the time she'd cut out twelve apron-shaped pieces, the girls were ecstatic.

'Coo, they look like aprons already, miss,' Edith claimed in surprise.

Encouraged by the girls' enthusiasm, Sarah let them choose one piece each and was just passing around matching silks when the door opened.

'What is the meaning of this? And who said you could move my benches around?' Miss Green snapped, her beady eyes taking in the scene before her.

'Good afternoon, Miss Green,' Sarah replied sweetly. 'In your absence, I have shown the girls how to pin a pattern and then cut out the aprons ready to sew them up for the Christmas Fayre.'

There was a heavy silence as the woman put her hands on her hips and glared around the room. 'That was not what I had intended them doing this afternoon, Miss Sullivan. Believe you me, they will make a pig's ear of that material.'

'We's not making piggies' ears, miss, we's making aprons,' Maisie announced, puffing out her little chest proudly.

'As I am here now, Miss Sullivan, you may leave me to conduct my intended lesson,' the schoolmistress ordered.

Sarah glanced at the clock on the wall and shook her head. 'There is only fifteen minutes remaining so that's really not enough time to start something new. It will be advantageous to finish what we are doing anyway,' she replied. 'Obviously you are welcome to sit and watch,' she added as the woman bristled.

'I shall inspect every single stitch, Miss Sullivan. As you may be aware, my sewing is second to none.'

'Yes, you did say, Miss Green,' Sarah responded. 'Right, girls, you have done extremely well so far. Unfortunately, we don't have much time left, so if you'd like to gather around, I will show you a basic hem stitch.'

'Hem stitch,' the mistress screeched. 'They can't do that.'

'If you'll permit me to demonstrate, Miss Green, they will then see how it is done.'

'No, I simply cannot allow you to come into my classroom and interfere with my lessons,' Miss Green replied, placing emphasis on the word *my*.

Aware the girls were watching, Sarah bit down a retort and forced her voice to remain civil. 'I believe it is you who are interrupting my lesson, Miss Green. Right, everyone, you will notice how, having chosen green gingham, I have threaded a needle with matching silk.' As she held the needle up for the pupils to see, the schoolmistress gave a smirk.

'You may think you're smart, Miss Sullivan, but I won't be requiring this position for much longer and neither will you,' she announced, flouncing out of the room and slamming the door behind her.

'Oh dear, I fink you've upset her,' Kitty observed. 'She's a nasty bit of work, ain't she?'

Although Sarah agreed, she shot the girl a stern look.

'What did she mean about you not needing this position for much longer, miss?' Edith asked, her brows furrowing in consternation.

'Don't take any notice, Edith. She was just upset to find me teaching her lesson. Now, shall we carry on?' she asked, then proceeded to show them how to hem.

Even though Sarah enjoyed the lesson, by the time she dismissed them at the end of the afternoon, her head was pounding. She'd done the very thing Harry had warned her about and fallen out with Miss Green again. Although she imagined the woman's threat had been an idle one, there had been something akin to triumph lighting her eyes that worried her. Perhaps she'd better mention it to Harry.

She made her way around to the kitchen, but could see no sign of him. Oh well, plenty of time to admit her failing after supper, she mused. She hoped he wouldn't be cross, for she really looked forward to the short time they spent catching up on things when the day was done. He certainly wasn't the hard-nosed master she'd first thought him. In fact, as far as the pupils were concerned, he had a sensitive side that quite surprised her.

'Ah, Miss Sullivan,' Mrs Daws greeted her. 'Everything all right?' she asked as Sarah went over to the range and held up her cold hands.

'It's absolutely perishing in that schoolroom. The fire in the grate was so minimal it hardly took the chill off the fireguard, let alone the room.'

'I did tell you November was a trying time. Still, come the middle of next month we'll have a coal delivery and Pip will be able to make more of a decent blaze.'

'I'm surprised the children don't freeze,' she muttered.

'Most of them are used to far worse conditions,' Mrs Daws chided.

Remembering Kitty and Luke, Sarah felt contrite. 'How is Luke today?' she asked.

'Thriving on that potion Dr Hawkins mixed for him. He'll be up tomorrow, creating havoc, you mark my words,' the woman chuckled. 'Mind you, we've virtually got a full house now.'

'Which means more work for you, Mrs Daws. You must tell me what I can do to assist.'

'You already do a lot, Miss Sullivan. But if you wouldn't mind cutting the bread while I mash these hard-boiled eggs, that would be a help.' The two women worked side by side in easy silence for a few moments before Mrs Daws spoke again. 'I went into town this morning and everyone seemed to be talking about the inspection.'

'Really?' Sarah asked, looking up from the loaf. 'Why would anyone be interested in that?'

'Well, there's those kind-hearted folk who hope the school passes and stays open. Then there's those toffee-nosed ones round here who are determined to see it close.'

'Surely they must see Red Cliffs gives these children a chance in life,' Sarah said.

'There's some only interested in having things their own way,' Mrs Daws snorted. Remembering Miss Green's outburst, Sarah nodded and was about to mention it, but the housekeeper was continuing her story. 'I bumped into the vicar on my way back and he said he's never seen the Misses, as he calls them, so animated. Apparently they explained the idea they'd come up with about form-ing a sewing bee to make uniforms for the children.' The housekeeper raised her brows.

'Their idea, eh?' Sarah smiled, thinking Mrs Knight's plan had worked.

'Honestly, they'll take credit for anything, those women. Anyway, the vicar said he was pleased because if they were busy with this sewing bee, then he might get a bit of peace.' Mrs Daws chuckled.

'Well, as long as the children receive their new clothes, I suppose it doesn't matter if people think it was their idea,' Sarah replied, not wishing to give Mrs Knight's ploy away. 'Talking of sewing, I've just taken the girls through the rudiments of cutting out an apron and basic hemming stitch.'

'Ah,' the woman said, knowingly. 'I thought I saw Miss Green stalking off down the driveway. Her nose were that high up in the air, I'm surprised she didn't bump into something. She wouldn't have liked her lesson being taken over, and that's a fact.'

'She didn't . . .' Sarah began but her explanation was cut short as Pip came into the room, his limp more pronounced with the cold weather.

'Mrs Daws, the coalman's outside. He says he has a delivery for the school. Shall I let him in?'

'But it's only November,' the housekeeper frowned.

'It's all right, Mrs Daws,' Harry said, coming into the room. 'I received a communication from our benefactor earlier. Apparently, our supply of coal has been ordered early this year, so let's not look the gift horse in the mouth, as they say.'

'Don't know about a gift horse, but the coalman's got his carthorse waiting,' Pip grinned.

'Then let him in and make sure you count the sacks as he empties them, young Pip,' the housekeeper ordered.

'And, as from tomorrow, you can make the fires up to their winter strength,' Harry said. Pip waved in acknowledgement then disappeared back outside.

'Well, that's a turn-up. In all the years I've worked here, I've never known our coal delivery to arrive before December. It means we can light the fires upstairs too,' Mrs Daws grinned. 'I don't know what we've done to deserve this, but I for one won't complain.'

'And we can work on the Christmas Fayre projects in the evenings now. Talking of which, how did the sewing lesson go?' Harry asked. 'I saw Miss Green striding off down the path as though the very devil was after her.'

Sarah sighed and put down the bread knife. 'She took exception to the fact that I taught a lesson she hadn't scheduled. As she only turned up fifteen minutes before the end of the afternoon, what were the girls meant to do, sit twiddling their thumbs?'

Harry frowned. 'Well, for your own benefit, make sure you record exactly what happened, noting down the timings, et cetera. Mr Green's daughter or no, a schoolmistress cannot get away with things like that. It's unfortunate with the inspection coming up, but there we are,' he shrugged.

'I shall also record her refusal to obey my orders. Those aprons could have been further advanced by now. There's just one thing, though. She insisted she wouldn't be requiring the position here for much longer and that I wouldn't either,' Sarah admitted. 'I trust she doesn't know something we don't.'

'Probably just an idle threat because she'd had her nose put out. I wouldn't worry about it. Do you want me to sound the gong, Mrs Daws?' he asked, seeing the woman carrying plates through to the dining room.

'Yes, please, Master Higgins. I don't think I can face Maisie's vigorous bashing today.'

After supper, while the children cleared away and carried out their duties around the house, Sarah and Harry sat together over a second cup of tea. As the gas globes hissed and popped, casting a cosy glow around the room, Sarah found herself relaxing at last.

'I saw Dr Hawkins earlier,' Harry said, giving Sarah his lazy smile. 'The boy will be well enough to join the others tomorrow morning.'

'That is good news,' Sarah replied. 'How is Kitty settling in? I don't know what you said to her yesterday, but she's following Edith around like a mother hen.' She flapped her arms and Harry laughed.

'She told me she wasn't a charity case so I pointed out that the ethos here is to help everyone, then gave her Edith as a project. Hopefully, they will support each other,' Harry explained. 'Dr Hawkins also said he will give each child a thorough check-up and update their school records before the inspection.'

'I didn't know they had school records,' Sarah said, giving him a searching look. 'Where are they kept?'

'They are locked safely away in a cupboard in the schoolroom. A note is made about each child when they first arrive here. Name, where they've come from, age if we know it, health issues, et cetera. The local authority makes a thorough inspection of each one when they visit so it's vital they're kept up to date.'

'There's so much I still don't know,' Sarah sighed.

'Running this place is quite a complex business, but look on the bright side, you know a lot more than you did when you arrived,' Harry smiled. 'Have you heard anything more from Fothergill?'

'No, why should I have?' she asked, looking at him sharply.

'With Mr Lawrence contesting the will and calling for an inspection, I would imagine Fothergill is following proceedings carefully.'

'He did say he thought my godfather had tied everything up securely as far as Red Cliffs is concerned, but I guess . . .'

'We can't count our chickens, and it's no use conjecturing on things that may not transpire. But we could make something interesting happen this Saturday evening,' he suggested, gazing at her intently.

'And pray what might that be, Master Higgins?' she teased.

'That date with a fish supper, perhaps.' He grinned in a way that made funny tingles run up and down her spine. 'I take it you are free?'

'On Saturday evening, you mean?' she asked.

'Actually, I meant free *per se*. I wouldn't be treading on anyone's toes?' he asked, looking so serious Sarah hurried to reassure him.

'Goodness me, no,' she replied.

'Well, if you don't mind being seen walking out with a humble schoolmaster, we'll leave these scallywags to the mercies of Mrs Laver and Mrs Daws for bath night and head into town.'

'I'll look forward to it,' she replied, smiling up at him. He leaned closer, and for a moment, Sarah thought he was going to kiss her. Her heartbeat quickened, but then April came bounding into the room, and the intimate moment was broken.

'Ooh, hope I'm not interrupting anything, Miss Sullivan, Master Higgins,' she giggled.

30

When Sarah stole downstairs the next morning, she was surprised to find Monday sitting on the chair beside the lit range with the ginger cat on her lap.

'Goodness me, someone's up early,' Sarah said, smiling at the little girl.

'I has to come and see me Ginger early 'cos once the others get up he runs away. Mrs Daws let me give him his breakfast,' she announced proudly.

'That cat's got a soft spot for you, Monday, and no mistake,' the housekeeper replied, looking up and smiling at the little girl before continuing her kneading. Just then, the kettle gave the homely whistle that Sarah loved. Lifting it off the hob, the housekeeper poured boiling water over the used leaves that were awaiting reuse in the big brown pot. 'Might be a weak brew,' Mrs Daws commented. 'Still, it'll be wet and hot so we should be grateful for small mercies, eh?'

'Mother used to say that,' Monday said softly. Sarah and Mrs Daws exchanged a look of surprise, for this was the first time the girl had spoken about her mother.

'Did she?' Sarah asked softly.

Monday nodded, then went back to stroking the cat. 'She gave me milk most of the time, though, 'cos she said it would make me strong. If we was short, she drank her tea black. Said it would put hairs on her chest but I never saw any.' The girl cuddled the cat tighter and its contented purring filled the room.

'You must miss her, dearie,' Mrs Daws said gently.

'Yes,' the little girl sighed. 'She was my friend. Still, I got Maisie now.'

'Indeed you have, young lady. And if you don't hurry upstairs and get dressed, she'll think you've gone to London to see the Queen,' the housekeeper told her.

Monday giggled, kissed the cat's head then put him gently on the floor. 'Ginger says it's time he scarpered anyway 'cos the others will be down soon,' she replied.

'I can't believe how matter of fact she is,' Sarah commented, watching as the little girl skipped out of the room.

'Children are more resilient than you think, although who knows what will happen when her father turns up. Sometimes it's the familiar that triggers a memory. Now, let's drink our tea, then we'd better make a start on the porridge.'

'Good morning, ladies,' Harry said, diving in through the back door and shaking himself on the mat like a drenched dog. 'It's raining yet again,' he sighed, walking over to the range and holding his hands out to warm. He darted Sarah a tender look, and remembering the previous evening, she smiled and turned away before the house-keeper noticed.

'I see you've fed old Marmalade already, Mrs Daws. That cat's getting as portly as Sergeant Watts,' he teased.

'You can blame Monday, Master Higgins. She slips down here first thing before the others wake and makes a right old fuss of him. He loves it, of course, don't you, old boy?' she crooned. Harry winked at Sarah, and despite herself, she found her pulse racing.

'Monday mentioned her mother this morning,' Sarah smiled.

'Well, that's a healthy sign. Perhaps I'll encourage her to draw a picture of the woman to help with her memories,' he mused. 'And talking of mothers, I mentioned the sewing bee to mine last night and she seemed really interested. In fact, she even intimated she would like to help.'

'That would be good for her, Master Higgins,' Mrs Daws commented. 'She always were beautiful at stitchery.'

'It's the first time I've seen her animated since Father died,' he agreed. 'Anyway, Miss Sullivan, when I told her you intended calling on Mrs Knight this morning, she said she might pay a visit herself. I've a feeling it might be you Mother wants to see, though,' he admitted, a flush creeping up his cheeks.

'Really?' she replied, staring at him in surprise. 'Why?'

'Apparently, I've spoken so much about you, she'd like to meet you. Mothers, eh, Mrs Daws?' he grimaced.

'I wouldn't know, Master Higgins, being as how I never had one myself. Well, I mean, obviously someone birthed me, but whoever that were saw fit to leave me in a box on the orphanage bins.'

'Oh, Mrs Daws, I'm so sorry. I had no idea,' Sarah cried, staring at the woman in horror.

'No reason why you should. It were a long time ago, obviously,' she sighed, thumping the lump of dough vigorously. Sarah couldn't help thinking of her own mother. She might have been taken from her early but at least Sarah had known she was loved.

'Well, the children here are lucky to have you,' Sarah said, patting the housekeeper's shoulder.

'Somebody's got to keep them in line,' the woman replied brusquely, but Sarah could tell she was pleased.

'I suppose this weather means the children will be confined to barracks,' Harry sighed.

'Well, if they can't go outside for their exercise, they can get it by cleaning and polishing the house,' Mrs Daws chuckled, having recovered her composure. 'It's an ill wind, as they say, or in this case a black cloud. Tea, Master Higgins?'

'Thank you, Mrs Daws. Why don't you get Pip to run you around to Mrs Knight's in the trap, Miss Sullivan?' he suggested. 'You really shouldn't be walking the streets by yourself.'

'Why ever not? We are in the twentieth century now, Master Higgins,' she retorted. Then, seeing him flinch, she could have cut out her tongue. 'Although it was a kind thought, thank you,' she smiled. 'Well, if I'm to meet your mother, I'd better find something smarter than this to wear,' she added, grimacing down at the old dress she'd donned first thing.

'There's still some nice bits and pieces in the front room, but make sure you have a bite to eat before you go out, Miss Sullivan,' said Mrs Daws. 'There's hardly anything of you as there is.'

'Oh, I wouldn't say that,' Harry replied with a grin, his good mood obviously restored. 'I gather Dr Hawkins is happy with young Luke's progress, so I'll introduce him to the rigours of the schoolroom after breakfast.'

*

Although Mrs Daws had set the children the task of cleaning and polishing the house, it was evident that their labour hadn't tired them out, for they exuberantly pushed and jostled their way into the schoolroom. Harry groaned, knowing his patience would be tested to the limits.

'Single file, you heathens,' he roared, staring at them sternly.

'Coo, that fire's 'alf decent, sir. I can even feel a bit of heat,' Bunter called, pointing to the coals that were glowing brilliantly in the grate. Luckily, the black metal guard was securely fixed in front of it and Harry silently thanked Pip for the meticulous way he carried out his duties.

'It is indeed, Bunter, which means your brain will be warm enough to start ticking this morning. Right, young Luke, I understand that you are five years old?' he said, consulting the record card he'd made out when the boy had arrived at Red Cliffs. Luke gripped his sister's hand tighter and nodded. 'Then you will sit here alongside Maisie and Monday for your lessons.'

'But them's girls,' he complained.

'He's quick,' Edith chortled.

Harry opened his mouth to respond but Kitty was already giving her the evil eye. She put her arm around the young boy's shoulders.

'Now, Luke, you bin given the chance of a decent education so you got to make the most of it,' Kitty told her brother. 'Then you'll get a good job and make sumfink of yourself. I'll go and sit with Edith over there so I'll only be just behind you, right?' The boy nodded and sat in the seat Harry indicated.

'Good morning, everyone,' he began.

'Good morning, Master Higgins,' the class responded.

'Why does we have to say good morning when we saw you at breakfast?' Kitty asked.

'Because it signals the beginning of lessons,' Harry told her. 'Now, whilst I settle young Luke into our regime, please get out your name cards and copy the letters onto your slates in your best writing.' After much rustling and scraping, the children finally settled down to do as he asked.

'Now, Luke,' he said, hunkering down beside the boy. 'Have you been to school before?' The lad shook his head. 'Do you know how to write on a slate?' At this, the boy smiled and nodded. 'Good, now watch carefully as I write the letters of your name so you can copy.' As Luke concentrated, tongue between his teeth, Harry let out a sigh of relief. If the boy was willing to learn it would certainly make his job easier.

'That's it, Luke. If you carry on like this you'll be a star pupil,' he encouraged. Distracted by a noise at the back of the room, he looked up to see two boys staring out of the window.

'Black, Brown, sit down,' he roared.

'Hey, sir, that rhymes,' Maggie chuckled.

'He's a poet and he don't know it,' Edith laughed.

'Enough,' Harry bellowed.

'But, sir,' Black began.

'Don't give me cause to get out the tawse,' Harry muttered, only too aware that he'd rhymed his words again. 'Brown, are you going to sit down or . . .'

'There's a big man trying to get in the school gates but Pip won't let him in,' the boy persisted.

Harry hurried over to look and saw Pip shaking his head at a burly man wearing a well-worn blue serge suit and a vest that may once have been white.

'Right, Kitty and Edith, you are in charge whilst I go and see what that man wants,' Harry stated. 'Continue with your writing, please. Any mischief and there will be trouble.'

'There won't be, sir,' Kitty declared. 'An' I won't need that whip eiver.'

Head down against the rain that was still falling from the leaden sky, Harry hurried outside. As he neared the gates, he could hear Pip saying, 'I know all the children, sir, and I can assure you there is nobody here by that name.'

'But Sergeant Watts said she'd been brought here,' the man insisted.

Closer up, Harry could see that, although the man was unkempt and unshaven, he wasn't some thug as he'd feared.

'Can I help you, sir?' he asked. 'I'm Harry Higgins, the schoolmaster.'

'The name's Denis Collyer, serving in the Merchant. I was explaining to this young man here that Sergeant Watts told me my daughter Violet Collyer's here.'

Harry frowned. 'Oh, you must mean Monday,' he cried, realization dawning. 'Let the gentleman in, please, Pip.'

'Right you are, Master Higgins,' he replied, swinging the gates open. 'I never thought he meant Monday, sir.'

'You were quite right to be cautious, Pip, thank you,' he told the anxious boy. 'Come indoors out of the rain, Mr Collyer,' he invited and set off at a brisk pace up the driveway. 'You must understand that Pip was only doing his job. It is our responsibility to ensure the safety of all our pupils.'

'It's good to know my Violet's been kept safe,' he replied. From the desolation in the man's eyes, Harry could tell he had only just found out about his wife's death.

Having dressed carefully in the coat she'd borrowed, Sarah was standing in the hallway, checking her reflection before going out. She had added a hat for good measure. It didn't quite match her outfit but at least she looked respectable, she thought. As she lifted her hand to the latch, the door opened. Harry was standing on the step, a broad-shouldered man beside him.

'Miss Sullivan, this is Mr Collyer, Monday's father,' Harry announced.

'Mr Collyer, do come in out of this dreadful weather,' she invited.

'Morning, ma'am,' he said, doffing his cap. 'I'm looking for the owner.'

'And you've found her. Do come through to my office, there's a fire in there,' she said, eying his clothes, which were dripping rain onto the parquet flooring the children had earlier polished. He had removed his cap and was twisting it around and around in his big, blackened hands as he followed her into the room. She gestured to a chair and he sank into it as though the weight of the world was on his shoulders.

'I've just found out about my Holly,' he murmured and Sarah could see him struggling with his emotions.

'Please accept our deepest condolences, Mr Collyer,' she said. He nodded.

'I've left the class in Kitty's hands, Miss Sullivan. I need to check on them, so would you like me to bring Monday in when I return?'

'If you would, Master Higgins, and could you ask Mrs Daws for some tea on your way?'

Harry nodded. 'I won't be long,' he assured her.

'She were the world to me, my Hol,' the man croaked. 'Then when Violet came along she just added to our joy. 'Cors, being in the Merchant, I'm away a lot but I always had them to come home to.' His eyes filled with tears and Sarah looked away tactfully as he dashed them off with the cuff of his sleeve.

'It must have been a terrible shock,' she murmured.

'Still trying to take it in. The sergeant was waiting as soon as the ship docked,' he sighed. 'How could that woman have been so heartless as to throw my girls out on the street and with Hol expectin' an all?' He shook his head.

'Monday, or rather, Violet, has been well looked after, Mr Collyer,' she assured him. 'Unfortunately, the shock of the . . . er, accident, left your daughter unable to speak for a while. She's fine now,' she hastened to assure him as concern sparked in his eyes. 'Anyway, as she was unable to tell us her name, we called her Monday after the day of the week she was brought here.'

'I'm right obliged to you for caring for her,' he replied. 'Well, it'll be up to me to look out for her now.' He came to a halt as Mrs Daws came bustling in with a tray of tea.

'You poor man,' she crooned. 'A terrible business and no mistake. Here, I've added extra sugar. It's good for the shock.'

He seemed to find a measure of comfort in the woman's fussing, for he smiled weakly. 'That's mighty kind, ma'am.'

'Not at all. She's a right bonny lass, your Monday,' she added. 'Now, I've promised Master Higgins I'll look after the class while he brings her over, so I'd better trot along.'

'What a caring woman,' he murmured as the door shut behind the housekeeper. 'You all have been really kind.' He shuddered to a halt. 'Forgive me,' he whispered, 'it's all come as a terrible shock. I was looking forward to seeing Hol . . .' As his voice trailed away, Sarah pushed his cup towards him.

'Have a drink,' she urged softly, not knowing what else to say to the broken man before her. As the fire shifted and settled lower in the grate, Sarah went over and added more coal, glad of the excuse of something to do.

Then the door opened and Harry came in, Monday tightly clutching his hand. She stood for a moment, staring at the burly man, before running over to him and throwing herself into his arms.

'Dadda,' she cried. 'Have you brought me anything?'

31

Sarah stared at Harry, not knowing whether to laugh or cry at the girl's reaction. Although he grinned ruefully, she could see he was touched by the emotional reunion, for the bereft Mr Collyer was hugging his daughter as though he'd never let her go.

'Well, that's a fine question to ask your poor father after he's been away at sea for so long,' he said, forcing a smile as he ruffled the girl's hair.

'You always brings me back a present, don't you, Dadda?' Monday replied.

'Yes, I do, pet,' Mr Collyer admitted, tears still flowing freely down his cheeks. 'But I was so keen to see you, I left it on the ship.'

'We can go and get it after school,' the girl replied, her eyes shining with excitement. 'Can Maisie come with me, 'cos she's my best friend?' Then she frowned. 'Why are you crying?' she asked, reaching up and wiping the wetness away. 'I suppose I'll have to look after you now Mamma has gone to be an angel in heaven,' she told him.

He stared at her for a moment then cleared his throat. 'An angel in heaven?' he whispered.

Monday looked at him sagely. 'The nice man with the white hair told me that.'

Mr Collyer looked enquiringly at Sarah.

'I think she's referring to my godfather, Dr Lawrence.'

Monday nodded. 'He told me Mamma wouldn't want us to be sad and one day when our bodies was tired, we'd see her again. Dr Lawrence has gone to be an angel too, so I expec' he's looking after her 'til you get there, Dadda.'

'Oh, Violet,' the man's voice cracked and he dashed impatiently at his tears.

'No, Dadda, I called Monday now,' she told him proudly.

Sarah opened her mouth to correct her, but Harry shook his head.

'It's for them to sort out,' he whispered, then addressed the man. 'The police managed to locate your wife's . . . I mean, Monday's grandparents.'

Mr Collyer's face contorted in pain. 'I bet they blamed me for everything,' he said bitterly. 'I'm not one of them, you see, and . . .' His voice trailed away.

'Don't concern yourself, Mr Collyer, we got the gist from Madam Rosa when she called here,' Sarah told him.

His bushy brows narrowed into a dark line. 'Madam Rosa, indeed,' he snorted. 'I'm surprised she didn't offer Violet a home in that fancy vardo of hers. She didn't, did she?' he asked anxiously. Remembering the ugly scene played out in this very room, Sarah looked awkwardly at Harry, but before he could reply, Monday was tugging at her father's hand.

'I told you, Dadda, I Monday now,' she said, wriggling down from her father's lap. 'I wants to go back to class and see Maisie,' she told Harry.

'I think that might be a good idea, Mr Collyer. Then we can discuss your daughter's future in private,' he replied.

'What's to discuss? She'll be coming with me,' the man replied quickly. Sarah's heart sank like a stone. Then she felt ashamed of herself. Of course Monday should be with her father. But it seemed the little girl had her own ideas.

'Maisie will be waiting for me, Dadda,' Monday told him. 'And Kitty says we gotta have an edu . . . edicatin,' she added, staring at him so seriously her periwinkle eyes turned the violet of her given name. 'I gotta learn so I gets on in life, see.'

Impressed by the little girl's determination, Harry's lips lifted at the corners, although he tried valiantly to suppress his grin. Perhaps his teaching hadn't been in vain. 'It might be best, Mr Collyer,' he said gently. 'Perhaps just for the rest of the morning?'

The man looked from Harry to his daughter and sighed. 'You're a right little bossy boots, just like your mother,' he told her. 'I guess we do have things to discuss, Miss Sullivan, so perhaps Monday should go back to her lessons.'

'I need to return, anyway, before the children run poor Mrs Daws ragged,' Harry pointed out. 'Come along, young Monday. Say goodbye to your father. You can see him at luncheon. Knowing our housekeeper, she will insist on you eating something before you leave, Mr Collyer.'

'You can see Maisie then, Dadda,' Monday said, giving him a dazzling smile. 'And I is glad you back.'

As the man gave a wobbly smile in response, Sarah turned to Harry. 'Perhaps you could ask Mrs Daws to bring us some fresh tea?'

'Her panacea for everything,' Harry nodded. 'I'll see you later, Mr Collyer.'

As the door closed behind him, Mr Collyer turned to Sarah. 'I see you're dressed to go out. Please don't let me hold you up any longer, Miss Sullivan.'

Sarah reached up and touched her hat in surprise. 'Goodness, I'd forgotten. Don't worry, Mr Collyer, getting Monday's future sorted out is the most important thing right now. You obviously want her to leave with you, but do you have anywhere to take her?'

The man slapped the side of his head. 'I'd not even thought. Forgive me, Miss Sullivan, this has all been such a shock. I still can't believe that terrible landlady threw my poor Holly out, and her expectin' too. Do you know, Sergeant Watts said she's renting out the place to holiday-makers? Makes more money out of them, apparently.'

Sarah sighed. 'I understand there is a lot of that going on at the moment,' she replied.

'Well, it ain't right, throwing decent folk out of their homes for profit,' he cried.

Sarah felt a prickle of unease creep up her spine, for worries about the school's future were never far away. Determined to focus on the man's plight, she pushed her own concerns to the back of her mind.

'Do you have any other family, Mr Collyer?' Sarah asked gently.

He shook his head. 'Ran away to sea when I was a nipper. Wanted the excitement of seeing a bit of the world, see. Then I met Holly and soon after we found she was expecting.' He stopped, looking embarrassed, but Sarah smiled encouragingly. 'Her so-called Romany parents didn't want to know so we got wed quietly and set up home. We was so happy . . .' His voice broke and he shook his head. 'Don't know what you must think of me, Miss Sullivan, blubbing like a baby.'

'You've had a terrible shock and it's natural you should want to have your daughter with you. However, until you find somewhere to live, would it be best for her to remain here for now?'

He didn't answer, just sat staring into the fire. 'I was goin' to take some leave then sign on again, but I can't do that now, can I? I mean, I've got nowhere to stay, have I?' he said eventually.

Sarah opened her mouth to respond but he continued muttering under his breath and she realized he was working things out in his head.

'Here we are, dearies,' Mrs Daws said cheerily as she pushed the door open with her behind and came in bearing the tea. She glanced at the stoker as she passed, then raised her brows enquiringly at Sarah. Not knowing what to say, Sarah shrugged. As ever, the capable housekeeper took charge. 'Shall I pour?' she asked, then without waiting for a reply, busied herself with the teapot.

'Here we are, dearie, you get that down you,' she said firmly, placing the man's cup in his hand. 'She's a right little charmer, your daughter. Only child in the place the cat doesn't run away from.' She chattered cheerily on, and after a few moments, the man made an effort to rouse himself.

'She loves animals. Came home with a ginger kitten once, determined to keep him, she was. Had to hide him from the landlady, of course,' he sighed. He was obviously about to return to his thoughts but Mrs Daws had other ideas.

'How long are you on leave for?' she asked, easing herself onto the chair beside him.

'The ship will leave after it's unloaded and restocked. I hadn't intended signing on for another trip straight away but now perhaps it would be better if I did. But there's Monday and . . .' He shrugged. 'The truth is, I don't know what to do.'

'Poor man. You've had a dreadful shock and, if you don't mind me saying, don't look in any fit state to make decisions. Why not stay and have a hot meal with us? Got a nice cheese and potato pie cooking, although it might be more spud than Ched, if you get my meaning.'

The man looked at the friendly housekeeper and slowly nodded. 'That would hit the spot and no mistake. We brought a goodly supply of provisions back with us, so when I go and get Monday's present I could speak nicely to the purser,' he said with a wink.

Mrs Daws smiled. 'The children would be most grateful, Mr Collyer.'

'Was everything all right in the classroom?' Sarah asked.

The housekeeper chuckled. 'Goodness me, that Kitty had them writing out their names like good 'uns. I just sat at the master's desk feeling all important while she ruled the roost. By the way, do you know you've got your hat on?'

'Yes, I was just leaving to see Mrs Knight when Mr Collyer arrived,' she replied, glancing over to where the man sat stifling a yawn.

'There's still time before luncheon, so why not go now? A bit of fresh air will do you good and Mr Collyer here looks all in, so he could have a lie-down in the little room behind the kitchen.'

'That sounds mighty tempting,' he admitted, looking at her hopefully. Then he frowned. 'Trouble is, what with the police waiting for me on the quay, I clean forgot to bring my sea bag with me things in.'

'Gawd love us, dearie, we've got plenty of spare things here,' Mrs Daws cried.

'That's sorted then,' Sarah said, getting to her feet. 'Try and get some rest, Mr Collyer.'

The rain had reduced to a mizzle and there was a brisk breeze blowing in from the sea. Taking deep breaths of the salty air to revive herself, Sarah set off at a brisk pace. She'd known this day was coming, of course, and it was only right that Mr Collyer would want to have Monday with him. Yet she'd be fooling herself if she didn't admit the little girl had become very dear to her.

Heavy black clouds hovered overhead and she pulled her coat tighter around herself. Then, as if he was standing right beside her, she heard her godfather's voice the day Madam Rosa had visited Red Cliffs. *I know you are fond of Monday but I must remind you to exercise caution, for we don't know how long she will remain here.*

'I tried, Uncle, really I did,' she cried.

As if he'd been listening, she heard him say, *There are many others needing your love and care, Sarah, remember that.*

'Yes, Uncle,' she replied, knowing what he said was true.

'Did you say something, Miss Sullivan, I mean, Sarah?'

Startled, she looked up to see Jack Wise had drawn up beside her on his bicycle.

'Oh, hello, Jack. I was miles away,' she explained. Then, pulling herself together, she added, 'That gingham material you kindly brought around is proving eminently suitable for the girls' apron-making.'

He beamed at her in delight, and as if seeking to prolong their conversation, made to dismount. 'You must excuse me, though,' she said quickly. 'For I am due to call upon Mrs Knight and fear I'm already dreadfully late.'

'You should get one of these,' he suggested, patting the shiny handlebars. 'It makes travelling around much quicker.'

Remembering an article she'd read only recently, Sarah nodded. 'What a good idea. Perhaps I should also abandon my skirts in favour of the knickerbocker?' she suggested, giving him a wicked grin.

A dull flush crept up his neck. 'Well, I, er . . .' he stuttered, staring down at his feet.

'Don't worry, Jack. I was only teasing. Now I really must be going,' she said, continuing on her way. She half expected him to suggest accompanying her, but he merely gave a nod then pedalled quickly away. Poor man, she really shouldn't have pulled his leg like that, she thought, then couldn't help chuckling at his mortified expression.

By the time she reached Mrs Knight's house, a double-bay-fronted property secreted behind a tall limestone wall, she had regained her equilibrium. The door was opened by a pretty young girl of about fifteen or so.

'Do come in, Miss Sullivan,' she said in a soft, melodious voice that Sarah found attractive. 'May I take your coat?'

'That's very kind but, as I can't stay very long, I'll keep it on. It's stopped raining so I shouldn't drip anyway,' she replied.

The girl smiled. 'My grandmother is in the parlour with the other ladies,' she said. As Sarah followed her down the hallway, the homely smell of baking wafted her way and she sniffed the air appreciatively.

'My first real attempt at cake-making,' the girl explained, showing Sarah into a light, airy room with high ceilings and tall windows that looked down over the bay. It was tastefully furnished with a grand piano in the corner. 'Miss Sullivan,' she announced.

'Thank you, Amelia,' Mrs Knight said, manoeuvring her Bath chair away from the sewing machine at which she'd been working. 'Miss Sullivan, how lovely to see you again,' she greeted Sarah. She was sporting an indoor bonnet, its ribbons matching the pink of her dress. 'As you can see, we are a hive of activity,' she said, gesturing towards the large table in the centre of the room that was laden with cloth and silks. 'Now you've met Amelia, my granddaughter. She is staying with me whilst her parents are abroad.'

'That's nice for you, Mrs Knight,' she replied.

'It is indeed. Amelia is such a help and plays the piano delightfully.' As Sarah exchanged smiles with the girl, she was struck by the similarity in their clear, grey eyes. 'You already know the Misses Snooper, Prior and Middle, of course.'

'Good morning, ladies,' she greeted them. They nodded graciously then bent their heads over the garments they were sewing.

'And last but definitely not least, I'd like to introduce Mrs Higgins, the mother of your schoolmaster,' Mrs Knight said, gesturing to a lady dressed in black. 'She has kindly offered her services to our little sewing bee.'

Mrs Higgins gave Sarah an appraising look, and she held her breath, wondering why it should matter that the woman approve of her.

'Miss Sullivan, I have heard so much about you,' Mrs Higgins finally said, giving her a warm smile.

'Nothing too shocking, I hope,' Sarah replied.

'*Au contraire*, my dear. In fact, if I hear your virtues expounded anymore I would think we had a veritable paragon in our midst.'

Not knowing how to respond, Sarah just smiled and looked around, taking in the delicate china tea service with matching plates on the trolley, along with the remains of a sponge cake, its damson-jam filling glistening temptingly.

'Amelia kindly made us that delicious cake to accompany our morning tea,' Mrs Knight explained.

'And extremely good for her first attempt it was too,' Mrs Higgins acknowledged.

'If a little lopsided,' Mrs Snooper sniffed. Sarah saw Amelia grimace and was about to say she thought it looked very appetizing when the woman continued. 'The verger was here earlier, Miss Sullivan. He waited for ages and kept looking out of the window for you,' she added.

'Then he said he was sorry but he'd have to leave,' Miss Prior added, her beady eyes boring into Sarah. 'That was a shame, wasn't it, Miss Sullivan?'

'Although it did mean more cake for us,' Miss Middle sighed, patting her ample stomach. 'We think our Miss Sullivan and the verger like each other,' she confided to Mrs Higgins.

As the woman stared at Sarah with a deadpan expression, she found herself growing hot. While I like the verger, it's your son I really care for, she wanted to shout.

32

'Of course they like each other, Miss Middle,' Mrs Knight said quickly. 'Being such nice people, they both like and see the best in everyone.'

'What I meant was . . .' the woman began, but was stopped mid-flow by Mrs Knight.

'I'm sure Miss Sullivan would like to see what we have achieved so far,' she cut in, her firm voice brooking no argument. 'Let's lay our work out on the table, then she can cast her expert eye over it.' Immediately, the ladies jumped to their feet and began pushing the silks, pins and buttons to one side before spreading out their sewing.

'While they are busy, let me get you some refreshment,' Amelia offered in her soft voice. Before Sarah could reply, she'd glided over to the teapot, which was covered in a beautiful floral cosy, and began pouring. 'Milk and sugar?' she asked. Sarah nodded, then watched as she deftly cut a slice of the sponge and arranged it on one of the delicate plates. Her movements were graceful, and she moved elegantly in her flowing day dress. Sarah felt like a carthorse in a blanket beside her.

'Do come and see what we've done,' the ladies chorused in unison. Sarah smiled at Amelia and, cup in hand, wandered over to where they were eagerly waiting.

'We haven't stopped sewing all morning,' Mrs Snooper sniffed. Sarah stared down at the six matching pinafore smocks that were already taking shape and gasped.

'These are superb,' she cried. 'The local authority won't recognize the children this smartly turned out.'

The ladies beamed and began singing 'Busy Bee' as they resumed their sewing.

'I'm so pleased you like them,' Mrs Knight said. 'Of course, we still have quite a few more to do and then there are the boys' shirts to make, but hopefully we'll have time. Have you heard exactly when the inspection is to be?'

'No, we are still awaiting a letter of confirmation. In the meantime, I asked April and Pip to write down the measurements of all the children,' she said putting down her tea and drawing a sheet of notepaper from her pocket.

'That's splendid,' Mrs Knight replied. 'Have you everything else prepared? I know what those official bods can be like, begging your pardon, Mrs Higgins,' she added, glancing towards the master's mother.

'Don't mind me, Mrs Knight. There is nothing I want more than Red Cliffs to pass this inspection with flying colours. Then perhaps Harry will be able to relax.'

'It has been very fraught recently,' Sarah agreed. 'Still, things seem to be looking up, for we've had a delivery of coal which means the rooms will be warmer. Apparently it doesn't usually arrive until December, but this year, for some reason, it's come early.'

'Ah yes, that would be Charlie. She . . .' Mrs Knight's voice tailed off as Mrs Higgins sent her a warning look.

Sarah stared at them in surprise. 'She? You mean our benefactor is a lady? Can you tell me about her?'

'Oh, don't mind me, Miss Sullivan,' Mrs Knight said quickly. 'Those ladies are making such a dreadful din I can hardly think. Now, what was it you were saying about them seeing Miss Green in the draper's, Mrs Higgins?' she asked, looking at the woman pointedly.

'Apparently they saw her looking at bridal material,' she said, looking over at the ladies who were still singing at the tops of their voices. 'Of course I dismissed it as idle chit-chat.'

'I know she's been walking out with the doctor's nephew but I can hardly see him proposing to Miss Green,' Sarah replied, laughing at the unlikely thought. 'Now I really must be getting back.'

'Before you go, I hope you don't mind my mentioning, but that hat and coat really do not sit well together. I have some trimmings in my workbasket which would remedy that. If you're agreeable, I could quickly transform your hat whilst you finish your refreshments.'

'Well, that is most kind of you, Miss Knight, but . . .' she began, determined not to be fobbed off by this diversion.

'Do let her, Miss Sullivan,' Mrs Higgins urged. 'Your attire is hardly, and forgive me if I'm frank, but it is not appropriate for the proprietor of Red Cliffs to walk around in mismatched apparel.'

'Put like that, I can hardly refuse,' Sarah replied, biting down her resentment. It was hardly her fault she had to resort to hand-me-downs, was it? Quickly, she removed her hat and handed it to Mrs Knight.

'No hatpin?' she tutted. 'What would you do if a strong gust of wind came along?'

'I'm sure you could find Miss Sullivan one, Grandma. You have so many, there's bound to be one that's a suitable match for the material,' Amelia said in her gentle voice.

'You're right of course, my dear. Perhaps you would place my workbasket on the table by the window.' Sarah watched as the girl did as she'd been asked, then wheeled her grandmother over to the light.

'I hear the little girl's father turned up this morning,' Mrs Higgins said.

'How do you know that?' Sarah asked in surprise.

The woman chuckled. 'The butcher told the postman who told the verger . . .' She shrugged.

'Perhaps I should ask the butcher when the inspection is to be,' Sarah replied, shaking her head in disbelief, before taking a bite of her cake. 'This sponge is delicious, Amelia.' The girl looked up and smiled then went back to helping her grandmother. Moments later, Mrs Knight was brandishing Sarah's hat aloft.

'Come and see it now,' she called. Immediately, the ladies fell silent then watched agog as Sarah went over to see what the woman had done.

'Goodness,' she exclaimed. 'I can't believe it's the same hat, Mrs Knight. Why, it truly matches this coat now.' The woman beamed and triumphantly held up a pin to match. 'I can't thank you enough,' Sarah said, placing the hat on her head before carefully inserting the pin.

'A little petroleum jelly combed through your frizzy hair would tame it a treat,' Miss Prior advised.

Sarah forced another smile. 'Thank you, ladies, for everything,' she replied. 'Now, if you'll excuse me, I really must be getting back to help supervise the luncheon. Thank you again for all your hard work.'

'I'll see you out, Miss Sullivan,' Amelia said, leading the way to the front door.

'Thank you for the refreshments and for your part in making those delightful smocks.'

'I really love sewing, so it's a pleasure,' the girl replied.

'I'm teaching the girls how to make aprons to sell at the Christmas Fayre and I only wish their stitches were half as neat as yours. Their enthusiasm far outweighs their talents, I'm afraid,' Sarah said, raising her brows as she recalled the antics of the previous evening. Amelia smiled and looked thoughtful for a moment.

'Would it be all right if I popped along to see them sometime? I'm a Sunday school teacher back home and rather miss being involved with children.'

'You'd be most welcome. It's dark in the evenings now, of course, but the girls also work on their projects each Saturday afternoon.'

'I'll drop by when my grandmother takes her afternoon rest,' Amelia smiled.

'See you then, Amelia, and thank you again for that delicious cake.'

What a lovely young lady, Sarah thought as she made her way back to the school. The girls were going to be so pleased with their smocks, and as for her hat, she mused, her hand going to her head. Who would have thought a tatty old felt bonnet could be turned into something as stylish as it now was? Complete with matching hatpin too. Just wait until she told Harry. Then she frowned. After the ladies' comments, she hoped Mrs Higgins hadn't found her wanting.

Her head was still reeling by the time she reached the school. Walking briskly up the driveway, a sudden movement on the roof caught her eye. Surely that was Mr Collyer. Oh no, the poor man, she thought, remembering how distraught he'd been earlier. She hurried indoors, ready to warn Harry, and narrowly missed bumping into April who was rushing down the hallway with a bucket in her hand.

'Can't stop, gotta take this upstairs. The rain's been pouring in onto the little 'uns' beds,' she explained breathlessly. Sarah nodded as she entered the kitchen, but didn't take in the girl's words.

'Mr Collyer's up on the roof,' she gasped.

Mrs Daws looked up from the pans she was juggling on the range. 'It were him that spotted the leak. Lying on the bed, he was, in the room behind,' she nodded her head towards the wall, 'when he noticed a damp spot on the ceiling. He's up there taking a look at the tiles. Like as not, more have slipped. Happens every year,' she sighed.

'You mean the roof's leaking?' Sarah muttered.

'That's what I said, Miss Sullivan,' she frowned. 'Why, you're as white as my baking flour.'

'I thought, I thought . . .' Feeling as if her legs were about to buckle under her, she slumped into a chair. 'Does Master Higgins know?'

'Yes, and very pleased he was when Mr Collyer offered to take a look. The master's busy supervising luncheon at the moment. That Miss Green's in there an' all. Don't rain but it pours,' the housekeeper sniffed.

'But it's not her afternoon for teaching,' Sarah protested.

'Sailed in here like she owned the place, and soon as she heard you were out, demanded a meal, if you please. Bold as the brass on the front door knocker, that one. Poor April's busy upstairs with buckets and whatnots, so she offered to supervise the girls' luncheon.'

'And what a good job I did, Mrs Daws,' Miss Green replied, appearing in the doorway of the dining room. 'I've never seen such disgraceful table manners in all my time as a teacher. They use the cutlery incorrectly, talk with their mouths full of food. It's quite disgusting,' she sniffed.

'I don't think that can be right, Miss Green. The children are not permitted to speak at the table,' Sarah informed her.

'They gabbled and grunted all the way through. It won't look good on the inspection report, you can be certain of that,' she added, ignoring Sarah's comments.

'May I enquire what you are doing here, Miss Green? This is not one of your afternoons for teaching at Red Cliffs.'

The woman gave Sarah a haughty look. 'I have come here today instead of next Thursday afternoon.'

'Might I ask the reason for you taking it upon yourself to change your schedule without seeking my permission, Miss Green?'

'Well, it wouldn't be fitting for me to be here whilst the inspection was being carried out, would it? Especially as my father . . .'

'Just one moment,' Sarah said, holding up her hand. 'Are you telling me the inspection is to take place next week?'

'That's what I said, didn't I?'

'But we usually get a letter telling us the date,' Mrs Daws protested.

'And I graciously offered to bring it with me,' the schoolmistress smirked, opening her reticule and drawing out an official-looking envelope.

'Like I suspected, there's a gapin' hole where the tiles have slipped. Been letting in the rain for a while, I would say,' Mr Collyer said, coming in through the back door. 'I can see water dripping right through onto the bedding.'

'Oh, what a shame,' Miss Green said, triumph sparking in her eyes. 'What will the inspectors have to say about the children sleeping in wet dormitories?'

'It's only affecting the one nearest the chimney,' Mr Collyer informed them.

'That'll be the girls' room, then,' Mrs Daws sighed.

'Don't worry, we'll think of something,' Sarah said more confidently than she felt.

'Dadda,' Monday said, coming out of the dining room. 'This is Maisie, my bestest friend,' she said, smiling to the girl who was holding her hand.

'Hello, Maisie, nice to meet you,' Mr Collyer replied, wiping his dirty hands on the cloth the housekeeper had handed him.

'This is hardly a social gathering,' Miss Green sniffed. 'It's time for lessons.' She ushered the little girls towards the door. 'Come along, you lot,' she called to the girls who were staring at them curiously from the dining room.

'See you later, Dadda,' Monday called as she followed the huddle of girls. 'Then we can go and get my present.'

The stoker shook his head. 'Little 'uns, eh? Not sure I like the look of that school marm, though.'

'So, Mr Collyer, what's the verdict?' Harry asked. 'Oh hello, Miss Sullivan, I didn't realize you'd returned,' he added when he saw Sarah. Then his eyes clouded with concern. 'Are you feeling all right? You're looking rather shocked.'

Sarah held up the letter and sighed but before she could answer, Mr Collyer spoke.

'That roof needs a fair bit of work doing to make it watertight. Some of it needs retiling and you'll not get that done by next Thursday.'

'We've not got the money to get it retiled at all. Why next Thursday?' Harry asked, staring at the man.

'That's when the inspection is to be. Miss Green kindly brought this letter with her,' Sarah said, waving it towards him.

'Did she indeed . . .' he began, then realized the boys were standing nearby listening. 'Right, boys, take your-selves off to the workroom and busy yourselves with your woodwork. I will be along shortly. Go along, scoot,' he urged. 'Bunter, you're in charge, and remember, if there's any trouble, you will answer to me.'

'Sir,' he called, and there was the thunder of pounding feet as they charged outside.

'I think we all need some tea,' Mrs Daws said, pouring water onto used leaves in the pot. 'Might be a bit weak, mind, but at least it'll help us think. Come on, sit down. A bit of planning is needed here.'

Like children, they duly obeyed. Sarah wrapped her cold fingers around her cup, and as the warmth penetrated, felt her spirits reviving. Realizing she hadn't actually read the letter, she unsealed it and scanned the contents.

'The inspectors will be here at 8 a.m. next Thursday,' she confirmed.

'Inspectors?' Harry frowned. 'We've only ever had one inspector before.'

'It definitely says inspectors,' Sarah confirmed, hastily checking the details. 'They will be here for the whole of the day, and if luncheon could be provided, that would be appreciated.'

'Oh, it would, would it?' Mrs Daws sniffed. 'I'll bring out the fatted calf then.'

Harry patted her hand. 'All your meals are feasts, Mrs Daws. The question is, what can we do about the roof?'

'I'd be happy to help,' Mr Collyer said. 'There's some stuff on my ship that would patch up the leak but it would only be a temporary job,' he warned.

'We'd be most grateful, if you're sure you're up to it,' Sarah replied. Then, aware he might have taken her words the wrong way, she added, 'I mean, you've had a terrible shock and . . .'

'I appreciate your concern, Miss Sullivan, but when Mrs Daws told me Violet, I mean Monday, had found comfort in the school routine, it made me think. Keeping busy will probably be best for me too.'

'Any help you can give would be most appreciated, Mr Collyer,' Harry replied. 'We are determined that Red Cliffs should remain open.'

'I'll go back to the ship right away,' he said, draining his cup and getting to his feet. 'Got to get Monday's present anyhow, or I'll never hear the end of it.' He raised his brows, but it was evident he adored his little daughter.

'Well, that's a relief,' Sarah said after he'd put on his cap and left. 'How has Monday been since he returned?'

'Same as ever. Apart from reminding him about her present,' the housekeeper chuckled.

'I'll finish my tea then go and see what Miss Green is up to. I've a feeling she won't be encouraging them to sew their aprons like I asked.'

'And I'd better return to the boys and their woodwork. Let me know when Mr Collyer returns, Mrs Daws. He may well need some help,' Harry said.

'Yes, Master Higgins,' the woman replied, frowning at the mountain of dishes waiting to be washed. 'Them scallywags have only cleared off and left me to tidy up. Well, it will have to wait 'cos I need to see how April's getting on upstairs.'

'I need more buckets, Mrs Daws,' April said, her face bright red as she appeared in the doorway. 'The rain's coming down in stair rods, and as quick as Pip and I empty the buckets, they fill right up again. It's a right mess up there and no mistake.'

33

'Oh, April, dear, I should have come upstairs before,' Mrs Daws cried.

'Is Pip still up there?' Sarah asked.

The girl nodded. 'He's emptying the water into the large bucket on the landing and I'm emptying that into smaller ones and bringing them down fast as I can,' she gasped. 'But we need more. The bedding on at least five of the beds is already sodden.'

'Well, as I said to Miss Sullivan, it doesn't rain so much as pour,' the housekeeper sighed. 'Bring the wet things downstairs, April. At least there's warmth in the place to help dry it out.'

'There's plenty of space in my bedroom so we can move the dry bedding into there,' Sarah suggested. 'Mr Collyer is hopefully going to effect a temporary repair when he returns.'

Now she was upstairs, the hole in the roof was only too evident. Water was pouring into the buckets in a steady stream, and Pip was busy piling the dry covers into a heap away from the leak.

'Can you carry that bedding through to my room, please?' she asked the boy. He nodded and began doing as she asked. His movements were laboured, though, and Sarah could see the damp air was affecting him. 'When you've done that, go downstairs and have some of Mrs Daws' soup.'

'I can't do that, got to stop the water coming in,' he replied, his voice coming in gasps as he staggered under the weight of the covers.

'Mr Collyer's gone to get some materials to do just that,' she told him. 'You've both done a sterling job,' she added as April appeared with another bucket. 'I'll carry on here whilst you go and get some hot food inside you,' she said, her heart going out to the conscientious youngsters, who weren't much more than children themselves.

As they nodded and disappeared down the stairs, she heard a scraping noise coming from the rain-spattered roof. Then a face appeared through the gap left by the missing tiles.

'Managed to cadge the stuff off the ship, so I'll get on with the job right away. You mind yourself, Miss Sullivan. Don't want you covered in this black sticky goo now, do we?'

'Do be careful, Mr Collyer,' she urged him. 'Shall I go and get Mr Higgins? He did offer to help.'

'He's already down there holding the ladder steady,' the man called.

Then she heard a thud followed by scraping. The room went dark as the daylight stopped showing through the roof. Making a quick assessment of the state of the dormitory, Sarah gave a sigh of relief. Thanks to April and Pip's admirable efforts, it seemed the damage had been contained to the far end. Seeing there was nothing else she could do until the repair had been completed, she made her way back down the stairs to empty one of the buckets.

The best thing would be for the girls to move into her room for the night. It would be a squeeze, but there were extra blankets in the big airing cupboard at the end of the hall, and they could bed down on those.

'Mrs Daws said inspection is to be next week,' April said, looking up from her bowl of soup as Sarah entered the kitchen.

'Yes, Miss Green brought the letter with her,' Sarah replied, patting her pocket so that the envelope crackled.

'Not given us much notice, have they?' Pip frowned, his hazel eyes darkening to brown. 'The doctor used to spend weeks getting everything ready.'

'I reckon that witch has had that letter for ages,' April muttered. 'It's the kind of trick she'd play.'

Sarah stared at the girl in surprise, for hadn't she been thinking the same thing? 'Well, the date is set and we shall do our best to be ready,' she replied, keeping her voice light. 'Talking of Miss Green, I really must see how she's getting on.'

'Mrs Daws has gone to see if Mrs Laver can come over for a couple of hours to help with the bedding,' April said. 'She said we were to find ourselves some dry clothes from the donations. I'm fed up with being a charity basket, not that people aren't very kind giving us things they've finished with,' she added quickly as Pip nudged her. 'It's just that it would be nice to wear something that's been made just for you.'

Sarah patted the girl's shoulder. 'And so you shall, April. Mrs Knight has set up a sewing bee and the ladies are making new smocks for all the girls and shirts for the boys of Red Cliffs, so . . .'

'You mean that includes us?' April gasped, staring at Sarah in surprise.

'As two of the most important people at Red Cliffs, both you and Pip need to look smart for the inspection, don't you?'

'Well, I'll be,' April murmured, sounding for all the world like the housekeeper. 'Did you hear that, Pip? We're to have our very own tops.'

Pip, more interested in his food, merely nodded.

Sarah smiled at the look of wonder on April's face, but as she made her way to the schoolroom, she had a dreadful thought. Everyone had expected the inspection wouldn't be for a few weeks yet. Would the ladies have enough time to finish their work? The strident tones of the schoolmistress broke into her thoughts.

'Get back to your work, Edith Curdy, or do you want to be locked in the coal store again?'

'No,' the girl cried.

'Then do as you're told,' the woman snapped.

Sarah threw open the door and stared around the room. Far from working on the aprons, as she'd instructed, the girls were sitting despondently stitching their samplers. Then she saw Kitty trying to console Edith, who was trembling so much she could hardly hold her needle. Incensed beyond words, Sarah took a deep breath to steady herself.

'What is the meaning of this, Miss Green?' she asked, endeavouring to keep her voice steady, as she was conscious the girls were watching.

'I'm sure I don't know what you mean, Miss Sullivan. The girls are learning their stitches as they normally do during my lesson,' the mistress replied, placing emphasis on the word 'my'.

'I would remind you that I expressly asked that you supervise their apron-making during the needlework classes.'

'And I would remind you that you are not school-mistress here, Miss Sullivan, I am. It is up to me what I choose to teach and how I conduct my lessons,' the woman responded, drawing herself up to her full height. 'Besides, with the inspection taking place next week, I'd have thought you would be doing everything to comply with regulations.' As the woman stood smirking in front of her, Sarah felt intense loathing spread throughout her body. Inspection or not, there was no way she was going to be blackmailed.

'She were going to shut Edith in the coal store, miss,' Kitty piped up.

'Kitty Bawden, get your miserable body out here. I will show you how we deal with common little sneaks,' the woman snarled, snatching up her ruler.

'Put that down at once,' Sarah ordered.

The mistress curled her lips. 'You are making my position here untenable, Miss Sullivan.'

'Then I suggest you remove yourself from the prem-ises,' Sarah said coldly.

'You'll be sorry,' the woman warned, grabbing her bag. 'I shall inform the local authority immediately.'

'I'd be obliged if you would, Miss Green. Good day to you,' she added.

As the door slammed closed behind the woman, a cheer went up from the class.

'You told her good and proper, miss,' Kitty chuckled.

Sarah smiled tremulously then sank onto the chair the mistress had vacated. What had she done?

'Would you like a drink of water, miss?' Monday asked. 'Mamma always got me water when I was feeling icky.'

Seeing the concerned look on the little girl's face, Sarah smiled. 'That's very kind, Monday, but I'm feeling much better now, thank you,' she replied, making an effort to pull herself together. 'Right, girls, it's time for break. Go into the kitchen and have a hot drink. Then we will work on our aprons in the dining room for the rest of the afternoon,' she told them, thinking it would be good for them to be away from the site of the recent unpleasant scene. Slowly following after them, she reflected on what a day it had turned out to be and how she couldn't wait for night and the sanctuary of her bed. Then she remembered she'd be sharing her room with at least six others and sighed. It promised to be a long night as well.

'Everything all right?' Harry asked, as she passed. He was holding the ladder steady. From above came the sound of banging. 'You look all in. Haven't overdone it, have you?' he asked, his eyes clouding with concern.

'I think Miss Green has left Red Cliffs for good,' Sarah admitted. Taking a deep breath, she began telling him all that had gone on.

'We can't have Edith locked in the coal store and I know your feelings about physical punishment,' he replied. 'I can't deny it's bad timing, though.'

'Especially as she's threatening to tell the authorities her position here is untenable,' Sarah sighed. Then she remembered what Mrs Higgins had told her, but before she could tell him, there was a shout from above.

'Finished up here. I'm coming down,' Mr Collyer called, peering over the edge of the roof at them.

'Right, I'll steady the ladder then,' Harry called. 'You go on in, Sarah. It might not be raining now, but it's getting cold, and we can't have you catching a chill, can we? Besides, the children probably need supervision by now.'

As Sarah opened the door of the kitchen, she was met by the smell of wet laundry. Mrs Laver was helping the housekeeper hang the bedding on the pulleys, ready to be hoisted up over the range to dry. April and Pip were valiantly tackling the pile of luncheon dishes, whilst the children were standing around watching as they supped their afternoon drinks. When the last pulley was in place, Mrs Daws rubbed her hands on her tea towel then bent and opened the oven door. Immediately, the room was suffused with the fragrant aroma of baking.

'Hey, ugly cakes,' Bunter cried.

As the children clamoured excitedly around the big table, Mrs Daws waved them back. 'Calm yourselves. These need to cool. Besides, as that nice Mr Collyer brought the dried fruit and sugar back with him, it's only manners to wait until he joins us. I suggest you all go and wash your hands so you're ready when he comes in.'

'Did he bring my present?' Monday asked.

'If you run along with the others you'll be back in time to ask him, won't you?' the housekeeper said, flapping her hands as she shooed them all outside.

'I was thinking, Miss Sullivan,' Mrs Laver said. 'If this inspection is to be on Thursday, the kids will need bathing and shearing on Wednesday night, so do you want me to come in then?'

'If you would, Mrs Laver, that would be helpful.'

'Might give me a bit of extra for me Christmas box,' the woman hinted.

'Of course,' Sarah agreed. 'And we really do appreciate your help today.' The woman grinned, her rosy cheeks flushing redder with delight.

'We've made up the girls' beds in your room, Miss Sullivan,' April said, looking up from the dresser where she was stacking the dishes. 'But where are you going to sleep?'

'I had thought the back room,' Mrs Daws said. 'But I'm not sure how long Monday's father will be staying.'

'He isn't,' Mr Collyer said, appearing through the door with Harry close behind. 'I've been mithering on what you said about Monday needing the security of routine, Mrs Daws. I had a chat with her earlier and can see she's happily settled. She told me she wants to stay here. Quite insistent, she was.'

'Well, Maisie is her friend,' the woman replied diplomatically.

'So she keeps telling me,' he grinned wryly. 'Then whilst I was fixing the roof, it occurred to me that keeping busy would be best for me an' all. So, if you've no objection, I'll return to my ship directly.'

'Probably best,' the housekeeper agreed. 'But you'll stay for tea and ugly cake, I hope. It's rare to have a treat mid-week, so we're mighty obliged to you, Mr Collyer.'

He stared at the cooling cakes on the tables and nodded. 'Don't mind if I do, but that cake looks mighty fine, so why is it called ugly?' he asked, looking puzzled.

'The children take turns in baking, and believe you me, the name often reflects the look of them,' the housekeeper chuckled and they all joined in.

'Well, it were hungry work and no mistake. Still, that patching should last you for a while, Miss Sullivan.'

'I don't know how to thank you, Mr Collyer,' Sarah replied.

'You already have by looking after my Monday. That name's quite growing on me, by the way,' he smiled. 'If you agree to her staying, perhaps we could talk terms like. I earn a good wage so 'tis only right I pay for her keep. I'll set about finding new lodgings then I can spend all my time with her when I'm on leave.'

At his words, Sarah's heart lifted. Monday would be staying *and* spending time with her father. 'That would appear to be the ideal solution,' Sarah agreed. 'And of course, we can review the situation as time goes on.'

'Well, that's a weight off me mind,' he replied. Then his face clouded. ''Tis goin' to take some time gettin' used to not having my Holly to come home to.'

'If we can do anything to help . . .' Sarah began but he was lost in his thoughts.

'Well, young April, I can hear the kids returning, so come and help me slice up these cakes,' Mrs Daws said. 'I'm sure we're all starving after the shenanigans we've had today.'

'Did you get my present, Dadda?' Monday asked, running ahead of the others and hurling herself at him.

'Maybe,' he replied, making an effort to pull himself together. 'Then maybe not,' he added, scratching his head.

'Don't worry, Maisie, he always teases me like this,' Monday told her friend, raising her brows in an adult manner.

Seeing the others growing impatient, Mrs Daws clapped her hands. 'I think you should all go through to the dining room and sit nicely at the tables.'

'Off you go, pet, you can have your present when you've finished. We need to have another little chat anyway,' Mr Collyer told Monday. The girl nodded then followed Maisie. Sarah saw him look wistfully after her, but Mrs Daws patted his shoulder.

'Monday will be fine here,' the housekeeper reassured him. 'Now, sit down and have your drink. It's a rare old treat to have tea that's good and strong, and I for one appreciate it.'

'Me too,' Harry agreed. 'It was thirsty work holding that ladder.'

'How long do you expect to be away for, Mr Collyer?' Sarah asked.

'The next trip's six months,' he replied, then frowned. 'Of course, that's a long time to be away from Monday now that her mother . . . Will that be a problem, do you think?'

'Sometimes, in circumstances like this, it is best for a child to have time to adjust,' Harry pointed out.

Mr Collyer nodded thoughtfully. 'Happen you're right. Like I said, I'm that relieved Monday is happily settled. I'm willing to pay a fair price for her board.'

'We would be grateful for a contribution, Mr Collyer, and as long as we pass the inspection next Thursday, there should be no problem with Monday staying until you return,' Sarah assured him.

'And if we don't then God knows what we'll do with them all,' Harry muttered to Sarah.

34

After the upsets of the day, the children were late going to bed and then the girls were so excited with their new arrangements, they took ages to settle. Monday had been so thrilled with her present from her father, she'd insisted on sleeping with the little globe of the world under her arm.

'What a day,' the housekeeper said, stifling yet another yawn.

'Up the wooden hill, Mrs Daws,' Sarah urged.

'I can't deny the land of nod's calling,' the woman agreed, looking around the tidy kitchen. Marmalade purred at her from the chair beside the range and she smiled. 'You've got the best place in the house, young man. Well, everything's ready for the morning, and with any luck and a following wind, the bedding will be dry by then. Thank the Lord Mr Collyer was able to fix that leak, albeit temporary like.'

'We can discuss what to do about that and everything else in the morning,' Harry told her. 'You go on up, Mrs Daws, you've had an exceptionally busy day.'

'Goodnight, both.'

'Goodnight, Mrs Daws,' Sarah said.

'Sleep tight,' Harry added, straddling his seat. Sarah poured more tea into their cups then pulled her chair up alongside the range.

As she idly stroked the cat's ginger fur, Harry smiled. 'So, you're an ailurophile like Monday, then?'

'A what?' she asked.

'It means you have a love of cats,' he explained, giving his lazy grin before drawing a chair up beside her.

'Master Higgins, I do believe you swallowed the dictionary when you trained to become a teacher,' Sarah quipped.

'And I still enjoy perusing a compendium,' he replied, quirking his brow.

Sarah was too tired to rise to the bait. 'It's been a long day,' she said, stifling a yawn. 'Still, it's good news Monday will be staying.' As Harry shot her a knowing look, she hurried on. 'Although I feel sorry for poor Mr Collyer. It must have been a horrible shock to find the police waiting when his ship berthed.'

Harry nodded. 'Timely for us, though, for I don't know how we would have stemmed that leak so quickly without his help. Did you see Mrs Daws' expression when she went into the pantry and saw the provisions he'd left for her?' Sarah smiled, for the housekeeper had been beside herself with joy. 'How did you get on at Mrs Knight's?' Harry asked. 'Did Mother pass muster?'

'Goodness, so much has happened since then, I'd almost forgotten. Your mother was most congenial, but I fear it was me who was found wanting,' she sighed. 'Still, I'm sure you will hear her verdict when you return home.'

He looked at her enquiringly, but not wanting to elaborate on the shortcomings of her appearance and the comments about her friendship with the verger, she swiftly moved the subject on. 'The ladies have made such a concerted effort with those smocks, I only hope they have time to complete them all and fashion shirts for the boys. I'll have to pay another visit and let her know the inspection will be sooner than anticipated,' she sighed.

'I'll get Mother to tell them. If Miss Green informs the local authority her position here is untenable, we're going to be asked some rather awkward questions about staffing and will need to have our answers ready.'

'I don't see the problem,' Sarah replied. 'The girls can join the boys full time in the classroom for the time being, surely?'

Harry shook his head. 'If it were up to me, then yes, of course they could. However, there are some subjects on the girls' curriculum for which a female teacher is deemed essential. With the recent addition of Monday and Kitty, Red Cliffs now has more girls than boys in its care. We are up against it, Sarah, make no mistake about that. I've also noticed Mrs Daws is looking extremely tired these days,' he sighed. 'We need more help yet don't have the funds.'

'I'll help Mrs Daws as much as I can,' she assured him. 'As for Miss Green, I can't help feeling there's something behind her behaviour,' she mused.

Harry looked at her curiously. 'What makes you say that?'

Sarah shook her head. 'Women's intuition plus something I heard today. I think that woman has an ulterior motive for wanting to leave her position.'

'You'll need to be more specific than that,' he told her, his expression grave.

'I need to ask some questions to clarify,' she said, not wishing to elaborate until she was certain.

'It's just regrettable she took such a dislike to you. Not that it's your fault,' he added quickly. He let out a long sigh, and Sarah wondered, not for the first time, if she could have handled her dealings with the schoolmistress better. Yet the children's welfare was paramount. It was an impossible situation, she thought, trying to blink back the tears that threatened.

'So it will be my fault if the school fails,' she sobbed.

'Don't cry, Sarah,' he murmured, pulling her close. 'Nobody could have worked harder than you.'

'But it was me who upset Miss Green and if Red Cliffs has to close as a consequence, I will have let my godfather and everybody here down,' she cried as the tears finally spilled over and rolled down her cheeks.

'Oh, Sarah, don't take on so,' he whispered, staring at her tenderly. Pulling out his kerchief, he gently dabbed at the droplets. Overwhelmed by his sudden closeness, she stared into his eyes. He gave a groan then leaned forward and kissed her lovingly on the lips. But even as shivers of anticipation tingled through her, he moved quickly away.

'Sorry, out of order there,' he murmured. 'Remember, we are in this together, Sarah.' He gazed at her so warmly, the flecks in his brown eyes gleamed like liquid gold in the light from the range. Then, as if someone had snapped their fingers, his manner became brisk. 'Go and get some sleep. We have a lot of planning to do tomorrow. I'll come in early so we can work on our strategy for the inspection. Goodnight, Sarah dear.'

As Sarah lay in the narrow bed in the little room behind the kitchen, she felt warmer and more comfortable than she had for a long time. It must be because this room is cosier than the bigger one upstairs, she thought, her fingers straying to her lips. It was only as her eyelids fluttered closed that she remembered Mrs Knight had referred to their benefactor as being a she. It was a shame Mrs Higgins had sent her a warning look or she might have learnt more. Giving a yawn, she vowed to tackle Harry first thing in the morning.

Despite the upheaval of the day and her unanswered question, she fell into a deep sleep where brown eyes shone gold as warm lips met hers.

'You're late, Harry dear,' his mother greeted him as he let himself into their home. As he bent to kiss her cheek, she gave him a knowing look. 'I met your Miss Sullivan today.'

'She did mention it,' he replied.

'Dorothy Knight is certainly good at getting the best out of those ladies of the church. They are the most dreadful gossips, you know, and gave the verger a terrible time.'

'Oh, what about?' he asked, settling into the comfy chair opposite her and holding out his hands to the fire.

'Your Miss Sullivan, actually,' she said, giving Harry another of her looks.

'Spit it out, Mother, you look like a broody hen,' he said.

'Such a vulgar expression, son,' she tutted. 'The misses think Jack Wise is beguiled by Miss Sullivan and say the pupils of his eyes go heart-shaped whenever her name is mentioned.'

'Really, Mother,' he snorted. 'That's far-fetched even for you.'

'I wouldn't like to see you hurt, son,' she murmured, staring at him fondly. 'Oh, you might play the stern schoolmaster, but I know you're soft on her.' Harry frowned and she changed the subject quickly. 'Dorothy Knight nearly let slip the identity of the Red Cliffs' benefactor,' she sighed. 'Miss Sullivan wanted to know about her and I think she should be told.'

'What?' he gasped. 'But we were sworn to secrecy.'

'By the doctor, and you respected his wish whilst he was alive. But think about it, son. He left Red Cliffs to Miss Sullivan, so he must have had a high regard for her. Charlie was his special friend, without whose help, I might add, the school would have gone under long ago, so . . .' She left her words hanging.

Harry stared into the fire and stroked his chin thoughtfully. 'Perhaps it is time Sar . . . er, Miss Sullivan knew, especially as the roof has sprung another leak and it looks as though we shall have to go cap-in-hand again. Luckily, Collyer was able to effect a temporary repair.' Then he stopped. 'Oh, of course you wouldn't know about him.'

'Monday's father, you mean?' She grinned at his look of surprise. 'The purser of his ship told the butcher, who told . . .'

Harry held up his hand. 'So the Torquay turkeys have been gobbling as usual. That's not all, though,' he sighed. 'We heard today the inspection is to be next Thursday, and as if that wasn't bad enough, Miss Green is to inform the authorities her position at Red Cliffs is untenable.'

'Goodness,' Mrs Higgins muttered. Then she stared at Harry. 'Next Thursday, you say? Why, that hardly gives us time to finish the smocks let alone begin making the shirts for the boys.'

'Or for us to prepare,' he sighed and stared mournfully into the fire.

'I've promised to help with the sewing again tomorrow, so I'll let Dorothy know when the inspection is to be, shall I?'

'That would be helpful,' he replied, remembering his promise to Sarah.

'Harry, er . . .' his mother began, then looked away, embarrassed. 'I was wondering if we should make Miss Sullivan something to wear for the inspection. She looks so, well, what she wears hardly befits the proprietor of a school, and you know how important appearances are.'

'She looks all right to me, Mother,' he muttered, as a vision of her mane of wavy hair and eyes shining like conkers in the autumn flashed into his mind. 'Well, I'd better turn in. I shall be making another early start tomorrow. Miss Sullivan and I have to plan our strategy.'

'Oh goodness, Harry, I quite forgot to tell you, the Deaconess asked that you call by on your way to the school. She has something extremely important to ask you.'

Sarah woke full of joy that she would be seeing Harry first thing. She was certain that, despite all the obstacles being thrown in their way, they would work out a strategy together that would get Red Cliffs through the inspection. Although she was dressed and at her desk bright and early, Harry didn't appear. Disappointment flooded through her and she snatched up the letter from the local authority and perused it thoroughly. Just as she'd suspected, the schoolmistress had been holding on to it, for it was dated some six days previously.

Determined to be on top of her game, she was jotting down ideas when the door opened and Harry came in followed by a pretty young girl of about ten. She was wearing a coarse grey woollen dress covered by a pinafore and was gripping a small bag as if her life depended upon it.

'This is Miss Sullivan, Sally. I told you about her on the way here, didn't I?' he said gently. The girl surveyed Sarah curiously, then nodded. 'Sally has come to stay with us for a little while, Miss Sullivan,' he explained cheerfully. Sarah smiled at the shy little girl, then looked askance at Harry. After their conversation the previous evening, he surely wasn't serious about taking in another female pupil? Before she could reply, Mrs Daws came bustling in.

'I thought I heard voices. Hello, dear. What pretty ringlets you have. So what's your name then?' she asked, bending down and stroking the girl's long fair hair.

'Sally Jane Jefferson, miss,' she replied in a well-modulated voice.

'I was just explaining to Miss Sullivan that Sally is going to be staying with us for a while,' Harry said quickly.

The housekeeper stared at him in surprise then turned back to the little girl. 'Well, Sally Jane Jefferson, I expect you're hungry?'

The girl smiled up at the housekeeper and nodded. 'I haven't had my breakfast yet because unfortunately Madam the Deaconess is ailing.'

'Well, I'm sorry to hear that on both counts. Why don't you come along to the kitchen with me and we'll see what we can find?' she invited, holding out her hand. ''Tis going to be a crying shame, cutting off them beautiful curls,' she whispered as she passed.

'But she's such a pretty little thing, surely her head won't have to be shorn?' Sarah asked as the door closed behind them.

'Rules of the house, I'm afraid, and we can't treat anyone differently,' Harry sighed. 'Sorry to spring another pupil on you, but the Deaconess is very poorly indeed. She is in urgent need of an operation, then will require bed rest for some months. When she asked me if I'd take in Sally, well . . .' he shrugged, 'what could I do? The rest of her pupils are boys and are being temporarily accommodated at the orphanage. Sally, however, has a weak chest and the Deaconess didn't feel she would be up to the more robust regime they have there.'

'Poor Deaconess and poor Sally. She is so nicely spoken. Whatever is she doing in a home, anyway?' Sarah asked.

'Apparently her mother died last year and her father didn't feel he was up to the challenge of bringing up a child alone, especially a female one who requires extra care. He pays handsomely for her keep, and the Deaconess insisted on us having this,' he said, passing over a purse full of coins. 'That should help swell the coffers,' he joked, but Sarah was thinking of the little girl being passed from pillar to post.

'Poor little thing,' she reiterated, idly tugging at a wayward lock. Harry watched in fascination and only just stopped himself from reaching out and smoothing it back into the knot on the back of her neck. Remembering his mother's words of the night before, he cast a surreptitious glance over Sarah's attire and had to admit she had a point. Whilst there was no denying Sarah was a beautiful woman, her mismatched clothes didn't inspire confidence.

'Is something wrong?' Sarah asked, looking so stern he almost chickened out of saying anything.

'Mother said how pleased she was to make your acquaintance. When I told her about the deadline she offered to let Mrs Knight know this morning and, er . . .'

'What?' she said as he faltered.

'She thought you, that is, we might benefit from new outfits for the inspection as well,' he added quickly before his courage failed.

'New outfits!' she exclaimed. 'We have a roof that is leaking, a schoolmistress who has resigned, not to mention an inspection in a few days' time and you're worrying about what we should wear? Ye gods, Master Higgins, just what planet are you on?'

'I thought it was Earth, Miss Sullivan,' he teased, then ducked as a wad of paper came flying at him. He caught it deftly then grinned as she stood there, hands on her hips, pools of red flaming her cheeks. Without thinking, he took a step closer. 'Although last night I did wonder if I'd gone to heaven,' he murmured.

'Here we are, dearies, thought you could do with a nice cuppa,' Mrs Daws said, nudging the door open with her behind and entering the room with a tray of tea. As they sprang apart, she stood staring from one to the other. 'Well, well, well,' she chuckled.

35

As Sarah followed Harry through to the dining room, her head was swimming with details of the strategy they'd finally begun putting together.

'Think positive,' Harry murmured. 'Oh, and fish and chips,' he added, grinning as he made his way over to the boys' table.

Sarah couldn't help smiling back, until she saw Sally. Although the girl seemed happy enough standing with Edith and Kitty behind their chairs, Sarah could have cried at her changed appearance. The dress she was wearing fitted well and was obviously another of her own, but the beautiful ringlets had been cut off and her head shaven like the others. Was it really necessary in this day and age? she wondered. Yet in her heart of hearts, she knew it was. Head lice spread like wild fire when children were in such close proximity. That reminded her; she needed to send a message to Dr Hawkins. Although Sally had come from the prestigious school the Deaconess ran, the rules of Red Cliffs decreed all new pupils be examined on entry and, as the little girl had a weakness, she didn't want to take any chances.

As Harry put his hands together for grace, Sarah saw Mrs Daws beckoning her from the doorway. Quickly she made her way over to where Sergeant Watts was waiting in the hall.

'Good morning, Sergeant. You're out and about bright and early,' she greeted him.

'A policeman's lot is a busy one, Miss Sullivan. The citizens of Torquay are only able to sleep easy in their beds because the likes of us are busy patrolling the streets,' he replied, puffing out his chest so that his silver buttons strained, ready to pop.

'And a wonderful job you do too,' Sarah acknowledged. 'Now, how may I assist you in your enquiries today?'

He frowned for a moment before his lips curled upwards. 'Very good, miss. Although I do have some questions for you as it happens,' he said, putting on his glasses and flipping open his notebook. 'I believe one Christian Lawrence, nephew of the late Dr Samuel Lawrence, is known to you, miss.' He looked up from his book enquiringly.

'Oh, yes, we know him,' Mrs Daws muttered.

The sergeant nodded. 'And when was the last time you set eyes on the aforementioned, er, gentleman?'

'Must be a while ago now,' Sarah replied. 'It was when I was returning from my visit to the solicitors.'

'And you've not seen him since, miss?'

'No, thank the Lord,' Sarah replied.

'Why, what's he been up to?' Mrs Daws asked.

'He's disappeared, that's what,' the sergeant grunted. 'Just when we needed to ask him about a few matters. It was something that young girl . . . er,' he consulted his notebook, 'Kitty, that's it. What Kitty said got me pondering, and when Sergeant Watts gets his thinking cap on no villain–is safe, believe you me. Why, I remember . . .'

'You mean you think Christian's a villain?' Sarah interrupted, wishing the man wouldn't digress.

'I mean we are seeking this man to help us with our enquiries,' he replied officiously.

'Good heavens. Can you tell us in what connection?' Sarah asked.

'I'm afraid not, miss.'

'Well, if we see him, you'll be the first to know,' Mrs Daws told him. 'Now, can I get you a cuppa, Sergeant?'

'Very kind, I'm sure. However, with the long arm of the law to uphold, I must be about my business,' he replied, snapping his notebook shut and placing it in his pocket. With a brisk salute, he marched out of the door.

'Well,' Mrs Daws exclaimed. 'Whatever can that Christian have been up to?'

Sarah shook her head, not liking to voice the suspicion that was forming. 'I'm sure we'll find out in due course. Goodness, the children have finished eating already,' she exclaimed as the boys bounded from the room and out into the grounds. 'Thank heavens it's stopped raining so they can let off steam.'

'Here, miss, 'ave you 'eard 'ow Sally talks? Dead posh, it is,' Kitty said, coming out of the dining room, her arms linked with the new girl and Edith. 'Tell miss 'ow you says your name?'

'My name is Sally Jane Jefferson,' the girl said in her well-modulated voice.

'I wish I talked posh like you, Sal,' Kitty said. Sarah stared at Kitty, surprised she should worry about such things.

'And she talks French,' Edith added, gazing at Sally in wonder. 'Tell miss your name in French,' she said.

'*Je m'appelle* Sally Jane Jefferson,' the girl softly intoned.

'My present from Dadda's got France on it,' Monday said excitedly, holding up her globe. 'He's been there and everywhere else in the whole world,' she exclaimed.

'Well, let's see if this wonderful globe can show you the way to the classroom,' Harry chuckled, ushering them out of the door.

'Goodness, somebody has made an impression,' Mrs Daws said, staring after the new girl. 'And there was me worrying they'd be taking the mickey out of her posh little voice. There's just no telling with kids, is there?' she said, going over and letting down the pulley. 'Or grown-ups,' she added, giving Sarah a knowing look.

'Let me help,' she replied quickly, only too pleased to hide her flushing cheeks behind the blankets. 'I'm glad Sally has made friends so quickly, and Monday's globe seems to have proved a hit too.'

'You're telling me,' April said, coming out of the dining room with an armful of dishes. 'She and Maisie spent half the night chatting about where they were going when they were old enough to leave here.' She would have added more but there was a rapping at the door.

'Postie,' a voice called.

'Blimey, it's quieter in the music hall on a Saturday night,' Mrs Daws tutted. 'Come in, Robert. Gracious, what's all this then?'

'Morning, Mrs D. This one's heavy and no mistake, it's from your accountants, so it's probably your books,' he added, sliding the parcel onto the table. 'There's a letter from your solicitors as well.'

Sarah shook her head. There was no privacy around here, that was for sure. 'Is that all?' she asked.

He nodded. 'Suppose you'll be busy getting ready for the inspection next week, miss?'

'Yes, it's going to be a hectic time.'

''Specially with the leaky roof and all. They frown on things like that, these official bods. Well, mustn't stand chatting, got the Queen's mail to deliver.' He gave a cheerful wave and disappeared down the path.

'Well, no need to tell you what's in the post then,' Sarah chuckled.

'Looks like you're going to have enough to do, Miss Sullivan. You take that lot through to your office, April can help with these,' she said, nodding to the bedding. 'At least it's all dry so you can have your room back tonight.'

'Actually, I was thinking I might claim that little room behind here permanently,' she told the woman.

'But the room upstairs is much bigger, Miss Sullivan,' the housekeeper replied, staring at Sarah in surprise.

'And would be better used by the girls,' Sarah said. 'Their numbers have increased even in the short time I've been here.'

'They have been crammed in,' April agreed. 'And now we've to make up a bed for young Sally as well.'

'Well, if you're sure, Miss Sullivan,' the housekeeper said doubtfully.

'I am, Mrs Daws. Now, if you'll excuse me, I really must get on.'

350

In her office, she swiftly opened the letter from Mr Fothergill, and assuming it would be about the dispute over her uncle's will, quickly scanned the contents. Instead, it contained a new offer from the developers who wished to purchase Red Cliffs. When Sarah saw the amount they were now willing to pay, she almost fell off her chair. It would certainly solve their financial problems, she thought, but then they'd have to find new premises, which would not be an easy task.

However, Mr Fothergill went on to say that whilst there seemed to be no substance to Christian's claim on her godfather's estate, until this was finally proven, nothing could be done. He felt it his duty to apprise her of the situation. She carefully put the letter in her drawer, knowing her uncle would turn in his grave if his beloved school was sold.

The parcel, just as the postie had decreed, contained the ledger showing the audited accounts.

'We would be grateful if you would verify and sign that you concur with our findings, before the inspection,' the letter stated. 'We have pleasure in enclosing our invoice for work carried out and would respectfully remind you that our terms are for settlement within seven days.'

Sarah gasped at the amount stated, then let out a long sigh. As if she didn't have enough to do, she'd have to make an appointment to see the bank manager. For, apart from needing to draw the money to pay the accountants' fees, she had to establish their current financial position in order to pre-empt any questions the inspectors might ask.

*

Sarah spent the next couple of days meticulously going through the audited books and setting up her own accounting system. Having been told it would be up to her to answer any financial questions the inspectors might pose, she was determined to be on top of everything.

Although Harry had included the girls in his lesson on Thursday afternoon, what they were going to do on the day of the inspection, she really didn't know. She'd offered to take the class herself, but Harry had deemed this inappropriate. April could have supervised their sewing, but while the girls respected and heeded what she said, by her own admission, her stitching was wonky.

'Sarah, don't forget our fish and chip supper this evening,' Harry called, popping his head around the door after luncheon on Saturday. 'It's raining again, so instead of taking the boys to the farm we'll be doing carpentry in the workshops. How's it going?' he asked, pointing to the open ledger on her desk.

'If I never see another column of figures, it'll be too soon,' she grimaced. 'Gosh, is that the time? April kindly brought me luncheon here on a tray and said she'd see to the girls until I'd finished, but I'd better not take advantage,' she said, getting to her feet and stretching her back.

'You're looking tired, Sarah. A night out will do you good,' Harry said, staring at her tenderly. 'In fact, after the inspection, I shall get the doctor to prescribe us one every Saturday evening.' He grinned.

'Sounds good. Meantime, the walk to the classroom will have to suffice.'

Sarah had just settled the girls to their aprons when there was a knock on the door and Amelia appeared.

'I hope I'm not interrupting,' she said, gliding into the room.

'Amelia, how kind of you to come,' Sarah greeted her warmly. 'I was just showing the girls how to attach the straps to their aprons, so you've arrived at a good time. Girls, I'd like to introduce you to Miss Amelia Knight. She is one of the ladies who have been working hard to finish your new smocks in time for Thursday.'

'Are they ready yet, miss?' Edith asked eagerly.

'Manners, Edith,' Sarah rebuked the child, but the girls were looking at Amelia expectantly.

'That's all right, Miss Sullivan. You will be pleased to know they are almost finished.'

'Coo, you talk posh like Sal,' Kitty marvelled. 'Wish I spoke all nice like.'

Amelia smiled then turned to Sarah. 'Before I forget, Grandma has been stitching a dress for you to wear on Thursday and wonders if you would be kind enough to try it on. I said I'd let her know any adjustments that need making,' she said, holding up a parcel wrapped in tissue paper.

'Oh,' Sarah murmured, not knowing whether to be pleased or insulted. 'How did she know my size?'

Amelia smiled. 'My grandmother has worked in the trade for so many years she's developed a skill for estimating people's measurements.'

'I see. I'll try it on when we've got these apron straps sorted,' she finally said.

'I know Grandma can be a bit bossy but she means well,' Amelia said quietly.

Immediately, Sarah felt ashamed. There were all these kind people giving up their time to help smarten them up, and she was acting like a martyr.

'I'm sorry. I appreciate her generosity, really I do,' Sarah assured her.

Meanwhile, in the workshop, Harry was patiently helping the boys with the finishing touches to their toys. Never before had he seen such brightly painted boats. He couldn't fault their enthusiasm but, despite his encouragement, their skills left much to be desired. Still, knowing the generosity of the people who attended the church fayre, he knew they'd sell anyway.

'Hey, sir, do you think this tug would look nice with red spots on it?' Brown called, holding up his boat.

'I think it looks decorative enough already,' Harry said, trying not to sigh at the lopsided line painted along the side. 'Why not move on to another one?'

'I'm already on my third one, sir,' Black bragged.

'We must remember it's quality not quantity that counts,' he reminded them.

'Unless it's Mrs Daws' cakes,' Bunter sniggered.

'Here, sir, there's a smart toff trying to get in. Shall I go and open the gate?' Pip called from his position by the window.

'If you would, Pip,' Harry said, 'but come and get me if you need assistance. Right, now, young Luke, let's see how you're getting on.' Harry knelt down beside the young boy. Then he blinked in astonishment, for although the boy was conscientious, he was usually slow in his work. 'Why, Luke, that's a masterpiece,' he said, holding up a diabolo the boy had put together. 'Wherever did you learn to do that?'

The boy flushed with pleasure at the master's praise. 'Da taught me 'afore 'e died. 'E were clever like that. I still miss 'im,' he mumbled.

Seeing the little boy's face crumple, Harry quickly called the class to attention. 'Gather around, boys, and if we ask him nicely, Luke might show us how to assemble the parts of a diabolo like this.'

Seeing he was the centre of attention, the boy beamed. ''Tis easy, really. What you do is this . . .' he began, picking up two sticks and some string.

'Hey, sir, that toff has come to see Miss Sullivan,' Pip said, limping into the room. 'Did you ask his name?' Harry asked.

'Yeah, and he said it were none of my business. He's right mean-looking and his eyes is too close together for my likin',' Pip growled. 'He were carrying one red rose. I mean, if I were courting a woman I'd at least take her a whole big bunch.'

'Courting?' Harry asked, looking at Pip sharply.

'Yeah, I wasn't going to let 'im in on account of 'im being rude like, but he said he were her betrothed, so I fort I'd better,' he sighed.

'Betrothed?' Harry growled. 'Are you certain?'

'Yeah, I fort it was weird too, but 'e said 'e'd come from Plymouth and I remember her saying that's where she were from. 'Ere, sir, are you all right? You've gone all red,' Pip exclaimed.

But Harry didn't hear him. As a roaring sound pounded in his ears, he slumped into his chair. Sarah was betrothed? She'd never said anything. And all this time he'd been thinking she liked him. Why, he'd even been making plans for the future. Like a mirage, a picture of her sweet, smiling face rose up before him and he shook his head to clear it. He'd not be taken for a fool. The boys stared anxiously at their teacher.

'You shouldn't have told him that,' Bunter whispered.

'Why not?' Pip asked.

''Cos he's sweet on miss, that's why,' Brown said.

'Yeah, his voice goes all funny whenever he sees her,' Black nodded.

'Oh 'eck,' Pip muttered. 'I wondered why miss was all smiley when she saw him.'

36

'Rodney, whatever are you doing here?' Sarah exclaimed, hurrying into her office. When Pip had popped his head around the classroom door to tell her who was waiting, she was certain he'd made a mistake.

'Sarah, my dearest, how are you?' Rodney replied.

At this endearment, Sarah stared at him in surprise, for he'd never been one for sweet talk. 'I'm well, thank you, and yourself?' she asked politely.

'I'll be better when I'm out of my wet things,' he replied, taking off his great coat and handing her the dripping garment. 'And this is for you,' he announced, presenting the long-stemmed rose with a flourish.

As Sarah gazed down at the bloom, its petals crushed and bruised, memories of the way he'd left her for another came flooding back, and she felt a rush of empathy for the broken little flower. 'Thank you,' she said coolly, placing it on her desk before hanging his coat on the peg. 'How is . . .' She paused and pretended to ponder on the name that was indelibly printed upon her mind. 'Molly, that's it,' she said.

'Milly, er, Millicent actually. We are no longer together,' he said, looking at her as if expecting a joyous response. 'She wasn't you, you see,' he added when she remained silent.

'Well, no, obviously,' Sarah replied.

'I've missed you, Sarah,' he continued in the silky-toned voice she remembered him using when he was trying to get around her. 'Dare I hope you've missed me too?'

She stared down at the broken flower and reflected upon his question. She'd missed him terribly when he'd moved on to pastures new, but she'd been so busy these past few months, she'd hardly given him a thought. Besides, now there was Harry. Unbidden, a picture of his warm eyes and that roguish grin popped into her mind, and she couldn't help comparing them to Rodney's judgemental grey eyes and cool demeanour. Rodney saw her staring and his lips curled into a look of . . . triumph?

'That motto reflects us, doesn't it?' he asked, pointing to the sign above her desk.

'I don't see how,' she replied.

'Like us, love never faileth. I have come here today to offer you back your ring,' he announced grandly, placing the familiar little square box before her.

Sarah almost choked at his gall. 'You mean, you think we can just carry on as though nothing has happened?' she asked, shaking her head in astonishment.

'Indeed I do. Now that your father is dead, you will be able to devote all your time to me. That was the only reason I left, of course. A man's needs are paramount, even more so a husband's,' he smiled condescendingly, as if explaining something to a child.

Sarah opened her mouth to remind him her father had been dead for some time. For once, words failed her. As ever, Rodney was thinking only of himself, just as he always had. Mistaking the meaning of her silence, he gave another ingratiating grin.

'I can see you are overwhelmed, my dear,' he said, getting to his feet and walking to the window. 'When I heard you'd inherited property in this neck of the woods, I was staggered. Admittedly, it's a bit run down, but with some renovation it will make us a good home. Did the old boy leave you any money?' he asked, turning to face her.

'Old boy, money, good home?' she repeated.

'Always the parrot, Sarah. You really are going to have to start thinking for yourself. Of course, as your husband, you will have me to guide you. Even so, as my wife you will be expected to act with decorum, keep a good house and above all, my dear, dress with some semblance of style,' he told her, his eyes narrowing as he took in her mismatched top and skirt. 'Now, do put on your ring then we can go and present ourselves to the vicar.'

'The vicar?' she squeaked.

Rodney gave an exasperated sigh. 'To discuss the calling of our matrimonial banns. Do hurry up with that ring, Sarah. I don't have all day.'

Sarah stared from the stern expression on his face to the little box on her desk. Slowly her hand moved towards it.

'For heaven's sake, Sarah, let me,' Rodney snapped, all pretence of charm evaporating like morning mist in the heat of the sun.

As if waking from a bad dream, Sarah snatched up the box and thrust it at him. 'You can take your precious ring and bullying ways back from whence you came,' she said.

He stared at her sadly, then shook his head. 'Oh Sarah, dearest, I'd forgotten how you hated surprises. Let me take you out for a nice meal. We can have some wine and discuss our future in more salubrious surroundings,' he said, looking around the sparsely furnished room and sniffing.

'There is nothing to discuss, Rodney. And if you require a handkerchief, I'm sure you will find one in your pocket,' she said, grabbing his coat from the hook and throwing it at him.

'Well, if that's how you feel, then I'm sure Milly will be pleased to have this,' he said, dangling the little box in front of her.

'If she's happy with such a pathetic offering then she might also appreciate this as well,' Sarah retorted, placing the rose on top of his coat. 'I'll see you out,' she said.

Closing the door firmly behind him, she didn't know whether to laugh or cry. To think he'd really expected her to fall at his feet. Of all the pig-headed, conceited, overbearing people she'd ever met, Rodney had to take the prize. To think she'd once contemplated marrying the man, she thought, going back into her office and sinking into the chair.

As she fought to regain her composure, she noticed the parcel Amelia had given her. Tugging at the string, she saw a beautifully cut charcoal-grey dress with lace collar and cuffs attached. Shaking out the folds, she hurried to the mirror in the hall and held it up against herself. She could hardly believe the transformation. Gone was the dowdy woman in hand-me-downs; in her place stood the smart proprietor of Red Cliffs. 'If only you could see me now, Rodney,' she chuckled. But, like the dowdy woman, Rodney was gone and it was time she resumed her responsibilities.

Hurrying back to the classroom, she was surprised to find the girls sitting in a circle around Amelia. Not only were they sewing, they were chanting as well.

'You sound as though you're having fun,' Sarah said.

Amelia smiled. 'I hope you don't mind, Miss Sullivan, but the girls asked if I could teach them how to speak properly. As they were *au fait* with what they were doing, they've been stitching at the same time.'

'Hello, miss,' Kitty said, her face wreathed in smiles as she carefully pronounced the 'h.'

'How are you, miss?' Edith enquired, eager not to be left out.

'How, now, brown cow,' the class chanted in unison.

'We's speakin' proper, miss,' Maisie said.

'We are speaking properly,' Amelia gently corrected.

'That's what I said,' Maisie agreed, nodding vigorously.

'Well, I don't know what to say,' Sarah replied weakly.

'You speaks proper all the time, miss, so you don't need to say anything,' Monday smiled at Sarah, who felt her heart swell with pride.

'We are all going to speak posh like you, aren't we, Sally?' Kitty said, turning to the new girl.

'I didn't actually realize I spoke any differently until you said, Kitty,' she replied in her serious way.

'See,' Kitty cried, clapping her hands in delight. 'That's 'ow we're going to speak.'

'Perhaps you'd like to inspect their sewing, Miss Sullivan?' Amelia suggested quickly. Sarah nodded and went around the group, checking all their aprons. Their stitching, whilst not perfect, was certainly passable. Then she saw Edith's apron and gasped.

'Goodness, that's absolutely wonderful, Edith.' The girl shrugged but Sarah could tell by the flush on her cheeks she was pleased.

'I told old Lettuce I could sew but she wouldn't listen,' she muttered.

'Well, you have all done very well, girls. Those aprons have come on a treat. It will soon be supper time, and if I'm not mistaken, Mrs Daws has just finished baking something nice,' she told them, remembering the spicy aromas that had been wafting along the hallway. 'Carefully pack away your sewing things, return your seats to their normal places, then go and wash your hands, ready for your meal.'

As the girls did as they'd been bid, Sarah turned to Amelia and smiled. 'Thank you so much, Amelia. I don't know how I'd have managed without your assistance. The girls have obviously taken to you and their sewing has progressed nicely. I can't believe they want to learn to speak properly.'

'They are a delight to teach and want to learn some songs next. Do you know, Sally sings like a little lark? The Deaconess encourages her to spend an hour each morning performing scales, as the exercises are good for her breathing.'

'My, you have found out a lot this afternoon, Amelia. Perhaps we can get Sally to teach the girls one of her songs,' Sarah suggested, staring at her in admiration. Amelia smiled then hesitated. 'Did you wish to ask me something?' Sarah prompted.

'At break, Mrs Daws mentioned Miss Green has left Red Cliffs. I know you are busy preparing for the inspection and was wondering if you'd like me to take the children for sewing on Tuesday afternoon?'

Sarah stared at Amelia in surprise. 'You are the answer to my prayers,' she cried. 'As your dear grandmother has been,' she said, holding up the charcoal dress. 'This is absolutely perfect. Please thank Mrs Knight for me.'

'I will, although in truth she cut out the material and I did the stitching. If there's nothing else you need, I'd better go and see how Grandma and her sewing bee are. They have made a start on the boys' garments and are determined to have them finished by Wednesday.'

'That is marvellous. I can't believe how kind everyone has been,' Sarah told her.

'We were all fond of Dr Lawrence and want his good work to continue,' Amelia replied. 'I remember he always had a sweet for me,' she sighed. 'I'll see you on Tuesday, then. Good afternoon, Miss Sullivan.'

'I want to hang up my dress so I'll see you out, Amelia. Thank you again for all your help.'

By the time Sarah went through to the kitchen, preparation for dishing up the supper was under way.

'Something smells nice, Mrs Daws,' Sarah told the woman. Then, remembering the fish and chip supper she was to share with Harry, she added, 'Although I won't be requiring any this evening.'

'As you wish, Miss Sullivan,' the housekeeper sniffed.

Thinking the woman was offended, Sarah asked if there was anything she could do to help. 'No, you go and do your paperwork,' Mrs Daws replied shortly.

Feeling she'd been dismissed, Sarah hurried through to her little room and set about tidying herself up as best she could. She toyed with the idea of wearing her new dress but decided against it. It was only a fish and chip supper after all, she thought, picking up the brightly coloured shawl before making her way back to her office to wait for Harry.

She lit the gas lamp and pulled the flimsy curtains, then set about entering the bills that had come in during the week into the new ledger. As she worked, butterflies of anticipation skittered around her stomach and she found it hard to concentrate. The little clock she'd placed on the fireplace chimed six, then the quarter and half hour, and still he hadn't turned up. Perhaps Dr Hawkins, having received her message, had called by to inspect Sally. Being the conscientious man he was, Harry always made time to talk to him. By the time the clock struck seven, she gave up all pretence of working and decided to go and see what was holding him up.

Mrs Daws was busy chopping vegetables on the big table and didn't look up when Sarah entered.

'You're not still working, Mrs Daws?' she asked.

'Well, these vegetables aren't going to turn themselves into soup for the Sunday children, are they?' the housekeeper replied tersely.

'Oh goodness, I'd forgotten it was Sunday tomorrow. We could do without that, couldn't we?'

'I'm sure the street children wouldn't be happy going without their weekly meal, Miss Sullivan,' the woman replied pointedly, before attacking a turnip with her knife.

'Sorry, I wasn't thinking. Have you seen Master Higgins?'

'Not since he went home, no.'

'Home?' Sarah said in surprise. 'But we were supposed to be going out for supper.'

'Happen he changed his mind then.' The woman sniffed and disappeared into the pantry.

'The children are all bathed and have their clean clothes ready for church tomorrow,' April announced, coming through with an armful of wet towels. 'Oh, I thought you were Mrs Daws,' she muttered, glaring at Sarah before going out to the washroom.

Sarah stared after her in dismay. What on earth's the matter with everyone? she wondered, sinking onto a chair. Even the cat stared at her disapprovingly before going back to sleep. Sighing, she poured herself a cup of tea from the still-warm pot and waited for Mrs Daws to reappear. When she did, she was labouring under the weight of a sack of flour.

'Let me help you,' she said, jumping up and taking it from the woman. 'You're looking tired, Mrs Daws. Couldn't this wait until the morning?'

'No.'

'Well, at least let me help.' Sarah said, reaching for the large mixing bowl on the dresser.

'I can manage,' the woman snapped, taking it from her.

Sarah watched as the housekeeper poured water onto the flour and began mixing it together with more force than was necessary.

'Miss Knight has offered to teach the girls on Tuesday,' Sarah told her. This was greeted by a thump as the dough was turned out onto the floured table. April came back in, shooting Sarah another glare as she passed. Then Pip came hobbling through carrying the boys' towels. When he too shot her a disparaging look, Sarah decided enough was enough.

'Stop right there, Pip, if you would. Now will someone please tell me why I'm either being ignored or glared at?'

He exchanged looks with Mrs Daws then sighed. ''Cos you've been leading Master Higgins up the garden path. He's right upset.'

'Never seen him looking so miserable,' Mrs Daws muttered. ''Tis a crying shame, what with him being a decent man and all.'

'Let me get this straight. You're saying Master Higgins has gone home because he's upset and it's my fault?' Sarah asked.

'Yeah, proper unhappy he was,' April said, coming back in with more dirty laundry.

'But what has that to do with me?' Sarah asked.

'He really liked you, miss,' Pip said.

'And I really like him, so what's the problem?'

'You already got a fella, that's what,' April retorted.

'Wouldn't have had you down as the type for twice-timing,' Mrs Daws sniffed. 'Still, you can never tell.'

'Twice-timing?' Sarah asked, perplexed.

'You mean two-timing, Mrs Daws,' April explained. 'With that toff who came.'

'Oh Rodney, you mean,' she cried, realization dawning.

'Yeah, him, the one with his eyes too close together,' Pip nodded. 'Poor Master Higgins went all crumpled when he heard your betrothed had come calling.'

'But Rodney is not my betrothed,' Sarah cried. 'I mean, we were many months ago but he broke it off. When he came back today wanting to resume our relationship, I said no and sent him packing.'

'So this Rodney ain't your feller then?' April asked, her face brightening.

'No, most definitely not,' Sarah vehemently assured her.

'Oh 'eck,' Pip muttered.

37

Sarah sank into bed, her feeling of dismay turning to anger. That Harry should have such little faith in her, hurt more than she cared to admit. Determined to have it out with him the next morning, she fell into a restless sleep. It was late when she woke. She dressed quickly and hurried through to the kitchen.

'Good morning, Mrs Daws,' she greeted the housekeeper.

'Is it?' the woman sighed. Thinking she was still being blamed for the misunderstanding of the previous evening, Sarah opened her mouth. 'Master Higgins hasn't turned up. I can't think what's happened to him,' Mrs Daws cried, staring at Sarah as if she had the answer. 'I'm sorry if I was hasty in my judgement of you last evening, Miss Sullivan. I was that worried the master was hurt, I wasn't thinking straight.'

And what about me, Sarah wanted to scream, but seeing the concern on the housekeeper's face, she bit back her retort. 'He's probably waiting at the church gates for us,' she replied, turning to Pip and April who were hovering in the doorway. 'Get the children into line, please.'

'Ooh, miss, do you think the master's jumped into the sea and drowned of a broken heart?' April cried, putting her hand on her chest dramatically.

'No, I do not, April,' Sarah replied firmly. 'Now, please hurry along. It would look bad if we arrived after the service has begun.'

'Miss Sullivan.' Sarah heard Mrs Knight call as she was making her way outside after the service. 'Now the inspection has been brought forward, I'm afraid there's no way we can get the boys' shirts made in time,' she said, her grey eyes clouding.

Sarah's heart sank. She'd set her heart on all the pupils appearing in some sort of uniform.

'Never mind, Mrs Knight,' she replied, swallowing hard. 'You and your sewing bee have done a fantastic job fashioning the girls' pinafore smocks and I can't thank you enough for my smart dress. It fits perfectly.'

'Good,' the woman replied. 'We understand how important this inspection is, and don't want to let you down. Therefore, hoping you'd be agreeable, we have already started sewing red waistcoats for the boys instead. Oh, and one for Master Higgins too, of course. I see he's not with you today, and neither is his mother. I do hope everything is all right?'

'I'm sure it is,' she assured the woman quickly. 'Waistcoats for the boys would be marvellous, Mrs Knight,' Sarah cried, her spirits lifting. 'You have all been so kind, I hope you and the ladies will allow us to show our gratitude by joining us at Red Cliffs for tea one afternoon.'

The woman nodded enthusiastically, setting the feathers on the side of her elegant hat fluttering. 'That would be delightful. In the meantime, Amelia can bring all the garments that are finished when she comes on Tuesday.

I'm sure our verger here will oblige by delivering the rest on Wednesday afternoon.'

'Indeed I will,' Jack Wise said, appearing at her side. 'If you are ready, Mrs Knight, I will see you safely home before presenting myself for one of Mrs Daws' splendid lunches.' He beamed at Sarah, and despite her whirling thoughts, she couldn't help but smile back.

'Good morning, Mrs Knight,' she bid the woman. 'I'll see you later, then, Mr Wise.'

'I'll look forward to it,' he replied, rubbing his stomach in anticipation.

Sarah caught up with Mrs Daws, then followed the crocodile of children back to Red Cliffs.

'I can't help worrying about the master,' the woman murmured.

'I'm sure he'll be waiting, ready to help with the luncheon. His mother probably required his services for something,' Sarah assured her.

She certainly didn't have Harry down for sulking, but then you didn't really know with men, she thought, remembering the way Rodney had flounced out of her office. Misunderstanding or not, the reactions of Mrs Daws, April and Pip made her realize that mixing business and pleasure was best avoided. From now on, Red Cliffs and its pupils would come first, she thought, dismissing the sinking feeling in her stomach.

The master was not waiting when they arrived back at the school. Under the guidance of April and Pip, the pupils served the urchins their soup, then ate their own luncheon. Having cleared away, they were letting off steam in the grounds when he finally made an appearance.

'Master Higgins, whatever do you look like?' Mrs Daws cried.

He put his hand to the livid bruise on his cheek and the dressing covering one ear and grimaced. 'Got set on by thugs,' he muttered. 'I was passing by the station when they tried to nab my wallet. Gave me this for stopping them.'

'You poor thing. Sit yourself down and have a cuppa,' the housekeeper ordered, lifting the big brown pot. 'Thanks to Mr Collyer, we've got good strong tea. I was saying to Miss Sullivan this morning, in all the years you've been at Red Cliffs, I've never known you not show up.'

'I'm sorry to let you down, but the police insisted on escorting me to the hospital to have my ear checked, then I had to accompany them to the police station to identify the thugs.'

'My, my,' Mrs Daws clucked. 'How many were there?'

'Two set about me but they've also arrested their ringleader. I think you'd better sit down too, Miss Sullivan, for what I'm about to tell you will come as a shock.' Sarah was about to refuse but seeing the look in his eye, took the chair furthest from him.

'Bet it were that toff I told the sergeant about,' Kitty said, appearing in the doorway.

'Whatever are you doing in here?' Sarah asked.

'I was waiting for Master 'iggins to show up. Word on the street says they got the toff for them train robberies.'

'Word on the street?' Sarah asked, frowning.

'Yeah, one of them urchins told me when I gived 'im 'is soup. Said 'e were 'idin up the gypo camp near Yalberton.'

'Now then, young lady, it's none of your business . . .' Mrs Daws began.

'It is if one of them was the guv who beat me up,' Kitty protested. 'It were 'is patch, see?' the girl explained, looking at Harry.

'You're right, Kitty,' Harry replied. 'Sergeant Watts had apprehended him previously, then let him abscond in order to lead the police to the rest of the gang.'

'You mean 'e's banged up now?' she cried. He nodded and she punched the air in delight. 'Hope they frow away the key,' she screeched. 'An' were the toff the leader?'

Harry nodded and took a sip of his tea. 'Yes, he was found hiding in Madam Rosa's vargo,' he admitted.

'You mean, Monday's grandmother?' Sarah gasped.

'Wait 'til I tell her,' Kitty cried.

'Don't . . .' Sarah began but the girl had already scarpered.

'Let her go. Monday will find out soon enough,' Harry sighed. 'Look, Sarah, the thing is, the ringleader of these delightful men turned out to be the doctor's nephew, Christian Lawrence.'

Sarah raised her eyebrows, then nodded thoughtfully. 'I thought as much.'

'You did?' Harry asked, surprised by her reaction. 'I thought you'd be astounded.'

'I had my suspicions when Sergeant Watts was questioning Kitty.'

'To think the poor doctor had a nephew as crooked as a dog's hind leg,' Mrs Daws sniffed. 'He'd be turning in his grave, if he had one.'

'At least they've caught up with him, that's the main thing,' Sarah said, ignoring the reference to her uncle's lack of grave, which she still found hard to understand.

'And he'll be put away for quite some time, from what the sergeant said,' Harry told them. Then he winced and put his hand to his head.

'Time you was heading home for a rest, Master Higgins,' Mrs Daws said gently. 'You've had one heck of a time by the sound of it.'

'It certainly wasn't the way I'd planned to spend Saturday night,' he replied, looking pointedly at Sarah.

'Like Mrs Daws said, you should go home and rest,' she told him, not wishing to be drawn into a conversation. He opened his mouth to protest, then, as if it was too much effort, got to his feet.

'I'll be fine by the morning and we can discuss everything then,' he said, giving Sarah a rueful smile.

'We'll certainly need to finalize our strategy,' she told him, then looked quickly away as hurt sparked in his eyes. He might still have the wrong idea about Rodney, but she could not forget the way he had abandoned her the previous evening without even asking her for an explanation. 'However, I have an appointment with the bank manager first thing and then have to put the finishing touches to my new filing system, so it will have to wait until after supper.'

The bank was busy that Monday morning, and despite having an appointment, Sarah had to wait. She spent her time watching the customers as they came and went. Their stylish attire made Sarah felt quite dowdy and she wished she'd thought to put on her new charcoal dress.

The trouble was, now there were so many children at Red Cliffs, her clothes were invariably the worse for wear by the end of the day, and she was determined to look as smart as she could on Thursday. She now knew how April felt about wearing other people's cast-offs, and resolved her first task after the aprons were finished would be to show the girls how to adapt the donated clothes to fit them.

'Miss Sullivan, my apologies for keeping you waiting,' Mr Collings greeted her as he ushered her through to his immaculately tidy office. 'Now, how may I help?' he asked when they were both seated and he'd dispensed with the small talk. He listened attentively, then glanced down at the file on the desk in front of him.

'I can certainly let you draw the sum you require to pay your accountant, Miss Sullivan,' he told her.

'Thank you. I would also like to discuss the possibility of taking out a loan,' Sarah told him.

The man frowned then sat back in his seat. 'What would be the purpose of this money, may I ask?'

'The roof has been leaking. Although a temporary repair has been effected, I have been told the tiles need replacing, which will be quite an expenditure,' she told him.

'Indeed,' he agreed. 'Tell me, Miss Sullivan, if the bank were to agree a loan, exactly how do you propose repaying it?'

Sarah swallowed hard, for in truth she had no idea, but he was waiting for her to answer. 'I've thought of things the school could do to raise funds for the repayments,' she assured him. 'We shall grow more vegetables to sell and the girls are becoming quite proficient at sewing so . . .' Her voice tailed off as the man smiled, not unkindly.

'Small fry, Miss Sullivan. Whilst your intentions are to be admired, it will take more than a spot of fundraising to meet the repayments, and I'm not sure that . . .'

'The important thing is the children have a secure roof over their heads,' she interjected.

'Again, I admire your sentiments, Miss Sullivan, really I do. However, in order to secure sufficient funding, Red Cliffs would have to be held as surety. Have you received confirmation that Red Cliffs now belongs to you? I was given to understand your godfather's will was being contested.'

Sarah swallowed again. Was nothing private around here? 'That's true. However, Mr Fothergill doesn't think the claim will stand up in court. He is taking advice on the matter and will confirm as soon as he hears. Besides, Mr Lawrence has been arrested and is being held in custody.'

'So I understand, Miss Sullivan. However, he has yet to stand trial and even that wouldn't alter his claim, I'm afraid. I had a healthy regard for your godfather, and there's nothing I would like more than to be able to help. However, even if it is proven Red Cliffs is your property, I wouldn't be able to advance you such a sum of money without proof you could make the repayments. The interest on such a sum would be quite considerable, have you thought of that?'

'Yes, of course,' she replied, returning his candid gaze.

He smiled knowingly. 'Look, my dear, your determination to keep the school open is to be applauded. However,

I would not be doing my job if I didn't point out that were you to secure a loan and then found yourself unable to meet your repayments, the bank would have no alternative but to seize the property and then where would the pupils go? Better a leaky roof than no roof, eh?'

Although he smiled kindly, Sarah could tell he meant what he was saying. 'Well, thank you for your time, Mr Collings,' she replied, getting to her feet.

'I just wish I could be of more help, Miss Sullivan.'

Whatever had she been thinking of? she thought, making her way out of the bank. Even if she had managed to secure a loan, once the roofer had been paid for his time and materials, there would be no money left to meet the repayments. If the inspectors insisted the roof needed replacing, the property would have to be sold and Red Cliffs would shut anyhow. It didn't matter which way she turned, she was stuck between a rock and a hard place.

Having paid the accountants and secured a receipt, she was hurrying down the main street when she bumped into Miss Green coming out of the draper's. The woman grinned superciliously and turned away, but Sarah was not to be put off.

'Good morning, Miss Green. I see you have had a busy morning,' Sarah said, indicating the large parcel under the woman's arm.

'I have indeed, Miss Sullivan,' the woman smirked. 'I'm surprised to see you out and about. I would have thought you'd be preparing for the school's inspection.'

'Everything is taken care of, Miss Green,' she replied, crossing her fingers behind her back. 'Which is just as well, since I saw from the date on the letter that you failed to hand it over in a timely manner.'

The woman bristled, her smile replaced with a scowl. 'It isn't going to make any difference. Red Cliffs will be closed and then me and . . .' The woman stuttered to a halt, aware she'd said more than she'd intended. 'Red Cliffs will get what is coming to it.'

'You believe in karma, Miss Green?' Sarah asked.

'Eh?' the woman frowned.

'I too believe what goes around comes around,' Sarah smiled. When the woman still looked blank, Sarah added, 'Whatever ye sow, so shall ye reap.'

Aware they were drawing curious glances from passers-by, Sarah bade Miss Green farewell. As she hurried away, she could feel the woman's eyes boring into her back and hoped her hunch had been right.

Leaving the town behind, she strode along the seafront, hardly noticing the plush hotels with their ornate frontages and well-tended grounds. How could she secure funding for the repairs to the roof? One more storm and they would be in serious trouble, as Mr Collyer had warned them. Catching sight of a large ship crossing the bay, she wondered where he was now. At least Monday was happy, she mused.

Feeling drained after her eventful morning, she leaned against the wall and stared out over the rolling waves. How she wished some of their mighty energy might transfer to her, she thought, idly watching as a cork float bobbed on the sea. Valiantly, it rode the waves, making its journey out to deeper waters only to be swept back again by the incoming tide. Two steps forward, three back, just as her life had been since coming here, she thought. She sighed, remembering the hurt in Harry's eyes earlier. Had she been too hard on him? Yet trust was everything, wasn't it?

As Pip let her back in through the gates, he gave her an even brighter smile than usual. 'Me and April have had a word with the master about that Rodney,' he whispered, tapping the side of his nose. 'He's been pacing the kitchen floor for ages waiting for you to come back.'

'I see, well, thank you,' Sarah replied, not knowing whether to be pleased or annoyed at their 'help'.

It was going to take more than their intervention to put matters right, she thought, hurrying through to her office. Truth to tell, she was still smarting from Harry's hasty assumption and failure to speak to her. Moments later, there was a knock and Harry's face peered around the door.

'About last night,' he began.

'How are you feeling after your ordeal?' she asked, deliberately choosing to misunderstand him.

'Oh, er, I'm fine,' he replied, awkwardly rubbing at a mark on her desk. 'I was thinking, er . . . It's a shame about our fish and chip supper and . . .' His voice trailed off.

'Yes, it was,' she replied.

'Perhaps we could try again next Saturday?' he asked, staring at her hopefully. His expression made her heart beat faster but she wasn't about to let him off the hook that easily.

'I think we should concentrate our energies on the inspection, Master Higgins,' she finally replied. 'So let's discuss our strategy for the inspection.'

'Yes, of course,' he muttered.

38

The rest of the week passed in a flurry of activity as Red Cliffs prepared for the inspection. On Thursday morning, the freshly bathed children lined up in their new outfits, ready to be inspected, and Sarah felt a lump in her throat when she saw how smart they all looked. Even Mrs Daws was sporting a new white apron, which the ladies had made for her.

'You looks right pretty in that grey dress, miss, don't she, Master Higgins?' April cried.

'Yes, she does,' he replied, giving Sarah a warm glance.

'And sir looks right dandy in 'is new red waistcoat, doesn't 'e, miss?' Pip prompted.

Although Sarah had determined to keep her dealings with the master on a professional level, it seemed April and Pip had other ideas.

As they waited for her to answer, a cry went up from Maisie. 'I feel 'ick,' the little girl wailed and promptly was, all over her new pinafore.

'Oh, Maisie, dear,' Sarah cried, hurrying over to the little girl, who was swaying from side to side, her eyes shining feverishly against her pale skin. She was about to scoop her up when April intervened.

'Mind your dress, miss. Come along, Maisie, let's get you cleaned up. 'Tis bed for you. Oh blimin' 'eck, them inspectors will be wanting to check the dorms. I can hardly put her in there, can I?'

Before Sarah could reply, there was an insistent ringing of the front doorbell.

'Oh 'eck, they're here,' Pip groaned. 'Shall I let 'em in, miss?'

'Yes please, Pip. We'll be in my office,' Sarah replied. 'Put Maisie in my bed, April,' she called over her shoulder. 'And let me know how she is, please.'

'Right, everybody, make your way quietly out of the back door and around to the classroom. Pip will join you in a few moments,' Harry ordered.

'Me is goin' with Maisie,' Monday protested.

'No, little sproglet. She needs a good wash. You come with me,' Kitty said, taking hold of her hand.

'There'll be extra cake for those who behave themselves,' Mrs Daws called.

'I must remember to be good, then,' Harry quipped as he followed Sarah, but she was too nervous to respond.

'Mr Green and Miss Harmon,' Pip announced grandly, as he showed the inspectors into the office.

'Good morning and welcome to Red Cliffs,' Sarah greeted them.

'The new proprietor, I presume?' the man asked, placing his file on her desk. Although his demeanour was haughty, Sarah noted the cut of his suit was poor. The way his nose twitched reminded her of a weasel.

'I am Miss Sullivan, and Mr Higgins you already know.' The man grunted at Harry, who smiled in response.

'My colleague Miss Harmon and I would like a conducted tour of your premises, then we will check your accounts. They have been audited?'

'Of course,' she confirmed. The man grunted again.

'We would like to discuss the children's welfare,' Miss Harmon said.

'As we act *in loco parentis*, their welfare is of the utmost importance,' Harry agreed.

'Must be a difficult job, controlling those disturbed ragamuffins,' Mr Green snorted.

'We prefer to think of them as children with challenges,' Harry replied.

'That is infinitely better,' Miss Harmon agreed. 'We would also like to sit in on the children's lessons, if that would be agreeable?' she asked Sarah.

'As my dau . . . I mean, Miss Green has informed me she can no longer work here, I imagine that might pose a problem for your afternoon curriculum?' Mr Green cut in.

'Not at all, Mr Green. Although she had to leave us so hurriedly, we have been fortunate enough to engage the services of Miss Knight who has proved to be an admirable replacement.'

'What?' the man blustered, raising his bushy eyebrows. 'Why wasn't I informed of this?'

'I'm afraid as your daughter left very suddenly, in the interest of our girls, we had to take immediate action.'

'She found them rude and unteachable, Miss Sullivan.'

'And in return we found her disciplinary methods outmoded, and her inability to teach what was asked of her inexcusable,' Sarah replied, ignoring Harry's warning look.

'My daughter found her position here untenable and insisted her agreement be terminated immediately,' Mr Green continued, ignoring Sarah's outburst.

'I believe her to have an ulterior motive for that. She is soon to marry, is she not, Mr Green?' Sarah asked sweetly. The man opened and closed his mouth like a landed fish.

'Is that so, Mr Green?' Miss Harmon asked, staring at the man in surprise. Grudgingly, he nodded.

'In that case the point is academic, for Miss Green would have had to resign her position anyway,' Miss Harmon replied, opening her notepad and jotting something down. As the man flushed, Sarah felt like cheering. Round one to Red Cliffs.

'Allow me to show you the kitchen and dining room,' Harry said, breaking the awkward silence.

As the man began gathering up his coat and file, Sarah turned to him. 'Your belongings will be quite safe here, Mr Green,' she told him. He frowned but reluctantly replaced his things back on the desk.

'This is Mrs Daws, our *Dux Coquorum*,' Harry announced as he showed them into the kitchen.

'I'm the housekeeper,' she replied. 'I'm just making your coffyn, Mr Green,' she told him. Sarah nearly choked but the woman added pleasantly, 'I remember how you like a nice pastry crust on your meat.'

'Everywhere looks spick and span,' Miss Harmon commented, looking around the room. 'And your baking smells delicious,' she added, pointing to the fruit cakes on the dresser.

'The children made those,' the housekeeper informed her. 'Good little bakers, they are. You can try one with your afternoon cuppa if you like,' she offered.

'I'll look forward to it,' Miss Harmon replied. 'And this is the dining room?' she asked, wandering into the next room. 'Goodness me, what a marvellous view,' she exclaimed, staring out over the bay.

'More suited to a family room,' Mr Green muttered. 'I doubt the children even notice.'

'Maybe not,' Sarah conceded. 'However, continually breathing in the sea air does wonders for their health.'

'And is that a vegetable plot out there?'

'It is, Miss Harmon. The children grow all the produce for their own meals as well as the Sunday soup kitchen. Sometimes there is even surplus, which they sell to help raise funds for the school,' Harry explained proudly.

'Admirable,' Miss Harmon said, clapping her hands in delight.

'We have yet to see the dormitories,' Mr Green grunted. 'I understand you have problems with the roof? My daughter told me there was water pouring in all over the beds.'

'I think that was a slight exaggeration,' Sarah laughed. 'We did have a problem with a couple of slipped tiles but they were immediately fixed. The number of girls here has grown these past weeks so it gave us the opportunity to reorganize the rooms. If you'd care to follow me, I'd be pleased to show you.'

'I was given to understand the whole roof needed retiling so I will need to check that out,' Mr Green grunted. 'As our time is limited, I will go through your accounts and your housekeeper can show Miss Harmon around upstairs.'

'If you'll excuse me, I need to take the children for their morning lessons?' Harry asked the inspector politely.

'Very well. We will both join you in the classroom later, Master Higgins.' As Harry pretended to cut his throat behind the man's back, Sarah had to turn away to hide her grin.

'Ah, April, how is Maisie?' Sarah asked quietly as the girl passed by, dirty clothes in hand.

'She's asleep, bless her,' April replied. 'Probably a touch of the collywobbles. You know how she is.'

Relieved the young girl wasn't suffering from anything serious, Sarah led the inspector through to her office. She was pleased she'd studied the audited accounts, as Mr Green asked innumerable questions. Eventually, he put down his pen.

'You seem to have a good grasp of things here, Miss Sullivan, which makes things easier for me.' Sarah was just about to thank him when he dealt his blow. 'It is abundantly clear Red Cliffs needs an injection of funds to keep going.'

'We are still awaiting monies from the local authority for the new pupils we have recently admitted,' Sarah pointed out.

'Money which will be paid when the LA has also audited the school's accounts,' he confirmed.

Sarah's heart sank, for they'd been relying upon the funding to take them through to Christmas. 'And how long will that take?' she asked.

'It depends,' he shrugged. 'However, I'm more concerned about the lack of money available for the upkeep of the building itself, which you must admit is run down and dilapidated.'

'Really, Mr Green,' she protested. 'I agree the building does need some updating but it is hardly . . .' Her voice trailed off as Miss Harmon popped her head around the door.

'Come in, Miss Harmon,' he ordered. 'How did you find the state of repair upstairs?'

'All dry and cosy in the dormitories,' she confirmed.

The man frowned. 'Really?' he said, looking disappointed. 'Well, as I said earlier, Miss Sullivan, the local authority will require an inspection report on the condition of the roof,' he said, getting to his feet. 'Now, please direct us to the classroom.'

Sarah had to hand it to Master Higgins. Unperturbed by the inspectors' presence, he took the children through their arithmetic followed by a history lesson. He made the details of the latter so vivid, the children joined in enthusiastically, asking question after question.

At the back of the room, Mr Green frowned and wrote copious notes while Miss Harmon listened attentively. When the gong sounded for luncheon, even the children seemed surprised.

'I have set your meal out in the front room,' Mrs Daws greeted the inspectors. 'I know how nit-picky they are,' she muttered to Sarah under her breath.

'How is Maisie?' Sarah asked.

'Still sleeping. Don't worry, we're keeping an eye on her. We'll see to the children too,' she added.

'Thank you, Mrs Daws,' Sarah murmured. 'If you'd like to follow me,' she said, turning to the inspectors.

'Here's your coffyn, Mr Green,' April said, placing the man's meal in front of him. 'Mrs Daws says she hopes it's the right size.' As the man looked at her sharply, the girl smiled sweetly. 'Can I get you anything else, sir?'

'This looks delicious,' Mrs Harmon said. 'Are the children having the same?'

'Of course,' Sarah exclaimed.

'Don't look so surprised, Miss Sullivan. It is not uncommon for teachers to eat well whilst their pupils survive on scraps,' Mr Green advised her.

'Unbelievable, isn't it?' Miss Harmon said, seeing Sarah's look of astonishment.

'Unforgivable, more like,' Harry snorted.

'I must say, I thought the children all looked very smart,' Miss Harmon said. 'I was given to understand they went around in rags,' she added, staring at her colleague.

'I wonder who or what could have given you that idea?' Sarah replied, staring at Mr Green.

As soon as he'd finished his meal, Mr Green opened his notebook. 'As I've mentioned before, Higgins, your teaching methods give cause for concern.'

'Whatever do you mean?' Sarah exclaimed.

'Firstly, you still persist in seating girls alongside boys when we prefer them to be segregated.'

'They are seated by age, Mr Green, in order that they may be taught lessons in keeping with their comprehension. It is a method which works well, I find,' Harry replied.

The inspector grunted. 'To encourage good discipline and obedience, children are expected to observe silence for the course of the lesson, not ask questions, Higgins.'

'We find children learn better by interaction and engagement.'

'And there was no evidence of any punishment being meted out.'

'Children learn better if they are encouraged rather than punished. Although I admit to having a tawse as a deterrent, I am proud to admit I have never actually used it.'

'That is a thought-provoking theory, Master Higgins,' Miss Harmon said. 'I shall be interested to see what the afternoon brings.'

'Master Higgins will be taking the boys for carpentry in the workshop while Miss Knight teaches the girls in the classroom,' Sarah replied.

'What are they making, Higgins, rulers?' the man snorted.

'Actually, they are making boats, diabolos and simple toys to sell at the Christmas Fayre,' he replied mildly. 'Next term they will be fashioning purpose-built shelters . . .'

'To house them when your roof leaks?' the man chortled.

'To house the chickens the farmer is letting us have.'

'Fresh eggs for the children, marvellous,' Miss Harmon cried.

'Accepting charity from the locals now, eh, Higgins?'

'Far from it, Mr Green. As you well know, the ethos of Red Cliffs is that the children help to pay their own way. In this case, the hens will be payment for sweeping out the farmyard and barns and helping the farmer's wife with her dairy and poultry. Now, if you have finished your meal, I think we should be making our way back to the children.'

'You take the girls and I'll inspect this woodworking class,' Mr Green told Miss Harmon, obviously put out. 'Though why we waste good time and money on educating females, I really don't know. I mean, what good can it possibly serve?'

'Mr Green, your attitude is outmoded. It is vitally important the girls learn in order to better their prospects and those of their children. After all, they will be the mothers of the future generation,' Sarah told him, leading the way out of the room. She was just thinking what an obnoxious man the inspector was when Miss Harmon spoke.

'I must say, I'm finding this day quite fascinating, Miss Sullivan. Will the girls be participating in this Christmas Fayre?'

'They have been busy making aprons to sell,' Sarah confirmed. 'Of course, they'll help with the refreshments as usual, but I feel it is important they are encouraged to earn funds like boys.'

'I quite agree, Miss Sullivan.'

'Good, now let me introduce you to Miss Knight,' she said, opening the door of the classroom. Immediately the girls rose to their feet.

'Good afternoon, Miss Harmon,' they chorused, emphasizing the 'h'. Sarah grinned at Amelia. 'Good afternoon, Miss Sullivan.'

'Good afternoon, girls,' she replied. 'Please continue with your lesson, Miss Knight,' she added.

'We's going to use my globe,' Monday said proudly.

'That's right, Monday,' Amelia said. 'After we've finished our sewing we are going to use your globe to follow the routes used for trading. Now, as we have finished our aprons, we are going to make a start on peg bags. Isn't that exciting?' There was a chorus of enthusiastic cheers.

'Would you mind if I sit with the girls?' Miss Harmon asked, once the commotion had died down.

'Of course not, Miss Harmon,' Amelia replied in her dulcet tones. 'Please feel free to ask any questions.'

'Well, I do have one I would like to ask,' she said, smiling at the girls. 'You seem to be enjoying your lesson, girls. What about Miss Green? Was she a good teacher?'

'She said when we was ripe we had to close our legs,' Ellen told her.

'Yeah, else we'd have baby bunny rabbits coming out of our tummy,' Maggie added. 'I still don't get that.'

Looking bemused, Miss Harmon turned to Sarah. 'That was Miss Green's idea of teaching them morality,' Sarah explained. 'Oh, please excuse me,' she added, looking up and seeing April beckoning her from the doorway. 'I'm needed indoors so please carry on with the lesson, Miss Knight.' Sarah rose to her feet. 'What's the matter April?' she asked.

'It's Maisie, miss, she's boiling up and talking gibberish.'

39

'I'm worried about Maisie, Miss Sullivan. She's that feverish, I think we should call Dr Hawkins,' Mrs Daws said, getting up from the chair beside the bed. 'April and I have been taking turns to sponge her down, but it's not making any difference.'

Sarah stared at the girl, who was thrashing about and muttering in her sleep, and frowned. 'April, can you run and get him?' she asked.

As the girl hurried from the room, Mrs Daws shook her head. 'I can't understand it. She was fine when the doctor checked them over last night. It's probably nothing but . . .' She shrugged.

'You look all in, Mrs Daws. Go and make a cuppa. I'll sit with her until the doctor comes,' Sarah said, sitting down in the chair the woman had vacated and taking the little girl's hand. It was only when the woman had left that Sarah let out a quiet groan. Supposing her being here with the sick child adversely affected the inspection? That Mr Green seemed to delight in picking on everything he could. Yet she couldn't just leave Maisie when she was ill, could she?

'Come on, Maisie,' she urged but the girl just mumbled again.

The minutes ticked by, and Sarah couldn't help wondering how the inspectors were getting on. Miss Harmon seemed genuinely interested in the children, whilst Mr Green was determined to find fault. Lost in thought, she jumped as Dr Hawkins appeared by her side.

'I'll examine the lass, if you don't mind, Miss Sullivan,' he said, drawing his stethoscope from his Gladstone bag. 'Perhaps you'd like to wait in the kitchen.'

'I'd prefer to stay, if you don't mind,' she replied.

'Hmm,' he muttered, his head already bent over the little girl. Finally, he replaced the bedcovers and went over to his bag.

'What's wrong?' Sarah asked, unable to contain her anxiety as she followed him out of the room.

'There's no sign of a rash but that fever needs to break,' he replied briskly. 'Continue sponging her down and give her this draft should she wake,' he said, placing a twist of paper on the table. 'I'll call back tomorrow morning before surgery.'

'Thank you, doctor. I'll see you out,' Sarah said.

'I'll sit with Maisie,' April offered, looking up from the potatoes she was peeling.

'Thank you, April. I'll be back as soon as I can,' she replied.

'Don't worry, we'll look after her,' Mrs Daws added. Sarah smiled her thanks, then led the doctor to the front door.

'She'll probably sleep but don't hesitate to send for me if you need me,' Dr Hawkins said.

'Thank you, doctor,' she replied. She was about to shut the door when Mr Green strode in from the schoolroom, closely followed by Harry.

'Was that Dr Hawkins I saw leaving?'

'Yes, one of our children was sick this morning and is running a temperature,' Sarah explained.

'Hope it's nothing contagious,' the inspector shuddered.

'How is Maisie?' Harry asked pointedly as he joined them.

'Feverish. The doctor's left a draft for when she wakes and . . .'

'Do you mind if we get back to business?' Mr Green enquired, frowning at his fob watch. 'Come along, Miss Harmon,' he called to his colleague, who was still outside chatting to Amelia.

'I'm not sure I should leave Maisie . . .' Sarah began.

Mr Green clicked his tongue in annoyance. 'We are here to discuss the future of the school, are we not?'

'Very well, we'll go through to my office,' Sarah agreed reluctantly, knowing she was between a rock and a hard place yet again. What a heartless man the inspector was.

'How was Miss Knight's lesson?' Mr Green greeted Miss Harmon as she came into the room.

'Fascinating. She had the girls switching from sewing to trade routes to elocution.'

'But she's not a trained teacher?'

'She already teaches at Sunday School and will be commencing formal training next year,' Sarah supplied.

The man gave a triumphant smirk then wrote something down in his notebook. 'Obviously, I can only give you a brief summary of my findings at this stage,' Mr Green told them. 'You will receive the official report within a month, but I warn you now, my recommendation is that that Red Cliffs be closed.'

'What?' Sarah gasped. 'But why?'

'I must say . . .' Miss Harmon began.

'You are not here to say anything, Miss Harmon,' Mr Green snapped. 'This house is not fit for occupation by children, its roof needs replacing and the books show you don't have the necessary funds. Besides which, your teaching methods are questionable, Master Higgins. Pupils should fear their master.'

'Like I've said before, we have moved on from the days of finger stocks and back straighteners,' he pointed out.

The inspector ignored him. 'Finally, the girls are being taught by an unqualified teacher,' he concluded, snapping his notebook shut. 'I also understand there is a dispute over the late Dr Lawrence's will.'

'You mean the claim made by Mr Christian Lawrence?' Sarah asked.

The man nodded. 'A respectable business man who intends turning this house back into a family home.'

'For when he marries your daughter, no doubt,' Sarah replied. This was met by shocked silence.

'Is this true, Mr Green?' Miss Harmon finally asked, staring hard at the man. He avoided her gaze and shrugged.

'I received this letter from my solicitor yesterday,' Sarah said, pulling an envelope from her pocket and waving it in front of him. 'It confirms my godfather's will is valid and that I am the sole owner of Red Cliffs.' As the inspector blanched, Sarah played her trump card. 'As for your respectable son-in-law to be, surely you are aware he is currently in custody awaiting trial for theft and extortion? I don't think we have anything left to discuss, Mr Green, so I'll bid you good afternoon.'

Mr Green stared at her in disbelief then got to his feet. 'The fact remains that you don't have the money to replace the roof,' he spat, striding out of the room.

'I do apologize for my colleague's behaviour,' Miss Harmon said. 'Rest assured, I shall be filing a report of my own.'

'I'll show you out,' Sarah said as the woman gathered up her things.

On the doorstep, the woman hesitated. 'I do admire your spirit, Miss Sullivan. From the way you are encouraging the girls to progress in life, am I correct in assuming you believe that women should have the right to stand alongside men in society?'

'I most certainly do,' Sarah assured her.

'In that case, perhaps you'd consider attending a meeting of the Suffrage Movement. We have an active branch here in Torquay and would welcome a person such as yourself,' she said, delving into her bag.

As the strident voice of Mr Green summoned her, she firmly placed a leaflet in Sarah's hand. 'Do join us,' she urged. 'It's time we women had our say.'

'Well, well, Sarah, you played a blinder there,' Harry said admiringly, as he came up behind her. 'I had no idea Christian and Miss Green were actually betrothed.'

'It was just a hunch after something your mother said,' she admitted. 'But that still doesn't solve our financial problems or the roof, does it?'

'True, and Mrs Daws and I have something to discuss with you after supper, if you can spare the time?' he said, giving her a warm look that sent little shivers rippling down her spine.

'Sounds intriguing. Now, I really must go and check on Maisie.'

'I was proud of our children today,' Harry told Sarah as they sat in the kitchen over a late-night cuppa.

'They did look smart, didn't they?' Sarah agreed. 'You should have seen Miss Harmon's face when Amelia explained they were going to use Monday's globe to discuss the trading routes.' She smiled and took a sip of her tea. 'Poor Maisie's still feverish, though. Dr Hawkins said he'd look in again first thing.'

'If Maisie's in your bed, where will you sleep?' Harry asked.

'On the chair beside her, then I can keep an eye out in case she wakes during the night.'

'I'll come down and take a turn, if you like,' Mrs Daws offered.

'That's kind, but you've done enough already today,' Sarah assured her.

'Yes, your cooking passed muster, Mrs Daws, which was more than can be said about my teaching methods,' Harry remarked.

'Since when have you cared a fig for the opinion of the local authority?' Mrs Daws scoffed. 'You'll carry on in your own way, as you always do.'

'Provided they don't close us down,' Sarah sighed. 'Thinking about funding for the roof, Mrs Knight said something odd the other day.'

'What was that, dear?' the housekeeper asked, supping her tea.

'She referred to our benefactor as being a woman.'

Harry and Mrs Daws exchanged smiles. 'That is what we wanted to talk to you about,' Harry replied.

'Although it's been so busy today, I told him you might be too tired,' Mrs Daws said, stifling a yawn.

'I think now is opportune,' Harry persisted.

'Well, I don't know about that, but I think it's time.'

'Whatever it is, please tell me,' Sarah urged, looking impatiently from one to the other.

'It's about our benefactor,' Harry began. 'Well, bene-factress, Lady Charlotte Chorlton, to be precise.'

'Goodness, a Lady? Well I never,' Sarah exclaimed. 'So how did she come to be involved with my godfather and Red Cliffs?'

There was an awkward silence as Harry and Mrs Daws once again exchanged glances.

'Well, er, it's, er, delicate . . .' Harry began.

'Oh for heaven's sake,' Mrs Daws clucked. 'Your god-father, the dear doctor, well, he and Lady Charlotte were friends for many years, very good friends, if you get my meaning.' She paused to let the message sink home. 'She were the love of his life, actually. Never had another lady friend in all the years I knew him. And she loved him too.'

'So why didn't they marry?' Sarah asked.

'Well, it was difficult. Her husband were a sea captain . . .'

'Oh, she was married. I see,' Sarah sighed.

'I don't think you do, dear,' Mrs Daws sniffed. 'The good doctor wouldn't behave in anything less than a respectful manner.' She stared at Sarah so disapprovingly, she had to apologize.

'Sorry. Of course not. Then . . .' She stuttered to a halt, not sure how to go on.

'Lady Chorlton's husband was a jealous man,' Harry said, taking up the story. 'When he died, he left certain conditions in his will. Lady Charlotte was to remain single or she would forfeit her entire inheritance.'

'How dreadful for her,' Sarah muttered.

'He were that possessive, see. Couldn't bear the thought of her being with another man. Jolly selfish if you ask me. Still, there's no accounting for some people. Anyway, he left her a very rich widow.'

'And she used some of her money to fund Red Cliffs?' Sarah suggested.

Harry nodded. 'She and the doctor had to keep their relationship secret, see,' Mrs Daws continued. 'Otherwise she'd forfeit her inheritance and lose her home, while he'd lose Red Cliffs.'

'Poor Uncle Samuel,' Sarah murmured. 'Now that it's been confirmed I own Red Cliffs, I should meet her and thank her for her help.'

'Oh no, you couldn't,' the housekeeper cried. 'We was sworn to secrecy and I'll probably burn in hell as it is.'

'Of course you won't,' Sarah replied, patting the woman's hand. 'My uncle would understand you're trying to save Red Cliffs.'

'Why don't you speak with Mr Fothergill and let him decide how you should proceed from here?' Harry suggested.

'I'll see him first thing in the morning,' Sarah declared. 'I'm so pleased you told me. Now I really must go and sit with Maisie and let April get some sleep.'

Sarah sat with the little girl through the long hours of darkness, sponging her forehead and listening for any change in her breathing. The events of the day played around and around in her head but she kept coming back to the same thing. Lady Charlotte. She was so pleased her uncle had known love and been loved in return. Yet how tragic it was that they'd been denied the opportunity to marry. Knowing what a highly principled man he'd been, he wouldn't have been happy conducting a clandestine affair. She must be some woman, Sarah decided.

She was so lost in her thoughts that she didn't realize the first light of day was stealing though the ill-fitting curtains, until Monday crept into the room.

'I've come to say goodbye to Maisie before she goes,' Monday whispered.

'But she's not going anywhere,' Sarah replied.

'She's goin' to be an angel,' Monday told her, staring at Sarah gravely with her periwinkle eyes. 'Bye, bye, Maisie. I'll see you when you's an angel,' she whispered.

As the small girl bent and kissed her friend on the forehead, Sarah felt a shiver tingle down her spine.

It was nearly noon and Sarah was still sitting at the kitchen table, trying to come to terms with Maisie's death. Had she missed something when she'd sat with her through the long night? She didn't remember any change to her breathing. She had regularly sponged the little girl's forehead and chest, but should she have called for Dr Hawkins? Yet there'd been nothing to report. Numbly, she got up and stared out of the window. Outside, Kitty and Edith were cuddling Monday close.

'How did she know?' Sarah wailed, dabbing at her eyes for the umpteenth time that morning.

'Got the gift, I guess. Sometimes children see things we don't,' Mrs Daws whispered, tears rolling down her cheeks. 'Don't seem right for such a little one to be taken.'

'Dr Hawkins said there was nothing any of us could have done,' Harry said. 'There'll have to be a post-mortem but he's pretty sure Maisie's heart was too weak to fight the fever. It's very sad, but for the children's sake we must try and carry on as normal. I'd better sound the gong and summon them in for luncheon.'

'To think I complained about the din young Maisie made. I'd give anything to have her banging the life out of it now. Oh!' The housekeeper sobbed, realizing what she'd said.

As Sarah comforted the woman, Harry called April and Pip over to supervise the meal. 'Couldn't eat a thing myself,' he muttered. 'I'll be in the classroom.'

'And I'll go and see Mr Fothergill,' Sarah said. 'I need to be doing something.'

Mr Fothergill stared at her over his silver-rimmed spectacles. 'After what you've just told me, Miss Sullivan, I feel I should acquaint Lady Chorlton of the situation.'

'And you will tell her that I'd very much like to meet her?' Sarah asked.

'I will indeed convey that message to her,' he agreed.

'Thank you, Mr Fothergill. I would be most grateful. She was such a good friend to my godfather, so I really should like to make her acquaintance. I would like to thank her for all she's done and explain that Red Cliffs might have to close.'

The solicitor frowned. 'I find it odd that the local authority, without having conducted a survey, should claim the whole roof needs replacing. Your godfather knew there was a problem, of course, but I was given to understand it was only to one elevation.'

'Well, Mr Collyer didn't have a problem effecting a temporary repair,' she explained.

'Leave it with me, Miss Sullivan. I will communicate with Lady Chorlton and advise you of her response. I can rely upon your discretion?' he asked, quirking his brow.

'Of course, Mr Fothergill,' she assured him.

He nodded. 'In the meantime, please accept my sincere condolences on the sad loss of one of your pupils. Death is never easy, but in one so young . . .' He shrugged helplessly.

'Thank you, Mr Fothergill. I shall await hearing from you.'

The service for Maisie was simple yet beautiful. Encouraged by the vicar, the children each placed a flower on the altar before standing together and singing the school anthem. As their clear voices were joined by the congregation, only Monday remained silent. Once again, she'd retreated into her own world.

Amelia, who had consented to stay on until a permanent replacement for Miss Green could be found, tried to encourage Monday to speak by pointing out places her father would be visiting on his voyage. Although the little girl eagerly traced the route on the globe with her finger, she didn't say anything.

In an attempt to lighten the atmosphere around the school, Sarah and Harry helped the children to finish the things they'd been making for the Christmas Fayre. They worked well together and relations were friendly between them, but there was still none of the easy banter that had existed before Rodney's visit.

Each day Sarah waited anxiously for the postman to arrive. Would their benefactor agree to meet her? And what would the results of the inspection be? Until she received the answers, the impending closure of Red Cliffs hung over her like the black clouds that persisted outside. Although her list of ideas for raising funds was growing, she knew in her heart that the projects would only realize a small amount. Whilst it would hardly make any impression on the sum that was needed for a new roof, at least she felt she was doing something.

40

As the day of the Christmas Fayre dawned, the two letters finally arrived.

'Mr Fothergill says our benefactor Lady Charlotte has agreed to my calling upon her when she returns from her vacation in the New Year,' Sarah cried excitedly. Harry and Mrs Daws exchanged relieved smiles.

'That is good news,' Harry said, but Sarah hardly heard him for she had torn open the other letter and was scanning the contents.

'Goodness, the local authority has given us six months to bring the property up to the required standard.

'I don't mean to rain on your parade but six months isn't that long to get everything fixed, Sarah,' Harry pointed out.

'Maybe not, but at least it will give us a chance to raise some funds and work out our next strategy. It's better than being closed down, isn't it?'

'That's very true, Miss Sullivan,' the housekeeper replied. 'A nicer Christmas present, we couldn't wish for.'

'That's right, Mrs Daws. I intend to do all I can to ensure Red Cliffs passes the next inspection. Now, come on, let's get ready for the Christmas Fayre,' Sarah cried.

They arrived at the church hall to find it festively decorated with holly and candles. As soon as he saw them, Jack Wise bounded up to Sarah with one of his dazzling smiles.

'Sar . . . er, Miss Sullivan, the good ladies have arranged two stalls for your pupils to display their handicrafts.'

As the children proudly set out their creations, Mrs Knight and her sewing bee ladies descended upon them.

'My, don't you all look smart,' Mrs Higgins exclaimed.

'And haven't you been busy?' Mrs Knight added, picking up one of the aprons. 'May I purchase one of these?' The girls looked at Sarah, who nodded.

'We've made you one each to fank you, I mean, thank you for our new clothes,' Kitty said as she and Edith handed each of them a brightly wrapped parcel.

'And you an' all,' Maggie, Ellen and June added, giving the three ladies of the church a package each.

'Yours is a peg bag, Miss Middle, 'cos we weren't sure if an apron would fit,' Maggie giggled.

'Mrs Daws hopes you will all join us for Christmas luncheon,' Sarah added quickly.

'But we never get invited anywhere on Christmas Day,' Miss Prior gasped.

'You're such a good cook, Mrs Daws,' Miss Middle added, turning to the housekeeper. 'We'd love to come.'

'We do all the cooking on Christmas Day, don't we, Pip?' April explained. 'But Mrs Daws keeps an eye on us, don't you?'

'I most certainly do,' the housekeeper chuckled.

The Fayre was well supported and the hall bustled with activity. All the things the children had made sold quickly. As the girls went around handing out the refreshments, Kitty winked at Sarah.

'We've made more dosh than the boys, miss,' she cried.

Sarah smiled. 'And we haven't finished yet. We're going to sing carols with the Salvation Army to raise money for the homeless.'

'Like we was, you mean?' Edith cried.

'Goodness, can you imagine what those children will sound like?' one woman remarked as she passed.

'They will sound just splendid,' Miss Snooper sniffed.

As dusk was falling on Christmas Eve, the town square thronged with people. Local tradespeople stood alongside the smartly attired visitors who had arrived to spend the festive season in the grand hotels or their own holiday houses. The tantalizing smell of roasted chestnuts and spiced wine mingled with the sound of high spirits and Christmas carols, while the children, who were swathed in woollen hats and mufflers, gathered excitedly around the huge tree, its myriad candles twinkling brightly in the gloaming.

'And now, the pupils of Red Cliffs will sing a special carol beginning with a solo by one of their gifted little girls,' the vicar announced. The band struck up the familiar chords and Amelia smiled encouragingly at Sally, who took a step forward and confidently began singing. As her dulcet tones rang out, the square fell silent. Sarah and Harry exchanged proud glances.

'Amelia's going to get Sally to show the others how to do the breathing exercises with a view to forming a choir,' Sarah whispered.

'Heaven help the vicar then,' Harry joked.

Then Amelia turned to the rest of the pupils. 'Remember "h",' she murmured, raising her arm to bring them in.

'Hark the herald angels sing,' they chorused, emphasizing the 'h' both times.

'It's hard to believe they're the same children,' Sarah sighed, as the last strains died away. Then Monday pointed excitedly to the figure sparkling from the top of the Christmas tree.

'There's Maisie,' cried Monday, hopping up and down excitedly. 'I said she'd come back as an angel.'

'Monday's got her voice back,' Mrs Daws beamed.

'Isn't it marvellous?' Sarah replied, staring at Harry in surprise. He gazed back so fondly, her pulse quickened. Then he moved closer and linked his arm through hers. A delicious feeling of warmth rippled through her, dispelling the last vestiges of reticence. She smiled happily up at him and their glances locked.

''Ere, look at the master and miss,' Kitty cried. As the children's giggles mingled with the Christmas music, Harry bent and gently kissed Sarah on the cheek.

'That'll really give them something to talk about,' he whispered.

'Remember, Sarah, *Love Never Faileth*,' her uncle's voice whispered.

Acknowledgements

To Pern for your continued support and encouragement. Teresa Chris for your wisdom and foresight. Maxine, Clare, Eve, Jenny and all at Penguin for your friendly assistance and invaluable expertise. You are all quite brilliant. Special thanks to Sally Bowron who kindly shared the notes on Ragged Schools she made during her visit to the museum.

More from Linda Finlay

Is the wedding dress of a Queen worth more than the happiness of an orphaned girl?

Is the legacy of her mother's love enough to survive alone?

Will her wish come true this year?

In crafting her future will she unravel her past?